FALLEN CREST UNIVERSITY

THE 5TH IN THE FALLEN CREST SERIES

NYT & USA Bestselling Author
TIJAN

Copyright © 2015 by Tijan
All rights reserved.
ISBN 978-1-951771-21-8

Visit my website at www.tijansbooks.com

Cover Designer: Lisa Jordan Photography

Editor: Jovana Shirley, Unforeseen Editing

Proofread by: Paige Smith, Chris O'Neil Parece, Pam Huff and AW Editing

Formatting by Elaine York/
Allusion Graphics, LLC/Publishing & Book Formatting

No part of this book may be reproduced or transmitted in any form or by any means, electronic or mechanical, including photocopying, recording, or by any information storage and retrieval system without the written permission of the author, except for the use of brief quotations in a book review.

This book is a work of fiction. Names, characters, places, and incidents either are products of the author's imagination or are used fictitiously. Any resemblance to actual persons, living or dead, events, or locales is entirely coincidental.

DEDICATION

Fallen Crest University is dedicated to all those readers and Tijanettes who love the Fallen Crest Series! You guys are awesome, for real. You pimp. You promote. You share. Your level of excitement is intoxicating and I know it helped me when I was writing this one.

There's a bit of a surprise for you guys at the end, so you're warned!

I also wanted to dedicate this book to Bailey. My little guy that's always there with me. Every day. Every break. Every time I go for some coffee, he's wagging his tail and just excited to see me. ;)

PROLOGUE

MASON

He was coming right, so I shifted, blocked his punch, and rounded with my own. My fist hit the side of his eye, and he doubled over. There was a crowd around us, but I couldn't hear them. They didn't exist to me. It was this guy. This was Sebastian's crowd. They wanted a fight. They got one, and this lackey would be the third guy I took down. It was a matter of moments before he gave in. He bent over, drawing in ragged breaths, and his hand raised to his head. He was checking out how much blood was there, and then the yells started to filter through my haze.

"*Get up!*"

"Let's go!"

They'd been screaming like that for the last hour. It never mattered. Each one of Sebastian's guys would get up, and I'd hit them back down. When one was knocked out, another would step in, and I'd fight him like the others—quick, painful, and without thought.

I hadn't fought in so long, but this felt good, finally being able to release the demons. Sebastian wanted to destroy my friendship with Nate. That failed. Nate left their fraternity instead, and they went after me. Their hit-and-run got Marissa instead. She wasn't innocent in some things, but she was an innocent of this war. And Sebastian won that battle.

He got to Marissa.

I didn't know what was promised or what was threatened, but she testified that she didn't remember anyone else being there. It was only me, her, and the speeding truck that came out of nowhere. The security cameras went missing. The only evidence I had on Sebastian was Nate's recording where he admitted that they didn't mean to hit the girl, but it wasn't enough to condemn their futures. The university didn't want a criminal case, so the fraternity was banned. Each individual member could attend Cain University, but not within their fraternity. That was it, though.

My revenge was simple. I burnt their house down.

They tried to get me expelled, but no evidence was found. They couldn't pin that on me. Months passed in tension. I knew they were going to fight back, but I was given a break—until tonight.

They were waiting for me after my last training session.

A third one came from the left at me. I bent down, swept an arm out, hooking him around the legs. I tossed him over my back, flipping him in the air. His back hit the ground, and he stared up at me, blinking in shock. I didn't give him time to think. My leg was up, and I brought it down. He twisted to the side, but I still clipped him in the head. It was enough to make him slow his attack. He rolled to the side and lay there, shaking his head clear.

A fourth was charging toward me.

I stood my ground, caught him by grabbing a fistful of his shirt, and hit him from the other side. My arm thrust out in a straight punch, connecting with him in the mouth. He stumbled backward, but a friend caught him and helped him to the background. There were more, all standing back and waiting their turn.

I took in a deep breath, my chest was tight, and my breathing labored.

This could go on forever. If they kept coming at me, they'd win. They'd wear me down. Some were surprised. Some wary. Others were just glaring with their hands closed in fists by their sides.

They were waiting for their leader, and then he came forward.

Park Sebastian.

He was clapping with an ugly smirk on his face and a gleam in his eyes. Stopping just outside of my reach, he stopped clapping. He dropped the smirk and lowered his eyes, locking his gaze on me as if he were going to charge. "Aren't you full of surprises?"

With the back of my hand, I wiped the blood from my mouth. Sebastian watched the motion and followed as I wiped it off on my pants.

He added, "I wasn't aware that you could fight."

I narrowed my eyes. He'd already tried to hit me with a car, knowing it would injure me and I'd be off the team. I could've been off the team permanently. No more football for me. No professional career either.

I tilted my head to the side. *What was he doing?*

"You took my house." He wagged a finger at me. "You took it in more ways than one. Although, in a way, you saved the university from rebuilding it."

"They did rebuild it."

"It's a fucking daycare now."

There was the Park Sebastian I knew. The cool and calm one wasn't the right one. I wanted to face the real one. I wanted him front and center.

"What are you doing, Sebastian?"

He nodded once, clipping his head up and down to himself. "I know what you're thinking. We could keep fighting, exhausting you, and we'd eventually win. We could do whatever we wanted to you." He pointed to my leg. "Maybe break that." He pointed to my arm. "Or tear the tendons in those so you can't catch a ball anymore." His finger moved up and down, from my head to my toes. "Or we could try it all over again. Run a truck over you, and you'd be done for. There'd be no going back, but here's my dilemma. The university would have to step in, and at some point, they'd let the law come with them. That's the dilemma."

He stepped back, his hands resting on his hips. "I don't want to go to prison because of you. Checkmate. You won. The fraternity is gone, literally in all ways. We're not allowed to function as a house of brothers anymore, but in our hearts, we still are. The other chapters know that, so even though we're not officially recognized as fraternity brothers, we still are. Outside of the university, outside of all the universities, we're *still* brothers." He tapped where his heart was. "You couldn't take this from us, but this is what I'm going to take from you."

Time slowed.

I knew. I'd always known.

Sam was sent to Boston. I wanted her to get away from Cain University, away from me, and even away from Logan in Fallen Crest. In some way of thinking, I'd thought that the farther away she was, the safer she would be.

His lips began to form her name, and I knew all that was for nothing. He was still going after her, and she would be at Cain University next year, coming right into the lion's den. I was delivering her to him.

His words were low and gravelly. I heard them through my alarm. A storm was going off in me, but his words penetrated me as he said, "I'm going to take your heart away."

No.

That damn smirk coming back to him, he added, "And you won't be able to stop me because she's not going to let you. That's going to be the best thing about it. You won't be able to do a damn thing about it, and the way I'm going to do it, she'll come right to me. I'm going to savor that day when she walks from you to me, and after I've taken your heart out, I'm going to take hers. I'm going to hurt her in a way so that she'll never be the same. I'm going to rip her soul from her body."

I snapped. One step took me to him, and before he realized what I was doing, I grabbed him and threw him down. I was on him, raining punch after punch, until his guys tore me from his body. They had to lift me off him, and even then, I kept going back for more.

I wanted to rip his insides out, but as I was trying to hurt him, I knew it wouldn't matter.

He was going after Sam.

CHAPTER ONE

SAMANTHA

Weddings were where two souls became one, but for me, it was a day where I was about to beat a bitch down. I was staring at that girl now as I opened the door, and Cass Sullivan was on the doorstep. Dressed in a tight skirt that ended below her knees with a slit up the thigh and a sequined top that dipped low between her breasts, she was ready for the wedding festivities. Her hair was pinned on the top of her head with curled tendrils that fell to frame her face. A normal person would've looked beautiful, but this was Cass.

I drawled, "This must be your dream come true."

Her heated eyes rolled upward before she sighed. "Seriously?"

Oh, yes. Seriously. I was trying to keep from gloating as I said, "You're finally showing up at the Kade house to see your boyfriend. You've got to be wet. This is what you've been salivating about for years, right?"

"Oh my god." She groaned. "Malinda said that Mark was here. You guys are all sleeping here for the weekend. Is he inside or not?"

A girl had to enjoy this torture. I had my fair share of enemies for four years now, but Cass was one that never went away. She had hated me since Mason and Logan became family, and she'd stuck like glue, refusing to go away. Her latest venture was as Mark's girlfriend, who would be my stepbrother after today.

I folded my arms over my chest. "Maybe."

"Sam! For real?"

I lifted a shoulder. "Maybe not."

I was being mean. I knew this, but after the crap she put me through, she deserved it. Once Mark's mom married my dad today, it would be official. Mark would be family, and that meant she had to be nice...*er* to me.

She took a step toward me.

I lifted an eyebrow.

Putting her mouth right next to my ear, she yelled at the top of her lungs, "Mark! Are you here?"

I cringed. I'd known it was coming. I'd known she was either going to hit me or scream. I'd thought I was prepared. I wasn't. "Shut up. My god. You killed my eardrum."

She grunted and rolled her eyes, smoothing her hands over her skirt. "Whatever. You should've called for him. I warned you."

Our gazes were locked in a battle, and that was when I knew. "You're still going to be a bitch to me, aren't you?"

"You thought I wouldn't be?" Her head reared back. "Where did you get that idiotic thought?"

Well, that sealed her fate. With a big grin on my face, I stepped back and shut the door in her face.

"Mature much?" she asked from the other side.

I shrugged. Any chance I got to shut a door in her face, I was going to take it. That made this more enjoyable. I turned the lock. Cass could knock and yell all she wanted. She was screwed. What she didn't know, I did, and that was the fact that

Mark was with Logan right now, and they didn't have their cell phones with them. They weren't even here.

Mason looked up from the table as I rounded the hallway for the kitchen. "Who was that?" A pad and pen were sitting in front of him as he was finishing up a speech.

Mark was the best man with Mason and Logan being the rest of the groomsmen. The other two snuck out for an errand, something to do with doves. I didn't want to know any details, so I hadn't asked. All I knew was that they'd left their phones for some reason, declaring they didn't want to risk evidence being recorded against them. As they had done that, Mark dropped another bombshell. He was horrible with speeches and he wasn't going to do one. No one trusted Logan to give the speech so that left one person: Mason. This was the reason my boyfriend remained behind with me.

Needing to leave to get my hair done, I was glad Mason and I were the only two in the mansion at that moment. It would be overrun that afternoon, but right now, I was trying to hold back from climbing onto his lap instead of sinking into the chair beside him. His hair was tousled and messy since he hadn't cut it most of the summer. It would be buzzed tomorrow for football season, so until then, I would enjoy running my fingers through it.

A shadow had formed over his jaw, but he was gorgeous. With striking eyes, angular cheekbones, a strong jawline, and an athletic build, which was sculpted to perfection from years of playing football and his extra training over the past summer, I knew why he was coveted by so many at Cain University.

My fingers ached to smooth some of the worry lines from his eyes as I said, "No one."

His eyebrows lowered. "That didn't sound like no one."

I shrugged and leaned close. "Trust me. No one important."

"Hmm." But he grinned and met me for a kiss.

With that gentle brush from his lips to mine, a small tingle went through me. We'd been together for two years now, and we had been through a mountain of troubles, but our time apart during the last year was coming to an end, permanently. After this weekend, all the cars would be packed, and Mason, Logan, and I would be moving to Cain University.

Mason would be starting late with his practices, considering his probation time from Cain U. After his last run-in with Sebastian, Sebastian's crew got suspended, and so did Mason. He was allowed to take all his finals online, and he didn't lose his football scholarship, but I knew he was antsy about returning to college.

As our kiss deepened, he sighed, and I could feel the tension in him.

Cupping the side of his face, I pulled back. "Everything will be fine."

The concern was heavy in his eyes. He lifted a hand to tuck some of my hair behind my ears, resting his fingers on my cheek afterward. "If they hurt you…if they hurt Logan…" The ends of his mouth tightened, and a flash of pain filled his eyes for a moment. "I don't know what will happen, Sam, if they touch you. I don't."

"It's not going to come to that."

Park Sebastian was the ringleader for the now officially banned fraternity, and he was the real reason behind Mason's feud with them. Mason hadn't wanted to play the fake who-are-you-related-to, how-wealthy-are-you-going-to-be-in-the-future, or you-scratch-my-back-and-I'll-scratch-yours games that Sebastian initially tried to recruit him for. The rejection wasn't taken lightly.

I ran my fingers through his hair and pulled back enough to gaze into his eyes. He was scared. I'd felt it during the summer. Each night, as he'd hold me, he'd grow more and more tense, the closer we got to this weekend.

I had no intention of being one of his weaknesses. "Mason, you don't have to worry about me. No matter what, we'll fight it. No one will hurt me. No one will hurt Logan."

His hand rested on the back of my neck. He was searching my face. He wanted to believe me, but he couldn't. Mason knew better. We'd been through too much bullshit to believe that everything would be okay, but I couldn't be his Achilles' heel.

No, it wasn't going to happen. I wasn't going to be used to hurt him.

I shifted closer to him. "I mean it, Mason. I'm here. I'm at your side. I'll do whatever you want."

"Sam—" he started.

I saw the struggle in him and shook my head. "No. Stop. I mean it. I get to have your back this time. And I will. No one is after me—no scorned lover, no obsessed stalker, not even a hateful bitch like Cass. No one like that will get close to me. Been there, done that. I know how to handle them."

I pulled him close, peering deeply into his eyes. He was torn, so I smiled and softly pressed my lips to his once again. I murmured against them, "Trust me this time. I know what we're getting into at school, and I'm here to help you. That's it. That's all."

He shook his head. "You shouldn't have to. That's what

pisses me off. I shouldn't have to worry about Sebastian going after you, but...he's capable of anything."

"Stop."

Mason always kicked ass. He'd stand in the line and dare people to go against him. He wasn't like this, unsure of the future. This wasn't a Mason I was used to, and that tugged at my heart even more.

"I will make friends, if that will ease your mind. I will surround myself with new college comrades, and when I come over to your house, I'll make sure to be careful. You or Logan can come pick me up all the time. How about that?"

He only said, "He can't hurt you. I don't know what I'll do if he does."

"He won't." I leaned close, pressing a kiss to him once more. I whispered, "I promise."

"Yo!"

As a shout came from the front door, and we drew back. A second later, Logan and Mark rushed in. Their cheeks were red. Beads of sweat were on their foreheads, and both had stupid grins on their faces.

Logan said again, "Yo." He stopped, his eyes narrowed, and he cocked his head to the side. "Did you two just beat it here?"

Mason's hand fell from my waist, and he rolled his eyes. "Logan, we're not like rabbits, humping all the time."

"Why not?" Logan grabbed the orange juice from the refrigerator and brought it over to the table.

As he set it down, Mark grabbed two glasses, and both sat down.

Logan added, "I would. You know, if I *could*...like we *could've been*—"

"Shut the fuck up." Mason glared.

Logan winked at me as he kept grinning, pouring the juice into his glass. "Come on, brother. I thought we were all fine with what was discussed. You know, the idea of Sam and me, that there could've been—"

Mason growled. "I punched you back then. I will do it again."

"What?" Logan gestured to his face. "Not this. It's gotta stay pretty. Mama Malinda will have your ass in a sling otherwise." He paused, his eyes alive and sparkling as they skirted between Mason and me. His lip curved even higher. "What do you think, Sam? What would they have called us? You and Mason are Samson. We could've been...Samog? No. That doesn't sound right. Sagan? Lotha? Those don't sound right either. What about just SamLo? Nah, still not right."

Mark poured himself a glass, and he was now watching Logan. His eyes kept glancing from one side of the table to our side. His hand tightened around the glass, and his Adam's apple bobbed up and down.

Mason reached for his pen and leaned closer to his brother across the table. "Shut up." He moved with lightning speed, bringing down his hand and slamming the pen into the table. As he sat back, the pen stayed upright, wedged between two of Logan's fingers.

Everyone's eyes got big.

Mason moved so quickly. We realized the precision of his aim after it was already done.

Logan was the first to react. A laugh came from him. It got louder and stronger. He was shaking his head at the same time. "I love messing with you."

"You're going to regret it."

The laughter died. Logan grew still. "What do you mean?"

"When you get a woman who you love…" Mason glanced sideways to me. "When she means the world to you and you're ready to do anything to keep her safe, I'm going to enjoy doing the same shit you've been doing all summer."

"Well," Logan's eyebrows bunched together, and the corners of his mouth curved down, "that won't be very nice of you."

"Karma's a bitch." It was softly spoken, but it was a taunt, and everyone knew it.

Logan looked at me. A question was there. He wanted to ask me something, but I shook my head. I was annoyed too.

Yes, there could've been a Logan and Sam, but it hadn't happened. Logan could've been a boyfriend, but Mason was my soul mate. The tension of that question, if Logan had feelings for me or not, had been plaguing us for a while. It was dealt with last year, right before the fraternity burned down. That truth came out, that there could've been an *us* with Logan and me. Mason took it easier than I'd realized.

And what Mason said was true. Logan had been making jokes about us a lot more lately. I couldn't help to think it had more to do with the fact that Kris and he were finally done. They'd broken up, gotten back together, and repeated that chain of events throughout the entire year. Their final, final breakup was four months earlier. Weeks before our graduation, Logan dumped Kris at a party, and he'd gone back to his man-whoring ways that night. There were rumors he'd gotten blow jobs from two different girls that night, at the same party, and he'd gone home with someone else.

Girls were friendlier to me now than they'd been when Logan was serious with Kris. I wasn't dumb. I'd learned to recognize the I-want-to-use-you-because-you're-close-to-Logan-Kade looks from a distance. I was able to evade their hooks. When I couldn't, my best friend, Heather Jax, had no problem removing the hooks for me.

Thinking about Heather now, I glanced at the clock on the wall.

I needed to go for hair primping with Malinda, her two sisters, and her best friend. I knew their daughters would be there, too. But no Heather.

"What?" Mason asked.

I asked back, "What?"

"You sighed. What's wrong?"

"Oh." Images of hairstylists, the smell of hairspray, and the sound of giggles and whispers all plagued me at once. I cringed. "I was just wishing that Heather didn't have to work today."

"Nate's coming tonight. He has some meeting at Cain U, but he'll be driving down later. Jax is coming tonight, isn't she?"

I nodded at Logan. "Yeah. She'll get off in time for the wedding dance."

"Thank god." He raked a hand through his hair. "She and Channing are on the outs now, aren't they?"

I stiffened. It was true. Heather and her off-again, on-again boyfriend from Roussou, Channing, were in one of their off times, and the feisty back and forth between her and Logan increased over the last three weeks.

The look in Logan's eyes didn't sit right with me. Still. If Heather wanted to sleep with Logan, there was nothing I could do. It wasn't like she didn't know what she would be getting into, but I heard myself saying, "If you do what I think you're going to do…" I paused to make sure Logan knew I was being serious.

He did. He moved in slow motion, so he was sitting at his highest height. The wicked glint he'd had when he came into the dining room now dimmed slightly. A more sobering look replaced it, and as he held my gaze, his head lowered just a bit. He was on my same level now.

I said, "You need to remember that she is the one female who's been a true friend to me. Do not shit on my friend's doorstep. You got that?"

His jaw clenched. "Jax isn't like the others, Sam. I respect her."

"Make sure to keep that respect afterward, too."

A phone buzzed from the counter, and Mark went to grab it. After he read the text, he looked up. "Uh, Sam?"

I already knew what was coming, and I started to stand from the chair.

He was still hesitant, glancing from me to Logan, as he said, "It's my mom. You're wanted at the house."

I nodded. "Hair appointment."

Mason grabbed my hand and pulled me back. He cupped the back of my head and kissed me. He murmured in my ear for only me to hear, "Have fun with your new mom. She already loves you."

A wave of something else went through me, and my throat closed up. I nodded and kissed him back again before pulling away and heading out of the house.

As I walked across the street to my dad's and Malinda's home, I wiped at my eye. No matter the undercurrents in our group, Mason was right. This was the day I was getting a new mom who actually loved me.

A weight lifted from my shoulders. I found myself grinning as I walked inside, already hearing shrieks and laughter from the kitchen. Today was the day Malinda would become Mrs. Malinda Decraw Strattan.

Malinda was there, her arms wide open for me, and she hooted, "Hot holy cannoli! It's my daughter. Come here, you beautiful, beautiful woman!"

CHAPTER TWO

Standing at the front of the church, as Malinda and my dad, David, made their vows to each other, I couldn't help but look at Mason. We were watching each other during most of the ceremony. It was a good feeling, being here, being a part of David's wedding, knowing he would get a good wife now, and also having Mason and Logan standing as groomsmen. It was like we really were a family now, like Malinda adopted all of us.

When it was my turn to walk down the aisle, after the minister proclaimed David and Malinda husband and wife, Mason tucked my hand over his arm. He leaned close, brushing his lips over my forehead.

The fairy-tale sensation took root, digging deep in me. As we walked together, the yearning to find the minister and make *it* official between Mason and myself was powerful. My fingers sank into Mason's arm, taking hold as if I were clinging to him so that I really wouldn't go and find the reverend.

A lot of Mark's friends were in the pews, and as Mason and I moved past them, Cass leveled me with a glare. I moved Mason to the side, and my bouquet narrowly missed her head. She drew in a breath, and I heard a curse from her, but we were moving beyond the others, like Miranda Stewart. Peter was her date. That was interesting. And there was Adam. Beside him were Becky and Lydia. I glanced to Lydia's side, but no Jessica. That was a shock. Jeff was there, too, and he lifted a hand to wave. Mason laughed under his breath, but Jeff just kept waving.

Jeff called out, "Looking good, Logan!"

Laughter pealed out over the visitors. Some girls giggled and whispered together, like they always did with Logan, but I knew others were still captivated by Mason. He'd been the prize when he was in high school. Mason was always the one they never got to grab. A part of me wondered if they were going to try tonight. There'd be dancing, music, booze, and probably some drugs. I wouldn't partake, but I knew others would. The old feeling of wanting to drag Mason away and keep him all to myself was filling me up again.

When we got to where Malinda and David were waiting to greet everyone, Malinda pulled me in for a hug, her hand rubbing over my back. "Hi, honey."

She squeezed me once more before letting David hug me. Mason hugged Malinda behind me, but when it was time to let me go, David didn't let me go. He whispered, his words choked up, "I love you so much, Samantha. You have no idea how much, and I am so blessed to have you in my life. I want you to know that."

More emotions were swimming in me, and tears were sliding down my cheeks. *My god.* I pulled back and saw the same wetness on his cheeks. We'd been through so much. I wanted to say that to him, but all I could say was, "Thank you for coming back for me."

I looked at Malinda, who was watching our exchange. She smiled at me, tears in her eyes, too. Her hand rested on her throat. "*Oh!*" Malinda threw her arms around us and hugged both of us. A second later, she motioned behind me. "Marcus, Logan, Mason—all of you, get in here. Family hug, everyone."

Mason hugged me from behind. Logan was beside him, and Mark brought up the rear, right behind his mother. All of them held us in one strong hug before we heard clapping from around us.

I stiffened. This was always the time when a taunt was thrown our way, but for once, none came.

Malinda pulled back and pressed her hand over her hair, making sure it was in place, before she waved her hand to the group that formed. "Come on," she said. "I've got a hug for each of you guys. Let's get it going, one big hug train here."

I asked David, "Do you need us to stay and greet people?"

He patted my shoulder. "Go ahead and have fun. Pictures are done. You guys are free to relax and enjoy. Just come to the reception in two hours."

"Wait, wait." Logan jostled, pressing up against my elbow so he could hear better, "We got two hours, you say?"

The easy grin slipped from my dad's face, and he tugged at his tuxedo collar. "Uh, you be there, and you be sober, Logan."

"Yeah, yeah." Logan slid his arm over my shoulder and bobbed his head up and down. Excitement seemed to be radiating from him, and he was barely containing it. "I don't want to piss off Mama Malinda. We'll be back, and we'll be sober…or we will *appear* to be sober."

"Logan."

He put his fingers to his forehead and saluted my father. "See ya later, Señor Strattan."

"Mason," my father spoke over Logan. "I want my daughter back, and she has to be sober. The chief of police will be at our reception."

Mason stepped up to my side. He removed Logan's arm from my shoulders and patted it as he guided it back to Logan's side, making a show of the gesture. He nodded to my father. "She will be. Logan's got a bee up his ass today, but don't worry."

Mason interlaced our fingers, tugging me to his side. He spoke over my head, "She'll be fine. Won't she, Logan?"

Logan rolled his eyes and jerked a hand over his shoulder. "Let's head out before the crowd gets here." As soon as we were outside, he made a beeline for Mason's Escalade.

He started to head for the driver's seat, but Mason called out, "Hell no. Back, buddy."

There was no argument.

Logan slid into the backseat but waved for us to hurry. "Come on. Hashtag Logan's thirsty, get a move on it."

"Oh god." Mason's hand released my elbow.

I went around to the front passenger seat.

As we got inside, Mason added, "Not the damn hashtags. I can't take them today."

Logan ignored him and began tapping on the ceiling. "Whatever. Let's go. I'm in the mood, the mood for booze."

As Mason started the engine, I saw Mark hurrying from the church. "Stop. Mark's coming, too."

Logan groaned. "Come on."

Those two words sent a new feeling in the air. Mason and I shared a look. Something was going on with Logan, more than the need for drinking, getting laid, and fighting. This was Mark, who was adopted into the group because he was my now stepbrother. The core was still us three, but those words were going to exile Mark.

He was almost to the vehicle.

I murmured, "Mason."

He nodded, already turning around and lowering his window. "I got it." He called out to Mark as he began to go around the vehicle, "Hey, can you give us a minute?"

Mark braked, and he frowned. "Uh, sure…"

He looked at me through the windshield, and I held a finger up, indicating one moment. His eyebrows furrowed together, but he leaned back and shoved his hands into his jacket pockets. I didn't like keeping him out, but this was our family business.

Mason twisted around in his seat. "What is your problem?"

"Nothing. I want to drink." Logan continued to tap on the vehicle's ceiling. "Let's head out."

"And Mark can't come?"

He jerked up a shoulder. "He can come. I was wrong to say that."

I was dumbfounded. Logan hadn't been this back and forth in a while, but he was pissy earlier when he and Mark got back from whatever they did. That made me wonder. "Did something happen with your prank earlier?"

"Nah. Malinda wanted a bunch of doves to be set loose during the reception. We talked the guy into a few white pigeons, too—ones that will drop some water balloons on people." He laughed to himself, but the sound came out sharp, edgy, and abrupt. "We thought some of the doves could do that, but he said pigeons would be better. They can be trained for that stuff."

"Who's getting the water balloons?" Mason asked.

Logan shrugged again. "Some bitch-ass people." He stopped tapping the roof and met Mason's gaze. "Quinn."

Mason flashed him a grin.

Logan looked to me. "Miranda Stewart."

That was fine with me.

He added, "I wanted one to be dropped on Cass, but Mark refused. Said it would mess up his chances of getting it in tonight."

"If nothing's wrong with Mark because of the prank, what then? What's going on with you?" I asked.

"Nothing. Like I said, I was wrong to say that." He let out a soft curse and opened his door. "Come on, man. The interrogation's over."

Mark was hesitant when he got in.

Mason glanced at him in the rearview mirror. "Sorry. Logan was being an ass. We wanted to hash it out quickly."

Mark waved his hand in the air in a dismissive motion. "No problem. I get it." He snuck a look over his shoulder. "But, um…can we get going? I'm pretty sure my girlfriend is going to be looking for me soon."

I groaned. "Punch it, Mason."

I looked too, and as Mason pulled out of the church's parking lot, Cass came out from the front doors, squinting with a hand shielding the sun from her eyes as she looked all around the lot. Miranda, Peter, and the whole Academy Elite group were right behind her, and they began scanning, too.

I faced forward in my seat again. Yeah, no. I did not want to hang out with that group again. Dealing with Cass being Mark's girlfriend was bad enough. Now, I needed a drink and when we got to the Kade mansion, Logan went behind the bar in the basement. I was heading for the bathroom, when he held up a shot he had poured. "Sam, get over here."

"I'm going to the bathroom."

He shook his head. His eyes darkened, and he held the cup higher in the air. "You can piss later. Let's drink first."

I glanced at Mason, and saw that he was fed up. He moved to stand in front of me, saying, "Okay, that's enough. What the fuck is up your ass?"

"Nothing."

Mason reached for the cup, but Logan moved it out of the way. He extended it to me again. "Sam, come on. Team player here."

My chin lifted. That was a direct burn against me. Logan didn't do that shit. He didn't take his anger out on me—others, yes, but not me.

Mason took the cup from Logan's hand. "You want to explain that little dig right now?"

Mark moved farther into the background. He was glancing between all of us, and I didn't blame him. Mark was family, but he wasn't in the core three. All our disagreements were normally held until we were behind closed doors. He was getting a front-row seat now. Logan and Mason were scary when they stood against others, but they were downright dangerous when dealing with each other. There was love and a fierce loyalty between them, but they wouldn't hold back either. This was one of those moments.

I moved forward so I was standing beside Mason. My hand grazed against the back of his, just enough so he knew I was there. He reciprocated by turning his hand to the side. His pinkie wrapped around mine and he squeezed it before letting it go again. "I mean it, Logan. You can take shots against others but not us. What is going on with you?"

"Nothing." He drank the shot that was intended for me and downed the shots poured for Mason and Mark. "Just nothing."

"Maybe I should go—" Mark started to say as he began heading for the stairs.

"Oh, no, Mark." Logan stopped him. There was a savage bite to his tone. "Why would you leave? You're actually *family* to Sam now." He poured another shot and waved it between himself and Mason. "Not like us. We were supposed to be, remember?" His gaze settled on me, and a burning anger was there. "Back in the day when your mom was faking it. She was supposed to marry our dad, and seriously," a bitter laugh came from him, "I hated your mom. I know Mason did, too. We wanted nothing to do with her. Here you came, right alongside her, and there went all that hatred out the window."

He stopped and closed his eyes. His head hung down before rearing back up. He downed that shot before continuing, "She brought us you, Sam, but we're not your family. We're not your stepbrothers. That's him now."

Mark cleared his throat.

Mason let out a soft sigh. "Logan."

"Just stop, okay?" Logan bit out. "Mark's her family. You're going to be her husband one day. Maybe then I'll officially be family to Sam."

I narrowed my eyes. Logan *was* family. This was bullshit. I didn't believe him for a second, and I didn't hold back. "You're such a liar, Logan." I felt the tension in the air double at my words, but I didn't care. I knew he was full of shit, and I jerked forward, my chin lifting in a challenge. "What's really going on?"

"I think I just spelled it ou—"

"You are family," I cut him off. "You know it. Mason knows it. Everyone in Fallen Crest knows it, so drop the bullshit. What is this really about? My mother?" *Wait...* "No, your dad. She didn't marry your dad, not yet, but she took him away."

And Logan would be off to college after this weekend—when his dad wasn't here and hadn't been for an entire year.

I said softly, "That's what this is about, isn't it? Your dad."

Logan's eyes darkened to a dangerous level. He wanted me to shut up, but he couldn't say those words to me. I read him when almost no one could read Logan Kade.

I shook my head. "Logan, your dad—"

He bit out, "Is a fucking asshole, but he's not here, is he? And, yes, Sam, your mom took him away. He's been at her side for a year now. He's not here, not for his son's last year, but I shouldn't be surprised. He's never been around. Always gone. Always screwing some woman. Of course, he'd fall in love and actually be the good guy to a psychotic evil woman like Analise Strattan."

"Logan—" Mason started.

"Don't even start, Mason. You were so pissed at him and for longer than I was. You're the one who wanted to beat his ass all the time, not me. Give me this one time when I'm just fed up and spewing some anger out. I mean, why shouldn't I?" He gestured to Mark, who was plastered against the wall now. "We're celebrating his mom's marriage to Sam's dad. His mom, who is awesome and loving and a better mother in one day than Analise will be in her entire lifetime. I mean, this is great news for Sam. She's getting a family who will love and support her. Finally, right? Finally. While you and I—we're stuck with our fucking father." Logan leveled his brother with a hard look. "You and I, Mase—we're on the outs. That hug just proved it. Mama Malinda is great, but Sam's real family is them now, not us."

That wasn't true. I started to shake my head, but I was

reeling inside. I couldn't believe he was actually thinking this. "No, Logan."

He snorted and poured more shots. This time, Mason took one, and he handed one to Mark.

When Mark hesitated, Logan gave him a half grin. "Sorry. None of this was meant as a personal attack. I'm just," he raked Mark up and down, and his half grin fell slightly, "jealous, I guess. Not an emotion I'm used to feeling."

Logan nudged the last poured shot my way. "Forget my ramblings. I'll get over it. What do you say, Sam? It's your time to celebrate. You got the family you wanted. Finally."

I glanced at Mason and saw he was torn as well. Logan was jealous, like he'd said. They came from money, but that was the only benefit from their family. It was a broken home. Their dad abandoned them on more than one occasion. It was enough that Mason wasn't saying a word right now, and I knew it was because he understood his brother's pain. That hurt so much more, that both of them shared in their abandonment. And they felt I was abandoning them, too, even though they rationally knew I wasn't.

I squared my shoulders back and grew firm inside. I took the shot and held it up, but I said to Logan, "You." I looked at Mason. "You." I skirted between both of them. "You two are my family. My mom left me. My dad left me. You two stuck around and held me up. You are the definition of family to me. No one else can even come close, and this stuff you're talking about, how I finally have a loving family, is bullshit. You two were it for me for years. You two *are* it for me, no matter what. Drop the pity act, Logan, and enjoy the fact that Mama Malinda will start buying you Christmas gifts now because that's the only thing changing. You both are in the family with me. They aren't accepting only me. They're accepting you two, too." I leaned closer, making sure they were watching my eyes and could see the promise I held in there. "Deal with it. No one's *fucking* replacing the two of you."

A look of pride came over Mason as Logan was fighting to hold back a grin, and Mark sighed in relief beside me. I held my glass up, and they raised theirs.

I said, "To fucking family!"

Each of us downed our shots.

Logan grinned as he wagged a finger between Mason and me. He remarked, "In the literal sense for you two."

No one commented.

The old Logan was back.

CHAPTER THREE

MASON

My brother was a dick.

After we took our shots and went back to the reception, I knew Logan got inside Sam's head. This was David and Malinda's day, but it was Sam's too. She got a mom. She didn't need to feel guilty about that, which is what Logan did. He should've let it go.

We weren't being replaced.

Seeing him make a beeline for Heather Jax now, I knew this wasn't going to end well. His hand was on her arm. He was looking down at her with a cocky smirk on his face and a look in his eyes like he was too cool for her.

Heather didn't get pulled in by Logan's tricks, but as her eyes darkened in lust, it was going to happen. She moved in closer. Her lip curved up in a seductive expression. She sucked in her breath, pronouncing her chest out more, and Logan's gaze fell down, right where she wanted it to be. He wet his lips, and their eyes met again. I saw the look passing between the two.

They both knew where the night was headed. That was when I stepped in. Clasping the back of Logan's neck, I grinned down at Heather. She jumped back. Her cheeks flushed, and she blinked up at me for a moment.

"Sam's dancing." I gave them both a knowing look.

Guilt flared in her eyes, and she looked down. "Oh, yeah. I should go say hi."

"Yeah."

Logan stiffened under my hand.

Fuck it.

I was getting the vibe that my brother didn't care what he was doing. He was going to have his fun with Sam's best friend. There was no point in keeping quiet. "You two are going to fuck tonight."

Logan remained under my hand and his nostrils flared, while Heather bit down on her lip and swung her gaze in Sam's direction. Neither of them corrected me. She felt bad. Logan didn't give a shit.

"Jax," I drew her gaze back to me again, "I'm going to violate my brother code right now."

Logan sucked in his breath.

I didn't care. "Logan wants to pound you. He always has, but he's held back for a few reasons. Sam's family. It would hurt her friendship with you. He doesn't love you. You're not the long-haul girl for him. And the last reason is Channing. However, my brother is not in the right frame of mind. He's not thinking clearly, and he's not caring about the consequences right now."

"Fuck off, Mason." Logan ripped himself from my hold. "Who gave you the right to play god for us?"

"I don't have the right, but this is going to hurt Sam." I looked through the corner of my eye. Heather had stepped back from us. She was thinking, and she was seeing that I was right, but hell, she was in pain too. I saw it there. Channing hurt her.

I added to my brother, "You can't hurt Sam and definitely not on this day."

Logan expelled a ragged breath, and he raked a hand through his hair. His head tipped back, and he let out a, "*Fuck.*"

As if hearing him, even though I knew she couldn't because of the deejay's music, Sam turned in our direction. She wore a bright smile on her face, her eyes sparkling and her cheeks were red from laughing. She lifted a hand to wave at us, but saw our faces. It was like watching a sunset falling fast. The liveliness left her. The smile dimmed. Her eyes grew worried, and the redness turned pink as her hand dropped back to her side. Just like that, with one look at us, seeing the storm over all three of us, it was like we'd sucked the life from her.

I gritted my teeth. I said to Heather, "Go and make her happy." I said to Logan, "You and me—we're going for a drive."

Heather started away but stopped at my words. "Um…"

I shook my head. "Tell Sam we're going on a keg run. We'll be back in a bit."

"Okay. Yeah." She frowned at Logan, but he wasn't looking at her.

Everything I'd said earlier to Sam was still weighing on my mind. Sebastian was a problem. I needed my brother with me to deal with Sebastian, and Logan was half himself right now. He didn't fight me, falling in line with me. Both of us weaved our way through the groups. As we got to the parking lot, some people yelled out our names. It was like high school again. Logan and I ignored them and went to my Escalade.

As we started to climb inside, a truck braked right next to us, and a window rolled down.

"Hey!"

Nate was grinning at us. He had on a dress shirt with the top unbuttoned, and his hair was spiked up.

Logan grunted out a short laugh. "You sure you left the fraternity, Nate? You're only missing a crew sweatshirt for your neck. You'd be the image of Yale assholery."

"Missed you too, Logan." Nate rolled his eyes and gestured around the lot. "Let me park my baby, and I'll hop in with you to wherever you're going."

I was about to decline, but he headed toward a parking spot. As he did, I glanced to Logan. "I'll tell him—"

"Let him." Logan shook his head, letting out a long sigh. He leaned back in his seat, his head falling to the backrest. "I'm the asshole. I'll get my shit together. I know what you were going to do, and we'll talk. I promise. I'll let you know what's going on, but you're right. I know you want my head in the game." He rolled his eyes. "I've been an asshole almost all year, but we have Seb-*ass*-tian to deal with. Monson will have the latest updates on him. We need to hear what he has to say before heading back to the reception."

I was slightly relieved. "Thank you."

"I know. I know. Trust me. I want nothing more than to pound Seb-*ass*-tian's head in, and it's game time." He grinned at me. "You have no idea how boring senior year was. No one to fight. No one to deal with. It was all too easy. Maybe I got bored. Maybe that's the problem."

He laughed to himself as Nate climbed into the backseat.

Logan remarked, "Maybe I need a war to get all my demons out."

"What?" Nate was reaching to shut the door, but he heard Logan's last statement and froze. "Huh?"

Logan said, "Nothing. You'd better have the latest and greatest on Seb-*ass*-tian."

"I do." Nate leaned forward as I eased out of the parking lot.

The Elite formed in a small crowd outside the door, but I didn't think they would do anything against Sam while we were gone. Heather was there. It was Sam's parents' wedding and Mark was her stepbrother now.

Logan saw the group, too, and met my gaze. We were thinking the same thing.

I murmured, "She'll be fine. Mark will step in if he has to."

"He better."

Nate was talking, but he stopped and looked between us. "What?"

"Nothing. Can you start over? I wasn't listening," I said.

"Yes." He started as I drove away, "Sebastian was allowed to buy a house off campus, but their place is only a block away."

Logan cursed. "Let me guess. All his roommates are the same douchebags from his fraternity house?"

"No."

"No?" Logan's eyebrows shot up. "That's surprising."

"Campus stepped in. They thought the same thing, so they set a rule in place that no more than five members of their fraternity could live in the same place. If they have more, they're violating the rule and can be expelled. No clue if that's legit or not, but if they want to be students there, I guess it's allowed. They can have non-students live there or guys who weren't members of the fraternity."

"How many are in the house?" Logan questioned.

"They're allowed three, and have two more guys who weren't members of the fraternity."

"Well," Logan snorted, "that's something."

"They're a block off campus?"

Nate nodded. "None of the members are allowed to live on campus unless they're in the dorms."

I knew the rules. I'd been there at the hearing when they were instated, but Sebastian had connections. He had money, too. Those rules could've been bent from last spring until now.

"Good," I said. This was good. Cain U was enforcing their policies.

Logan was watching me. "What are you thinking?"

"I'm thinking Sebastian is waiting for us to come back. He's getting all his ducks in a row, and when we're in place, he'll start again."

"You think?" Nate was looking between the two of us, his hands dangling over the sides of our seats. "So much damage has happened."

Not to me. That was the bottom line.

I shook my head. "Sebastian wants to hurt me, and it hasn't happened yet. He hit Marissa in the hit-and-run and when they jumped me, I hurt them more than they hurt me."

Logan grunted. "Prick. Prick. Prick. He's a super prick…in my asshole."

Nate and I paused, glanced at Logan, and then skipped over that one.

I said, "Sebastian always gets his way. He pushes people around to do what he wants, and I didn't do what he wanted. He wanted to control me, and I said no. Every time he's tried to hurt me, it hasn't worked." I sighed. "I don't want Sam to be a part of this. At all."

Logan and Nate gazed at me.

Nate nodded, saying, "Fine with me."

Logan frowned, narrowing his eyes. "She is a part of this."

"Not this. Not this war. She's out."

"He'll go after her anyway."

"We can't include her in this. That means all talk about Sebastian, anything we do against him—she can't know about it. If she's involved with anything, we're giving him an excuse to hurt her. I know it sounds ridiculous, but if we separate her from this, he might not focus on her as much." I was wishing, but I had to try something.

I gripped the steering wheel with white knuckles. My brother had no idea how dangerous this would be for her. "This will be her freshman year. I want her to have some semblance of a normal year. New friends, dorm room, feeling lost—that bullshit."

A grin teased at the corners of Logan's mouth. "Sometimes I forget how much of a softie you are inside. If that's what you want, that's what we'll do, but first, can we stop at that liquor store? I really do want to get some booze."

I pulled in and he went inside. The conversation was dropped, and when Logan came back with enough liquor for half the wedding, his whole attitude was gone. The rest of tonight was about having fun.

Tomorrow we were heading to Cain University.

CHAPTER FOUR

SAMANTHA

It was College Move-in Day and the day I used to dream about.

It was the epitome of freedom to me. Freedom from my mother's tirades. Freedom from the unhappiness in the house. Freedom from her highs and lows. Freedom from her. Even when we'd first moved in with Mason and Logan, I'd still longed for when I could go away to college. That was the last link in the chain. Mason and Logan protected me from her, but I hadn't been physically free from her until James took her to a hospital. College was the final breakaway from her, and here I was.

I was free. Finally and for real.

Mason and I walked past a mother and daughter hugging each other with tears in their eyes. That wasn't me. I was on cloud nine. Malinda offered to come, but I didn't want her and David to wait one more day for their honeymoon. They deserved to be happy, and with Mason beside me, this was my happiness.

This day was finally here. Literally. We were at my dorm room.

Mason opened the door and went inside to put my bags on the nearest bed. He stood back and watched me come inside.

My dorm room was one large square. Behind the door were two dressers. The beds were pushed up against the far wall, set on top of each other, and a window was in the corner. A desk was next to it, along with two dressers against the third wall. The second desk was right next to the door.

I nodded to the bed where Mason already put my bags and put my bag on the desk by the window. I wanted that corner area for myself. I wanted the window view, looking out over a quad surrounded by sidewalks and trees. A group of guys were throwing a football around, and two groups of girls were laying out, already reading books or studying.

It was my little corner of home.

Mason asked, "Are you sure you don't want to live with us?"

I ran my hand down the desk, feeling the wood and the little indent of someone's initials carved into it. I shook my head. "No. I want this year."

He nodded. "I know."

We talked about it at length before. Mason was worried about Sebastian, thinking he was going to try to hurt Mason through me, but that was the problem. If Sebastian were going to use me to hurt Mason, that meant Mason would have to know about it. I didn't know what Sebastian had in mind. I was assuming some form of mental manipulation, but he'd have to line up. I had gone against some of the best. It wasn't going to work, so here I was. Mason was worried about me. I was worried about him.

Mason, Logan, and Nate had been hush-hush about their plan to battle against Sebastian. I was not to be a part of it—that was all I knew—but they didn't know my plan.

I would not allow Mason to be hurt. I was protecting my man this time. It was my turn to keep secrets. This was going to be the one and only secret I would keep from the man I loved.

Mason would never know how Park Sebastian was trying to hurt me.

"Oh." A nervous laugh came from the doorway. A very tall, very slender, and very beautiful girl with almost white-blond hair stood there, holding on to two bags slung over her shoulder. She adjusted one of the straps and flashed perfect, white teeth, smiling at us. "Hey. I'm Summer." She focused on me. "You're Samantha?"

I nodded. "Sam."

"Oh, nice." She came in, putting her bags on the floor. "I was nervous I got the wrong room. Again. Apparently, we have floors that go that way and floors that go this way. I didn't realize our floor was one of those that went this way." As she talked, her hands made motions to the left, to the right, and back again.

I was mesmerized by her languid motions. As she moved, it was like she was gliding or floating. I'd never seen anything like it. Heather was sexy, and she commanded that attention, but Summer was different. It was like she was a gazelle or a goddess.

Sparkling bracelets slid over her arms as she was motioning, still talking and laughing, now explaining how maneuvering through the packed hallways had gotten her even more lost. She was saying this to Mason, her eyes transfixed on him. She tilted her head backward, lifting her hand to tuck a strand of hair behind her ear before grazing her fingers down the side of her cheek and lingering there for a second.

That was when the momentary spell was gone. *Poof.* I snapped to attention. Her eyes were dilated, and her lips were plumped out a little bit.

My roommate was attracted to my boyfriend.

I interrupted whatever she was saying, "Mason's my man."

Her voice cut off, and she looked at me. Her eyes were wide, surprised. "Uh…yeah."

Mason coughed, frowning at me. "I already told her that."

"Oh." *He did?*

"He was telling me that he had a brother here, too."

I frowned, glancing at the hallway. "Logan was supposed to help me move in."

"Speaking of Logan, I'll go find whatever freshman dorm room or closet he's in." Mason passed me, his hand grazing mine in his own way of reassuring me. He glanced over his shoulder. "I'll be back with more of your stuff from the car," he said before disappearing into the hallway.

My roommate started for her desk but swung back around. "Wait. Mason. Does he already go here?"

I nodded.

Her eyes started to light up. "Is he a sophomore this year?"

I gave another slow nod.

"Is his last name Kade? As in, Mason Kade?"

"You've heard of him?"

"Have I heard of him?" Grabbing my arms, she pinched into them. "He's supposed to go pro next year. He's Cain University's premium wide receiver. Of course, I've heard of him. Mason Kade is a legend. My dad is friends with the coach, and they've talked a ton about him. I can't believe it. Oh my god." Her chest began rising, picking up pace, and she let go of my arms to wrap her arms around herself. "I need to calm down. I'm getting too excited."

"Are you a fan of him or of football?"

"Both." Her cheeks were flushed red, and she was fanning herself. "Did you turn the heat on?"

I gestured to the open door.

"Oh." She grinned at me, still waving her hand to fan herself. "Sorry. I'm not normally this fangirlie, but, man." Her smile turned lopsided. "I can't believe he's your boyfriend. Mason Kade is dating my roommate. Wow. When I tell my dad, he's going to freak."

I was still giving her the side-eye. She was beautiful. She was tall. She was thin. She had bone structure that went through her ass. She could be a model. And she was going all gaga over my man? If she moaned his name in her sleep, I was going to go apeshit. Damn the consequences.

She must've noticed my reaction. Her mouth dropped open. "Oh! No! I'm not interested in him like that. No, no, no. I'm a *huge* football fan. You have no idea. I am not normal. I can give two shits about the guys. It's all football for me. I inherited my dad's genes."

I narrowed my eyes.

"Wait. Not that I could give two shits about guys like *that*. I'm not like that either. I like guys. Well, it's not that I don't like girls. I mean, I do. Oh my god." She groaned, pressing her hands to her temples. "I am making a fool of myself, and I don't normally do that. Seriously. People make fools of themselves around me, not the other way around."

One of my eyebrows went up. *Really?*

She groaned again, shaking her head. "And right there, I came off super arrogant, didn't I? I am not like how I'm coming across. Not at all. I'm not arrogant. I just don't adhere to certain rules of society. Now, I'm sounding like a major dork." She flung a hand out, gesturing to me. "It's you. You're super cool, and you're dating Mason Kade, whose career I've been following for years. His brother too, but not as much."

"You know Logan?"

Her eyes were still wide as she slowly moved her head up and down. Her cheeks were becoming pink again. "I know *of* Logan. Who doesn't? Do you not realize how *known* your boyfriend and his brother are? I know their football stats. I know how many games they played together. I know they were a force to be reckoned with. Mason graduated, and Logan still did amazing with Fallen Crest's record last year. How many did they win? Are you from Fallen Crest? I guess I don't even know that. You may be from somewhere else. Wait. How did you meet Mason? I know I'm being really nosy, but I can't help asking. I'm fascinated with everything. My dad wanted to go pro, and I think he knows their dad, too—something about business. Okay, I'm shutting up. I keep babbling and babbling, and you're looking at me like I'm a psycho stalker. I'm not. Promise." She patted herself on the chest before forcing herself to sit down on the bed and tuck her hands under her legs. "I just really like football. That's all. I don't want to get into either of their pants." She squeaked, her entire face flaming up. "Shutting up. Now."

There was a moment of silence.

The girl was stunning, and she was rattling off things about football, about Mason, about Logan, and even about James. I glanced at the storage totes she'd brought in with her and glimpsed a stack of magazines. The plastic was clear, and the images were blurry, but I could tell the pictures were of her.

This girl was a model and a football fan. "Logan's going to try to hump you like crazy."

"What?" Her head swung back up. She was confused until she saw where I was looking. "Oh." She bit down on her lip. Her hands pulled from under her legs and twisted onto each other. "Yeah." Her foot nudged the closest storage tote. "That's my secret. I'm a model—or I was a model. I quit, so I could come to college." A bitter laugh left her. "My stepmother's not happy."

"Your stepmother?"

"My dad got himself a new wife a few years back. It's been…" She hesitated before continuing, "Difficult, I guess. But what did you say about Logan? He's going to hump me?"

I grunted, moving to start unpacking my own things. "He's going to try." *Damn, my roommate was a model. How cliché was that?* "A model, huh?"

She let out a sigh, giving me a smile. "Former model. College student now, no matter how famous my mother would like me to be."

"Your mom?"

"Yeah." She turned and lifted a tote to her bed before pulling things out. She glanced up, tucking her hair behind her ears. "That's the one thing my mom and my stepmom have bonded on—me. They both want me to keep modeling and do college when I can. But that's not me. Neither cares about what I want. It's what they want, you know?" She frowned slightly. "Look at me, burdening you with all my stuff. I'm sorry. I don't mean to dump this on you, especially on the first day we're meeting. And Mason Kade. Hello! I'm still buzzing from knowing that I know him, you know?"

I grinned. The ball of tension was loosening. "Well, we do have an entire year to get to know each other. I think this was appropriate first-day conversation."

She laughed, her grin spreading wide. "I like you. Most girls instantly hate me." She grew thoughtful. "Not you, though."

"Trust me. I've had my fair share of chicks hating me." *Kate. Miranda. Cass. So many others.* "You won't get that from me." *Not unless you hurt me or my loved ones. All bets are off then.*

"Hot damn, woman!"

A whistle sounded from farther down the hallway, and I knew I had two seconds to give my model roommate a warning.

Logan was coming.

CHAPTER FIVE

MASON

Sam's new roommate was Logan's wet dream, which he made sure she knew. After watching the girl squirm for a good half an hour, I directed my brother to the hallway, kissed Sam, and said our good-byes. The roommate looked relieved.

Sam grabbed my hand before I slipped from the room. She asked, her voice hushed, "You okay?"

I cupped the side of her face. "Yeah. You?"

She nodded. Her hand fell to my chest, and she spread her fingers wide, just touching me there. I wanted to close my eyes, pull her into my arms, and take her to bed and forget Sebastian, forget his threats, forget Sam's roommate, and even forget Logan waiting outside for me. I wanted all of that to go away in that instant, so I could be inside Sam like I'd been earlier that morning. *Fuck.* Something was telling me that the whole plan where she'd stay in her dorm every night for the first month wasn't going to go as planned.

Sweeping a hand down her back, I rested it on her hip and tugged her into me. *Fuck the roommate.* I touched her chin and bent down, my lips brushing over hers. They opened, waiting for me, eager for me. Still holding her chin in place, I grinned against her mouth.

She murmured, her lips moving against mine, "What's that for?"

"It's nice knowing that you'll not be driving three hours back to Fallen Crest." My hand slid inside her shirt, rubbing over her hip bone.

She tilted her head back. "You're telling me." Her hand started its own exploration, moving up my arm, slipping underneath my sleeve, and spreading over my shoulder.

I wanted to close my eyes and let her feel anything she wanted, but the roommate and the brother—I groaned. "I'm picking you up later this afternoon."

A husky laugh slid from her, and she pressed her lips back to mine. "Sounds like a solid plan."

Her hand fell down between us. I knew where she was going, and I adjusted my back so that the roommate couldn't see anything. As soon as I did, Sam's hand found where I was straining against my jeans. She added, "Like I said, solid."

"That's not fair." I couldn't touch her where I wanted.

Her grin grew wider. She was enjoying this little torture session.

Goddamn. I wanted to take her hard. Leaning closer, I whispered into her ear, my teeth grazing her earlobe, "You're starting something—"

She stopped me by pressing a hand to my chest, and then she finished for me, "That I am going to thoroughly enjoy."

"Later."

"Later."

"Thanks for letting me know," Logan said from behind me. "From the hallway. From where a bunch of other strangers are. We all know when my brother's getting his boys rocked, but do we know where? Tsk-tsk, Mason. You need to share this information. I need to know where to set up the sex-tape equipment."

Sam pulled herself from my arms and her hand was up before I could hold her back. Her finger was pointing, and she was in his face. "You don't even joke about that, Logan. You'd never do that. Say it. Right now."

He held up his hands, taking an exaggerated step backward. "I was just kidding. The two of you were all over each other." His hand rested on his chest where his heart was. "Show some consideration for us newly single people."

Sam's roommate moved next to me, watching the exchange.

Logan caught sight of her. A smirk appeared. "Because I am. I'm newly single and hurting. Painfully. I'm lonely."

Sam rolled her eyes. "You broke up six months ago."

"Three months ago."

She narrowed her eyes. "You hooked up three months ago."

"Well," Logan's eyebrows pinched together, "technically, we last hooked up three days ago, but I'm counting three months ago. We had a weekend fling, so the old relationship wounds were reopened." The sides of his mouth curved down, and his eyes grew somber as he looked to Sam's roommate. "Sometimes, I just need to talk. It's more about the talking, the emotional connection."

Sam hit him on the back of his head. "You're a man-whore."

Logan ignored her. "Or even just holding hands. That gentle small touch can be so intimate, you know?"

Sam started to shove him down the hallway. "Go. Get out of here. Stop trying to get into the model's pants."

Logan twisted around her, looking at the roommate. "Model?"

Sam paused. "Huh?"

"You said model. Your roommate's a model?"

She looked at me for confirmation.

"You did."

Her eyes closed, and her head fell back. "Now, there's no stopping him. What did I do?"

The roommate started laughing.

I glanced sideways at her. "You might want to make up a boyfriend. It's the only thing my brother will respect unless you enjoy getting hit on every time you see him."

"Yeah," Logan said over Sam as she was herding him down the hallway. "Right there. I don't mean to brag, but I'm kinda a big deal. I don't usually have to hit on girls, but for you, any day. You want a pick-up line? Give me a call. Give me an order, and I'll supply it real fast. I'm like a fast-food joint. Need a self-esteem boost? Give me a call. Want to get something rubbed?" He winked. "Give me a call. I don't offer these services to just anyone."

Sam had him by the stairs. "Stop hitting on my roommate. I swear, Logan. Stop."

Logan turned his attention from the girl to Sam, and his stance changed. His shoulders tensed up. His eyes focused in attention, and the corners of his mouth tightened. The mischievous side of my brother was coming out. I shook my head, heading toward them.

"Hey, Sam." Logan waited. His smirk was too much now.

"What?" She stepped back, instinctually coming toward me as I grew near.

"Wanna switch places? You can have my room, and I'll have yours?" His gaze darted past her shoulder to the roommate.

I glanced back. The girl was watching us, but she wasn't

watching from fascination or interest. That wasn't what I was sensing from her.

The chick was gorgeous. That was obvious, and I hadn't been surprised when Sam let it slip that her roommate was a model. She had the height, but there was something different about her. While Logan was hitting on her, she'd seemed more interested in me, but I hadn't gotten a sexual vibe from her. It was like she was just…interested?

Her eyes were on me, and she jerked backward into the room. Before she did, I caught the surge of color on her cheeks.

I frowned. "Is your roommate okay?" I asked.

Sam and Logan turned to me. The attitude from both of them changed instantly.

Logan's eyebrows dropped together. "What do you mean? Like, in-the-head, okay?"

"Yeah," Sam shared a concerned look with Logan before turning back to me. "What do you mean?"

"She seems…different."

Sam waved that off. "She's an avid football fan. She was talking my ear off about your and Logan's stats before you came back with the rest of my stuff."

Logan's mouth dropped. "I did all that work, and she knows my stats? What the hell? I even did the fast-food joke. Most girls drop their pants for that one."

"She's a model."

"So? Models can like me, too."

Sam added, "She's probably used to guys hitting on her left and right."

"That's true." Logan rubbed his chin. "My stats, huh? Football turns her on?" His eyes flickered to me, and he laughed. "Talk about awkward. You can never bone Sam in her dorm room. You don't know her level of fandom. She could be daydreaming that you're boning her or worse." He shuddered. "My joke about the sex-tape equipment just took on a whole new meaning."

I rolled my eyes but asked Sam, "She's a fan? That's it?"

She nodded. "I'm surprised she didn't ask for your autograph. Her dad is friends with your coach or something. And she knows your dad, too."

That got Logan's attention again. "Our dad? James?"

"That's what she said."

I relaxed a little bit. "Find out her dad's name, but that makes me feel better. You'll be safe with her?"

"I think so. She didn't come off as scary to me."

"Scarily hot, you mean," Logan shot in, grinning.

"Can you turn down your moods?" Sam frowned at him. "You go from pissy to being drunk. You're hitting on my roommate to I don't even know what, and now, you're back to being sexually suggestive?"

"What? That's what being Logan is all about. I'm like a ping-pong ball. I'm all over the place. Too fast for you to catch."

Sam shook her head. "I'm going back to my room. I'm unpacking. I'm going to meet my floor advisor and maybe go get my textbooks with my roommate." She glared at Logan. "I'm leaving. I'm going to try to be normal."

She pressed a kiss to me before squeezing my hand.

"I'll text you later."

She nodded, waving to us before going through the crowd of girls and mothers who were still watching us.

Logan noticed them, too, and frowned. "Check it out. All the dudes are probably inside, putting the bunk beds together." He gestured to himself and pretended to do a curtsy. "Logan Kade.

You heard the name here first." He threw to Sam, "Normal's overrated, by the way."

"Screw off, Logan."

Some of the women broke out in laughter. One mother clapped, but Sam went back to her room. She was safe. That was all I was worried about. She had to be safe.

"Let's go." I headed for the stairs.

Logan waited until we were closer to the vehicle before he asked, "You didn't see anything unusual up there?"

I knew what he was referring to. Climbing into my vehicle, I waited for him to get into the passenger side before I pulled out of the parking lot. "No. I checked every room. Did you?"

He nodded. "All chicks. I didn't see anyone with a picture of Park Sebastian in their room." He paused and then said, "Sam's going to be pissed if she realizes we were up there, canvassing her floormates."

I didn't care. "We needed to make sure she would be safe."

"The back door locks, so no one can get through that way."

I nodded. "I asked around. A front-desk clerk is always on duty, so no one can sneak her in and out that way."

"Sam might be safe there, maybe safer than if she lived with us. There are lots of witnesses, you know."

"That's my thinking."

That was the entire reason for heading up with her to the room. Helping her move everything up was the other reason, but the main one was to scope everything out—her resident advisor, her neighbors. The place was an all-girls dorm, but I wouldn't put it past Sebastian to get some girl to help spy on Sam.

Logan was right. Both of us had been in and out of the rooms. We took turns, one slipping in as the other distracted whoever was helping the girl move in or hurrying inside if a room was left empty for some reason. Everything we saw didn't show any connections to Sebastian, but that didn't mean there wouldn't be any.

Logan sighed. "You should just hire security."

"I already did."

"Serious?"

I gave him a look. "You're not weirded out by that?"

"Fuck no. Sebastian's crazy and an egomaniac. He'll do anything to hurt Sam because that means hurting you. I'm glad you already got security on her."

"He starts tomorrow."

"Are you going to tell her?"

I gave him a look.

Logan grinned at me. "I idolize you and your deceitful, dark ways. Hey," Logan tapped my arm, "pull into that parking lot. The bookstore's over there."

"The bookstore?" But I did as he'd asked, and as we got out of the Escalade and headed for the store, I said, "I'm not telling Sam to lie to her. I'm not telling her because she'd hate having a shadow."

A group of students were standing in front of the doors. Some were smoking. Others had bags of their textbooks and were talking. A few more were standing there, looking through their books. Logan and I bypassed them, heading inside, but as we were going in, Nate was coming out.

"Hey!" A big grin came from him. We stepped back outside with him and he finished zipping up his backpack. Shrugging it on, he looked between Logan and me. "What are you guys doing here? Wait. The store. I got it." He cringed. "Don't roast me."

Logan and I shared a look. I had no intention, I never did, but with Logan, one never knew. When he kept quiet, Nate and I shared a look instead. That surprised both of us.

"What?" Logan must've noticed the look. "Sam just tore my ass in half. I'm not going to start pounding on someone else."

A few of the girls closest to the door whipped around, watching us and Nate burst out laughing.

I frowned at Logan. "You had to use those specific words when you were talking about my girlfriend?"

Logan smirked. "She's my future stepsister too, you know."

All of the girls on the left side of the door looked over, hearing that last statement. Ignoring the attention, I asked, "You're done getting your books?"

"Yeah." Nate was waiting, watching me.

I rolled my eyes. I'd get Logan back later at the house.

"Let us get our books and head to the house. Is it too early to start partying?" Logan moved forward but stopped short.

Looking over his shoulder inside of the door, I saw the reason, and a chill filled the air. Park Sebastian and three of his friends were coming from the basement door that led into the bookstore. The tension dramatically went up. My jaw clenched. I wanted to go for him, but Nate saw Sebastian the same time I did. Nate's hand clamped down on my shoulder, as if anchoring me in place. Logan was in front of me. I didn't know if he was going to hold me back or lunge for the dickhead himself.

If this was going to happen, I glanced over my shoulders—there were witnesses here. I wanted it to be done where there were none so I went inside. Logan and Nate followed behind.

"Look who it is. The current stars for *Fraternity Assholes: Where Are They Now?*" Logan said.

I shared a look with Nate. I hadn't realized how thankful I was for having my brother with us until that instant. As if sensing my thoughts, Logan moved to the side, and I stepped next to him. We were shoulder-to-shoulder, gazing down at Sebastian and three of his friends. Judging from the hostility on their faces, I figured they were fraternity exes as well.

Park Sebastian.

My eyes roamed over him. He looked like the same preppy dick that he'd been last year. His hair was blond, gelled and combed to the side. Polo shirt. Khaki cargo shorts. A bag of books in one hand and a flask in the other.

"Logan Kade." Sebastian showed his perfect teeth. "And the big brother with his best friend. Well, this is lovely. All three of you together." He met my eyes for a second. A sinister dark look passed there, and he craned his neck to look behind us. "Is that it? Just the three of you? No one else?"

My eyes narrowed. He was looking for Sam.

I started forward, but Logan beat me to it. He slapped a hand on the wall next to me. His arm blocked my advance as he drawled, "Who do you love, Sebastian?"

Sebastian tensed. "What do you mean?"

"Girlfriend? Sister?" Logan's voice chilled.

He fights. I talk. That's our thing. His old words filtered back to me, and I knew that was what he was doing. He was doing his job.

Nate moved around us, and Logan slid over, making room for him. When Nate stood in front of me, Logan took a step with him. Both of them were edging me backward just slightly. They were protecting me.

"Why are you asking?" Sebastian's question was wary.

"I need to know who to target." Logan grinned at him. "I'm very, very single this year, if you didn't know, and since you enjoy threatening someone we care about, I figure it's the least I could do. You target ours. I'll target yours."

"I think you've already taken enough from me."

Logan touched his ear and leaned forward. "What was that? What did you say?"

Sebastian gritted his teeth. "You heard me."

"No, no." Logan pretended to clean his ear out and stepped forward again. "Seriously, I couldn't hear you. What did you say?"

"I said," a low growl emanated from Sebastian, "you've already taken enough from me."

"What are you talking about? I think I have a wax problem." Logan threw me a smirk over his shoulder. "Who knew a buildup of discharge could be such a problem?"

He was going to hit Sebastian. I saw the promise in Logan's eyes and knew he was getting closer for a sucker punch. Sensing my tension, Nate glanced at me from the side of his eye. He knew something was going to happen.

I couldn't fight.

Sebastian would use it against me.

That was what I was telling myself. *Not here. Not now.*

Logan edged forward one more step.

He was going to, no matter what. I looked up and around. If my little brother was going to hit Sebastian for me, I could help in some way. There was a camera in the corner of the doorway. It was rotating around the entrance and the other set of stairs that led to the top floor of the bookstore.

Logan and Sebastian were still talking, but I eased forward. Logan glanced at me, and I nodded to the camera.

He looked up and shifted backward an inch.

A sudden rush of air left Nate, and I knew he figured out what was going on.

He muttered under his breath, "We're doing this?"

Sebastian couldn't hear him. He was still fixated on Logan.

Nate added, "Okay. Tell me when."

I threw him a side grin. He got it, grinning back at me.

This, right here, was what I'd been missing all last year—besides Sam, of course. She was the constant, but this camaraderie with Logan getting a person worked up and Nate ready to join in.

Sebastian got silent, looking between us.

Logan sent Nate and me a small glare. I flashed Logan a grin back. *Relax.* I moved forward and snuck a peek to the camera. It was rotating back, moving at a slow pace.

Logan caught the look and gazed up as well.

In ten.

"I'm not sure if you're aware of this threesome dynamic," Logan started.

Sebastian's eyes narrowed. Logan was too cocky, too sure of himself. Sebastian's head lifted to the side as he kept skirting among all three of us.

Nine.

I was next to my brother. They came from the basement section of the bookstore, so Sebastian was blocking his friends from us. His three friends were down a few steps, too far but close enough where they could catch Sebastian.

Eight.

Logan continued, "But the three of us…" He gestured to all of us. "Well, technically, it's the Fearsome Foursome with Sam, but she's not here." His tone lowered, growing more serious.

"And she's not a part of this, so I guess, right now, you can call us the Threesome Fearsome."

Seven.

Sebastian was almost ignoring my brother. He was solely focused on me. *Fine.* I let him see the threat in me and murmured, "My brother's not kidding, you know."

Logan quieted, edging back so that I was now in the front.

"About what?" His tone was clipped.

Sebastian knew. He was remembering Logan's threat.

I reminded him. "Your sister. Your girlfriend."

Six.

"I don't have either one of those," Sebastian shot back.

Logan piped in, "But there's someone."

I added, "There's always someone."

Sebastian grew silent, looking between the two of us.

Five.

Nate spoke up, "They're talking about who's vulnerable to you, Sebastian."

"You shut up," Sebastian snapped at him. "You left the house. You don't deserve the right to talk to us."

His three friends got riled up at that. They moved forward, and I started eyeing the big one closest to Sebastian. He was a big motherfucker.

Four.

"Nate never should've been with you," I said, commanding all of their attention. We were close. The camera would rotate back. I wanted their focus on me, not Logan. "That was a mistake he rectified."

Three.

Sebastian's eyes narrowed to slits. "I'm going to make both of you sorry that you came back here."

"What about me?" Logan smirked at him.

No. I wanted Sebastian watching me.

He turned. "I already tried to get your acceptance revoked."

Well, holy shit, I hadn't expected that response.

Two.

Logan opened his mouth. His eyes flashed in anger, and he was going to say something to piss Sebastian off. I blocked him. I needed Sebastian and friends' eyes on me.

"Time's up," I said calmly, quietly.

It worked. They all turned to me, and Sebastian's eyes widened. He started to rear back—

One.

I rushed forward.

Sebastian lifted his arm to block my launch.

I soared past him.

He frowned.

It happened in the blink of an eye. I opened him up to Logan, and I checked the Big Motherfucker against the wall, holding him back.

I looked over my shoulder.

Logan threw the first punch. Sebastian was looking over his shoulder, following where I went, before he realized his mistake. Logan got him clear across the face, on top of the nose, and then it was game on.

Time slowed for that first hit but slammed back, and everything that happened afterward was so quick.

I had the bigger guy against the wall. He couldn't move to help, and Nate rushed around me to stop the other two from going forward. Logan's hit did the deed. Sebastian fell back, but he didn't fall down the stairs. He fell into Nate's back, and I clamped on Sebastian's arm. One hit was fine, but having the guy getting more injuries or worse from falling down the stairs would be another thing entirely. His arm reached out and grabbed me. He didn't know who was holding him. One of Sebastian's friends slipped past Nate, but I maneuvered Sebastian, and shoved him so he fell into his friend's arms.

Logan was at the door, waiting.

Nate reared his arm back, ready to deliver a hit of his own, but I caught his arm and ripped myself from the Big Motherfucker.

I dragged Nate behind me, and all three of us scrambled from the entrance. Once outside, I looked back. The camera was circling back to sweep where we'd left.

Logan tucked his hand into his pocket so no one could see the swelling.

We held firm. Nate started toward the parking lot, but I shook my head. This was Manipulation 101. We waited, and it wasn't long before the door flung open.

Sebastian and his three friends flew out, searching for us.

We were right there, standing calmly.

Sebastian frowned, stopping himself, but he couldn't hold back his friends. The three of them rushed us.

The Big Motherfucker came at me. The other two squared against Logan and Nate.

As the big guy swung, I dodged and scooted back, holding up my hands. "Hey, hey, hey."

Here was the slimy part. I hated doing this, but it was needed to deal with Sebastian.

I lied through my teeth, "What the hell? Come on."

The girls outside gasped. Two of them screamed, and I glimpsed a few grabbing for their phones. One girl sprinted into the bookstore.

"Stop," Sebastian cried out.

He reached for his friends, but they weren't hearing him.

The big guy swung again. I blocked his punch. I could've delivered a good uppercut, but I hadn't. I shoved him away and held my hands up again. "Come on, man. What's your problem?"

Logan was doing the same as me, ducking and dodging.

Nate started to throw his fist, but he caught on to us, and his arm fell back to his side. The three of us kept scooting around as Sebastian's guys continued to throw punches.

"*Guys!*" Sebastian yelled at them.

They still weren't listening.

Suddenly, they were grabbed and shoved backward. A wall of guys stepped between them and us, and it took a second before I realized what had happened.

Some of my football teammates were there. Drew, the quarterback, and a few others. Drew was standing in front of me with his back to me. The rest were literally a wall between Sebastian and his guys and us.

"Hey, man," Sebastian started, moving away. He held his hands up, like I had moments ago. "They started this."

A girl spoke up, "No, they didn't. Those guys came out, and then those other guys just started hitting."

Logan glanced at me. We shared a look. This hadn't been planned, but it was like Sebastian delivered himself to us on a platter.

"We didn't," the Big Motherfucker huffed back at her. "The one guy hit Sebastian, and then they ran. We were just following. They started it."

Drew turned to me before saying to Sebastian, "Well, it

doesn't matter. They have witnesses. You don't. I'd suggest you walk and walk fast before campus security gets here."

It was then when Sebastian figured it out. His anger spiked, and he glowered at me. Drew was studying me, too. I kept my face blank. I felt bad. Drew and the guys weren't supposed to be there, but this was my fight against Sebastian. A lie to my quarterback was collateral.

Sebastian didn't want to go. He lingered, but his friends were the smarter ones this time around. They grabbed his arm and pulled him down a sidewalk. He was glaring at me the whole time.

Good.

I wanted him to glare.

I wanted him mad.

I wanted him off balance. He'd mess up, and when he did, I would win.

Drew shook his head. He said under his breath to me, "That took some balls."

"What are you talking about?"

He murmured so that no one else could hear, "Be careful, Mason. Okay?"

I was going to deny whatever he thought I was doing, but I saw it in his eyes. He knew. They were knowing, a little awed but also cautious. Instead, I nodded. "I will."

CHAPTER SIX

SAMANTHA

Mason trailed kisses down my throat, lingering between my breasts, before groaning and lifting back up to meet my lips.

My god.

He pushed farther inside me, going deep, and I sighed from contentment as his mouth moved over mine.

I loved this man. The harder he went, the more I would unravel for him. The deeper he moved, the more I'd want to match him, thrust for thrust. Harder. Rougher. Deeper. As he moved, so did I. Our hips were glued to each other. I gasped, pleasure coursing through me.

As soon as I'd walked through his bedroom door, he pinned me against it and started kissing me. Not many words were shared. We didn't need them, but as he readjusted his hold on my hands above me, I knew something was wrong. He was hungrier than normal, like he was starving to be one with me.

His hand swept down my side and gripped under my leg. I had a second to realize what he was doing as he reared back to thrust once more into me. He lifted me from the door and carried me to the bed. He held me up like that, and the sheer force of it rippled through his back. His arms were taut, holding me in place, and a thrill of adrenaline shot through me. This man, as he laid me down and gently fell with me, had so much power and strength.

I reveled in his caresses, loving every inch of him, as he went back inside before moving out and then back in. He was on top of me, but his weight was welcome. My wrists were stretched above me again, and then he lifted his head, watching me. He gazed down through lidded eyes, the stark need for me so bright and obvious in their depths. It was like an extra layer of emotion swimming over the surface. I saw it in his eyes and the way his mouth looked to be in pain from needing to touch mine again. It was even in how he grabbed my hip and moved it to the side, aligning his hips, so he could go deeper. He was all the way in, sheathed there, as he held still for a second.

I was his.

What he wanted from me, I'd give.

I panted. I wanted to reach for him and pull him back to me, but he kept my wrists in his hand. This was for him.

He groaned, dipping back down to my lips. I felt his yearning once again, and I lifted up, pressing all of my body against his. We were both slick from sweat, so we seamlessly moved together, almost gliding against one another. He pulled out before going back inside me.

"Mason," I murmured. I wanted his mouth on me, anywhere on me. I wanted him to go faster. I wanted to feel the ride.

The sensations were building. I was going to come.

"Sam," he whispered, bending over so that his lips grazed my ear. He kept moving.

I felt his body tensing and knew he was right with me.

He cursed, gasping. "I love you."

We both came together. I pulled at his hold on my wrists, but he held me, still pinned. I looked up to find he was watching me. A lazy smile adorned his face, and his free hand went to rub between my legs, right at my opening.

"Mason!" I jerked against his hand, feeling the sensations triple, as he started rubbing in a circular motion.

He pressed harder, but not too hard. I felt the buildup once again. Two waves were pressing onto me. I strained against him, trying to pause his caresses. I was going to come undone.

"Mason," I whimpered. *Please.*

He kissed under my ear, finding my spot, and his hand moved faster and then slower before picking up speed, and pressing down. I couldn't do anything. I was helpless.

He whispered, "Let go. This is for you."

I was coming…

His hand kept rubbing.

He pulled out, but his finger dipped in me.

I gasped again. My back was off the bed. My hands, head, and legs were the only things touching.

Mason kept going. A second finger slid into me.

"Mason!"

He started kissing my throat, moving up the side of my chin to the corner of my mouth. He held there, a teasing caress. I wanted his mouth on mine again. I always felt home when he was there. I turned my head, seeking his lips, but he moved back.

My eyes flashed in warning. I was going to get him back for this.

He grinned, his hand pumping in and out, as he rubbed at my tip.

"I'm—" I couldn't talk. I was panting again.

This man…he was going to be the death of me.

Mason stilled his hand. He let go of my wrists, and I curved into him, holding on to him, as I rode out the sensations. My body continued to tremble as wave after wave crashed over me. I was a puddle of nothing by the time they stopped. I could die happily.

"Fuck. You." I rolled to look at Mason.

He bit out a laugh before dropping a kiss to my mouth. "Did you enjoy that?"

I curved my hand over his shoulder, savoring the feel of his muscles. "I'm going to get you back. You know that, right?"

"I hope so." He sat up. His eyes darkened once again as he took in the sight of me.

My breasts were full and erect. I was perspiring, and my eyes must've looked crazy. He trailed a hand down from my throat to my stomach, ending right between my legs. "I missed you so goddamn much."

So goddamn much.

So goddamn much.

I remembered the texts we shared a while back. A wave of nostalgia rose up, and my throat swelled. We'd been apart during that time. My hand cupped the side of his face. "Hey," I said softly, rising up to my elbow, "what's wrong?"

We're together. We're fine. Nothing will come between us, I tried to tell myself, but his rigid shoulders were causing me to worry.

"Hey," I tapped the underside of his mouth, "talk to me."

He grinned before lightly kissing me. Dropping to his back, he lay next to me and scooped me, so I was curled halfway over him. His hand fell down my back, causing a trail of tingles in its wake. "It's nothing."

It wasn't nothing. I had two guesses, but I only needed one. "You saw Park Sebastian today?"

He sighed. "Yeah."

"And it didn't go well?"

"It did, but…"

I was done with his hesitation. Sitting up, I fixed him with a stare. "Talk. Now."

He started to reach for me, but I caught his hand. "Tell me what's wrong."

He sat up, resting against the headboard, watching me. "Logan threatened to go after someone Sebastian loves, someone who's vulnerable."

I waited, hearing what he wasn't saying. "You and Park Sebastian are not the same."

"You're right." Mason gave me a half grin, but it didn't reach his eyes. "He's a monster that hurt a friend of mine where he was vulnerable. I'm the monster that let my brother threaten someone Sebastian loves." He shook his head. "I don't see how we're that different."

"Threatening someone so that he's scared is completely different than actually doing it."

"But Logan would do it."

Our eyes caught and held. He was right.

I swallowed. "Logan wouldn't do it unless he was forced, unless he had no other option."

"Sam…" Mason tugged on my arm, drawing me closer to him.

I was almost kneeling on his stomach.

He caught and held my hand on his lap. "I know what you're saying. I'm just worried that we've bitten off more than we can handle."

His gaze was focused on me, but I had a feeling he wasn't

really watching for my reaction. He was watching me. He was worried about me.

I squeezed his hand. "Hey."

I shifted until I was straddling him, and his hands rested on my hips, holding me in place.

"You and Logan are not monsters. You protect. You take care. You shield those you love. Yes, you're ruthless. Yes, you go to lengths others don't, but you do it so that no one—and I mean, no one—can hurt you or even try to hurt you. That's why you do what you do. That's why you're who you are and why you're loved by me and wanted by so many others. That's why you're respected. You protect and you love and you don't let anyone take that away from you."

I leaned down until my forehead rested against his. I was staring right into him, and I felt like I could see his soul. He was stripped bare to me, like I had been moments ago for him.

"Do not let Park Sebastian get into your head. Handle him how you handle everyone. You go right through them, no matter what fight they put up."

He grinned and his lips nipped at mine. His hand caught the back of my neck, and he held me still, adjusting our hips. I had a second's notice as he said, "I love you so damn much." He pushed inside me.

I closed my eyes, leaning back, and he started moving in and out of me again.

I loved him, too.

And I would tell him right after—

He held me to him and rolled, so he was on top of me.

I grabbed his hips and began to move with him.

Yes. Right after this.

"How do you like your roommate?"

I peered up at Mason, lying next to him. I was half-tempted to glare at him and give him the silent treatment. He hadn't let me return the favor for his earlier torture that was…delicious. I didn't know why, but something was still bothering him. I wouldn't push it though.

I answered, tugging my tank top over my head, "She seems nice. We went to get our books after you guys left."

"Right after we left?" He'd been rubbing my stomach, but his hand stilled.

I shook my head. "No, like two hours later. We visited for a while, and her parents brought a bunch of stuff to the room."

He went back to rubbing in a circle. "Did you like her family?"

He was acting funny.

I shrugged. "They were okay. Normal parents." I grinned. "Not like any of ours anyway."

Mason waited until I pulled my arms through my top. He caught one of my hands and toyed with my fingers. "I didn't do the dorm thing. I lived in the football house right away. Do you do things with your whole floor, like to get to know each other?"

I took a moment and stared at him, fighting from smiling.

He noticed. "What?"

"You. Being so cute." I nudged him with my elbow. "You're trying to be coy, but I know you want to make sure I meet people."

He rolled his eyes and sat up to rest against the headboard. "Ha-ha. I honestly have no clue what the dorm thing is like, but yeah, I think it'd be smart if you became friendly with your neighbors. The more support you can get, the better."

"I will, and yes, we had a floor meeting. Everyone went to get ice cream today, too."

"Did you?"

"No." Just looking at him, my mouth started watering. Again.

His green eyes were piercing me, and his firm lips were grinning back at me. Mason always had a chiseled face and strong jawline, but they were beckoning me once more. I ached to run my fingers over them.

"I came here instead."

"Sam."

I heard the reprimand coming, but I put my hand up, stopping it. The lust was held at bay. "It's fine. They're doing a movie and popcorn night in the lounge. I'm going to go back and join in with that. I figured any bonding I could've done while walking to get ice cream could be done while I made popcorn for everyone tonight."

He nodded, but his face closed off. I couldn't read him anymore, and I frowned, but I knew what was bothering him. It had been the same since he came back to Fallen Crest with a busted face.

Leaning over him, I cupped both sides of his face in my hands. "Hey."

His eyes looked up.

"Let me in."

And like that, his wall slid away, revealing the concern that I knew was there.

I whispered, "I will be fine."

"You don't know what he's like."

We both knew who *he* was.

We both knew what we were talking about.

I asked, "Do you think he'll physically attack me?"

"He did with me." His hands rested over mine, rubbing my wrists. "I don't think he would with you. That'd be…there's no going back from that, but I can't promise he won't. I don't know."

"Well then, I'll carry a Taser with me, and I promise not to go anywhere alone. Would that make you stop worrying so much?"

"Sam," he started.

His stomach muscles contracted, and he caught me around my waist, holding me in place, as he lifted himself back up, so we were sitting face-to-face, like we had been an hour earlier. He added, "I'm always going to worry. When it comes to you, there's nothing I won't do, and he knows that. That's my weakness—how much I love you, the lengths I'll go to protect you. Sebastian's smart. He'll use that against me." He shuddered, running a hand down the middle of my back and over my spine. "Promise me that if you see him, you'll call me or Logan. Promise."

"I will."

My words didn't matter. The storm of unrest was still with him, but it'd have to do. We'd have to see how things progressed as we went.

I wasn't the mastermind that Mason was. I couldn't predict people's behaviors like he could, but I knew one thing. I'd gone against my fair share of formidable enemies. Park Sebastian was a guy. The only thing he had over my other enemies was his physical strength. I didn't think he could outcast me like Jessica and Lydia tried my sophomore year at Fallen Crest Academy. I didn't think he'd have a group of girls assault me in a restroom, and I didn't think he had the mojo to make me fall in love with Logan. The only other threat that we'd endured was my mother, and she was long gone. I knew she wasn't coming back.

I sighed, pressing a kiss to Mason before crawling off his lap and heading for the shower. "I need to get going. Floor movie and all."

"I'll take you back."

I flipped on the light and stepped under the water. Mason was dressed and sitting on the edge of the bed, waiting for me when I came back out. My eyes narrowed, but as he looked me up and down, a slow grin tugged at the corner of his mouth, and I started to forget the small hope I'd had of him joining me. Raking a hand through his hair, I tugged his head to look up and into my eyes.

His hands rested on my hips, and he pulled me to stand between his legs.

I said fiercely, "I will be okay." I paused and then asked, "Okay?"

His hands tightened once before relaxing. "I know you will be."

Logan was in the living room when we passed, heading for the vehicle. He grinned and waved his fingers to us. "Toodles, lovers. Don't screw in the parking lot. I heard they ramped up their security guard detail." His gaze shifted to Mason. "Something about a fight by the campus bookstore."

"Really?" I frowned. "I hadn't heard anything. My RA would've said something—well, I think she would've anyway."

He went back to the football game on the television and shrugged. "Hmm. Yeah, well, maybe she's not in the know, like I am."

"Logan." A low warning came from Mason.

Ignoring him, Logan raised a hand in the air again. "Tell your roommate she's hot, Sam. I'll be stopping by for morning coffee and crumpets."

"Toodles and now crumpets." I rolled my eyes, following Mason out the door. Bypassing him as he stopped to hold the door for me, I said, "Your brother needs to stop watching the BBC network."

Logan shouted from inside, "I heard that, and never, woman. BBC holds my heart like no vixen ever shall."

I groaned.

Mason grinned and let go of the door so it could swing shut. "He's hyped up for a good fight. He was bored last year in Fallen Crest when all the action was here. He's been in a Monty Python phase lately. Don't get him going on the burning of witches."

I glanced up at him as he said that, rounding the car for the driver's seat. I tried to judge if there was an undertone or hidden meaning in his statement, but as Mason got into the car and started the engine, he didn't seem to hold on to anything. His shoulders were relaxed. He grinned at me and reached over to grab my hand when I got inside. He held my hand the entire drive back.

The tension from in the bedroom seemed to have lifted off his shoulders—at least for now—but I knew some of that was because Logan was here.

We were all here.

CHAPTER SEVEN

The house that loomed in front of us was large and in charge.

Music pounded from it. The lights were bright through the windows, spilling out onto the backyard. And people were everywhere. I glanced around the group of girls who opted to skip the movie night for this house party, and most looked scared. A couple were already drunk while my roommate was busy checking her phone. She had a bored expression on her face. I frowned, unsure of how to take that, but I understood the nerves from the rest. This was their first college party. To be honest, I was a little unnerved, but I thought it was more because I hadn't told Mason I was going to this party. He thought I was safe and sound, sitting all cozied up with a bowl of popcorn, a blanket, and maybe even a wine cooler.

That was the plan until the movie reserved by the resident advisor sucked. After thirty minutes of most people spending time on their phones or taking restroom breaks, she let us go and threw in an invite to a party she'd heard about. It was her way of making up for the suck-ass movie. We were given directions and a few guidelines on what kind of guys to stay away from, and then she gave us the green light along with a request to save the puking for outside and not in the floor's restrooms.

That led to a group of nine of us trekking across campus and down one block.

"So…" Summer cleared her throat, putting her phone in her pocket. "What do you say, ladies? Are we going to tackle this bitch or stare at it all night?"

Another girl, a little heavyset with red hair, smacked herself in the chest. She nodded firmly and declared, "Hell yes, we are." She paused before adding, "Tackle this bitch, I mean. Not just stare at it all night. I, for one, want to meet a man, and that ain't happening if I hang out with only you ladies this year."

Summer thrust her fist in the air. "That's the whoring spirit we want."

I grinned.

The red-haired girl nodded again to us. "That's what I have. Not a whore, but I have spirit. I have the drinking spirit tonight."

Another girl, shorter than the rest with striking, blue eyes and white hair, piped up, "We need to buddy up. Sexual assaults happen at parties like these, so we need to check on each other."

Summer grabbed my hand, holding it in the air. "My roommate's mine."

As they found their buddies, their hands joining ours in the air, Summer leaned closer to me. "I'm glad you came. You looked unsure about it before."

I shrugged. "My boyfriend has enemies on campus. He worries."

"Stay close to me. My mom worried about the same thing, so she made me take self-defense classes. You know," her cheeks flushed as she lowered her voice, "because I'm a model."

I glanced around, but the others hadn't heard. "I know how to fight a tiny bit, but don't be embarrassed about that. I get it. I really do."

"I know. I just…" She waved a hand down the line of girls. "Most get jealous when they find out what I used to do for money."

"Are you talking about the whoring spirit?" The heavyset girl joined our conversation along with the little female next to her.

"What?" Summer asked.

"What you used to do for money."

"Oh. Uh…" My roommate was a deer in headlights. Her eyes were wide, and she went pale.

I stepped in, channeling some Logan, "She used to clean ass."

All three of them snapped their attention to me.

I grinned. "She was a nurse's aide. That's what they do, but she didn't want to let you know. All the jokes, you know?"

"Oh." The heavyset girl scratched the side of her face. "That's…completely understandable. I was a sandwich artist all through high school. It may sound great, but there's really no art involved, if you get my drift." She held her hand out. "I'm Kitty, by the way. With my name, trust me, I really do understand not appreciating the jokes."

We all stared at her.

She glanced at each one of us and then explained, "Kitty's not a nickname. It's my real name. My mom was obsessed with Pink Kitty."

"Oh." I frowned. "I'm so sorry."

"Ah, what can I do?" She waved it off and nudged her elbow to the white-haired girl. "This is Nina."

"Hi." Both Summer and I nodded and introduced ourselves.

Nina waved but glanced over her shoulder at the house. Most of the girls had gone inside.

Seeing this, she asked, "Shouldn't we have a plan, so no one gets lost? And are we all walking back together to the dorm or going with our buddies? We are not prepared for this house party at all. Do we even know who's hosting it? I heard some fraternity got disbanded last year. It's not those guys, is it?"

I tensed, wondering what else she had heard, but Kitty had the answer. "Oh, no, I talked to Ruby."

"Who's Ruby?" someone asked.

Kitty's eyebrows knitted together. "Our RA. Don't you guys listen?"

Summer grinned at me.

Kitty was already saying, "She told me where some of those guys were holed up, and it's not the same house. These guys are just a group of friends. She knows them. She said they're pretty harmless, except for those two creepers she warned us about. Oh, and she was going to call to give them a heads-up that some of her girls were coming." She pointed at us, including the group who had gone inside the house. "That's us."

Summer sucked in her breath, fighting back a grin.

"I think we should do a four-person buddy system. You two look out for us at the end, and we'll do the same," she said with precision and a firm head nod.

I glanced down, expecting her to do a little footstep. It'd sounded like she was starting a cheer. As I was waiting for the toe-heel movement, she linked her elbow with Kitty and began prancing up the hill to the house. Her free arm was swinging widely. Her head was high. Her shoulders were back. She even tossed back her hair with a head shake. Nina was ready to take the world on, one house party at a time.

Summer groaned next to me. "Oh my god, we're surrounded by dorks."

"Not our whole floor." But I wasn't sure, and *dorks* wasn't the nicest word to use, but I had to agree a little bit. "I would say that they…" I was searching. "Um…they're not as practiced with house parties as we might be?"

"Speaking of, you've barely blinked since we got here."

We started after the other two after Kitty hollered for us to get our spirit butts in gear.

"But from the stories I've heard about Mason Kade and his brother, I'm not surprised. I have to admit that even I've heard about the Kade parties. I wanted to go to one, but I could never talk my friends into crashing one with me. They were too scared. They'd heard the girls who went to them were like savage beasts."

"You're not far off with that one." Kate and her pack of four could howl with the best of them. "And," using her phrase, I said, "you've barely blinked yourself."

The music grew louder as we stepped onto the porch. Reaching for the door, Summer murmured before opening it, "I've been to a few discos overseas. These don't compare." She winked as she drew back the door.

The music overwhelmed us.

So did the laughter and conversation.

So did the heat from all those bodies inside.

So did the smell of weed, booze, and sweat.

I couldn't believe it. My first college party really looked like a scene from *Animal House*.

Just inside the door, Kitty, Nina, and some of the rest from our floor were huddled together, gripping their red plastic cups.

Summer frowned at them. "You guys already have beer?"

At that moment, a guy wearing a toga came around the corner, holding a row of red cups. A guy came with him, holding a pony keg on his shoulder. As they both saw us, wide smiles lit up their faces.

The guy with the cups said, "Well, hey there! Two newcomers. Hold on, ladies." He knelt and pulled out one cup, holding it underneath the keg's spout.

The second guy was nodding his head in rhythm to the bass, looking glazed over as he pushed on the spout, and the beer started flowing.

When they were done, the guy with the cups stood back up and held a hand out to Summer. "I'm Blaze, and Ruby's a friend. She said you all were coming, so no worries. Only good guys here. All the bedrooms are locked up anyway. No one can use them. There's a bathroom upstairs. There's one on this floor, but I wouldn't recommend it. Sy keeps plugging it. It's disgusting, so if the upstairs one is full, there's one downstairs, too. If you guys need anything, let me know, and I'll try to help you out. I'm the host extraordinaire."

The second guy kept bobbing his head, now closing his eyes. His pony-keg duties were done. Still in rhythm, his hips began moving back and forth as he moved away.

"Oh." Summer shook Blaze's hand and stepped back into me right afterward. "I'm Summer. This is…" She started to point to me, but her gaze slid over my shoulder, and she trailed off.

Her eyes got big as an arm rested around my shoulders, and I was pulled in close to a hard body.

I closed my eyes. I knew who it was, even before he said a word.

"And this is Samantha, my stepsister." Logan grinned at Blaze. "I'm Logan."

Stepsister? Summer mouthed to me.

I shook my head. Too long of a story for right then.

Blaze's eyes lit up. "Logan Kade?"

"That's me."

The two shook hands, and Blaze lingered for a moment longer than Logan before letting go. He pointed the column of cups at him, a wide smile growing. "I've heard about you. Holy shit. I heard about everything. Last year. The fight today. What they tried with your brother." His eyes were threatening to bulge out now. "Mason Kade is your brother! Holy fucking fuck. That's awesome." He looked past him with a question falling from his lips. "Is he with you?"

I had already been tense, and I became even more so now.

Logan replied, clasping me even tighter to him, "Nah. He's got football practice tomorrow. He had to go over new plays tonight, but this is Nate."

Blaze's arm swung to Nate, who stepped to Logan's other side. "I'm crapping my pants. You're Nate Monson. I've heard all about you, too. You were with those motherfuckers last year before you gave them the middle finger."

Nate shook his hand. "Yeah," he said to the guy, "I was pretty stupid in the first place to join them." He glanced to me. "Hey, Sam."

Blaze took in the greeting and bounced the cups up and down, pointing at me with them. "You. You, I have to tell Ruby about. She's going to flip out. You're connected to legends. Do you have any idea?"

Logan was suppressing laughter. I felt it from his chest.

I frowned. "Tell us what you really think."

"What?" Blaze's smile never dimmed. "I hate Park Sebastian. Ruby loathes him with the passion of ten thousand fire ants. Whatever you guys want," he swept his gaze over the entire group, "let me know. You got it. You want pizza? I'll order it right now."

"No." Logan held out a hand, stopping him before he could rush to the phone. "We're good, but," he took my beer, "Sam might want another beer."

"Oh, yeah." He turned and hollered, "Gus! Get over here. We need the pony ASAP." He said to Nate, "We'll get a beer for you, too. Be right back."

I'd only officially met Kitty ten minutes earlier, but she shoved her way through the group to my side when Blaze went in search of his pony-keg friend. Summer was elbowed to the back. She seemed more startled than offended by the move, but I was elbowed in the side, too.

Kitty said in a loud voice, "Who are your friends, friend?"

Kitty was on a one-man mission.

She seemed hesitant of Logan but warmed right up to Nate, even going to his side as she refused to let go of his hand. Nina replaced Kitty by my side, but she didn't look inclined for an introduction. She had her arms wrapped around herself and half of a sleeve stuck in her mouth. Summer was watching her too, and as we shared a look, she shook her head. Nina would have to get over her social shyness or whatever her issues were if she was going to enjoy college.

That was exactly what I was going to do—enjoy college.

And still protect Mason.

Logan curved his arm around my neck, hooking me, as he and Nate began to move through the house. I went with him, and trying to peek over his arm, I saw that Summer was following behind us. Kitty and Nina were attached as well since Kitty was right next to Nate's side. His hands were shoved into his jeans pockets, but she grabbed ahold of his arm. He grimaced, but Kitty was a determined woman.

Going through the dining room and then the kitchen, I was surprised, even though I shouldn't have been at the amount of people who were already saying hello to Logan. Word about who he was spread fast, and guys were coming over to introduce themselves. The girls were checking out him and then the entire group with interest in their eyes. We were people to know, and I had an understanding to how it must've been for Logan growing up.

He was a Kade. The name was known and respected. They were feared by some and wanted by others.

As Logan was saying hello to the guys, the girls were becoming attracted to him. The more he talked, the more they were falling under his spell. I had a moment of sympathy for whoever managed to tame him.

As the night wore on, Logan charmed the majority of people at the party. We took up residence in the basement near the pool table, and I recognized the near-worshipful looks from Kitty and Nina, too.

Even them.

Even Kitty, who had been hesitant and latched on to Nate, had the stirring of lust as she watched Logan bend over the pool table and lined up a shot.

Summer had gone to get a new pitcher of beer, and she came back, placing it next to me. "Man." She propped her elbows on the counter behind where we were sitting and maneuvered her chair so that her back was to it.

We were both watching Logan and Nate at the table.

"The stories were not exaggerated. I don't know if half these girls could keep their load in if Mason were here, too. Your boyfriend and your *stepbrother*?" There was a question attached with the last word before she added, "They're something else. I don't think Cain University realized who they were getting when they accepted both of their applications."

"Technically, they only accepted Logan's application. They knew Mason and me ahead of time. We both got full scholarships."

"You did?"

"In track."

Her perfectly trimmed and outlined eyebrow lifted up. "You're a runner?"

I nodded. I had gone earlier this morning, but I was feeling the itch to de-stress with an hour-long jog already.

Logan caught my eye. He'd been watching the conversation and holding his pool stick, as he waited for Nate to miss his shot. He lifted his own eyebrow now in a silent question to me. I shook my head, tucking my hands under my legs. I was fine. He didn't need to save me.

Logan didn't care. He came over anyway and wedged himself between Summer and me so Summer had to scoot her chair down a bit. It was a subtle move and one that others wouldn't register, but her eyes narrowed a little bit. Summer got it.

That told me she was smart or at least knowledgeable about the different tactics people could use, like how Logan had her move over but not me. I was protected behind him, as he was half-turned to her. His head swung my way, so I was still included in the conversation, but he put a safe amount of distance between Summer and me.

It was nicely done.

He asked, intently watching her, "Roommate of Sam's, tell us about yourself."

She swallowed before replying, "Uh…what do you want to know?"

I poked Logan's side. "I told you she modeled."

"Aha, and the intrigue builds." He grinned, his teasing tone evident. "Seriously though, you're Sam's roommate. I know I was a dog before, but I love Sam. She's family, so that means a few things."

Summer glanced at me. I was watching Logan.

He added, giving her a smirk, "You need to tell us more of your deepest, darkest secrets."

Her eyes moved back to him, now glued to his face. She didn't look like she was breathing.

Logan grinned. "For real, be honest. I know you're a Mason superfan. The thing we really need to know is if he boned Sam in your dorm room, would you pretend it was you instead?"

"Logan!" I hit his chest.

He was undeterred, still studying my roommate.

Her cheeks flooded with color. "The asshole part of your reputation is true."

"You didn't answer the question."

"Logan." That was enough. I started to get off my chair.

He grabbed the chair and blocked me from sliding off it. I had to stay or be forced into brushing against him in an awkward position. I loved Logan but not like that. I sat there, captive by my almost-stepbrother, as he interrogated my roommate.

"Yes," she croaked out. "I'm a fan of Mason's because he's a god in football, and I'll continue to be a fan when he goes pro. But will I daydream that he's screwing me when he screws my new friend and roommate? Hell no." Her eyes sparked at him, heated. "And how dare you even insinuate that of me. Who are you to ask a question like that?"

Logan moved in closer to her, his face impassive. "I'm her family, and I have every right to make sure she's not getting screwed over."

"Logan." It was time. I tapped his arm. "Move."

He didn't.

"Logan!"

He relented and slowly stepped back. He was still holding her gaze, an unspoken threat going between the two.

Well, if my roommate hadn't already hated him before, she did now.

I stood from my chair and tried to give her a reassuring smile, as I latched on to Logan's arm. "Excuse us for a bit. I have to go and chew my family member out." I turned and shoved him forward. I added over my shoulder, "In private."

Logan motioned at Nate, pointing to Summer. Nate frowned but went over and took my empty chair.

Once we were outside, I whirled on him. "What are you doing? She's my roommate."

"I want to establish the boundaries early on." He climbed on top of a table, his feet resting where people would normally sit. His elbows went to his knees, and he clasped his hands together, watching me with an unrelenting intensity.

He didn't care. That stopped me. Whatever lecture I had stored up, ready to deliver, would fall on deaf ears. I'd be wasting our time. I sighed instead, sitting down next to him. "Did you have to be such an ass to her?"

"Yep." He grinned at me, moving an arm to hug me to his side. "Like you would be for me."

He was right. I would. "Still."

He squeezed me to him. "I like her."

Of course, he did. "I'm not surprised."

"She's got balls." He grinned, laughing to himself. "She's kinda like Heather, but Heather's tougher. That make sense? And she's got a football boner for Mason. I can tell. Every time Nate and I talked about football stats, her eyes would light up. She was listening to every word."

I frowned. "You were talking about football stats?" What had I been paying attention to? Oh, right—all the girls who were starting to watch him like adoring fans. I was looking out for future Logan Kade stalkers. "Never mind."

"Hey." His voice dropped.

A tingle of awareness ran down my spine. The serious side of Logan was coming out. I sat up.

"I'm kinda glad you're here tonight."

"You are?"

"Yeah." He frowned at me. "You didn't let Mason know?"

I shook my head.

He shrugged. "Listen, don't feel bad about that."

For real?

He saw my look and grinned. "I mean it. Mason wants you to have a normal college experience, and yes, that means going to parties. Why do you think I'm here? He knows you're smart, and you can take care of yourself—"

"Do you?" I cut in. "Because I wasn't getting that sense when you were being an ass to my roommate."

"Sam." His eyebrows pinched together. "You don't even know her. Why are you defending her?"

He was right. She wasn't my best friend, but I was trying to make myself believe she was. "I'm sorry. Thank you. You were right to do what you did."

"She's not Heather," he said softly.

I shot him a look. "Speaking of which..."

He leaned back, hearing the suspicion in my voice.

I asked, "You're not going to fuck up my friendship with Heather, are you?"

"What are you talking about?" He glanced away.

I saw the guilt in that one movement. Logan completely knew what I was talking about.

I poked him in the leg. "I know you two slept together."

He cursed under his breath, rubbing a hand over his jaw. "Mason told?"

"Mason knew?"

"Uh." He looked back, alarmed now. "I mean—"

I waved that off. It didn't matter. "I'm not an idiot. You two were slow dancing half the night, and you both disappeared at the end. I texted you guys, but neither of you answered. I'm not dumb. She and Channing are on a break anyway, and you two always had chemistry."

He leaned forward, dipping his head, and he raked his hand through his hair before letting it drop back to his leg. "I'm sorry, Sam. I didn't mean for you to know that."

"I'd be a shitty family member and friend if I hadn't put two and two together."

He groaned. "Mason chewed us both out. He didn't want you to know. He didn't want either of us to take away from your night—you know, from you finally getting a family. I'm sorry."

Mason did that? An emotion swept through me, warming

me up. A stupid smile came over me, and I couldn't wipe it off right away.

Logan saw it and snorted. "You're going to crawl into bed with him tonight, aren't you?"

I sighed happily. "Probably. That was sweet of him."

A dark look flashed in his eyes, but his mouth straightened.

I waited, knowing there was more. He was holding back. Figuring it had to do with something more sinister, probably Park Sebastian, I didn't push for answers.

Instead, I gestured to the house. "Can you not be a dick to Summer anymore?"

"I won't." His fist lightly tapped under my chin. "I wanted her to know not to mess with us."

"You thought she would?"

He lifted a shoulder. "She's a model, Sam. She's got an ego. I can tell. Girls like that think they can walk all over anyone and get away with it just because they can. I wanted to let her know that, yeah, she's hot, but she ain't the only hot chick around. Enough about her." His voice dropped again, back to that seriousness from earlier. "I was going to come find you tomorrow anyway, but we're here. I know Mason wants you to call him if you see Sebastian, but I want you to call me instead."

"Why?"

"Because Mason's hands are tied behind his back."

My eyes narrowed.

"He can't do anything—at least, not in public. It could hurt his football career. As much as Mase hates to admit it, he's like a freaking politician now. He's gotta watch everything he does and says. Nothing can blow back on him."

A shiver was winding its way down my spine. The consequences Logan was talking about became even more real to me. Fear started in my gut, building with urgency. I had to make sure nothing happened to Mason.

I nodded, feeling Logan's gaze on me. He was waiting for my acknowledgment.

I gave it to him. "Yeah. Okay."

"I mean it. Don't call him. Call me. I can get kicked out of school. That's no problem for me. I can go to the college across town. Whatever. It's not a D League, but it's still a good school. I can handle the blowback. I need to, for Mason. Nothing can happen to him. I can fight. He can't. He has to be really careful, especially with this dickwad. He's not a normal dickwad. He's got some brains."

I nodded, forcing my head to move up and down, as my neck muscles seemed paralyzed.

The serious moment was done. Logan added, his voice more carefree, "It's like he's a dick who has serious sperm in his wad, if you know what I mean." His knee nudged mine. "Hey. Hey? You know what I mean? It's like he's extra fertilized, but we have to keep him from spraying all over us—"

I shoved back at his knee and hopped off the table. "We're going back to the party, and I'm going to drink. You," I pointed at him as he was trying to hold his laughter in, "stop talking to me about dicks, wads, and who's fertile or not. Call Heather if you want to have that conversation. I'm sure she's got her own theories for that stuff but not me. That's gross."

He laughed as he climbed off the table and started to follow me back inside. Right before we got to the door, he grabbed my arm, stopping me. The jokes were gone again. "This doesn't have to do with Sebastian, but it's about Jax."

I waited. He never explained anything about Heather before. I wasn't sure if I wanted to know, but I kept quiet.

"Jax and I—it's not a thing, and it won't hurt your friendship."

I studied him, looking up at him in the moonlight.

He shrugged and looked away. "That was the first ground rule Heather put down. Whatever happens, it won't harm you. We promise. Both of us."

I nodded. "Good enough for me." I gestured over my shoulder to the house. "And can you kinda be a dick to the other two girls from my floor? I can see that they're both already falling in love with you, and I don't want to deal with that, especially when I go to the restroom. I don't want some chick trying to hop into my stall, asking for a date with you."

"Ah." Logan's shoulder straightened. His usual smirk adorned his face, and just like that, the serious Logan was gone and the womanizing one was back in play. He pretended to crack his knuckles, stretching his arms over his head. "I'll see what I can do, but, Sam, I'm like a god among mortals. I can't help who falls in love with this." He gestured up and down his body and winked at me. "Girls are going to love what they can't have."

It was my turn to snort. "Please. You give plenty of yourself away."

He barked out a laugh, catching the door as I pulled it open. His arm came over my head again, and he held the door for me. Going back inside, the music seemed even louder, and when we saw most of our crew was on the dance floor or on the couches, I knew all the serious conversations were done for the night.

It was time to have fun.

Summer saw me from the dance floor—her arms winding up and down above her head, her hips moving in rhythm with the music—and she motioned for me. With the bright smile she was giving me, I figured Logan hadn't put too big of a wedge between us.

Making sure he saw where I was going, I headed to meet her on the floor. Kitty moved away, making room for me in their makeshift little circle. I spotted Nina on the couch. Blaze was sitting next to her, still wearing a toga, and he had the pony keg this time. She looked ready to launch into outer space. He put his arm around her, and I started to laugh. She grabbed her legs, as if forcing herself to stay on the couch.

I had a feeling things with this group of people were going to be okay.

Step one was done.

I made some friends.

CHAPTER EIGHT

MASON

"You're dragging, Kade."

I was doing sprints, and I stopped, heaving for breath, as Drew came over and lined up next to me. He was right. I was.

Sam crawled into bed with me the night before, and I'd loved every minute of it, but an hour later, we'd both decided she should wake up in her dorm room. The whole commitment to staying in the dorms for the first month was going to be taxing on both of us, and that meant another hour of being awake because I'd driven her back. I walked up with her, and for another fifteen minutes, we'd stood outside her door before she went inside. I was dragging, but I didn't care.

Remembering Sam as she'd straddled me, leaning back and letting her hair fall down so that the tips of it grazed my legs, gave me enough of a boost, so when Drew and I both took off, racing each other now, I pulled ahead halfway.

I was waiting at the end as he finished his sprint. I drawled, grinning at him, "Who's dragging now?"

He grunted, bent down, and tossed a towel at me. "You're a smart-ass."

I used the towel to wipe my face. "Someone has to be. Matteo's gone."

Drew sobered as we walked to the side bench for water. The first part of the morning was spent running around the track. Afterward, we were herded into the locker room for a quick talk with the assistant coaches, and then they'd let us back out to do individual drills. Mine had been sprints. Drew caught me at the tail end of doing thirty. I'd have to go back and do another thirty before calling it quits and going to class.

Walking with me around the track, he said, "Matt called last night. He said his dad was hit by a drunk driver."

"Does he have to miss school?"

Drew's mouth tightened. "I don't know. He says so. He's got to take care of the family until his dad is out of the hospital and rehabbed enough to start working again. They come from old values. The man takes care of the family and all that jazz. With his dad out of commission, it falls to his shoulders to take over and work for the family. He's got little siblings still, and their mom's a housekeeper somewhere."

It sucked all around. It just sucked.

Drew glanced sideways to me. "Coach talk to you yet?"

I nodded. An anchor fell to the pit of my stomach. "I'm benched for the first two games."

Drew cursed. "You serious?"

"I missed the first month of training."

"That wasn't on your part. That was the school's decision."

"But because of my involvement with Sebastian, the blame has to be on me."

Drew didn't know about the house. No one did, except for Nate, Logan, and Sam. I was innocent in everyone else's eyes. That anchor turned inside of me, digging into my sides and making me feel some guilt. Drew's tune would be different, but

I didn't regret what I had done, not after what Sebastian tried to take away from me first—my future in football.

Drew swore again. "Whatever. The whole thing is fucked up, but I am happy you put him in his place. When that fraternity fell, that was a big deal on campus. I know you made Matteo proud and Lane, too, with how Sebastian could've helped with his scholarship two years ago and didn't, letting it get stripped from him after being injured. Sebastian's a greedy bastard. He's slime." There was a warning in his voice. "Just watch your back. You know he's looking for payback."

My jaw clenched. Drew didn't have to remind me. I more than knew the stakes at hand.

"Football, school, and my family—those are my priorities."

"Good. We'll watch your back. You know that."

"Thanks."

We were coming to the end of our first circle around the track.

"Kade!" a coach shouted from the bench. "Finish your sprints and take off. You got class to attend."

Drew nodded to me, veering to the left, as I crouched back down for another sprint.

SAMANTHA

The smell of coffee woke me up, and I was greeted with the image of Summer coming in the door, dressed to the nines in a flowy, white top that slipped off one of her shoulders and hung past the middle of her thighs. It looked like a dress she could wear to a nightclub. She was wearing skintight jeans underneath with high heels. Her bracelets jingled against each other as she placed a cup of coffee on my nightstand.

"Ruby has a latte machine in her room." She inhaled a whiff of her latte, and a dreamy smile came over her face. "I'm in love with our RA." She pointed at me with her cup as she sat at her desk. "She's in love with you. A little Blaze bird was gushing to her about your stepbrother sometime this morning, and she wants to meet his obsession."

I cringed. "Really?"

She watched as I climbed out of bed.

I grabbed the latte first. My robe was second. I had priorities. Even before slipping on the robe, I had to take a sip. It was caramel heaven. "Thanks for this."

"If you can't find me, don't be surprised if I'm camped out on Ruby's floor. She knows the best way to make friends with freshman girls hoping to fight the freshman fifteen—feed our caffeine addiction."

I grinned, putting the latte on my desk.

"So..." Summer took another sip, her eyes darting to my bed. "I couldn't help noticing you this morning, right before I almost stepped on you." She rolled her eyes. "Why I chose the top bunk, I'll never know. Can I be a nosy roommate who's hoping to be a good friend and ask about your change of heart last night? I thought you were getting a ride back with Logan?"

"I was." I yawned, stretching my arms above my head. A little chill swept over me, and I finally pulled on the robe. "I went back with him and crawled in bed with Mason."

A sigh left Summer's mouth. "The football legend."

I stopped. "Uh, yeah. Anyway, Mason brought me back. We're doing the whole thing where I actually live in the dorm, at least for a month."

"I don't mean to sound all creepy, and I'm not lusting after your soul mate because he's gorgeous, but I've had a thing for Mason Kade for years. I know almost all his records and stats since his sophomore year in high school. It's a football thing for me. For real." She blinked at me a couple of times. "Most girls would be thinking of eight different ways to kill you, so they could take your spot, but that's not me. It's the football. That's all."

I narrowed my eyes. She seemed sincere, and she had gotten wistful the night before when Logan and Nate were sharing old football memories. But she was a girl. And Mason was Mason. I frowned. I should've heard alarm bells clanging against my skull, but there was none.

I shrugged. "I've had girls go nuts and try to hurt me, but if you're going to try, good luck." I kept my eyes level as I stared at her.

Things were nice and demure between us. We'd been getting to know each other at a slow pace, but this was different. I let her see the hardness in me. She did, straightening in her chair, but she didn't look away. That was a good thing.

As she held my gaze, I said, "I'm not being a bitch when I say this, but you'll lose. If you do want him and you're trying to lie to me here, trying to deceive me in any way, it won't work. I've had tougher and more ruthless girls try to, and they never won. They never will, so if that's your agenda, drop it, or move out. You won't be fighting just me. You'll be fighting Mason and Logan, too. The three of us are family. No one will get between us."

A slow grin curved over her face. "There she is." Her head went down, like she was staring at an approaching lion. There was no fear, no caution. There was just recognition and something similar to excitement. She put her latte on her desk but never broke eye contact with me. "I've been wanting to meet the real Samantha since I realized who you were."

"What are you talking about?"

"It wasn't just Mason and Logan that I heard about. You lit your dad's car on fire. You put Budd Broudou in jail, and you got Brett Broudou to protect you. I mean, damn, girl. I get all hot and bothered by a sixty-yard touchdown run, but a lot of other girls get just as hot and bothered about whoever tamed Mason and Logan Kade."

"Girls?"

Her grin was a full smile now. "I know a few lesbians who'd love to get your number. When I go home, I'll have to fight 'em off with a baseball bat when they figure out that we're roommates."

I cocked my head to the side. "Should I be alarmed that you knew about me and didn't tell me until now?"

"Okay." She tucked her hair behind her ears, her eyes eager. "Maybe I should've been up-front that I knew about you, but I didn't want to sound like a creeper. When I found out who my roommate was, I almost pissed my pants. I didn't know before coming here yesterday. The housing place sent me a letter saying my assigned roommate changed due to complications, and I was supposed to notify them if I was unhappy with my new assignment." She snorted to herself, picking up her latte again. Her legs crossed at the ankle as she perched on the edge of her chair. She rolled her head back and forth before resting it against the wall, too. "Hell to the no. As long as you can put up with my football obsession and the fact that I think you're awesome and I'm kinda wondering if I'm a lesbian, too. I think this year will be *awesome*."

I shook my head, uncertain of how to take all of that in. Mason would go with his gut. That was what he'd tell me, so it was what I did. My gut was comfortable. It was only uncomfortable that I wasn't concerned about her, so I shrugged, sipping from my latte.

I said, "Okay."

She leaned forward. "Okay…as in, we're good? As in, I didn't scare you away?"

I nodded slowly. "I guess. Okay then."

She whooped and thrust a fist in the air before covering her mouth with it. "Sorry. That's the football nerd in me. You won't want to sit with me at the first game we go to. Seriously, I'm nuts."

I gripped my latte in front of me. "You know more about me than I know about you."

Summer stilled. "Want to hear some embarrassing model stories? You think you've dealt with psychotic, catty bitches? You have *no* idea. I was at a shoot one day where one model mixed cream in with a girl's fat-free milk, so she'd gain two pounds before another casting call the next day. Another girl changed the labels on cans of soup, so this other girl thought she was eating the light-calorie soup, but she wasn't. She was eating the one loaded with calories. Ruthless, I'm telling you." She shuddered. "I had one girl try to mess up my heel, so I would fall and break an ankle. She told me to 'break a leg' with such enjoyment that I knew she'd meant it literally."

"Whoa."

"Yeah. If you want tips and tricks on how to make a starving psychopath foam at the mouth, you've got an invaluable asset rooming with you. I've dealt with all of them."

I could already hear Heather's voice in my head. *Do it. Get the info.* One never knew when information like that would come in handy. I started to chuckle, but the laugh subsided.

I hadn't brought up Logan to Heather before we left. We said our good-byes. It'd been awkward, but I knew most of that was because Heather was fighting back tears. I was already missing my afternoon shift at Manny's. I knew Heather would want to know all about Summer. She would think it was hysterical that I was rooming with a model obsessed with football.

"Sam?"

"Huh?"

Summer was standing in front of the mirror, picking at a seam in her shirt. She pointed to the ringing phone next to me. "You want me to get that?"

Ring.

The phone was doing that.

I slumped back in my chair, but I jerked, almost spilling my coffee, as I reached for the phone. "He—" My coffee spilled over. I cursed, catching it and righting it before any more could get all over the desk. "Sorry. Damn coffee. Hello?"

"Samantha?"

I frowned. "Malinda?"

Summer stood and motioned for the door. "I'll be in Ruby's room."

I nodded, and once she closed the door behind her, I said to Malinda, "Aren't you and Dad on your honeymoon?"

"We are, but that doesn't mean I don't have time to stalk my new daughter-in-law." She laughed. "Your father kept me from calling yesterday. I tried your cell phone, but Mason answered. He gave me your dorm number, and I'm supposed to tell you that he'll track you down today to give you your phone."

I groaned. "I forgot it in his room."

"And I see you two are really sticking to the whole dorm-room-for-a-month thing." Her tone sobered up. "I think that's commendable of you."

I sighed, standing and trying to reach for my clothes with the phone tucked between my ear and shoulder. "We'll see how long it lasts. I haven't lived with Mason in over a year. Everything in me wants to go and find him already and just be with him, not stay here with people I don't know yet."

"Yet. *Yet* is the operative word, and I'm so proud of you, Samantha. Your father is, too, and he's harassing me, so he can get on the phone."

I frowned, pausing, as I reached for a shirt in the closet. "No, he's not. He was probably leaving the room as you said that, wasn't he?"

She was silent for a moment before a rueful chuckle slipped out. "You and your father. You two can be in each other's presence, and you think that's bonding. You two should talk more."

"We do talk."

"Only when you have to."

She was confused, and she had reason to be. I asked, "How's Mark doing?"

A hiss came through the receiver before she grumbled, "That damn son of mine. I love him, but he can be an idiot sometimes. He decided to take a page from your book and prove he's so independent. I wish he wouldn't have. He locked himself out of his car and wouldn't let me go to his campus with him. When he finally did get the keys, he didn't have enough cash to pay the locksmith. He had to get a ride with the locksmith to a nearby ATM. He paid the guy and ended up paying an extra ten dollars just to get back to his car. He forgot to lock his car after all of that."

A foreboding sense started building in me. "Oh, no..."

"'Oh, no,' is right. His car was stolen. Everything he had was gone. We ended up wiring more money to him once he did a report and got to his dorm room. I had the airplane tickets booked, and we were packing to fly to him when he called last night. The cops found his car, and some of his stuff was still there. As soon as we're back from the Bahamas, we're going right to his place and making sure he has everything he needs. That boy is going to be the death of me, I swear." A wistful sigh left her. "But I'll be damned if I couldn't love him any more than I do. I feel like I'm bursting with pride with the two of you, even with Mark's mishap."

I grinned. Some of that happiness I heard from her was contagious. I made a mental note to let Logan know about Mark's adventure. Mark would wish the next family holiday wouldn't happen because of all the teasing he'd endure.

"Okay. Your father is motioning for me. If we don't leave now, we'll miss the horseback riding on the trail." She whispered into the phone, "And your father wants to miss that, but no way, honey, I won't let that happen. I need to get that stud on another stud just so I can take a picture and Instagram that back to Fallen Crest. You know how much ribbing he's going to get about that one?" She ended with a hurried, "I'm so excited! Bye, Sammy. I love you!"

Sammy.

I was slightly stunned as she hung up, and the dial tone started in my ear. I didn't remember if I'd said good-bye back or not, but she'd called me Sammy.

I was still sitting there, hearing that name on repeat, when Summer cleared her throat.

Her head poked around the door. "Uh, sorry." She winced, and her eyes fell on the receiver now blaring in my hand. "Oh, good. You're done. Uh…I have to warn you about something."

"What?"

She slipped in and shut the door with a soft click behind her. Her hands remained behind her back, still on the door handle. "Kitty and Nina are camped out at the end of the hallway. They've asked me four times when I think you might be heading for class. After last night, they're in love with Logan Kade, and it's sad to say, but that made them your personal stalkers." She rolled her eyes. "I told them you don't have class until lunch, but they don't believe me. I think they're going to wait you out and do the thing where you have to walk with them to your class—you know, where they're super friendly, so friendly that you'd be completely rude to even try to ditch them." She shuddered, one corner of her lip curving up. "Such beginners. If only I could school them better, they'd be proper stalkers."

She laughed. "Just kidding. For real, but, uh…" She cleared her throat. "We need to come up with a plan so those two are distracted while you slip down the back hallway door. They really should have one positioned in the lobby and the other by the back door. It only locks from the outside, and the alarm's not turned on during the day."

"What?"

She clapped her hands together. "Exactly. Operation Distract and Dash needs to commence…" She looked at my pajamas. "Whenever you're dressed, that is."

CHAPTER NINE

Summer went past the two girls, who really were camped out by the doorway. Nina was holding her backpack in her lap while Kitty had a strand of hair pulled over her face. She was furiously picking at it. Summer strolled past them and pretended to trip over Nina's feet. Kitty didn't seem impressed, so Summer spied the water bottle next to her and somehow lunged for it, knocking that to the ground, too.

I waited as both girls got up. Nina helped Summer while Kitty grabbed her water bottle before it fell down the rest of the stairs.

It was my time.

Both were distracted, and I slipped down the back stairs. I went all the way down and through the back door. Summer was right. A girl soared through the door two seconds before I hit the last set of stairs. No alarm sounded, so I went outside.

I was waiting by the bike rack as Summer came out, laughing. She was barely holding on to her coffee cup, which she'd told me she was going to refill in Ruby's room right before activating Operation Distract and Dash.

She had a second cup for me and shook her head, tsking under her breath. "Logan was not enough of a dick to put those two off. I think he only cemented that they both want to marry him. What will Nate think? Kitty loved him first."

"I think Nate will sleep just fine at night."

"You never know. She could've been the love of his life." Summer sped forward as we began walking toward the classroom buildings and turned around so she was walking backward. She wiggled her eyebrows. "What if Kitty actually is the girl he's meant to be with? I mean, who knows? He could end up going down the completely wrong lane in life. Do you believe in stuff like that?"

I slowed, frowning. "What are you talking about?"

She sped up, still walking backward and motioned for me to keep up with her. "I mean, the decisions you make today could alter your future. Things like that. Maybe I wasn't meant to be your roommate. Maybe I was supposed to be someone else's, but something happened. Say, for instance, she did something horrible. She made one decision that changed her future, so it changed ours, too. You and I weren't even going to meet, much less become the best buds that we will be. Thank god she made that horrible decision, right? Or maybe not. Maybe whoever that girl was might have actually been the love of Nate's life, or maybe even Logan's. Let's get ambitious here. Do you think about stuff like that?"

"No." I scratched my head. It was spinning a little bit. "Why the hell would you?"

Summer laughed, twirling around so that she was walking side by side with me again. She lifted a shoulder, her head falling down. "I don't know. I think it's the aftereffects of hating my stepmother. She did a real fucking doozy on my dad. I always think, what if they hadn't met at that bar? What if my mom and dad hadn't fought that night? What if I hadn't come home late, so they wouldn't have ended up fighting because of me?

Things might've been different." She sounded so serious now. "Things might've been happier."

I stopped walking. People streamed around us. A few shot us dirty looks, but most just zipped around us, hurrying to their classes.

I'd known her a day.

That one moment told me so much more about her than all the other hours we'd spent together.

She was unhappy.

She hated her stepmother.

She wished for her old life.

And she blamed herself.

As if she realized she'd given me a full window to her inner workings, Summer grinned at me, looking at me sideways. "*What* are you looking at?"

A broken daughter.

I shook my head. "Nothing."

Me. I was looking at myself.

I pushed forward. "Let's go to class. Where's your first one?"

Summer pointed to a brick building across the courtyard. "In there. I checked the map yesterday when we got our books. The store is right over there." She moved to the smaller building right next to where her classroom was.

Students were everywhere. A line was outside of the bookstore, weaving down the sidewalk. People were milling back and forth, some dashing around the line and moving into the brick building. The larger building extended higher, maybe four floors, and students were lingering outside those doors, too. Some were smoking. Others were talking with friends. Still more stood next to the bike rack. We were coming down a sidewalk that met five other sidewalks in a large stone circle in the middle of the courtyard, and people were coming back and forth.

As Summer checked her map again, I saw some others doing the same. We weren't the only lost freshmen. The thought was a little comforting.

"Yeah." Summer nodded before folding the paper up and sliding it into her folder. "That's my building. Where's your classroom?"

"In Ives. Room three-twelve."

Her forehead wrinkled, and she pulled the sheet back out. "Okay." She stopped. Her finger started to point, but she turned until it was aiming at the building right behind us. "This is your stop."

"Really?"

"Yep." She checked once more. "Ives. That's what my map says, so this is it unless there are two Ives buildings."

I was about to say good-bye and head inside when Park Sebastian stepped in front of me, blocking me. A smug smirk was on his face beneath his black sunglasses. His gelled hair was combed to the side. As he stood there, holding a book and a couple of notebooks in his hand, he looked like he stepped right from a college magazine shoot. His shirt hung from his wide shoulders, not too tight, and fell to his trim waist. He had on frayed cargo shorts, but they seemed like they'd been frayed on purpose.

I didn't think. I said the first thing on my mind, "You look like a douche." I pointed to his shorts. "That's trendy? If you're hoping to look poor, you're sucking at it. Your whole demeanor screams entitled rich prick."

Summer gasped quietly beside me, but she coughed, trying to cover up her laughter.

Sebastian's smug smile didn't move. It began to spread, and he lifted his sunglasses. He started to take them off as I felt a presence beside me. Logan stepped in front of me. He was dressed in a T-shirt and similar cargo pants, but I kept my mouth shut about him. Logan could pull it off, looking like a rich bad boy who didn't give a shit. Then again, I knew Logan. That probably helped, but standing next to him, Sebastian looked even more like a poser.

Summer glanced nervously at me.

I shook my head. It was during the day. There were lots of witnesses around. We'd be fine. Nothing bad would happen.

Logan started. "Thought we told you to stay away from Sam."

It wasn't a question.

Sebastian moved back a step, letting his sunglasses fall back in place. He gestured to the building behind him. "I'm going to class, Kade. You're going to start a fight because of that?"

"You're in her way." Logan's hand slipped behind him, and his bag slid down his shoulder and his arm until the strap was hanging over his wrist. He held his fingers toward me. His bag slipped even further, and he motioned for me.

I took the bag from him and slid it over my shoulder. Maybe this was going to last longer than the few minutes I'd originally thought. I bit my lip, casting a concerned look to Summer. She didn't seem like she was going anywhere. A fascinated expression was on her face as she gazed first at Logan, to Sebastian, and back to Logan again.

"Again, I was just going to class."

Logan didn't move.

Neither did Sebastian.

Summer kept glancing between the two and to me. When she saw I was holding Logan's bag, her eyes got wide. I wanted to reassure her, but the truth was that I had no idea what was going to happen.

I kept remembering what Logan said the previous night. *Call him, not Mason.*

Mason couldn't get in trouble.

As if Logan knew the train of my thoughts, he shifted on his feet. My gaze jerked up and trailed past him, past Sebastian, and landed on Mason.

He was coming from the building where my class was located with my cell phone in his hand. A scowl was on his face, and his jaw locked in place. I swallowed tightly. Logan moved backward, stepping into me. I adjusted, knowing that he was herding me even more away from Sebastian.

I started to go to the side. I wanted to go to Mason, but Logan's arm swept me back. He caught me around the waist. He held me in place, right behind him. A memory flashed in my mind of another time when Mason had done the same motion for the same reason.

"Mom."

"*Don't!*" *Her head snapped back up, and her eyes were wild. "You always said, we'd be gone. He wouldn't marry me, and you were right. He won't. It's over. Finito. Finished."*

I stepped around Mason, but he moved with me. When I started to get closer to her, he moved another inch. He was blocking me. He didn't want me close to her, so I stayed put.

I folded my arms. "Mom, you're drunk. Everything will be better in the morning. I promise."

Park Sebastian wasn't my mother. I didn't have years of terror built inside me because of him. My mind was made up. I wasn't helpless, so I shoved Logan's arm down. Mason's gaze caught mine, and he narrowed his eyes. I caught the warning there, even before anything was said. It didn't matter. I would not let him get hurt because of me. I would not allow myself to be his Achilles' heel. Sebastian needed to learn that, so I started forward.

Logan caught me again, but I sidestepped him. He went to the right to block me. I feinted left. Because of the movement, I was now face-to-face with Sebastian. Logan groaned a little bit, but I tuned him out.

"Sam."

I shrugged off Logan's hold.

"Sebastian." Mason's tone stopped everything. He was quiet but foreboding.

Sebastian, who hadn't realized Mason was right behind him, straightened abruptly. He kept his glasses on, but his jaw clenched, and he moved to the side so he wasn't surrounded on both sides anymore. Mason adjusted, coming to stand next to me. Logan circled to stand on his other side. We were now a unified front while Summer crossed her arms. Her head kept going back and forth between us and Sebastian. I didn't dare look over to see what she was thinking. She was getting a good view as it was.

The entire atmosphere shifted once Mason made his presence known.

Sebastian's smirk fell flat.

The aura of tension and danger was around us. Students dashed for their classes, but they slowed and then stopped to watch the standoff.

No one said a thing. I wasn't sure if I was even breathing.

Sebastian laughed—or tried to laugh. It fell short and came out sounding angry. "Mason, nice of you to sneak up behind me."

I tensed.

Mason pushed something against my hand. "I was waiting for Sam."

Opening my hand, I took my phone from him and tucked it into my purse.

I could feel the anger rising in Mason. He wasn't doing or showing anything, but I felt it from him. His arm brushed against me, and it was rock solid, like cement. He was like cement on a normal day, his body toned and perfected from his training during the past summer, but this was more. The strength in him was radiating out, and everyone else was noticing, too.

As I looked at the crowd that formed, I knew the tension between Sebastian and Mason would be known by the end of the day, if everyone on campus didn't already know. Phones were pointed at us, recording, and I only hoped Mason really wouldn't do anything now. That would be blatant evidence against him.

Logan must've been thinking the same thing. He laughed and folded his arms over his chest. "Look at you, Sebastian. All alone. It's like a rare sighting in the wild. You usually travel with your pack, don't you?"

Sebastian shot back, "You would know." He gestured to Mason. "Always in your brother's shadow, right? He's the leader. He's the football talent while you…what are you?"

Sebastian's eyes flicked to me, and I knew where he was going.

He added, taunting, "Couldn't get the gi—"

I surged forward, stopping him. "You'll stop right there."

"Or what?" His eyes sharpened.

Yes, he hit a nerve, and I was the one to let him know that.

Lovely.

I opened my mouth. I had no idea what I was going to say, but Mason's hand rested over my arm. He pressed it down. I'd been lifting it, but I hadn't even known. Sebastian saw that gesture, too.

He laughed now. "Maybe I should feel sorry for the two of you." He looked at Logan and back to me. His gaze stayed on me, falling to my mouth. His eyes narrowed, lingering there. "Neither of you really matter. I mean, it's all about Mason, isn't it? He's the star wide receiver. You two came here, following him. And what for?" He pointed to my arm where Mason was still touching me. "To be told what to do by him? My, my. That must be so much fun for you both."

His sarcasm was evident.

I gritted my teeth.

Mason shook his head. "It won't work."

"What won't?"

"We're not normal," Mason continued. He was calm now. He was in control.

Sebastian didn't like that. I could tell as his mouth pressed into a thin line, the ends stretching tight.

Mason continued, "You can't try to bait them to see what they might say back to you. That's what you're doing—pressing some buttons that maybe others have. But it's not true. I don't tell Sam what to do. My brother isn't jealous of me. You're looking for a reaction because you'll know that's a weakness we have in our family, but you're underestimating the bond we share."

"What? You mean, you aren't a dictator? You don't control your girlfriend?"

I wanted to defend myself, but I wanted to defend Mason, too. His hold was keeping me contained—for now.

Logan started laughing. All attention went to him, and he was shaking his head. He pointed at Mason and to Sebastian, still laughing. "Honestly, have you not done your homework? Do you not know anything about us? If anything, Mason's jealous of me. Sorry, Sam." Logan flashed me a grin, but it was strained, too. He wasn't completely enjoying this, even though he sounded like it. "I love her. We're family, but my brother's going to enjoy only that one vagina for the rest of his life."

"Logan!" I snapped. "You want to piss me off, too?"

He waved at me, dismissing me. "See? You hear that? She's so uptight just because I mentioned her vagina. I'm sure it's amazing, Sam, but you have to give some sympathy to Mason. It's like he's in pussy prison. Everyone knows the two of you are going to get married, and he's in the prime of his life. He should be partaking in ass morning, noon, and night with a couple of afternoon delights, if you know what I mean."

"Logan," Mason murmured, "if you could get to the point."

"The point is pussy prison." He swung his head to Sebastian, and his grin widened. "My brother's wrong."

Sebastian's shoulders lifted and rolled back. He was getting ready for something.

Logan kept going as he brought one arm across his chest, stretching his shoulder. "I don't think you're here to throw bait at us, see what we bite on, and find a weakness in us. I think you came here, knowing where Sam's first class was, and you wanted to threaten her, maybe see if we'd be here, too, maybe see what might happen after that." He gestured to the onlookers who only doubled in numbers. "There are a lot of witnesses. No one can have a go at you..." His voice trailed off for a moment.

I frowned.

Sebastian shifted onto his heels.

Logan continued, "I don't think you're here for anything in particular. I think you just showed up to see what would happen, and you're safe. No one can hurt anyone." *Anyone* was code for, *No one could hurt Sebastian.* "Maybe that's why you're alone. Maybe you didn't want one of your guys taking a swing at us. Payback."

Payback?

Logan shrugged. Somehow, as he did so, he was a step closer to Sebastian. "All I know is that you've got something planned, but here's my warning to you. Don't do whatever you're thinking. Walk away. It can end today, but if it doesn't, if you do whatever you're planning on doing, things will end badly for you. Two words—pussy prison. That's where you're going to end up—in prison—and you're going to be someone's pussy. That's the only ending I foresee for you unless you listen to me right here and now. End whatever you're planning."

Prison...

A shiver went down my back. I hadn't thought it would get that ugly, but Logan was right. There had been an attempted hit-and-run. A house was burned down. And those had been the opening acts.

Shit got real.

I sucked in my breath. My hand flattened against my

stomach—no, that was Mason's arm. I moved closer to him, edging forward, as Logan was talking. Mason held me back.

I moved back a step, and he glanced down at me. There was a question in his depths. Was I okay?

I nodded, feeling my pulse skyrocket, as Logan's voice kept repeating, *"Prison,"* in my mind.

"You think that's where this is going?"

Logan craned his head to the side. "We've been on campus for two days, and both days, we've run into you. I don't think it's a coincidence, and I think you're stupid to pretend that they were."

"What are you saying?"

"Nothing." Logan looked around to the crowd. "Just telling you that we have no delusions where this is going and that we're not underestimating you." He glanced to Mason. "Though, I agree with my brother. I think you're underestimating us."

Logan is stalling.

The realization hit me like a ton of bricks. So was Mason. That was why his anger subsided. They were waiting for something. I studied Sebastian, and I noticed he was, too. No one was making a move against the other. The crowd grew more restless. They were like me, waiting for the fun to happen—not that it was fun. If this was a preview of what was to come throughout my entire freshman year, this was going to give me a heart attack by the end of the year.

"Okay." Summer stepped forward, standing between Logan and Sebastian. "I don't really know what's going on or even who this dude is." She jerked a thumb at Sebastian. "But I can tell that nothing's going to happen. Whatever pissing show this confrontation was supposed to fulfill, it has to stop. If you all keep talking, someone will eventually snap—oh…" Her eyes got big.

Bull's-eye.

Sebastian's mouth lifted in a quick grin before it vanished just as quickly as it'd appeared. That was what he had been doing after all. He wanted one of them to swing at him.

I frowned. That couldn't be the whole reason. Mason and Logan were right. That was too simple. That wasn't sophisticated at all, not what they were expecting from Park Sebastian.

An uneasy sensation took root in me.

Something was off.

Something wasn't connecting.

"Okay." Summer cleared her throat. "Whatever. It's not going to happen." She said to Sebastian, "They aren't taking the bait. They're not going to fight you here." She twisted to Mason and Logan. "And I think he got your message. You're not underestimating him. Check. Got it." Her head skirted between all of us, falling to me at the last second. Her eyebrow arched high. "Can we all move along now? Let's proceed until the next confrontation because, apparently, it's bound to happen. I, for one, am already late for my first class, and being late is one of my pet peeves. No model can be late for a shoot. That's been pounded into me by now." She winced at her choice of words. "I could've used a better word there."

They stood there for a moment after her speech ended. No one laughed at Summer's slip. Logan kept staring at Sebastian, and so did Mason. They were waiting for his next move. Knowing they'd stay there until he was forced to either attack or retreat, I slipped around Mason's arm and moved in front of him.

Still, no one moved.

I shook my head, catching Summer's eye. She realized what I was doing and lined up in front of Logan. I placed my hands on Mason's chest, feeling his pulse beating hard there, and ignored the little tingle of lust forming in me. I began lightly pushing him back, herding him through the crowd and toward my building.

Summer tugged on Logan, pulling him with us.

Logan held firm, still staring at Sebastian, until the moment was gone.

The tension suddenly lifted.

Mason and Logan went with us, and soon, the crowd closed off so we couldn't see Sebastian anymore. That was when Logan cracked a grin, wrapped his arm around Summer's waist, and lifted her in the air. She squealed, more from surprise than enjoyment, but a second later, a laugh came from her, and Logan threw her over his shoulder.

He grinned at her. "You got me. Where do you want me?"

She shook her head, still laughing, as she looked at him, hanging upside down. "You're crazy."

He winked at her. "And you've only known me for two days, too." He gestured to us. "I'm taking this one to her class. I'm going to make a big scene so she can slip in, unnoticed, and I will make my apologies to her professor, leave, and find out where my class is. See you two lovers later."

He headed off, circling around where our standoff just happened. As soon as they were gone, Mason's hand slid down, and his fingers entwined with mine. He pulled me inside my building and into a private classroom. Once the door was shut, he sighed. "I'm sorry that happened just now."

I shook my head. His other hand rested on my hip, and I lifted our hands to his chest, feeling his heart still racing.

"I don't really know what happened, but I guess it was inevitable that we'd run into him. Might as well have been the first day, right?"

I expected his pulse to slow down, but it didn't. It sped up, and I snuck a look under my eyelids. Mason wasn't looking at me. He was peering over my head with a scowl on his face, and the shiver returned to me again.

He'd been quiet during the exchange. I'd known he was angry, but I'd thought he relaxed a little bit. I was wrong.

I said, "Logan was stalling for you."

He still didn't look down at me. "What do you mean?"

"You were going to do something, weren't you?" As I said it, I knew I was right. It clicked into place.

Logan had known, too, and he took over the talking, giving his brother time to calm down.

"You were going to hit him." Or something worse.

Mason's jaw clenched. His hand tightened on my hip. His fingers dug into my skin. "Seeing him so close to you…I almost lost it. I would've if Logan hadn't been there."

Alarm rose up in me, mixing with that cold shiver. That couldn't happen, ever.

"Mason…" I spread our fingers over his heart.

I wanted to will him to calm down. He needed to be the old Mason—the cool and controlled mastermind. The fact that Sebastian got to him so easily by just being around me had me on edge.

Mason pulled our hands down, and he cupped the back of my head. Bringing me closer, he pressed a kiss to my forehead. "I love you, and don't worry. I'll get it together. Go to class. I think half of your classmates were outside anyway. You can slip in with them." He dropped a kiss to my lips. "I'll see you tonight."

He slipped out the door before I'd registered his words.

I was left standing there, actually scared for the first time in a long time.

CHAPTER TEN

MASON

Logan was at home, waiting for me. I asked as soon as I shut the door, "Nate?"

"Class. We're good to go. Sam, too?"

I nodded as I took the chair across from him. "She's worried, but she's not as worried as she should be."

Logan flashed a grin. "I like her roommate."

That was code for, *I'm going to bone her roommate.* I shrugged. I'd cared about Heather, only thinking it might hurt Sam. The roommate was probably worse because of her living proximity with Sam, but there were even worse things to be concerned about.

"He was waiting for her."

The grin dropped as Logan nodded. "I know."

The motherfucking asshole had been waiting for her. I shook my head. "That's going to be a problem."

"Yeah, but I don't know what else to do. You got that guy following her, right?"

"Yeah."

"Did you okay that with campus?"

"What do you mean?" I asked.

Logan lifted a shoulder. "Just that it's kinda creepy, seeing a security guy lurking around campus. He could get reported, and then what?"

"No. He blends in with the students. He won't get reported."

"Oh, yeah?" He clapped me on the shoulder. "When do I meet him?"

I shook my head. "You don't."

"What?"

"No. I'll deal with this. I want you and Sam to enjoy your first year. When I know something or when something happens, I'll tell you." I held his gaze, making sure he understood I was serious. "Okay?"

Logan narrowed his eyes, but he didn't fight it. His lips pressed into an even line.

I said, "I'm using the same company that Dad did. You know they're good. They do their job."

"I think that's bullshit."

"Logan." No. "I'm pulling rank."

"What?" His eyes widened.

"Yeah. I'm the big brother. I'm the reason behind this." He was going to argue. His shoulders lifted. His eyes took on a defiant gleam, and he held a hand up. I interrupted him, "One semester."

"What?" His hand lowered.

"One semester. I will handle the security company for one semester. I'll bring you on board after that."

His eyebrows were pinched together. He was mulling it over, and then his face abruptly cleared. "Well. All I can say is that you picked a good company. They're top-notch." Logan winked at me, getting up from the table. He tapped his head before disappearing into the kitchen. "One semester, Mason.

And good job on hiring them. Way to think ahead. That's your job. You think. I talk."

Hearing the refrigerator door open, I called out, "I thought the motto was that I fight, and you talk?"

Logan came back with a beer and sat down. "I should be nice and offer it to you." He popped the lid and took a big pull before he grinned over the top. "But I know you're in training, and you're wrong. That *was* the motto, but it's changed. I added a section last night. We *both* fight. We *both* talk. What *is* my job? I joke. You never joke. Your humor sucks."

Again, there were worse things to be concerned about. I grunted. "Like I give a shit."

Logan laughed. He tipped the bottle back for one more drag. "I'm so damn thankful we're living in the same house again." He paused and lowered the bottle back to his lap. "What?" He gestured to his face. "You got the whole look like, 'Grr, I'm Mason. Let me piss on you while I beat your face off at the same time.' What did I do wrong?"

We talked about it already. I shouldn't say anything again. *Fuck it.* It was still with me, always in the back of my mind. "You could've been for Sam."

"Oh my god." He tipped his head back, groaning. "Not this shit again."

"We talked about it once."

"Yeah." His head bobbed up and down. "And you punched me later. Thanks for that, by the way."

"My pleasure." I flashed him a grin.

A low growl emanated from him. "You're the sun and moon to her. I would've been a fucking chandelier. That's it."

"Chandeliers are pretty."

"I said that last year to give you a different viewpoint. I'm like a chandelier. You're the sun and moon." Logan's eyes narrowed. "Perspective, asshole."

"I have it, asshole. The sun and moon are taken for granted. Chandeliers are put in magazines. People go ooh and aah over them." There was no heat behind my words anymore. As soon as I'd said the words, I was fine.

Bringing the whole issue up had been enough. It made Logan squirm, that made me feel better.

He shook his head. "You're being jealous."

I smirked at him. "Not to Sam. She doesn't know. You'll understand when you meet your other half and I'll love tormenting you, but until then—" I leaned forward and slapped his arm, spilling his beer. As he jumped up, I ignored his curses and said, "Let's go and do some scouting. I want to find out where Sebastian actually lives."

That was the plan until we got out the door and saw Drew and Nick, a lineman from the team, coming over from the team's house. The looks on their faces stopped us.

I asked, knowing something was wrong, "What is it?"

Drew handed a phone to me. "That was campus security. They found Nate in a parking lot just now."

I took the phone as a weird sensation started in my gut. It was blind rage, but it was being held at bay. A buzzing sound filled my ears as I grated out, "Found?"

Logan echoed, "What do you mean, *found*?"

Drew's mouth flattened, and his shoulders slumped down. "I'm sorry, Mase. They beat him up."

FALLEN CREST UNIVERSITY
SAMANTHA

My first day at college consisted of hiding from two of my floormates, being involved in a public showdown that could've been a brawl, and now wondering where the hell my boyfriend was. It was almost midnight.

My classes were nerve-racking, but when they'd mostly gone over each syllabus with a light lecture, I started to relax. Only one professor made us break into small groups to read and discuss an article.

Mason said he would call. He never did.

I wasn't sure about his football schedule, so when Summer and a bunch of the girls from the floor went to dinner, I tagged along. Afterward, Kitty and Nina wanted to hang out in our room. They'd brought movies and popcorn. Summer enlisted Ruby's help, so she'd moved them to her room with the excuse that she had a large projector for the movie. I'd slipped out within half an hour and changed into my running clothes.

When I started outside, I faltered.

I'd be running alone.

I didn't know the safe trails.

It was dark already.

But I needed to run. The need was almost an ache in me.

"Are you making a break for it?"

Summer flashed a grin. She'd come down behind me. Her hand scratched the back of her head, and she puffed out a burst of air, looking around the lobby. Her eyebrow lifted. "I'm surprised it's almost empty."

Two others were in the main lobby. One was on her phone and cast a glare at Summer, overhearing her. She went right back to texting a second later and slumped farther down in her chair. The other was in a chair by the wall, curled up with a book.

I lifted my foot, bringing it behind me to stretch. "Kitty was making me nervous. She kept looking at me with a weird evil-like Cheshire cat grin. I felt like a mouse being pulled in on an invisible string."

Summer shuddered. "Shit. That sounds horrible."

The corner of my mouth lifted. "Hence, why I needed to go for a run."

I cast another look over my shoulder. People were out there. I could hear low murmurs of conversation through the door that had been left open, but I hadn't thought this through. My normal routes were in Fallen Crest, three hours away.

"I probably shouldn't go running alone though."

"Would you like a running buddy?"

"More like, I just shouldn't go alone because it's not safe."

"Oh." She perked up. A smooth smile appeared, and she winked. "I was talking to a chap today. I think I have a solution."

"A chap?"

She laughed but held up a finger. "One minute. Let me go and grab some stuff. I'll be back."

I checked my phone while she ran to the room. Still no call or text from Mason. I thumbed through the six texts that I sent his way. Where was he? Was he okay? Why wasn't he answering? Should I start to freak?

He'd sent one text five hours ago, saying,

> **I'm okay. Talk tonight or tomorrow. Love you.**

I suppose it should've been enough to placate me, if it weren't for the hair-raising alarm. I wasn't going to call 911 and report a missing person, but Mason texted, and because of that, I hadn't texted Logan or even Nate. Mason was going to get back to me. I knew that. We'd been through enough battles, so I knew he'd follow through, but…I wanted to know now.

Or I wanted to run now.

Either of those would help to appease me.

Summer rushed around the corner with a backpack strapped to her shoulder and keys in hand. She dangled them at me. "Come on. We have to meet someone somewhere."

"Where are we going?"

She didn't answer. She just latched on to my arm. I was dragged from the dorm to the parking lot, and we got into her car. She drove around campus, and not long after, she pulled into the empty lot of the campus gym. *Empty* was the operative word.

I looked around as we got out. "Where is this going?"

Summer grinned over her shoulder, heading for a side door. "Relax. Come on. Trust me."

I grunted, "Not my forte."

She knocked once, paused, knocked again, and did a double tap right after. The door was immediately pushed open. A big guy wearing a Cain U sweatshirt stood on the other side. His hair was sticking up, and he rubbed his eye as he held the door for us. Summer and I slipped inside. I wasn't sure what to say, but Summer touched his chest.

Her hand lingered, and she gazed up at him, a soft smile stretching her lips upward. "Thank you, Dex."

"Yeah, yeah." He released the door but caught it so that it

wouldn't slam shut at the last second. It softly clicked instead. He went ahead and motioned for us to follow.

This was part of the football stadium where Mason trained. He would know where we were going, but I had no clue. The guy led us through dark hallways, and everything was a maze. We came to an open area. The air lightened.

Dex said, his voice echoing slightly in the room, "Hold up one second."

He left us. It was just silence after that.

I grabbed Summer's arm and hissed, "If he kills us, I'm haunting your ass."

She laughed, easing my hand from her arm. "Trust me."

She patted my hand, but I swatted at hers.

I repeated, "Like I said, not my forte."

"What isn't?"

"Trusting people."

"Oh." She grew quiet. "Well, trust me in the next few minutes because—" And as she said those words, the lights turned on, flooding a huge indoor running track.

I stopped listening. My eyes got big. My mouth was slightly ajar, but I didn't care how idiotic I looked. It was my own personal running track. Okay, not really, but this was why Summer brought me here.

I was gutted. "You're joking."

She squeezed my arm. "Nope. You need safe? Well, here you go."

Dex was coming back. He seemed more awake than when he'd met us at the door, and he rubbed a hand over his jaw, taking in my excitement. "Summer said you're a big runner. Have at it."

I held my hands up. "I'm not going to look a gift horse in the mouth. Just thank you."

The track was larger than regular sized gyms. I judged the distance and calculated that two laps would equal a mile. I'd go as long as my legs would take me.

Summer pointed to the starting line. "Go for it." She pulled a paperback out of her bag and went to a nearby chair, plopping down. "This is my seat for the duration. You do your thing, and I'll do mine. I've got a hard-on for Harlequin hotties."

Dex lifted a hand. "All right, I'm going back to bed. I've got early morning practice." He said to Summer, "Don't get me in trouble. All the lights have to be off. Don't mess with the sound system, and go out through that same door. It'll lock behind you."

Practice? As he left, I asked Summer, "Is he on the football team?"

She nodded. Her face was more guarded now. "Should I have told him who you were?"

She meant, who I slept with.

I shook my head. "I'll tell Mason tomorrow." *When he finally returns a phone call.* I gestured to where Dex had gone. "Do I want to know how this transpired?"

Summer opened her book, but she winked at me, running a hand down her leg. "I'm a model. Getting hit on by guys happens. Though," her forehead wrinkled, "I don't usually take them up on their offers, but Dex seemed fine. He wants in my pants. I know that. There's not the usual pressure I get from other guys though." She shrugged. "Who knows? Maybe I'll actually go on a date with him. Now, go. Shoo. Do your thing, roomie. I will be completely distracted here for as long as you need to run."

It'd be an hour, maybe two. I frowned. "It might be longer than you expect."

"You're mistaking me. I don't want to go anywhere for a couple of hours." She patted her book, holding it to her chest. "That's how long it takes me to really get into one of these suckers. If you finish in thirty minutes, I'll be pissed."

I relaxed as I heard that. I felt my mind tuning into the run. My earphones were plugged in. My music was programmed and ready to go. My phone was hooked to my arm, and my roommate was forgotten. Everything slipped to the background—where I was, the time of the day, and that I hadn't heard from Mason. All of it was shoved down.

It was me and the track.

I did my stretches and started off at a light pace. I wanted to close my eyes and just run, but I couldn't. I kept them open and focused ahead of me. I didn't need to worry about cars or people, but I needed to worry about any loose piece from the track. I had to find all the indentations as I rounded my first lap, but it was smooth. By the fifth lap, I felt comfortable with the track. My body was loose and warm. It was ready to go, and I kicked up my speed.

The bass in my ear melded with my running. I hit the track on the beat, and soon, it was just me. I was the music. We molded into one being as I kept going.

I wasn't running to forget something. I was just running. There was no mother. There were no enemies from the Academy. There were no enemies from Fallen Crest Public.

There was no relationship that hadn't been mended.

My mother was getting help. David was married to Malinda. I spent time with Garrett, my biological father. The only person was Sebastian, but in that moment, as I was doing what I did best, a surge of contentment flooded me. Mason and Logan would be fine. They would handle Sebastian like they handled everyone. They wouldn't be harmed. Everything would be fine.

I felt it in my gut, and as I kept going, now on my tenth lap, I was becoming stronger.

By my twentieth lap, I turned everything off.

I was running because that was what I did. My legs moved forward because that was their purpose. My arms pumped harder, helping as I sliced through the air, and my chest was tight, but my lungs still worked. Air was breathed in and released.

I was soaring.

I didn't know how much time had passed. It wasn't until Summer was waving her arms in the air that I slowed down. She waited for me to stop beside her.

Pulling my earplugs out, I felt for my pulse, and I automatically started counting as I asked, "What's wrong?"

"Nothing." A look of awe was on her face. Her eyes were a little glazed, and she was taken aback. "You weren't lying when you said you had to run. We've been here for two hours."

Two hours? I frowned. I'd stopped counting my laps. "Oh."

"You seem disappointed."

"I have no idea how far I went."

"Well, it was damn far. That's for sure. Do you need to know?"

Bending down to start my stretching, I wasn't sure. "I haven't met with my track coach yet."

"Uh...okay."

I shifted my leg, stretching the other. My head turned, so I could see her. "My last one wanted me to record everything."

"Wait." She held a hand up. "You're talking like you could keep going?"

I could. I'd run longer, but two hours was my normal max now. I hadn't gone past the two-hour mark in a long time. All I said was, "I warned you."

She laughed. "You did, but I had a real reason to stop you." She held up her phone. "Dex texted me a while ago. He remembered that the security guards sweep this place twice during the night. They should be coming around in thirty minutes."

I groaned, holding the bottom of my heel and pressing my forehead to my knee. She was right. We had to go, but holy hell, as I finished with that last stretch, I hadn't felt this alive in a long time. Mason and running—they were the only things that could achieve that feeling for me.

I grabbed my earphones and said, "I can finish stretching in the room. We can go now."

"You sure?"

I gestured to the hallways. "It might take us a while to get out of here. We might get lost."

"Ha." Summer flashed a grin and held up her phone again. "He texted me directions for that, too. Okay. Hold on. I'm going to be brave and turn off the lights. Don't leave without me."

As if that was really a question.

After she turned off the lights, she hollered from across the gym, "Okay. You're smart. This is going to take longer than I thought. Being in the dark was a whole lot scarier." As she kept talking, her voice grew louder and louder. She was slowly coming back to me. "I'm about ready to piss my pants. And I'll never watch another scary movie in my life. I don't think I'll even watch *Supernatural*. Oh my god—" Her voice started to veer off.

I interrupted, "Turn back. You sound like you're going to the left of me."

"Oh." A second later, she said, "Is this better?"

"Keep talking."

"Not a problem." A nervous laugh was there. "If anyone had night-vision goggles, they'd be pissing their pants, laughing at me. I'm stretching out my arms and legs in front of me, so I won't hit anything. And I'm waving my phone around, too. So far, the light hasn't helped with shit."

She was getting closer.

I could see the little light of her phone. "I can see you. Keep coming."

She snorted. "That's what *he* said."

I grinned, wiping off some of the sweat from my forehead. "Is this the wrong time to ask if you have two phones?"

The light stopped. Her voice dropped. "Why?"

Logan would be so proud. "Because I'm seeing two lights. Are you waving one behind you, too?"

Her light turned off. "Do not joke with me. I know where you sleep."

I was holding the laughter in and cleared my throat. My voice was calm as I said, "There's a light behind you."

She screamed. Her light was swinging back and forth, as if hitting someone. As she kept coming toward me, she yelled, "I don't see anyone."

I kept quiet.

"Sam!" Her panic picked up a notch.

I still said nothing.

"Oh my god!" Her feet sounded like a stampede, and she was sprinting for me now.

Her phone grew in size, and then she was right next to me. She grabbed my arm, and like before, she dragged me after her. We were both running through the hallways.

She kept chanting, "Oh my god, oh my god," under her breath as she was trying to read Dex's directions. "Go left here. Now, right." She yanked me with her. "Oh my god, oh my god."

No one was there, but her fear was intoxicating. It started to creep into me, too, and I pressed her to go faster. We were at the door, and we burst through it. I stopped to make sure the door would shut. Summer didn't. She hightailed it to her car.

Getting there, she saw I was still by the gymnasium, and she pounded on her car's roof. "What are you doing? Get in the car."

I couldn't hold it in anymore. My blood was buzzing from the adrenaline, my run, and Summer's terror. I folded over, and the laughter poured out of me.

"Wha—" She stopped.

Crap. I needed a ride. I tried to muffle the laughs as I went to the car.

Summer was glaring at me. Her hand crumbled over her keys and she choked out, "Do not tell me that you were fucking with me."

I got inside and secured my seat belt. She couldn't kick me out. I looped the strap around me a second time to make sure. I'd hold on to it like it was the only thing anchoring me in a tornado.

I waited until she got in and did her own seat belt. I said, "I might've been lying…"

She sucked in her breath.

I finished, "About the second light."

She was silent.

Then the screams came. "I actually pissed my pants! How could you? Oh my god!"

I waited it out. She kept screaming, but the hysteria slipped a notch, and she started her car before turning out of the parking lot.

Two blocks. I kept telling myself that. *We can make it two blocks.*

Summer kept ranting, "I'm going to make your life hell. Buckets of water when you're not expecting it. Your coffee's always going to be cold. And your shampoo. You'd better hide your shampoo somewhere else because, every chance I get, I'm pouring hair dye in there." She belted out a harsh laugh, turning into our parking lot. "So bad, Samantha. You're going to pay so bad."

She quieted as we got out.

I snuck a look. "I don't know what came over me. I think I channeled Logan. I'm sorry. I didn't know how scared you would get."

Her shoulders loosened, and a short laugh slipped out. She shook her head, her mouth curved up into a rueful grin, and another burst of laughter jerked from her. She shot me a dark look as we entered our dorm. "Oh, man. I'm calmer now. I abhor being scared. Hate it. Hate it with a passion. My boyfriends used to do that shit to me all the time."

My lips twitched. I wanted to laugh, but I didn't dare.

She cursed under her breath. We started up the stairs to our floor, and she motioned for me. "Go ahead. Let it out. I might've overreacted."

"You think?"

She laughed again, the tension easing a little bit from her. "I knew there wasn't a second light. I was looking, but it didn't matter. It was already in my head. What if someone was actually there? They were following me. They could've killed me. No one would've known, and they would've gotten you, too. Okay. My imagination was running wild."

Right as we topped the stairs for our floor, I murmured, "I will never prank you again."

She shrugged, letting out a breath of air. "It's my bad. I know it was a joke—at least, I think I knew it. I totally overreacted, but," she shot me cautious look, "this just means that I get to plan my payback."

A retort was on the tip of my tongue, but when our dorm room came into view, it died.

Mason was sitting on the floor outside our room.

He'd been waiting, and judging from the mask on his face, he wasn't happy about it.

CHAPTER ELEVEN

MASON

She was laughing. I heard it as she and her roommate were coming up the stairs.

She had every right to be angry with me. I ditched her. She didn't know about Nate or that we'd been at the hospital with him for the last six hours, waiting for all the tests to get done before they'd let us take him home. They would've kept him for observation, but the last bed went to a heart attack patient. That was what the nurse said when she cleared Nate to go with us. We were given instructions on what to check for, including his breathing, his skin color, his pulse every hour, and a few other things that Logan wrote down. As soon as I could, I went to Sam's dorm. She hadn't answered my calls, and as she came down the hallway, I saw the reason.

I stood, but they both quieted as they got to me. "You were running."

Sam didn't reply. Her eyes narrowed, and a shadow appeared underneath them. It was me. She knew something was wrong, and bags formed under her eyes. My mouth pressed flat. I hated being the cause of it. I couldn't lie, but I knew that I couldn't tell Sam about Nate. Those bags would become permanent, and she'd only worry.

She started to say something but waited, glancing at her roommate.

The girl continued to stare at me. Her eyes widened a fraction.

Sam cleared her throat.

"Oh!" Her roommate blinked rapidly, jerking forward. "Sorry. Um…" She pulled out her keys for the door but dropped them. "Shit." Grabbing them, she tried to insert the right key, but it wouldn't go. It took three more tries before she slid it inside and grimaced to us over her shoulder. "Sorry about that. I'll be, uh…I'll be in here." She paused in the doorway, still looking between me and Sam. "Oh, yeah. Okay. Bye." She went inside, and the door slammed shut.

Sam was frowning at it.

It opened again. Her roommate poked her head around it, biting down on one side of her lip. "Sorry. It slipped from my hand. Okay…again. Bye." She waved at us, her hand right next to her ear. "Take as long as you want. I'm going to bed."

Sam moved into me. I leaned against the wall, holding her to my chest, when their door opened again.

The roommate slipped out, holding a shower caddy. "Sorry." She kept her head bent, and her eyes forward. "I have to go to the restroom first, and then I'm off to bed. For real. Take your time."

I could feel Sam's silent laughter, but she didn't respond. We waited until her roommate made the trek to the restroom and went inside.

Sam whispered, looking up to me, "Maybe we should go somewhere private?"

I nodded, letting her take the lead, but when she started to head toward the parking lot, I caught her hand and motioned for the basement. "You have some rooms down there, right?"

Her eyebrows lifted high as she nodded. "A computer room. The movie room, and the kitchen are down there. There's another smaller lounge, too."

"Let's go down there."

"But…" She cast a confused look outside.

I entwined our fingers and started for the basement. "If we go to my place, you won't be leaving until morning."

I was already hard, imagining how it would feel to slide inside Sam. It would be heaven to me. I could forget about Sebastian and how he'd gotten to Nate. All of that shit could be forgotten, but that wouldn't be fair to Sam. She deserved normalcy. Spending time with her at her dorm was normal. Hearing her laugh with her roommate was normal. She'd get pulled into our war. I knew it was inevitable, but I wanted a little bit more time. That was all I was trying for. I was just holding that off.

She was happy.

I couldn't be the reason that went away.

No one was in the small waiting lounge. I headed inside, but Sam checked the movie room.

"Mason," she held the door open, going inside, "this is more private."

A large screen was on the far end of the room. Plush, large seats were placed in rows in front of the screen. The back of the room was made up with couches, and a side door opened to a back kitchen.

We picked a couch in the farthest corner, but Sam went to turn the kitchen light off. A small amount of light filtered in underneath the door from the rest of the basement. I watched as she made her way to me.

She was confident. She moved with purpose.

It hit me how much she changed from when she'd moved in with Analise. She'd lost everything. She hadn't cared about anything, and she had been a badass because of it—striking out, not giving a shit. Logan and I took her in, and then she had something to lose—me. She got scared. She was pushed around by the girls and bullied by her own mother, and through all that crap, she'd still fought. She'd clawed her way back up, protecting and loving Logan and me at the same time.

Good god. I wanted to pull her on top of me. I wanted to lose myself in her.

When I sat on the couch, Sam had a knowing grin, and she sat right where I wanted her, right where maybe she shouldn't have. My hands held her hips as she straddled me. She looped her arms around my neck and rested her forehead to mine.

Her grin never dimmed, not even as she teased, "Why do I feel like we're in high school, and I don't want my mom to catch us making out in the basement?"

Shit, I love this woman.

A smooth and lazy low laugh flitted from her lips. I waited for her to find my mouth with hers, but she didn't.

She held back and her eyes traced over my face. "What happened today?"

I wasn't going to tell her. *More time.* I needed more time. "Logan took us out of town. He heard about some park or something, but we got lost, and we didn't have cell phone reception. I'm sorry." I cupped the side of her face. My thumb rubbed down over her cheek, falling to linger at the corner of her mouth. The ache to kiss her was building—along with another ache. Well, that ache was just permanent. I had an eternal hard-on for the woman I loved.

"Logan took you out to some park?"

"That's what he was trying to do." The lies came so easy, and I smiled, knowing I was a dick. "We never found it. Said some swimming hole with a waterfall was there."

"Oh." Her hands fell down to the bottom of my shirt. She was toying with it. Her knuckles brushed against my stomach every now and then.

The small touch was driving me crazy. I should still her hands. I didn't. I was going to hell, and we were going to be indecent in two minutes if she kept that up.

"You went on a run with your roommate?"

She shook her head, her eyes darkening in lust. "I ran. She read."

"Wait. What?"

A husky laugh slid out from her. "I ran around this track, and she read her book in a chair."

"The track? The running track in the gym?"

"Yeah. A guy let us in, but don't tell. I want to use it again. I need to find a place to run." She amended, "Somewhere that's safe anyway."

She'd been inside some building for at least the last two hours, and my security guy never said a word. That was one phone call I'd be making as soon as I left—or, hell, I'd just find him. He or his replacement weren't off duty until Sam was tucked into her own bed and sleeping.

"Sam," I lifted her chin so that she was looking right into my eyes, "don't go running at night by yourself."

"I didn't. That's why Summer went with me."

"But if she can't go with you, don't go. I mean it. Or call me. I'll let you into the gym, too. I have keys. All the football guys do. We have twenty-four-seven access in there for training."

"You do?"

I nodded, but she was right. She needed a place to run. I should've scoped that out for her already.

"Mason?"

"Hmm?"

She snaked a hand to the back of my hair and tugged me to her. "Will you please fucking kiss me?"

That was all I needed. Taking hold of the back of her neck, I leaned forward, taking her lips in mine. *Fuck the dorm.* I started to turn to roll her underneath me when she hit my shoulder and leaned back.

Her cheeks were flushed, and her eyes were dilated in shock. "Here?"

She was mine.

"What?" A low growl was fighting to be released. I wanted her. I wanted to take what was mine—

Damn it. Basement, basement.

We were in the motherfucking dorm basement. She had classmates, and a resident advisor.

That growl erupted, and I realized there could even be cameras. Checking the room, I didn't see any lights blinking, but I couldn't assume there weren't any.

Still…

My hand loosened on her neck and rubbed over her skin, caressing. I teased, "I could push a couch up against the door. No one would be able to come in."

"If you want to do that, let's go home."

She sank back on top of me. Her hands ran underneath my shirt and slipped up, and I closed my eyes, enjoying the feel of her. They were on me, no one else. I had no reason to be jealous or insecure, but damn, I loved knowing she loved me. I loved that I could run my hand down her arm, and she'd gasp from the sensation, like she did just now. I loved that I could linger right above her shorts with my fingers rubbing the skin underneath her shirt, like she was touching me, and her body would begin to tremble, like she was doing now. I loved that, as I laid her down on the cushions and rose above her, blocking her from any views there could be, my fingers could dip inside her shorts and hover over her opening, and she would arch her back up. She would come alive.

She closed her eyes, but she was watching me now. Her eyelids were heavy with desire. I grinned. My body was wound tighter than a nun at a *Magic Mike* show. It wanted release, and it wanted that in her. I fought against it. I pressed a kiss under her jaw, and feeling her silent intake of breath, I nipped at her collarbone. Feeling another shiver go through her, I exposed her stomach before dropping one last kiss under her belly button. I could live off making her shudder in my arms. That was my job—to make her happy, to make her climax, and to make her experience what so many could never imagine.

I closed my eyes and forced myself to stop. I wanted to keep going again but rested my forehead against her stomach, instead.

She could feel the fight in me and relaxed in my hands. Her hand swept through my hair, running down my neck. Her nails scraped the back of my head, and I grinned. It was my soft spot. That little touch could hold me in place for hours. She had that power, that knowledge over me.

I lifted my head, and the exhaustion from the entire day finally seeped into my bones. I could lay there, on top of her, and sleep until morning. I frowned, trying to remember why that was a bad idea, as her nails kept running up and down my neck.

I sank down on her. She welcomed me, adjusting her body so that she could comfortably hold me. I slipped to the side, my leg and arm over her. My head moved to the crook of her neck and shoulder. She kept scraping over my neck…until I fell asleep.

"Psst. Psst."

Some chick was bent over me, her finger to her mouth, with her knees together. Her hand dropped to twist with her other one, and she gritted her teeth. "Uh…"

I jumped up, landing on my feet right in front of her. It was Sam's roommate. I was not prepared to deal with this chick, especially after she woke us up.

"Holy shit," she squealed, startled by my sudden movement. She scooted back but remained in the room.

I scowled at her. "Get out."

"Uh…"

A snore sounded from behind me. Sam was curled on the couch, her knees pulled up to her chest. She was almost falling off, and I took a moment to stare at her. How she slept like that, I'd never know, but the girl could fall asleep whenever and wherever.

Wherever…

The couches weren't familiar.

I scanned the room and remembered we were in her dorm's basement. "Fuck!"

"What? Huh?" Sam flew alive, jerking upright on the couch. Her hand raked through her hair. She blinked at me and blinked at the chick, and her hand dropped to land with a thud against her side. "Summer?"

"Yeah. Hi." She moved closer a few steps, glancing nervously at me. "Uh, I got woken up this morning. Ruby came down to grab more coffee from the kitchen. She saw you guys and told me that maybe I should check on you. Here I am." She gestured between all of us, back to herself, and around to Sam and me again in a wild flying motion. "Checking on you. My job is done." She began edging to the door, backward, her gaze skirting to me and jerking back to Sam. Right before her back hit the door, she paused, and her hands did another abrupt movement. She looked like she was doing a cheer that was failing miserably. "So…okay. Anyway, in case you needed to be somewhere…"

The last statement was directed to me, but she wasn't meeting my eyes. Her head hung down, and she kicked at the floor.

I could almost hear Logan laughing in my head. *Dude, you broke the model. You scared her fighting spirit right out of her. Damn, you're good.*

I grunted, running a hand over my face, feeling my scruff. *Fuck. Fuck. Fuck.* I had to go. I gently touched Sam's shoulder, leaning over to press a kiss to her, and I whispered against her lips, "I have an early morning run." My lips moved to her ear, adding, "Love you."

She nodded, grasping the back of my head, and she moved, so she could kiss me again. "Love you, too. See you."

"Uh…" The roommate opened one of the doors. Her back moved, holding it open as she waited for our exchange. One arm was crossed over her chest with a firm grip on her other arm hanging down. It looked like she was holding on for dear life.

I had no time for her. I touched Sam's arm once more, and then I was off. It was seven in the morning. I'd missed my run with Drew by an hour. *Fuck.*

I called him as soon as I was in my car and on the street, heading home. He didn't pick up after the first time.

He did after my second call. "Shit, Kade. Where were you?"

"I'm coming now."

"Fucking hell. We're done. The guys and I are heading to get breakfast now."

I gritted my teeth. The urge to yank my steering wheel off and throw it at the nearest car was powerful. I let out an irritated breath instead.

"Dude, don't get pissed at me. You asked for the run and didn't show."

"I know. Something came up."

"Yeah?" His irritation eased.

Mine didn't. I took a turn rougher than I needed to, and I forced myself to slow down. I wasn't mad at Drew. I was mad about Nate. I was mad that I had to leave Sam—no, I was mad that I'd lied to her.

"Sorry. Okay. I'm going for a run by myself."

"You need someone to time your sprints."

"I'll make my brother do it."

"Okay." Drew sounded cheery all of a sudden.

I frowned. The asshat sounded too happy to get out of that.

Whatever. I shook my head, turning onto our street.

As I pulled into my driveway, Drew came out of the football house with his phone to his ear. He saw me and waved, heading over.

"Hey." Drew pointed to the football house. "If you want, we can wait. You could eat with us and do sprints this afternoon? Nick and Rome didn't join us this morning either."

The idea had merit, but as I was considering it, the door to my house opened. Logan stood there with a scowl. He waved at me to get inside.

"Or," Drew noted, "maybe not?"

"I should do my run anyway. I have a nine am class. I can get it done before."

"Okay. We have practice at three today."

I nodded. "I got the schedule. I'll be lifting in the evening with the guys, too."

"Good."

Some of the guys from the team were coming out of the football house. They all nodded in hello to me but waited on the sidewalk for Drew.

He started for them, pointing at me. "The guys miss you. They want to rib you about Sebastian. You know that, right?"

The group overheard him, and Rome yelled over, "Yeah, when are you going to finally smash that pretty face of his? I thought you were the all-star fighter, Kade?"

I shot back, heading for Logan, "You hit like a two-day-old kitten, Rome. You'd have better luck sneezing on him."

He groaned. "I should. That's my new weapon if someone gets in my face. Watch out. Here come my germs."

A couple of the other guys started laughing, but I got inside. Logan shut the door, crossed his arms over his chest, and lifted an eyebrow. He didn't say a word. I felt like I was being schooled by Mama Malinda.

I asked, "What?"

The corner of his mouth curved up. "Where have you been all night, son? I've been worried sick. I've been sitting in this living room, waiting for you, since the crack of dawn."

"I'm fighting the urge to slap you on the back of the head."

He dropped the facade and moved back, holding his hands up. "I surrender. Sorry. Thought some parental acting might make you feel loved."

"Is that Mason?" came from the second floor. "Is it? Logan? Is that Mason?"

I jerked a thumb up the stairs. "I take it Nate's awake?"

"Yeah." Logan's scowl came back. He glared up to the ceiling and gave it the middle finger. "That's what has had me up since the crack of dawn. He's been yelling for you half the night."

"Really?"

"Mason, I want to talk to you…if that's you." He paused. "Come up here if it is!"

A roar ripped from Logan, "Shut up!"

There was silence.

"You shut up! Mason? Is that you?"

Logan drew in an angry hiss and let loose, "Mason died! You're stuck with me, Monson! How are you going to handle that?"

Another beat of silence.

"That's not funny! You're not funny all the time, Logan! You're not funny half the time. How's that? You think that's funny?"

"Oh." Logan went to the stairs, but he waited at the end. He continued to shout upward, "So original, Nate! You know what else is original? If I flushed your pain pills down the toilet. That'd be *real* original."

"You—" he choked off. He sputtered out, "That's horrible. That would really be horrible. I can't even—I'm like this because of you and Mason. All the time, it's me. I get in the car accident. I get blackmailed. I get threatened. I get beat up. I'm sick of it! I want you guys to finally get hurt and feel what it's like…" His voice faltered.

Logan jabbed his finger in the air. His glare didn't lessen from when Nate was yelling back at him. Logan said to me, "That's his attitude. He said he's fed up with being the punching bag. He's taken our beatings for the last time. He's been griping about this shit since three. Where the hell were you anyway? Seriously. I am ticked that you've been gone."

Dropping my keys on the table, I figured it was time to deal with this. No early morning run and no breakfast with the team. It was time to do damage control with my own best friend. I said to Logan, "I went to see Sam. She called yesterday, and I never returned her calls."

"Oh." He frowned. The hostility was instantly gone. "Is she okay?"

"Yeah. She went on a run. Her roommate somehow got her into the gym where there's a running track."

"Yeah? The model roommate?"

I gave him a look. "The chick you want to bag, yes. But I doubt it'll happen. She's infatuated with me."

"No way." He was quick to protest. "She's got a football boner for your stats. That's it. The chick is cool."

I gave him a questioning look. "The chick is weird and awkward."

"See? Football boner." He pointed to my junk. "Show her the goods, and it'll probably cure her of her stupids."

I punched him. "You show your dick."

"Ouch." He shot me a dirty look. "What was that for? And she doesn't have a football boner for me. Seriously, Mase, the girl is wacky about football. That's all it is. She doesn't like you like that." He quieted, his eyebrows pinching together. "At least, I hope not. Otherwise, you really can never bone Sam in her own room."

"Mason?"

I glanced up the stairs. Nate was right about some of it. He got the brunt of a lot of payback that was headed our way. Some of it was accidental, and some of it was because he was the nearest link on our chain. He was owed an apology, at least from me.

I pointed upstairs. "I should go deal with him."

Logan crossed his arms over his chest.

"You're not coming?"

His only response was, "Good luck with that." He dropped the clipped tone. "I have to go to class anyway."

"Okay."

I started up the stairs. As I got to the floor, a girl came from Logan's room. She was freshly showered and was straightening her shirt. She didn't notice me at first, so she almost walked into me. I caught her by the shoulder and pushed her back. She gasped, her eyes wide in shock, and then she relaxed when she saw me.

"Oh. Sorry." She sounded breathless. "You're Mason, right? Logan's brother?"

I nodded.

"Mason?" Nate didn't sound as agitated. "You out there?"

"Yeah. Hold on."

"Oh, good." He was relieved. "Finally."

The girl tilted her head to the side, studying Nate's closed door. "He's been yelling for most of the night. Logan gave me some earplugs, so I could sleep through it, but I didn't know he was still yelling."

I didn't want to know anything. Not where she came from. Not who she was. Not how she came to be in our house or how Logan picked her up. The girl looked too chatty.

I pointed downstairs. "He's down there. Hurry. Catch him."

"What?"

"Please."

I wanted her gone. Having randoms in the house was normal but not when we just brought Nate home from the hospital.

She didn't move, though. She seemed frozen in place.

"Go find Logan. Now." I was being harsh, but I didn't care.

"I—"

My patience was gone. I heard it snap. "Better yet, get the fuck out of this house."

"Mase?" Logan came to the bottom of the stairs. His mouth formed an O as he saw his friend, and he grimaced. "Shit. I forgot."

"See?" I grated out to the girl. "We don't chat in this house. My brother fucks and forgets. That's what you are to him. You're a forgotten. Now, get out."

"Asshole!" she seethed.

I nodded. I'd take it.

She swept down the stairs and jerked around Logan, shoving out the door in the next second.

I scowled at my brother. "We *just* brought Nate home."

"I know." He cringed. His hand lifted and grabbed a handful of his hair. He pulled at it, making it stick up, before his hand dropped back to his side. "She called me at two. It was a booty call. I thought she left, and I got distracted by Nate yelling." He frowned to himself. "Where the hell did she sleep last night?"

"In your bed?" I grated out. "Just a guess."

"Huh." He grinned, shaking his head. "I thought that was just a really big pile of blankets, even though I couldn't remember having that many. Makes sense now."

"You gave her earplugs to sleep."

He waved that off, smirking. "That was right after I came on her. I was feeling friendly. I came back from the bathroom, and I thought she was gone."

"Mason?"

I groaned. This shit was too much. "Go to class. I'll take care of him."

"Oh, hey." Logan stopped me before I went into Nate's room. "The school called his parents. They're heading here."

Fucking déjà vu. Nate gets hurt. His parents get called. They sweep in and take him away from us.

I sighed. Maybe this time, that would be for the best. "Yeah. Okay. Thanks for letting me know."

"Mase!"

I opened Nate's door. It was time to deal with my best friend.

His arm jerked in the air, and I ducked back. I just saw the motion. I didn't see the book that he'd chucked at me, but it hit the wall by me. Catching it off the bounce, I tossed it back at him. Nate didn't duck, and it clipped him on the shoulder.

"Fuck you." He grabbed the book and hurled it as hard as he could toward his closet. The doors were shut, and the book went right through one of them, splitting a hole in the door.

I pointed at the hole. "You're paying for that."

"Fuck *you*!" One arm lifted, and his other arm clapped down on the opposite forearm. He gave me the fist and the middle finger. He collapsed against his headboard and groaned, cradling his head with his hands. "I *hate* this. I hate being like this. I hate being in pain. My parents are coming, Mase. You know what a headache they're going to be?"

He seemed calmer, so I eased farther into the room and perched against his dresser. I started to fold my arms over my chest, but I caught myself and let them hang at my side. I needed to be ready in case anything else was sent soaring my way. Nate had a right to be pissed, but I didn't want to get injured.

"My parents. My fucking uptight and self-righteous parents." Nate continued to grumble, "I feel like I'm in high school, and I'm going to be chastised. They're going to want me to move out. I'm going to have to fight them on that and screw that. They don't remember me until they get some phone call from the hospital, you guys, or jail. I'm an adult now."

If Logan had been in the room, he would've pounded his fist in the air, cheering Nate on. I did nothing. I waited for him to be done.

"They can't come in here and threaten me. That's what they always do." He lifted pained eyes to me. "If they cut me off, you're sharing your trust fund with me."

"Fuck that."

"Mason."

"That's my trust fund. No way. Stand up to your parents. If they cut you off, get a job."

"Right. Because that's what you'd do," he retorted.

"I can tell you one thing I wouldn't do," I grated out. My jaw clenched. "I wouldn't buckle under any threat. The only one that's come close was Sam's mom, and she could've screwed my entire future if she wanted. If my dad threatened to take away my trust fund, I'd go to the bank and put a bag of shit in his safety deposit box." I thought about that. "Or I'd have Logan do it. He'd do it."

"You don't get it."

"Yes, I do. Your parents are assholes. So are mine. Deal with them, or they'll do this to you all your life."

He ran a hand over his face, letting it drop, and he looked even more haggard afterward. "They've not been the same since my sister…"

I quieted. Nate never talked about his sister. An incident happened years ago, and she was shipped to a boarding school in Europe. He'd mentioned her one other time, but no details were shared. I wasn't certain what happened, but I could guess, and if that were my sister, I would've been seeing red.

He shrugged, slumping farther down in his bed. "Okay. You're right. Deal with them. That's the plan. I'll get it done." He started to look around and pointed beside me. "Can you throw me that robe?"

I tossed it his way.

It landed on his lap, and he shrugged it on. "Sorry I was a bitch before. I was mad. Just tell me you're going to get that fucker."

I nodded. "Somehow, he'll get taken care of. I promise, Nate."

"The asshole had his guys, my former friends, jump me while he was doing a standoff with you guys in public." Nate's eyes hardened. I heard the pain from him. He added, "I want him to fry."

"He will."

Nate looked up, catching my gaze. I let him see the promise there, and he nodded. Some of the pain slid away.

He murmured, "Thank you."

Park Sebastian did this shit to him. It went down as Nate said. Sebastian's friends jumped him in a back parking lot. He was going to his class when they showed up. They'd herded him to a back corner for more privacy, and then they let loose and pounded the crap out of him.

He couldn't walk. He couldn't even pull out his phone to dial 911. A security guard found him, and during that time, Sebastian was waiting for Sam.

He orchestrated the whole thing.

The message was sent.

The war had finally started.

CHAPTER TWELVE

SAMANTHA

It'd been a couple of weeks, and I fell into a routine.

Early mornings would be spent with the girls. Summer and I would walk to our classes together. When Ruby's latte machine broke, Summer and I began going to the campus coffee shop. Some of the other girls joined us, including Kitty and Nina, and it became a gossip session. Kitty and Nina no longer waited in the hallway for me after I'd evaded them for the first week.

Logan was given strict instructions not to come to my dorm. He came a second time, and Kitty took root on Summer's love seat in my room. She wouldn't leave. Nina tried getting her to leave, pinching under her arm and hoisting her legs in the air. She tried to roll Kitty across the floor to the door. Nina's plan had been to drag Kitty the rest of the way down the hallway to their room, but her butt had been too heavy for Nina. The ninety-six-pound girl was no match for Kitty, who was a solid one hundred eighty. When their Logan fandom lessened, once he had stopped coming by, they became more normal.

The afternoons would be spent going our own ways—to classes and to the library.

My evenings were split between running and seeing Mason. If I saw him in the afternoon, I'd run at night. Summer would go with me, reading her book in the stands as I circled the gym track. If I ran earlier, I'd see him later at night. There were no more sleepovers in the movie lounge. He hung out in my room a couple of times, but Kitty and Nina were scared of him. Summer got better with her starstruck ways. She wasn't as awkward, but when she caught herself staring at Mason, she'd leave and spend time in another room.

It was easier to go to his house, but it was nice when he was at my place, too. Since the torture from the movie-room night, we kept everything PG-13. If things were going to the R rating, we'd ease back or go straight to his place. Logan caught on. If I saw him on campus during the day, he'd ask if it was a fuck night or a no-fuck night. That was his way of asking if I'd be at the house later, so we could all hang out in the kitchen or living room or if I'd just be seeing Mason at my dorm.

It was that time of day when my path would cross Logan's. His class was in the same building as the post office and while I waited for him, I was in line to get a package from Malinda.

"Next." A lady at the counter signaled for the next person to step forward.

That was me. I waited for the guy in front of me to move aside. He stayed in place, so I moved around him and gave the lady my slip. As she went to get my package, the guy didn't move. I didn't look up, but I could feel his attention. He shifted to the side, resting his hip against the counter, and he folded his arms over his chest.

He was watching me, and he wasn't being bashful about it.

I waited, my jaw clenched. Guys were interested in me. I hadn't dealt with that attention at Fallen Crest Public because everyone knew about Mason, but it was different at Cain University. Mason was known, but our relationship wasn't. In some ways, it was refreshing. I could go to classes as I pleased with no attention, judging, or cutting me down if I wore a black shirt versus what was in style, but I assumed this guy was interested in more than my fashion sense. I was prepared with an easy lie to evade him, but he never moved back a step. He held firm, almost touching my elbow.

He was quiet, waiting for me to address him.

The guy was an asshole. I felt that much from him, by how brazen he was being. I gritted my teeth when the lady came back. She slid a box to me, and I was right. Malinda's handwriting was on it. She'd put hearts all around my address with quotes written on the sides.

Go for it, Sam!
Live life to the fullest!
I miss you, and so does your father.
David says, "Hi."
Mark says, "What's up?"
Don't let Logan get you into too much trouble.
Give Mason a hug for me.

There was more written, but those were the ones I glimpsed before I turned to leave. The guy blocked me. I couldn't go behind me. A large group of students were there, trying to get to their mail slots, too, so I had to go around the guy.

I stepped right, and so did he.

I went left. He did, too.

A growl formed at the bottom of my throat, and my eyes snapped. I didn't want to get hit on. I didn't want to deal with this. Everything froze in me.

I was looking right into Park Sebastian's smirking eyes. His hair was gelled and combed to the side. He wasn't wearing the polo like last time, but he had on a Cain University shirt with a pair of jeans. The outfit fitted his form nicely and screamed money. Others were wearing the same shirt, but they couldn't pull off the wealthy vibe like he could. They also couldn't pull off the arrogant asshole vibe like he was giving off either.

As our gazes made contact, the corner of his lip curved up. He was taunting me. He knew I hated this, hated having another male standing so close to me. He wasn't Mason. I began to back up, holding the box to my chest, but I was bumped into. Elbows ground into my back. Someone's hair whipped at my face as she turned abruptly. I was jostled forward.

My eyes got wide.

I was going right into Sebastian, and he knew it. His arm fell down and lifted. He was going to catch me.

I didn't want him to touch me. I couldn't stop it, though, and he caught my elbow. I was tucked into his chest, and he transferred us, rotating swiftly on his heel and bringing me to the other side of the line, where I could suddenly breathe. No group was suffocating me, pressing me back into him. He released me at the same time as I hit him with the box. I hoped whatever was inside wasn't fragile because I'd thumped it hard against his chest, jerking backward. All of that was in one swift motion.

"Hey," he said, falling back a step. His hands lifted in a quick surrender.

My nostrils flared. He was a joke. "Do not touch me. Ever."

A few waiting in line for their own packages heard my comment and looked over. They were confused. Sebastian wasn't touching me anymore. I looked hostile. I didn't care.

I said to him again, "Stay away from me. I mean it."

I turned to go, but Sebastian blocked me again.

He rounded in front of me, his hands in the air. "Seriously, I won't touch you."

"What do you want?"

He had watched me while I stood next to him, waiting for my package.

He knew who I was. I realized he had known who I was, even before going to the side of him. That was why he stayed there. He'd forced me to move to the side. He'd forced the entire situation, trapping me with that group behind me.

I thought about moving to his left side, away from the pressing group, but his bag was there. I had to go to the right side. He kept it open for me.

It was a move that Mason and Logan would do. Their enemy did it, too, and that sent my internal alarms from the ridiculous stage to the ludicrous stage. They were blaring, flashing in circles. I knew Park Sebastian was cunning and manipulative, but he was showing a new card to me.

He was even more calculating than I imagined, but I did what Mason would do. I took that information and put it to the back of my mind. It would help in dealing with Sebastian in the future, if he did anything else. As I stood there, regarding him now in suspicion, I knew he was going to.

My shoulders rolled back. *Screw it.* I said, "If you're going to use me to hurt Mason, it won't work."

His eyes widened a fraction of an inch. His top lip lifted in appreciation. I surprised him, and he enjoyed that. I frowned. I hadn't expected that, but I hugged my box closer to my chest. His gaze fell down to it, and he was reading the quotes Malinda put around it. I tried to cover them, closing my hands around the box. He moved to the next quote. I covered that, too. I looked ridiculous, and I felt my cheeks warming.

Enough.

I couldn't win like this.

I began to back away. I kept my eyes averted, hugging that box, and I was backpedaling. I could run into someone, but I didn't care. I had to get away from him.

"Samantha." He walked with me.

"Stop," I hissed at him.

He leaned forward, a slow grin tugging at the corner of his lip. He tucked his hands behind his back. "I'm not going to hurt you. Look. See?" He held his hands out again and made a show about tucking them behind his back. "Hands behind my back—literally."

"Good. Now, stay there." I kept scooting backward, but glanced around.

We attracted attention from the back of the line. Some were laughing. Others lifted their phones to record us. I cursed. Mason did not need to see that, so I ducked through the line and around a corner that led to the coffee shop. Even more people were milling around there since it opened to a sitting area by a bunch of water fountains.

Shit. I had nowhere to go.

I looked back over my shoulder.

Sebastian was there, grinning at me but trying not to grin. "I'm not going to hurt you."

"You knew I was behind you in line."

"I did. Yes."

An exasperated gasp left me in a sudden whoosh of air. *That asshole.* I knew he set the whole thing up.

"You waited on purpose, making me go to the right side where I'd be trapped. People come out there from the cafeteria."

"I..." He pursed his lips together and shrugged. "Yes, I did."

"Asshole."

His head clipped down. "Yes, I am. I'll take that."

"Go away."

"I…" He faltered again, his eyes skirting to the side. "I just want to talk. Is that so bad? I'm not going to hurt you, and I'm not going to use you to hurt Mason either."

I snorted. "Like hell you aren't."

His grin grew a centimeter. "Well, I would, if I thought I could, but you're not exactly naive." He leaned closer as he said that last word, his grin spreading even wider. A spark appeared in his eyes.

He liked our banter.

I scowled. "Stop enjoying this conversation."

That brought out a laugh from him. He cleared his throat to cover but couldn't. A second laugh slipped out, and he shook his head. "Sorry. You're different than what I remember. You remember meeting me? The first time?"

"Yeah." My scowl held firm. "You were friends with Nate and salivating over Mason, imagining all that you could use him for in the future." I scoffed, "Good times."

His grin slipped a little, and he drew upright. "Not nice."

If I were Heather, I would give him the middle finger. I refrained, but my upper lip curled in disdain. He got what I was feeling.

Tugging at his shirt collar, he cleared his throat a second time. "I've not done anything to harm you. I don't think I've warranted this reception."

I burst out laughing. "Are you fucking kidding me?"

The sound wasn't from amusement, and it drew attention from those by the coffee shop. I ignored them. This guy was insane.

"You tried to use my boyfriend. When he said no, you tried to destroy his friendship with his best friend. When that didn't happen, you tried to hit Mason with a vehicle. When that didn't happen, you tried to get him expelled—"

Sebastian lunged forward but caught himself.

I hustled back and held my ground, but I was elated. I'd gotten him to slip a little, and that one small movement drew even more attention. It was all about getting the other one to show their true colors. Sebastian looked pretty on the outside, but he oozed slime on the inside. I wanted that slime on the outside. I wanted everyone to see it, too.

"You're better than I thought." His nostrils flared up as he noted that with a look of admiration in his eyes.

No. I looked closer. That wasn't admiration. It was cunning. *Shit.* Maybe I had shown him my cards too soon. He knew I wasn't the naive girlfriend who needed protecting. I had fangs, too.

"Samantha?"

Kitty and Nina came through the door behind Sebastian. They walked around him but paused, taking note of the tension in the air.

I raised my chin. "Walk away."

"Wha—" Kitty started to protest, but Nina elbowed her in the gut.

I said anyway, "I'm not talking to you, Kitty."

It was all Sebastian. I didn't look away, and his eyes narrowed. I had him in the position I wanted. If he wanted to do something—intimidate me, proposition me, threaten me— he'd have to do it now, and he'd have to do it with an audience. He needed to play his cards, or he'd have to retreat and try again.

He didn't say a word, but he nodded to himself and swung around the girls.

He retreated.

I won this battle.

Closing my eyes, I let out a breath of nervous air. *My god.* Now that he was gone, I was full-on trembling. I checked my pants. No mess there. Another thing to be thankful about.

"Uh…" Kitty stepped closer to me, watching him, before he weaved around the coffee shop crowd and disappeared from eyesight. "What just happened here?"

Nina asked, "Who was that?" Her tone said it all. She was quiet and cautious. She knew something bad happened.

I met her gaze and saw the knowing look there. I rasped out, "Someone not good. That was who."

I didn't tell them about that meeting. Kitty liked to talk about everything. Nina liked to analyze everything, but for once, they seemed to adhere to my unspoken request. Neither said a word.

I skipped my next class, and those two girls were done, so the three of us went back to the dorm. It was Friday night.

Right before I ducked inside my room, Kitty called my name from down the hallway. She was standing in her doorway, her head poking out.

"Yeah?" I asked.

"We promise not to be weird at the game tomorrow."

That was right. I remembered. We were all going to the game together, and it was the team's first football game at home. The whole campus was buzzing. We were playing Grant West University, another Division One league team a few hours away. We were slated to win. Our football team was ranked high this year, and I knew Mason was part of the reason. Drew was another reason. Both of them were considered for The Heisman this year, but Mason declined. Drew was the frontrunner now, and together, the two were dynamic to watch. I'd gone with Logan and Nate to the other two away games, but the first home one was always on another level.

The fans were more hyped.

The team was more hyped.

And the pressure was even more.

"Okay." I laughed. "Thanks for letting me know."

She was talking about Logan and when he'd find us at the game.

"And tell your boyfriend good luck," she said in a rush.

"I will. Thanks, Kitty."

Nina poked her head around her roommate. "Tell him good luck from me, too."

"I will." I laughed again. "Thanks, guys." I went inside my room.

Summer was gaping at me from her desk, holding a pen. As I shut the door, she let it drop dramatically along with her mouth. "Did my ears just play a trick on me?"

"What?"

"Kitty and Nina are acting normal?"

"Oh." My chest was tight. I went to my desk, hoping she'd keep talking about Kitty and Nina. She couldn't notice that I was still upset about Sebastian. "Yeah. They must've realized that Logan doesn't come around anymore. Put two and two together maybe?"

Before she could reply, a soft knock sounded on our door.

I opened it and experienced a slight flash of panic.

Mason was standing there, his arms crossed, his eyes concerned. He looked so damn delicious that I didn't know if I should confess about my run-in with Sebastian right there or drag Mason to bed after I kicked Summer out. He looked freshly showered, so that meant he'd come from the locker room. He was wearing a Cain University shirt, and the irony was not lost on me that Sebastian wore the same one today. But with Mason's broad shoulders, cut form, and trim waist, he made my mouth salivate. I glanced at Summer, saw a drop of drool at the corner of her mouth, and knew I wasn't the only one.

"Hey." I cringed. That came out like a nervous squeak.

His eyes narrowed a little bit, and the corner of his mouth dipped down, but he shook his head, and an easy grin appeared next. "Hey back. What are you doing?" He saw the package in my hands. "From Malinda?"

"Oh." I looked at it. My hands were clutching it to me like it was my life raft. "Yeah. I guess this is what normal moms do?"

Summer murmured behind me, "Da fuck?"

She didn't know about Analise. I shared some things about my family with her, but I hadn't explained all the craziness or the reason for all the craziness.

Mason noticed my tension, and he gestured to the room. "Can I come in?"

"Yes. Yes." I shuffled to the side and closed the door behind him.

He paused and lifted his head. A low, "Roommate," came from him. That was his greeting to Summer.

She did the same, grunting out, "Boyfriend."

I rolled my eyes. "You guys can use each other's names. I live with her, Mason."

He lifted a shoulder, sitting down on my bed. "Roommate."

A soft growl came from Summer, but she stood and let out a big sigh. "All right, you two lovebirds, I'm off to my last class for the week." Grabbing her bag, purse, and keys, she halted right before leaving. She asked me, "Are you going to be around tonight?"

"Oh." I glanced at Mason. He gave me a blank look back, so I replied, "I'm not sure. I'll let you know."

"Sounds good." She waved before leaving. "Toodles, Sam… and her superhot boyfriend."

Mason scowled, but it lacked any heat. "She shouldn't talk to me like that."

Putting the package on the desk, I went and curled up in his lap. "She's a fan. She's getting over it."

"Still weird to me." He studied me for a second, his hand went to my mouth.

I caught it and drew one of his fingers into my mouth. My tongue wrapped around it. I wanted to forget about my afternoon and how I was going to handle that situation. I wanted to get lost in his arms.

Seeing what I wanted, Mason tipped us both back, cradling me on his chest as he lay down. I was securely in his arms, and he rolled me over, so he was looming above me. His eyes darkened, holding my gaze before dropping to my lips where a small smile showed, and I let go of his finger. The ache for him already started inside me.

A knowing grin formed on his face, and without saying a word, he slipped from the bed to lock the door and flip the lights off. My heart started pounding. The need for him was rising between my legs, and I licked my lips, watching as he took his shirt off. He was all muscle..I could make out every single one of them as he came back to me. The flames were growing hotter and hotter. I wanted to slide my hands over every inch of him. I wanted to feel his weight on top of me. I wanted to feel him inside me.

I wanted him to break the fucking bed for me.

I was going to lie to him. Even now, watching him coming back to me, I knew what I was going to do. Park Sebastian's name would take this from us. I wouldn't allow it. Mason would be upset, if he ever found out, but I'd stand by my decision. This lie between us was for us. It was for him. He protected me from so much.

I had no choice.

I loved him, but I was lying to him.

Guilt rose up in me, threatening to choke me, but I envisioned Sebastian winning. I envisioned the hurt on Mason's face. I envisioned what he would do to Sebastian. Then I envisioned the consequences afterward; Mason could get kicked out school. He could get kicked off the football team. That meant no football career, no fulfilling his dream; but worse—he'd be hurt because of me.

That. Could. Not. Happen.

I was wrong in what I was doing, but it was my turn to protect him. My turn.

He paused above me, leaning down so that his lips were just above mine, and he whispered, "We're going to the house after this."

I closed my eyes, feeling his hands under my shirt.

He added, taking my shirt off, "I want to do this all night with you."

Hell to the yes.

CHAPTER THIRTEEN

LOGAN

I weaved around a group of people. The girls looked good. The guys looked lazy. The redhead caught my eye, and normally, I'd stop, share a few jokes, and wait and see how the guys reacted to me. If they were pro-Logan, I'd stay and end up taking one of the girls back to the car for privacy. If the guys were anti-Logan, I'd keep going. The girls would find me later.

That was how it usually ended but not this time. The party was in the backyard of someone's house. It was on the outskirts of town, but my information was good. This was one of Park Sebastian's parties, and I only had so much time. Nate hurried to catch up, and he was casting nervous looks to the side, watching the groups of guys who were observing us.

Yes, bitches. A motherfucking Kade was in their presence.

The news would reach Sebastian before I could, so I hurried even faster. I wanted to get there first. I didn't want him to have time to strategize and round up his assholes. This was his territory, but I had the element of surprise...for the next few minutes.

"Logan." Nate veered close, dropping his voice so that only I could hear him. "Are you sure about this?"

I wasn't surer about anything else. "Yes." I gave him a dark look. "Don't turn chickenshit now. We're doing this."

"I know. And I'm not. I'm just," he kept going, "saying that we need to make sure we have everything worked out ahead of time. I mean, this is one of their parties."

I scowled. "You're turning into a chickenshit."

"I'm not, but why aren't we doing this with Mason?"

"Two reasons. One, my brother is making sweet, sweet love to his woman tonight, and two, because he can't do shit. He's on the football team. It's on us to do something."

"Mason has a plan."

I shot back, "Yeah, well, I love my big bro, but he's dragging his feet with this one. Sebastian needs to be dealt with. I'm tired of sitting on my hands. You backing out?"

"Shut it, Logan!"

"You are." I glimpsed his face.

He'd gotten worked over by them a few weeks ago. His bruises finally faded. I paused. Maybe I should send him back. But no, I needed backup just in case.

"Kade?" The guy came over with a beer in each hand. His hair was sticking straight up in the air, and he looked like a rejected has-been fraternity brother.

Recognition hit, and I flashed a grin. "You're Blazer. You're the Toga Kid."

"Uh, close." He held out the beer to me.

I held up a hand, rejecting it.

He handed it to Nate, saying, "I'm Blaze. I had that party at the beginning of the year. You were there with your brother's girlfriend, who lives on my friend's floor. She's Sam's RA."

Nate glanced at me.

The pudgy Toga Kid called her Sam. He didn't get to call her anything, except his friend's floormate, but since he was there, and I was remembering other conversations from that night, I held my tongue. I skimmed him over. He didn't look too drunk. He was happily sloshed. His smile was lazy. He wasn't teetering on his feet, but his shirt was unbuttoned, and the T-shirt underneath had a few stains from the night—ketchup, mustard, but mostly spilled beer.

He was drunk enough, and after he opened the second beer and was lifting it to his mouth, I took it.

A quick smile to smooth things over, I told him, "I changed my mind."

"Oh." His shoulders went up and down. "Sounds good to me. I can get more, but, uh..." He noticed the looks as well. "You do know where you're at, right?"

We were gaining more and more attention. The small frame of surprise was gone.

I nudged Nate with my elbow. "Maybe you want to bring the car around?"

"What?"

"The car." I shot a meaningful look at the fence beside us.

"Oh." He frowned. "But..."

He gave me another look, and I knew what he was thinking. I smiled back at him. I took his beer and gave it to the other kid, Blazer—no, Blaze.

The guy blinked in surprise and started to smile.

Oh, no, we weren't friends. I was going to use this son of a bitch who thought he could use Sam's name like he mattered.

Throwing an arm around his shoulder, I patted him on the chest and said to Nate, "Blazer will help me out."

"Blaze."

I patted him again. "That's the least of your problems."

Nate was shaking his head. "No, Logan. No, no, no."

Blaze was frowning. "What problems?"

I pointed to the street. "Get the car. I'll need it."

Nate let out an unhappy sigh. "I'm not okay with this."

I didn't care, and I jerked Blaze around with me. "Say, Toga Kid, where are all your friends?"

They'd claimed to hate Sebastian. It was their day to show their balls or let 'em shrink back up into vaginas. I had a feeling they were going to shrink, but either way, we were going to have some fun.

"Uh…" He wasn't fighting me. He was just confused as he replied, glancing across the crowd, "They're by the fence. Why?"

"Let's go say hello."

"Wait. What?"

Too late. I was almost dragging the kid to his buddies.

Mason was the mastermind in our family, but I wasn't a complete idiot. Sebastian knew I was there, and he'd know in two seconds that I was alone. These guys, as they'd proclaimed, weren't Sebastian supporters. The standoff needed to happen with them at my backside, not Sebastian's fraternity rejects.

We got to Blaze's group of pals when a sudden hush went over the group.

He was there.

I didn't know why I enjoyed these moments.

I had no support—or little support. The odds were stacked against me. Most people would run the other way, not seek it out. As the crowd parted and Sebastian stepped through with his A-holes behind him, I was feeling the tingle in me. It was low and spreading fast, but as it rose, it was becoming overpowering. It was the need to fight. Mason didn't have to fight. He didn't enjoy fighting, but I did. I loved it. I thrived on it. And right now, I was damn near climaxing.

I was so fucked up, but all I could do was smile at Sebastian, who looked way too cocky and self-assured for his own good.

"Logan Kade," he greeted, smirking, with a hint of laughter in his voice. "Are you lost?"

I could punch him now. One shot, and he'd go down, but his buddies would be on me, and that was not what we did. We fought, but we won.

"*Patience.*" I could hear Mason's voice in my head.

He'd go slowly. He'd make sure all the checkpoints were in place, and he would start the conversation, but he didn't like to strike first. I did. Mason liked to hit back once someone hit him. It was something that drove me crazy about him. Maybe I just didn't have the patience in me that he did.

I forced myself not to respond. Not yet.

Nate needed time to get to the car.

Sebastian moved closer, cocking his head to the side. "Or are you just deaf? You didn't hear me? Should I repeat myself?"

I still waited. If I started now, I didn't know how long I could stall. Better to hold off before fully engaging. Again. Mason would be so damn proud.

"Hello." He lifted his hand. He started to snap his fingers.

Okay.

My patience just ran out.

I caught his hand right before he could snap his fingers once more, and I narrowed my eyes. "Think twice before raising your hand to me."

His eyes went wide. He was startled by how fast I moved, and so were his buddies. I had one second before they got over it, so I shoved his hand back, hard enough that he stumbled back a couple of steps, too. I changed, my entire demeanor forming the same old cocky Logan Kade.

I grinned, winking at him. "Careful, Sebastian. I'll snap back if you're going to roll that way."

"What?"

My warning was filled with violence. He reacted to the threat of it, but my tone was light and almost flirting. The douche had no clue who the fuck I was. He was off balance. I could go in, sweep him back up, and could control the conversation instead.

I did as I said, "You've come to welcome me. Thank you." I glanced around the growing crowd. "You're one kind motherfucker if you've personally welcomed everyone here."

Sebastian's face went from confused to scowling. His eyebrows locked together. "What are you doing here, Kade?" He made a point of looking around. "Is your bitch hiding in the shadows?"

I shook my head, tsking him. "Come on, Sebastian. You left the gate wide open with that one. I have so many comebacks. 'Don't talk about your mama like that.' 'Oh, but she's not my bitch. She's yours. Thanks for loaning her to me.' Or even the typical, 'I know you're angry about your girlfriend jerking me off, but damn, you don't have to be petty about it.'" I drawled, "There are so many of them. I'll just leave all of them alone and come back with a pretty simple one."

I stared him down, letting the amusement fade away. He could see that I was serious. I'd waited long enough for Nate. It was time to get down to business.

I ended with, "You're the only bitch I see here."

It was a simple insult, but it worked. His anger went up a

notch. It had been there, simmering with my light jabs, but it was like I'd hit him with a straight-up uppercut.

I showed him my teeth. My smile didn't reach my eyes. "Come back at me now, bitch."

A second uppercut. Right there. Right to the face.

The crowd was deathly silent. I had a feeling no one insulted Sebastian—at least to his face. The ass needed to really learn who the Kades were.

He kept quiet. Ah, he was thinking. He was doing that thing that Mason liked to do. I'd pushed him, but he was rallying back. He wanted to get his feet on the ground and take control of the confrontation.

I wasn't going to let him do that, so I said, "You asked about my bitch before, but seriously, where's yours? I'd like to meet your girlfriend."

When he didn't respond, I looked around, craning my neck. "I don't see any chick who's worried about you. What does she look like? Wait." My hands went up, and I moved back a step. "Do you not have a girlfriend?" I moved a second step back.

Sebastian frowned. He noticed my retreat, but he didn't get it. I wasn't backing down. I was forcing Blaze and his pals to surround me. I wanted to draw Sebastian farther into this circle, farther away from his A-holes.

He stepped forward.

It was working.

I waited. He'd catch on if I took a third step backward. Blaze was to my right. His other friend, who had the pony keg, was on my left.

I asked Blaze, "Does Sebastian have a girlfriend?"

Blaze's eyes lit up. He didn't want to get drawn into this. Too late. I just pulled him in. That was the entire purpose of this venture. Sebastian thought he controlled everyone. He was ill-informed. I just needed to show him that he didn't and that meant forcing people to stand against him.

Sebastian looked at him. I was willing to bet good money that he had no idea who Blaze or his group of friends were. In fact, I was willing to bet even better money that Sebastian didn't know half the people at this party.

One match, one person—that was all it took to start a fire, so here I was. I was the fucking first spark.

Blaze couldn't go against what he'd already proclaimed at his party. There were witnesses, and like he'd said, his friend was Sam's RA.

Girls didn't respect cowards.

If Blaze backed down, he'd be a coward.

Granted, this was plan B, and yes, I hadn't thought of it until Blaze sauntered up to me at this party, but as agendas went, this was an even better one than my original idea. The crumbs were tossed on the ground.

I asked Sebastian, "Are you good friends with Blaze here?"

Blaze did a double take as I'd correctly said his name, but he looked back at Sebastian.

Sebastian was studying him, scratching at his jaw. "I don't believe I've had the pleasure." He glared at Blaze. "Who are you?"

"Uh…" Blaze shifted on his feet.

Yep, the kid didn't do confrontations well.

He started to hold his hand out.

I tapped it back down. "No, no, no. This isn't how you do it, Blaze."

"What?"

Sebastian was staring at me again. His eyes were locked on me, a fierce scowl there. He was starting to feel the insults.

I came to his party.

I insulted him.

I hadn't ran off.

I was continuing to insult him.

And, yes, I was still not leaving.

As he remembered this night over the next week, the sting of embarrassment would grow more and more.

Stages. Fighting a war took stages, and this was one of them.

"Enough thinking, Logan. Finish it." Hearing Mason's voice, I reminded myself about why I was there in the first place.

I hit Blaze on the arm and said to Sebastian, "Okay. All the jabs and jokes aside, you're right, Sebastian. I am here for a reason."

"I never asked why you were here."

I ignored him, gripping Blaze's arm. "My friend here, Blazer—"

"Blaze."

I looked at him. "Really? Again?"

He scoffed, shrugging his shoulders.

I turned back to Sebastian, noting that his buddies crowded in more. They were right next to Blaze's group, but feeling the threat, Blaze's friends moved forward, too. They were starting to stand off against them.

I continued, "He was telling me at his party a while ago how proud he was of me and of my brother, too."

"Oh, shit." Blaze sucked in his breath. He shot looks to his buddies. He'd just been clued in as to where I was going.

I added, smiling widely because this was so damn fun, "And he was even thanking me for going against you. You see, here's my public service announcement to you, Sebastian." I cupped my hands around my mouth and whispered loudly so everyone could hear, "No one really likes you."

Pause.

Wait a beat.

Let that sink in.

Now, keep going.

"Like all these guys." I gestured to Blaze's group. "They were all telling me how much they hate you. In fact," I moved a step toward Sebastian, "I've had a lot of people tell me how much they detest you. They were all happy when your house was burned down. They even wanted to thank whoever did that horrible thing." I winked at him. "So, I'm here," one more step toward him, and I was within swinging distance, "to help you out, if you think about it. I'd like to know who my enemies are—unless they're too much of a coward to stand their ground. But still, I'd at least like to know who the cowards are."

I waited.

The seeds were dropped.

Sebastian's nostrils flared. "You mean to tell me that you came here just to out these guys?"

"No." I shook my head.

"What?"

"No, I didn't come here to do that." I grinned at him. "I came here to start a fight, to be honest, but, uh…" I skimmed over his brothers. "I'm severely outnumbered, and you know, I've got some smarts up here." I pretended to knock on my head.

"Logan," Blaze hissed behind me.

A small amount of disappointment flared in me. The guy was calling me by my first name. *Last names, Blaze. Last names is how you do it.* I'd share that golden nugget of dumbassness with him later. First, I needed to start with what was my original intent.

I needed to start a damn fight.

Ignoring Blaze, I held my arms out. The beer was firmly held in one of my hands. "Thank you for your hospitality, Sebastian, but I should get going."

His eyes narrowed to slits. He started forward. They weren't going to let me leave in peace, but that was what I hoped.

And I turned, as if I were leaving. Then I saw what I was waiting for—Blaze's head snapped to the right. I felt Sebastian closing the distance between us, and I dropped down. His arm went over my head. I caught it with my arm. I jerked him forward and smashed my beer can on his forehead.

The fight was on.

CHAPTER FOURTEEN

A slammed door was my only warning for the impending arrival. Mason would be through my door in two seconds, and he wouldn't care that it was locked. He'd kick it down or pick the lock. I sat up and held the girl still on top of me. I pulled her hips down and thrust up one last time. Yep, there it was. My climax came, and holy shit, it was a good one. It was still rippling through me.

I used that last second to enjoy it. My door burst open just as I finished, and I collapsed back on my bed.

The redhead yelled, diving for the bed sheets beside me, and covered herself.

Neither Mason nor I paid her attention. Instead, I was locked in a heated stare with my brother.

One of my eyebrows lifted. "Yes?"

He scowled at me. "What did you do last night?"

"What you couldn't do."

He knew what I meant and gave me the middle finger. "Fuck you, Logan." He turned to go.

I hopped out of bed, but the girl cried out in protest.

Pressing a quick kiss to her lips, I patted her on the hip. "I gotta take care of this. Be a nice little lay, and get dressed."

"You're an asshole," she seethed.

I grabbed some pants, and I paused as I considered it. I was. I shrugged. "I'm not trying to be a dick here, but I picked you up at a party where I'd started the entire brawl. What did you expect?"

She sat upright, her entire face flaming in red. "Do you even know my name?"

No apologies here. "One, you never told me last night. Two, I never asked. I don't know what you expected when my exact words were, 'Do you want to go to my place to fuck?'"

She sucked in a breath and her lips pinched together.

With a shirt in hand, I started for the door. I needed to smooth this over with Mason, but the chick was becoming more of a problem than I'd thought she'd be. I paused in the doorway. "We fucked. You stayed the rest of the night, and we fucked again. Both times were good, even though I'm sorry I couldn't help you finish this morning." I nodded toward the hallway. "I'd thought I'd have more time before he exploded in here."

"Whatever." She scooted to the edge of the bed and began searching for her clothes.

I waited as she furiously dressed. The jeans were pulled up. The zipper and button were left undone as she reached for her bra and her shirt. She drove here, following Nate and me in the car, so that I wouldn't have to get a cab for her. She took her keys and brushed past me. I sucked in my breath, evading her elbow at the last second, and she cursed at me.

I followed her down the stairs.

She opened the front door and whirled around to face me. "You—" she sputtered. The redness traveled to her forehead and spread down her neck. She couldn't talk. She was so angry.

She was hot.

Her tits strained against her shirt. Her jeans slunk down to showcase her hip bones. She wasn't skinny. She had a nice amount of meat on her, enough where I could be a little rougher than normal, and she screamed for it last time.

Shit.

I knew I'd want another go with her.

When I laid my hand on her arm, her body tensed under my touch. She was getting ready to blast me, so I said softly, "I'm not trying to be a dick. I just need to make things right with my brother before his game today."

She relaxed instantly and shook her head, rolling her eyes. "My god."

"See?" I smirked at her, running my hand up her arm and curling it around her shoulder. I moved around her head. I cupped the back of her neck. "You don't know my name either. I'm Logan, not God."

She laughed but let out a different curse.

I drew her close and murmured, right before my lips touched hers, "I'm not the J guy either."

"Oh my—"

I pressed my lips to hers, shutting her up. My mouth opened even wider, and I took control of the kiss, becoming more demanding, until she sighed into me and pressed against me.

"You gotta stop calling me that guy's name." I pulled back but pressed one last kiss before I stepped away. "I'm Logan, and I'd like to call you again."

A rueful laugh slipped from her closed lips. "I must be out of my mind, but here you go." She grabbed a pen from the table beside the door and wrote her number on my hand. "Call me before I regret this."

I had every intention to, but once she was out the door, I

hurried to Mason's room. I paused right before his door. It was closed. I didn't remember seeing Sam's bag anywhere.

I wasn't sure if she was still there or not, so I knocked and opened the door an inch. "You decent?"

Mason yelled from his bathroom, "She's not here. I just got back from driving her to the dorm."

"Oh." I walked in, ignored the smell of sex, and held up my hands as he swung those accusing eyes my way.

Shit. My brother could kill someone just by looking at them. It hadn't happened yet, but I knew it would. He'd have the best defense ever. *No, Judge, he really only looked at the guy.*

"Logan."

"Right, right." Not a good time to be distracted. "I went there to start a fight."

He scowled. "Without me. What the fuck were you thinking?"

"To be honest..." I waited.

His scowl never lessened. He was waiting for my explanation.

I said, "The same thing since the beginning."

"What are you talking about?"

"You can't do anything, Mason. Your hands are tied. If you make one move against Sebastian, he'll go to the board about it. You'll get kicked off the team and expelled from school. I have nothing to lose. If I get expelled, so what? I'll just go somewhere else. I don't have a career in football that could be taken away from one punch. He's got you by the balls."

"You're wrong. I do have something planned, but it's going to take time." He went back inside the bathroom and turned the shower on. He came back to the doorway. "Stay out of it, Logan."

"No."

"Logan."

I held my ground.

Mason protected me. He planned out the best defeats, and we were firm together. He couldn't this time, but he was refusing to see that.

I shook my head. "I can't. Nate went with me. *He* went with *me*. If you could handle this fight, he never would've done that, and you know it. Nate's always true to you first."

"I—" Pain flashed across his face.

I didn't like seeing that, and I knew it was killing him to admit this, but for once, my brother needed to be the protected one.

I murmured quietly, "You know I'm right. It's why you haven't done a thing against him yet."

"You're wrong." But the fight was gone from him. Mason cupped the back of his neck and ran his hand up and over his head before letting it fall back to his side. "Can you just trust me? Something is in the works, but you're right. I have to go slow, and I have to wait some stuff out. It'll be worth it in the end. It will."

"What are you planning?"

"I'm…" He hesitated. "I'm waiting on something. That's all I can say."

"This is bullshit. We're supposed to be together on this. All of us—you, me, Sam, and Nate. The foursome fearsome, remember? What are you planning? And why can't you tell us? You haven't said a word to Nate about it, and I'm guessing you haven't said a word to Sam either."

"I'm waiting," was all he said.

"You're stalling."

"Logan." He was so damn resigned.

I gritted my teeth. That shit, that sound from my brother...I was right whether he'd admit it to me or not. He was waiting until football was done. That was what he was doing. It'd be too late.

"He's going to go after Sam," I said.

"Not if we don't engage him more."

I clipped my head back and forth. He wasn't getting it. I wanted to rip off his fucking door to throw at him, but I couldn't. Feeling a twinge of disappointment for the first time, I said, "You're wrong, Mase. He's going to go after her whether we wait or not."

"Yeah. He'll go after her for sure now."

"And you have one security guard on her."

His shoulders lifted, held in the air, and lowered slowly. He couldn't refute it. One guard for all of Sebastian's friends.

I asked, "What if he really tries to hurt her?"

"I'll fucking kill him."

"And that right there is how he's going to win this time. He does one thing to her, and you'll go after him. Boom, he's got you. Cops show up. He's got hidden cameras recording the entire thing, and he's won. Your career is gone. Your future is gone, and fuck, Mase, it could get bad enough to where you do time. All the crap we do, we should've done some time by now."

We were arrested before, but James got us out every time. That was over. If we got caught again, there would be no rich daddy to help us out. I tried again, "Let me handle Sebastian."

"Logan," he started, shaking his head.

"I'll run everything by you. How about that? You can help

me with the masterminding shit. I mean, holy dumbass, I took a page from your book last night."

"What do you mean?"

"My original plan was to go in, get a hit in, and jump over the fence and have Nate there, waiting for me with a getaway car. I couldn't do that, and I had to switch agendas."

"What did you do?"

"I thought you heard?"

"Drew called this morning. All he said was that you got into a fight with Sebastian's guys. That was it."

"Oh." My shoulders felt a little lighter. I almost felt pride as I told him, "I outed some of his enemies. I put them in a corner where they admitted to hating him, or they'd have to kiss his ass and slink away with their tails between their legs."

"And?"

"They fought *with* me."

Mason nodded, a look of admiration in his eyes.

My head lifted. My shoulders straightened again. I stood an inch higher. My brother was proud of me. "Fuck yeah." I grinned at him. "They were a little sore at me later, but those guys will fight with me again, if I need them. They think they're manly men now."

Mason nodded again, grinning back at me. "Good job, brother."

"Damn straight."

He gestured to the ceiling. "And sorry for interrupting. I knew you had a chick. I just wanted to be a dick back to you."

"Ah, I see. You're learning from me. I'm not just a smart-ass with my words. I can be a smart-ass with my behavior, and yes, barging in when you've got Sam straddling you, that's definitely a smart-ass dick way of doing things."

Mason narrowed his eyes at me and said ruefully, "Yeah, I must be learning from you."

"I'll teach you more ways, my student, but first," I lifted my hand to look at the number, "I might need to show up somewhere with a latte. If there's one thing I've learned from Sam, it's that girls love their lattes."

"Logan," he called out as I turned to leave.

"Yeah?"

The gravity on my brother's face made me pause for a second. I'd only seen that look a few times—when our mom left, when we found out Sam was beaten up in the restroom, and when Nate's vehicle crashed in front of us. There were other times, but those were the ones that ran through my memory.

He said, "Be careful with this one. He thinks like I do."

It wasn't an insult, but I knew what Mason was saying. Sebastian strategized. He analyzed. He thought five steps ahead, whereas I didn't. I was two steps ahead, if I were lucky.

I nodded and murmured, "I will."

SAMANTHA

It was fun to walk to the football game with the girls. I hadn't enjoyed hanging out with a group of girls in so long that I almost missed what it was like. Gossip. Laughter. A few tears, but I wasn't sure the cause for them. Some whispering. The occasional belch, followed by some farting jokes. This hadn't happened with my old group, and it was sad to realize that Jessica and Lydia were my last real group of girlfriends. Cattiness and competition came with them.

Who knows? I skimmed over the group of my floormates. If I grew closer to them, perhaps the same thing would occur.

So far, it hadn't. So far, I was protected. Maybe it was because I already had a boyfriend. Maybe it was because I was still kind of a loner. Maybe it was because my roommate had more to be envious about with her long legs and model cred.

A few envious looks were sent Summer's and my way. When we got to the stadium and sat down, those looks grew more and more. When Mason ran out onto the field and the crowd started a frenzied cheer for him, the whispers in the group tripled, and so did the envious looks.

Summer noticed the looks and narrowed her eyes at the closest girls. She asked with a bite in her tone, "Yes? May we help you?"

The two girls closest to Summer froze for a second.

One whispered, "Is her boyfriend Mason Kade?"

"Yes." Summer sat up as far as she could, so she was literally looking down her nose at her. "And, no, you cannot use Sam to meet him. They're in love. They're so in love that they make me want to vomit, and I probably would if I wasn't so starstruck by Mason Kade myself."

"Oh." The girl shrank back but fanned herself. "We've seen him in the hallway, but we didn't realize he was the same Mason Kade on the team. He's gorgeous."

A part of me was damn proud of Mason. The other part went on instant alert. If this were their reactions already, would I have another restroom fight on my hands? I hoped not. This was college. I wanted to assume violence like that only happened in high school and by the hands of girls like Kate.

Summer leaned in close to me. "Don't worry. They're all rug rats. Mason could easily step over them."

I gave her a smile—or I tried. It fell flat. If she only knew what I was actually worried about...

"Yeah, that's true."

She studied me, narrowed her eyes a little, and nudged me with her elbow. "They're not going to drug him or something. Besides, Mason is one dude who will not be coerced. You don't have to worry about him with other girls."

My head moved up and down. I was nodding. I was agreeing to everything she said, but her voice sounded from a distance. Football, money, looks—that was the world that Mason and Logan ruled, and I had been brought into their world. A shiver racked through me. I didn't even want to imagine how I would've been if those two hadn't welcomed me into their twosome family or if Mason and I hadn't fallen in love.

"You okay?" Summer was still watching me, now concerned.

"Yeah," I rasped out, coughing to clear my throat. "Yeah, I'm good."

"You sure?"

"Oh, yeah. I'm good." I forced another grin. "Peachy."

We were halfway through the game when Summer asked to use my phone. She forgot hers. I didn't think anything of it until the game was over. We won. Everyone was in good spirits, and I was proud of Mason.

My whole chest was full of it, but I'd forgotten that along with his fame came the thirst from others. They wanted him. They wanted what I had. They would plot, scheme, and deceive. They'd do what it took. I already knew it would end in failure, but they didn't. They'd go the gamut to try to destroy my heart.

"Hey."

We were following the girls through the parking lot, but I was looking for Mason's car. I was going to text him and say that I would wait for him by it. Summer caught my elbow as I started to veer for his Escalade.

She asked, "Where are you going?"

"I—" I was about to tell her when I stopped.

Logan hadn't come to sit with us, but I hadn't thought about it. I'd figured he wanted to steer clear of Kitty and Nina. I would if I were him. But now, I saw him standing a few yards from us. He wasn't looking at me. He was looking past me, and the expression on his face was like an invisible hand pressing down on my chest. But that wasn't the only thing. A large and nasty-looking bruise was on the side of his jaw. I looked over his other injuries—a cut lip, a bandage on the corner of his eye, and another bruise on his forehead.

He was focused beyond me, and it hit me. Logan was staring with hatred at whoever was behind me. The loathing wasn't hidden. It was there. It was in the open, and there was no hiding it.

A shiver trailed up my spine.

I knew who was behind me, but I turned, and everything went into slow motion.

Sebastian was staring right back at Logan. Sebastian's face was bruised. One of his cheeks was swollen. More bruises were on his neck. Through a small opening in the crowd, I saw his hand resting on his side. His knuckles were cracked open, all black and blue, too. The crowd covered his hand up, and I couldn't see him anymore.

Neither of them looked like they were going to approach the other.

I was almost invisible to them, but a second tingle shot up my back. A sixth sense had me looking, even before I'd realized it, and behind Logan was Mason. He had just come out of the doors.

He was standing there. His hair was wet, and I figured he'd showered. He was wearing a Cain U shirt that clung to parts of his chest that were still wet. His athletic pants only accentuated his trim waist and athletic build. He stayed there, holding a bag, as he looked at me. Concern and heavy wariness was there before he masked them and looked at his brother. He lingered, watching his brother, as his eyebrows jerked forward a split second. They smoothed back out, and his gaze moved past to Sebastian.

I couldn't look away from Mason. A dark ominous sensation took root in my gut. This was a standoff. The hairs on the back of my neck stood up, but I couldn't move.

Summer was talking to me. Her voice came in and out. It was as if I were submerged in deep water, and she was above me, calling my name, while I was fighting to break the surface.

Something bad was going to happen.

Someone else was saying my name, and I frowned. That person…

I tore my gaze from Mason and turned.

Heather was right there. She was right in front of me, and she was waving a hand over my face.

I broke the surface.

I could hear her plain as day.

She said, "She goes into these freaky trances. Don't worry. She'll break free. Usually, it just means she needs to jump Mason's bones—"

I didn't let her finish. Launching myself at her, I tightly wrapped my arms around her. I hadn't realized how much I missed my best friend until that minute.

CHAPTER FIFTEEN

"Are you going to tell me what was up with the weird stare-offs earlier?"

Heather was outside the house party, lounging in the backyard with me. She wanted a smoke, and I wanted some peace and quiet. My head had been full with too many thoughts.

After an awkward dinner with Mason, Logan, and Summer, they'd dropped us off at the dorm. The plan had been to grab some clothes for me, so we could sleep back at the house. It was more comfortable there, but those plans went awry as soon as we stepped foot on the floor. Kitty and Nina were going into Ruby's room, but they went wild when they saw us. Ruby's friend, Blaze, was throwing another party, and we were supposed to be the guests of honor. Ruby informed me later that Blaze now considered himself a badass, and he had near idol-worship for Logan. He became a man and wanted to repay Logan in beer and pussy.

Ruby cringed as she said the word *pussy*, but it was a direct quote from Blaze himself. She added, "Though, I have to be honest, I'm pretty sure Logan's being used to bring the pussy part. Blaze told me that where Logan Kade goes, pussy follows." She shook her head. "I'm sorry, but can you guys come?"

"Uh…" I'd glanced at Heather and Summer, the latter had been unnaturally quiet during dinner.

Both gave me blank faces back.

I'd made the decision. "Why not?" The evening couldn't get more awkward, could it?

When we informed Mason of the change of plans, he planned to drop us off and pick us up later. That hadn't lasted long. Logan got on the phone, and within five minutes, Mason's phone was ringing. Drew and half the football team wanted to go to the party, too. Mason's hand was forced, but I knew he was fine with that. Going to a party with Logan was like old times. The only reason Mason hadn't originally wanted to go was because he'd thought I'd want my girl time.

That was what I was getting right now. Hanging out in the backyard with Heather while everyone drank, flirted, shrieked, giggled, whispered, danced, and whatever else inside was fine by me.

That brought me back to her question, something that had not been discussed during dinner. I shrugged now, sliding down in my chair to get more comfortable. "It's Park Sebastian."

I chewed on my bottom lip. It was obvious Logan had been in a fight with Sebastian. Both were covered in bruises. When we got to the house, one by one, guys poured into the party, and they all had bruises, too. It looked like they'd been in a mass brawl.

Heather took a drag off her cigarette and flicked the end into an ash bowl set between the lawn chairs. The setup was already here when we'd come out. There must've been others in the house or at the party who smoked. I was grateful for some privacy, though.

"He's the current big bad villain?"

I nodded. "He's an asshole."

She grunted, taking one more drag. "Aren't they all?"

I peered at her, pulling my knees up to my chest and wrapping my arms around them. She looked good. Her blond hair had a slight curl to it. She was tanned, toned, and decked out in a simple black tank top. Her jeans were tight with holes and rips all over them. Underneath her ass cheeks were two slits in her pants, and as she had walked through the house before, all the guys had noticed. Her entire demeanor screamed sex and cool.

I sighed, grinning. "You look happy."

Her blue eyes flicked to mine, and her lips slightly curved down. "Really?"

I sat back up, straightening in my seat. "You're not?"

"I'm a fucking mess." She ground out her cigarette and pulled out a second one. Lighting it, she murmured, "I have no clue what's going on with me and Channing. And—" She stopped talking but glanced at the house for a second. She didn't say a word. She just stared at the house before her gaze fell back to the cigarette in her hand. "You know I screwed Logan, right?"

I nodded. "I knew that night."

"You weren't mad?" She seemed to have been holding in her breath.

I shook my head. "There's always been a flirtation between you two. I figured it would happen when you told me that you and Channing were on the outs."

"Oh." Her head dropped back down. "Fuck me. I'm a piss-poor friend. I'm sorry, Sam."

"For what?"

"I screwed him on your dad's wedding night."

I couldn't hold back a grin. "I screwed my boyfriend that night, too. It was a good night for some lovemaking."

A smooth and husky-sounding chuckle left her. She searched my face before putting the cigarette to her lips. "You're seriously not mad?"

My head moved from left to right. "I'd be selfish if I were. I know it won't last, and I know I won't be put in the middle, if anything does happen."

"It won't last. You're right there." She chuckled again. "What's up with your roommate?" She took a drag and gestured to the house with the cigarette. "She and Logan got a thing going? She texted me from your phone earlier. I forgot to mention it to you."

"She did?"

Heather murmured, "Said you could use a friend, but I was already coming."

"Oh." I sat back. That'd been nice of her. Remembering her question about Logan and Summer, I shook my head. "Not yet anyway. Why?"

"She got all quiet when he came over after the game. I caught her looking at him a bunch during dinner, too."

"Really?" Summer's football boner was for Mason, but I shrugged. "She's a big football fan. If she's got something for Logan, I have no clue about it. Logan hit on her the first day I moved in, but that was it. She used to be a model—"

Heather's top lip curved up. She spoke around the cigarette, "I was going to say, she could be a model. She must have guys galore crawling all over her."

"She does." *Come to think of it...* "I know she gets hit on a lot, but she doesn't talk about the guys."

With Dex, there'd been no word about him until the night we needed the gym, but there were other incidents. Pizza would be delivered from guys when we hadn't ordered any.

She would have flowers show up, too. I'd teased her the first few times, but she'd claimed there was no card. She'd said the flowers were for both of us, but I knew Mason never sent them. I'd asked him the first few times, and he'd denied it and asked if he needed to worry about another guy being in my picture. The whole thing was laughed off.

Now that Heather was bringing it up, I frowned. "Is that weird? I think she gets gifts from guys, but she doesn't make a big deal about it at all."

"Nah." Heather tapped on the end of her cigarette and leaned back in her chair. "Just means she doesn't want to deal with jealous chicks. She doesn't have to worry about you, though. You ever been jealous?"

Marissa. "Yes," I said matter-of-factly and quickly.

Heather was startled by the vehemence in my voice.

I added, "She got to go to school with him when I couldn't. I hated her for that."

"Oh." Heather grew quiet. "Well, the chick got hit by a car. I'd say that was karma." She grinned, waiting for my reaction.

I thought about it. I envisioned the truck hitting her and the look on her face in the hospital when she'd told me she loved Mason. I pressed my lips together. "I never thought that was funny." But the laughter was boiling up in me. I tried stifling it. It didn't seem right. I couldn't. I laughed. And I didn't stop. "You're right." Some more came out. I shook my head, wiping at the tear in my eye. "That's hilarious to think about."

Heather chuckled with me before she grew serious again. "Okay, for real. Where is that chick? Tell me you don't have to see her, do you?"

"She was going to come back, but Mason told me she

transferred. She'd e-mailed him during the summer to let him know he wouldn't have to worry about seeing her."

Heather groaned, throwing her head back. "That's the worst. What a passive-aggressive piece of shit. Good riddance. The psycho chick can move on to someone else."

It was nice. Marissa was a headache last year, but she'd been quickly forgotten with the migraine of Park Sebastian.

That reminded me. I said, "He cornered me at the post office on campus."

"Who?"

"Park Sebastian."

Heather swore under her breath. "Did Mason rip his head off?"

I started to feel a little numb as I shook my head so slowly from left to right. "I didn't tell him."

"You didn't?" Heather lowered her arm. It had been propped up on her elbow, her cigarette dangling in the air. As she watched me, she took notice. She swore again before asking, "Are you going to tell him?"

More numbness. My head moved again from left to right.

I was lying to Mason by not telling him. I should. We should have a united front, but it wouldn't have worked. Mason would've been upset by that mere conversation. I was scared of what he might do.

I asked Heather, my voice slipping to a whisper, "Was it the wrong thing to do?"

She frowned. Her eyebrows bunched, and she studied me, thinking. "No."

I held my breath. "Really?"

I didn't need the validation. It was me, myself, and I. I was the only one making these decisions, and the terror was almost paralyzing. I hadn't been thinking about it because I couldn't deal with it. But what if I were wrong? What if I were playing into exactly what Sebastian wanted? There was a wedge between Mason and me. It was small, and it was on my side, but it was there. I lied to him. The other choice was to let Sebastian win. He would hurt Mason.

No. There was no choice.

I said to Heather, "I think Logan's doing the same as me."

"What's that?"

"We're both keeping things from Mason."

"To protect him?"

"Yeah." That was it. It really was all about protecting Mason. That helped reaffirm my decision. "I was right with what I did?"

"Fuck yeah." She scowled, but it wasn't meant for me. "That asshole Sebastian needs to get fingered by some big-ass convict. It sounds like he's playing mind games. Meeting you at the post office or wherever it was. You're screwed either way. Don't tell Mason, and it's a lie between you two, or tell Mason and worry that he'll go bonkers and do something to ruin his career. This dickhead isn't normal from what I've been hearing. Is that what happened with Logan?" She gestured to her face. "All his bruises? He got in a fight. That Sebastian guy was in the parking lot, too, right? He was bruised up."

"Yeah, I'm assuming, but I haven't had time to talk to either Mason or Logan about it."

Just then, a collective cheer sounded from the house.

Heather looked back over and ground out her second cigarette. "Well, he's got buddies in there. Whatever happened, I'm guessing it was a win for our team."

She was right.

Hearing those words helped. My chest felt a little lighter. My shoulders lifted again. They weren't being pressed down by an invisible weight. Having Heather here and hearing her logic gave me new strength.

This was right. Whatever Logan and I were doing was the right thing to do. We were both protecting Mason in our own way.

"Thank you for coming to visit."

Heather looked over at me, and she softened. Her eyes opened wider, and some tears pooled there on top of her bottom eyelids. One corner of her mouth lifted as she held out her arm for me. "Aw, Sam. It was the first home game. I had to get up here to support you guys. Now, come here, and hug me again. I'm such a damn sobbing wreck with you. You make me feel all girlie and shit."

I laughed, but I went over and gave her another hug.

It felt damn good.

"Woohoo, my friends, where are you?" Summer's voice came from the door. She was peering out into the backyard with her eyebrows scrunched together. "I don't see anything. Is anyone out there?"

Heather called back, "Yep. Walk straight and go right. We're thirty yards from you."

"Oh. Good." She went down the steps and followed Heather's directions exactly. She saw us right away and dropped down to the empty seat. "I need to hide out. Ruby is insisting I'm her strip beer-pong partner." She shuddered. "No, thank you, Mrs. Blaze. And he's very drunk and hanging all over me."

"Blaze was?"

She nodded to me. "I'm pretty sure our RA hates us now—or hates me."

I scratched the side of my face. "But she asked you to be her partner?"

"I'm pretty sure she's the type who brings her friends close but her enemies closer. Yep, that's her. And now we know for sure, she's completely in love with Blaze, who is completely in love with me and Logan. I'm pretty sure he asked Logan for my digits tonight."

Heather barked out a laugh. "Typical dude. He could ask the RA, who probably has your number, but he didn't. He went to the other guy, also claiming bro code at the same time."

Summer leaned back and snapped her fingers in Heather's direction. "Exactly. Thank you. I'm not the only one who gets the inner workings of guys."

"Oh, no. Dudes can be catty, but it won't faze Logan. He won't even think about it, Blaze asking for your number. Don't worry."

Summer grew quiet.

Oh, damn. I felt a Heather moment. She was going to call out the truth, right here and right now.

Heather drawled, "If you've got the hots for Kade—and I'm talking about Logan—you can be reassured." She turned to me as she said her next part, "Yes, I'll probably be shagging him tonight, but it's done. After tomorrow, I'm going to fix things with my current guy."

"Oh." Summer's mouth was pressed in a flat line. Her hands sank into the chair's armrests before she forced her shoulders to drop back down. "You know, I can't blame you."

Feeling influenced by the sharing bug, I dropped my own bomb on both of them. "Not that Logan is exclusive unless he's in a relationship, but he has been spending time with a redhead."

Boom. I lifted my hands in the air. The bomb exploded. There it was.

Neither girl seemed fazed.

I slumped back down, my hands still in the air. "I felt like sharing that, even though I can see both of you don't seem to care."

Heather pulled out a third cigarette. "Just for that, I'm going to ride him really hard tonight."

My hands moved back in and fell to my lap.

The bomb just imploded.

The alcohol had me buzzing.

When we went back inside, I curled up on Mason's lap. He held me through the rest of the night as our whole group took over the basement. Kitty, Nina, and some of the girls from the floor danced in the corner, sneaking glances at the guys. Logan was the reigning champion of the pool table. When he wasn't aiming for a shot, he was flirting with Heather. Summer joined their conversation as well, which meant Blaze and some of his friends joined, too. The rest of the room was filled with Mason's football teammates. They were like him, seemingly content to lounge around, play pool, talk, or watch ESPN on the television, even though there was no sound because of the music blaring from the speakers.

After so many shots that Logan kept bringing me, I was relieved when Mason announced he was taking his drunk girlfriend home.

I raised an arm in the air and announced, "That's me."

Now, we were back at the house, and he was helping me to his bedroom. Logan and Heather came home with us, too. I wasn't sure where Nate was the whole evening. I'd forgotten to ask, but I hadn't seen him a lot over the last month.

The room seemed to be in high-definition color. The walls jumped out at me, and I jerked back, evading them and giggling at the same time.

Mason caught me from behind, murmuring, "Whoa there."

I pointed at the wall, wavering on my feet. "It jumped out at me." I swatted the wall. "Stay there."

"Okay, yeah. Here we go." Mason bent down, wrapped an arm around my waist, and picked me up.

Everything went whoosh. Now, the wall really was laughing at me. His arm was secure so I went with it. I was drunk, but it was fun. Ignoring the wall that kept watching me as he carried me to his bedroom, I focused on what was in front of me—his ass.

Nice. Firm. Supple. Ass cheeks.

I could just reach down and grab a firm handful of them, and I did. *Oh, yeah.*

The cheeks were tight. I could bounce a quarter off them. I kept squeezing them. I tried to lift them up and back down. Even there, not much bounce. My man was hella toned, and he was all mine.

These ass cheeks. I patted them again before grabbing hold once more. They were mine to play with. I could watch them as he walked around. I could lick them if I wanted, and that was a good idea. My eyes lit up, and I started to inch down. He had on his jeans, but that made them even hotter.

"Okay." Mason clamped down on my own ass. "Where are you going, sweet cheeks?"

"Sweet cheeks." That made me laugh even more. "I was admiring yours."

"You don't say," he remarked dryly. "Remember what you touch down there, I can touch up here, too."

That was right. He grabbed ahold of my pants, but his palm was pressed over my own ass cheeks.

I wiggled over him. "Feel me up, Mason. Go for it. Make my night complete."

I felt the silent laughter from him as his shoulders moved up and down. He nudged his bedroom door wider and ducked inside. I started to lift up, but he caught me. Shifting me down over him, my legs slid down the front of him to the ground, but he caught me before I touched the floor. One of his arms anchored me to his front as he caught the back of my neck. It was a firm and almost possessive hold. It was like I was his. He carried me as if I weren't human, like I was a doll, but I loved it.

A thrill went through me. His muscles contracted as he stopped right before his bed and looked at me. His gaze held mine, slipping into me and past my walls. It was like he could read my thoughts. Then again, when hadn't he?

I wound an arm around his neck and tilted his head to mine. "Do you know how much I love you?"

His eyes darkened. I saw his love for me shining right back. "Same for me."

"No." I shook my head. "Say it. I want to hear it."

I was becoming the possessive one now. He was mine. All mine. This perfect specimen of a man—who held me in his arms, who could make me shudder from ecstasy, who protected me from so many people—was my future. He was my soul mate.

He was the only one who mattered. I loved him with a passion that took my breath away. It was more than I ever felt.

He grew serious, letting me stand on top of the bed. I fell to my knees, looping both my arms around his neck. I kept him looking right into my eyes, not that he was fighting it. His grip fell to my waist and was just as strong as mine on him.

"Tell me, Mason." It was a quiet but commanding urge. "Tonight, I want to hear how much you love me."

"You do?"

I nodded. The emotion moved up to my throat. It was choking me, and I was holding back tears from it.

"You want to hear how much I love you?"

I couldn't talk, but I nodded again. The tears were right there. They hadn't fallen, but they were just waiting to go.

A tenderness came over him, and he laid me down on the bed. His hand gripped behind my shoulders, and the other was on my hip. I did nothing. I was like the most precious being to him as he lowered me down, so my head gently touched the bed. He stood above me, our eyes holding each other's.

His hands fell to my jeans as he murmured, "I have an entire list of why I love you, so this could take a while."

Please. I wanted nothing more.

He undid the button on my jeans, holding my gaze, and slid down the zipper. He paused for a moment and tugged them down past my hips. He murmured as he pulled them off, "I love how you crinkle your nose when you need to tell me something, and you're scared—like if I smell and you don't want to hurt my feelings, or earlier tonight, when I knew you wanted time alone with Heather, but you didn't want to make me feel left out."

I thought he understood I wanted time with her. We hadn't said the words, but I'd been right.

My lip started to tremble. Emotion like I'd never felt before was pressing down over me. My blood started to feel energized. I was excited for it. I was waiting for it.

Mason knelt on the bed, and his hand touched my flat stomach. His fingers spread out, flattening his palm, and he continued to touch me only there. "I love how your eyes kind of go wild, and you toss back your head when you're pissed about something." His other hand touched my chin. "You lift your chin, and you get this look, like you're going to bulldoze your way through a tornado if you have to. No one's going to stop you."

I pressed my lips together, trying to stop the tears.

It was useless. One slid down, making a lone trek to the side of my chin.

Mason caught it, touching it with his finger. He brought it to his lips like it was the most normal thing to do. He slid his other hand up my stomach, lifting my shirt with the motion. Deep flames of lust were licking at me. They were growing more and more, and I bit down on the inside of my cheek. As his hand rested over my breast, my entire body was trembling.

I wanted him to touch me. I wanted him to kiss me. I wanted more.

Arching my back, I moved up against his hand, but he pressed me back down. He was firm but so tender.

I felt like my heart was being shattered into a million pieces, but he was putting each of them back together, one by one.

He pressed a soft kiss between my breasts. "I love how you don't look at my family with contempt, but you could. You have every right to do so. My mom's a stuck-up bitch who thinks you're not good enough for me, but she's wrong." He lifted my shirt off me and came back down, cupping the back of my neck. He was still poised above me, so he wasn't lying on top of me or next to me. He was just above me. He dropped down to nuzzle behind my ear as he added, his breath caressing my skin, "She's so severely wrong because I'm the one not good enough for you, but she hasn't figured that out yet."

He was both wrong and right. His mom was a pretentious bitch, but I could never hate her. I got him from her. I wanted to say those words to him, but my throat ceased working long ago. I was helpless, only listening to the very words I asked from him.

Mason reached underneath me, undid my bra, and slid it off my arms. He drew it out, letting the bra act as a caress as he pulled it from me. He watched me the entire time, never looking away. "I love how you fidget with your shirt or your sleeves when you're distracted or thinking about your mom."

"I do?" There. I'd managed to get that out, even though my voice was hoarse.

He nodded and moved to his side. He leaned down, and his cheek grazed against mine from the movement. "You think about her more than you realize, and I know you miss her, even though you hate her, too."

The tears slid down now. I had no idea that I thought about Analise, but he was right. The tears weren't going to be stopping anytime soon. Grief hit me full bloom in the chest, but it was the good kind of grief. It was the kind that had been holed up there, submerged so deep that I hadn't known it had taken root. It was lifted now, pulled up to the surface, and I felt it lessen, even just slightly.

Mason whispered, pressing kisses down my throat, "And I really love how you love me. Completely. Irrevocably. Overwhelmingly. Selflessly. Unconditionally." He lifted his head, peering right down into me. His lips were just above mine. "Because I don't deserve it, but somehow, I got it, and I will never, ever do anything to lose it."

I was a mess.

Tears were flowing down my face.

I was smiling, crying, and trying to talk. All at once.

I wanted to reach up and hug him back. I wanted to tell him how much I loved him back, but no words could get out.

Finally, I just wrapped my arms around his neck and hugged him down to me. That was all I could do, but I hugged him with all the force I could summon. He wrecked me, but somehow, I loved this man even more.

Mason laughed into my neck. "I have more to say."

Oh god. I couldn't take any more. I couldn't talk with all the emotions swimming through me. I shook my head and pressed my lips to his.

He got the message, and it wasn't long after that before he slid inside me.

He'd completely gotten the message.

CHAPTER SIXTEEN

The next day was low-key. Heather, Logan, Nate, Mason, and I went for breakfast. There'd been no tension or awkwardness, but I wasn't sure if I should've been worried about that or not. Either way, Logan and Heather seemed fine with each other. After Heather left that afternoon, I went back to the dorms to study.

It was during my second class on Monday that I got a surprise.

"Psst." Logan dropped into the seat next to me and poked my arm with his pencil.

"You're not in this class."

He flashed me a grin, raking his hand through his hair. "Actually, I am." He grimaced. "I've been going to the wrong hour." He nodded to the professor, who just came into the room. "She informed me last week, so here I am. Correct hour, and lo and behold, who do I see?" His beaming smile gave me an indication.

I kept my face blank. "Batman?"

"What?"

"You saw Batman? No?" Logan started to say something, but I shot a hand up. "Wait. I have more sarcastic answers."

He was shaking his head, craning his neck backward. "Who are you? What have you done with my future stepsister?"

I winked at him, settling back into my seat. "Oh, come now, Logan. I've learned from the master."

His hand touched his chest, and he tilted his head, his eyes crinkling as he smiled at me. "*Moi?*"

"No." I didn't bat an eyelid. "Mason."

Logan burst out laughing and elbowed me in the arm. "College is good for you, Sam. You're funny. You used to mope way too much last year."

A shocked laugh choked out of me. *Mope?*

All the reasons last year and the previous year sucked were on the tip of my tongue. My finger lifted in the air as I was ready to list them off, but Logan shut me down when he grabbed my hand and pushed it back to my desk.

He leaned close and whispered as the professor called for attention, "Jeez. You *always* have to be the center of attention, don't you?"

My eyes threatened to bulge out. He thought I had to be the center of attention?

He laughed. "I'm just messing with you, but I actually did come over with something to say." He grew quiet and more serious.

I waited.

He remained quiet.

"Logan," I prompted.

"I forgot what it was."

"Ah, Mr. Kade," the professor called his name. "It's nice to see you in the correct hour and classroom this time."

All eyes turned our way—or at least the rest of the classroom that hadn't already been watching Logan. He was unfazed.

A lazy grin came over him, and he gave the professor a

thumbs-up. "Enjoy it, Stephanie." He indicated his thumb. "I only reserve this for the superhot professors."

Her slight grin vanished. Her mouth pressed into a flat line as she said, "It's Professor Baun, and not only was that inappropriate but it was also *not* entertaining. Do it again, Mr. Kade, and you'll be out of this class."

I closed my eyes. That was like a personal challenge to Logan. I knew what was coming.

He leaned back in his chair, gave her a cocky smirk, and asked, "To clarify, if I hit on you one more time in this class, does that mean I can go back to the other hour? Because I have to say, the other class worked better with my schedule, but this one has my brother's girlfriend in it." He threw his arm around my shoulders and patted my head. "See Sam? I'm never inappropriate when she's around." His grin grew as he showed his perfect white teeth.

A guy in the back coughed into his hand. "Bullshit."

Logan turned around and gave him the thumbs-up sign, too, and coughed right back. "Asshole."

"Okay, Mr. Kade." The professor snapped her fingers and pointed to the door. "Out. I'm not going to deal with this. You can come by my office immediately after this class ends." The glare she fixed on him meant business.

Logan stood, and another smart-ass comment was about to leave his mouth.

I clamped a hand on his arm. As he looked down, I shook my head. "Just don't."

The cocky smirk vanished, and he straightened, nodding to me. "All right. Wait for me afterward. I still need to talk to you."

As he went, the professor's gaze fell on me with a look of disappointment and derision. The old Sam would've shrunk back into her seat. I'd changed, and I stared right back at her. I enjoyed this class, and I enjoyed learning from her, but I'd done nothing wrong. If she was irritated with Logan, that had nothing to do with me, so I lifted my chin.

Mason's words from last weekend filtered back to me. *"You lift your chin, and you get this look, like you're going to bulldoze your way through a tornado if you have to. No one's going to stop you."*

I felt the same determination now. She wasn't going to bulldoze through me or try to intimidate me. I'd stand my ground. A second later, after she'd held my gaze, she dropped hers and pointed to the board behind her. The class continued after that, but tension filled the room from Logan's departure and my stare-off with the professor. I'd endured more than this awkwardness, so I sat back and gave everyone a silent fuck-you back.

I looked bored throughout the class period. People noticed. Some gave me disgusted looks. Others seemed more attentive to me. There were a few who nodded in approval.

For once, I felt like I could take the Kade name on. *I am Samantha Kade. Hear me roar.* That confidence lasted until the end of the hour.

"Miss Strattan." The professor plunged a knife through my daydreaming. She had the same disappointment and derision written over her face. "May I talk with you as well after class?"

A girl who was sitting two seats down from me sucked in her breath.

A guy muttered under his breath behind me, "Damn."

With that one request, the professor tainted me. Whatever her issue with Logan, it extended to me.

I'd done nothing wrong. *Fuck that.* I asked, "Why?"

She had forgotten me, gathering her papers, as everyone started to leave. At my question, they sat back down.

She looked around the room. "You can all go."

They ignored her.

She pressed her lips together and pinned me down with a stare. "I can explain in private, Miss Strattan."

Fine. My jaw was clenched shut, and I gritted my teeth, shoving up from my seat. I clutched my book, notebook, and bag in my hands. "I've not done a thing wrong. I want to make that clear for the rest of the students. I've not missed a day. I've never been late. All my assignments have been handed in and done well, if I might add, from the exemplary scores you've given me up until this point."

Her head cocked to the side, and she came around, standing beside her podium with an arm resting on the side. "Are you challenging my request to meet with you in private?"

"I'm making my record known to the rest of the class."

"Why?"

"Because, at the beginning of the hour, I was just another student. Logan came in, and he challenged you. He did that. Not me. Now, you're requesting to see me after class. I don't know why, but if you start downgrading my assignments, I want to make my history known to everyone else in case I might have to challenge you in the future."

Her nostrils flared. "Based on what?"

"Based on discrimination."

Her chest jerked up and held. Her fingers wrapped tighter on the podium, and her free hand pressed into her hip. "Discrimination of what?"

"Whatever feelings you have toward Logan. I don't want them projected to me as well, not unless I've earned them."

"I think you're earning them right now." Her lips were pressed tightly.

I had nothing more to say. I stated my case. I'd stood up for what I felt was coming my way, and I'd made it known. If she were going to paint me with the same disdain that she had for Logan, it wouldn't be fair treatment. I'd been treated unfairly by classmates but never teachers, so I wasn't going to let it start in college.

"Class dismissed." She swung her head around, giving the entire group a pointed look.

They'd all remained, waiting for the end of our exchange, and when I didn't say anything more, they began collecting their things and leaving the room.

A couple of girls walked by me, grinning at me over their shoulders. The professor noticed but didn't move. She didn't say a word. She stood in silence, just like me. A couple of guys walked by as well and nodded at me before slipping from the room.

Respect.

I earned theirs, and though it hadn't been my intention, it felt good. It felt liberating.

Once the last student was about to leave the room, she said to him, "Close the door, Frederick."

He paused and shot me a look, but he did as she'd said.

From the other side, he mouthed the words to me, *Good luck*, and he gave me his own thumbs-up sign before leaving.

I held my breath. I had a feeling I would need it.

"You think I'm going to treat you unfairly?" she clipped out.

"Yes."

"Because of one person?"

"Because of Logan, yes."

She paused, studying me. The disappointment and derision that I'd felt earlier seemed to fade. Her eyes swept me up and down. I raised my chin higher and felt like I was a chicken offering its neck for the slaughter. I lowered my chin but steadily gazed right back.

"Has that happened before?"

"Yes, but not by a teacher."

Her eyes narrowed. She grew thoughtful. "You've had other students treat you unfairly?"

"Because of Logan and because of Mason, yes."

The tension was gone. She dropped her attitude, and her tone softened as she said, "Well, I'm sorry to hear that."

I—

Wait…

I frowned. "What?"

"The reason I asked to speak to you in private was because I'd finally put two and two together. You're Garrett's daughter, aren't you?"

My head was swimming. "What?"

A low chuckle escaped her, and she grabbed the pile of books and papers from her podium. Gesturing to the door, she said, "Walk with me. And, no, Samantha, I'm not going to treat you unjustly because of your connection to Logan Kade or his brother."

She reached for the door and held it open for me. I went past.

She said, falling in line beside me, "I know your biological father. I went to school with him. Garrett Brickshire, right? You were raised by David Strattan. Analise is your mother?

Garrett told me last year Mason Kade was dating his biological daughter."

I winced. I hadn't talked about my mother in so long, but she'd been mentioned twice in the last three days. "Yeah. You know my dad?"

"I do." She pointed down a hallway, and we turned.

Logan was waiting outside a room, sitting on the floor. He stood to his feet as he saw our approach. His eyes narrowed, taking in my face.

She nodded to him, pulling out her keys. "Mr. Kade."

He ignored her and asked me, "You're upset?"

"I…" I was, but it wasn't warranted.

She looked between the two of us and nodded. "Ah, yes. Garrett did say the three of you, Mason included, were exceptionally close. I'll give you a few minutes to reassure him that you're fine, Sam, but come inside when you're done." With those words, she went inside.

Logan pulled the door shut. "What did she say to you?"

"Nothing." I waved at him. "For real. I'm okay. I…jumped to conclusions. She knows my dad."

"Garrett? Not David?"

"Yeah. She said she put two and two together when you came to class today."

He looked inside, watching her through the small window in the door, and smirked. "I bet she banged him."

"Logan!" I smacked his arm.

"I bet she did. She's hot. Your dad's hot. I bet they had a whole fling." He jerked his head back to me. "Oh, that reminds me, too. Well, he's not the reason, but Mama Malinda is. She called this morning. They're coming for parents' weekend this Friday."

"What?"

"Malinda and your dad—your *real* one, David—are coming up. She wanted to surprise you."

"Why are you telling me?"

"Because you hate surprises."

I scowled. The fact that he knew they were coming up before I did pissed me off. No, that wasn't right. I was jealous. They were my family, not his.

I sucked in my breath. They weren't my family. They were his, too. I had no reason to be jealous.

"Sam?" Logan was watching the myriad of expressions cross my face.

I shook my head. "I have to go."

"You okay?"

"Yeah, yeah, I'm fine." I tried to wave off his concern and pointed to the office. "Tell her I'll talk to her later. I…have to go to the bathroom." I needed a lie that Logan wouldn't hammer at me about, trying to figure it out. My mouth turned down, and I grabbed at my stomach. "Diarrhea."

"Ew, Sam. We're family, but I don't need to know details like that."

"Uh-huh." I raised my voice before turning and hurrying away. "Okay, yeah, gotta take a shit. See you later, brother dearest."

"Okay." He sounded confused. "Enjoy taking your shit."

"Yeah, yeah."

I rushed around the corner, then stopped and slowed down, but my heart didn't. It was pounding against my chest, trying to break through it. I stopped altogether.

Logan was my family. Mason was my family. I had no right thinking they weren't. Malinda, David, Mark—we were all family. I blinked back some tears. The sudden feeling of being lost wafted up, and I shoved it down.

I needed to go on a run.

MASON

I was waiting in my Escalade when Sam returned from her run. Logan said that she was upset earlier and lied about it, so I expected that she would go on a run. She was crossing the parking lot with her roommate clutching a book next to her. Sam was counting her pulse with her finger to her neck while gripping a water bottle in her other hand. They'd see the vehicle in a second—or Sam would. I took that moment to study the roommate.

Sam mentioned that she met the family. She mentioned a stepmother. My attention sharpened on the roommate as she glanced in my direction. Our gazes caught and held, but she didn't mask the fear that flashed for a split second. It was there and then gone, and her face went back to being pleasant. She murmured something to Sam, who looked in my direction. Sam said something to the roommate, and the two parted ways. The roommate headed for their dorm while Sam came my way.

I sat back, my eyes trained on the roommate, until Sam opened the door and climbed inside.

"Hey." She'd probably been running for two hours, but she wasn't winded. She had a glow to her face.

I grinned back at her and leaned over. She met me halfway, her lips fitting perfectly to mine. I held there for one more second. She was a break from reality.

With her hand coming to rest on my cheek, she pulled back

with a slight frown. She asked, her hand falling to my chin and staying there, "You okay?"

I had two objectives in mind. I went with the easiest one. "Logan said you committed the ultimate crime."

"What?" A quick laugh left her, but her eyes narrowed.

"He said you brushed him off."

"Oh." A second laugh came out, more relieved. "It was nothing."

"Sam?"

"It was stupid." She sat back, facing the front. Her head leaned back against the headrest. "I just freaked for a second. It's ridiculous."

"What was it?"

She groaned before saying, "I got jealous."

She fell quiet again.

I prompted, "Of?"

"Of Logan."

I frowned. I hadn't expected that answer. "Of what?"

"Because Malinda told him, not me, that they were coming up for parents' weekend. I…" She faltered again. "I got jealous." A sheen of tears were on her eyelids. "They're my family, not his, and I got jealous about that." She wiped at the tears with the back of her hand, even though they hadn't fallen yet. "It's so, so, so dumb. You guys are my family, and so are they. I shouldn't have felt like that. I have no right."

"Sam." *Shit.*

She was beating herself up over wanting a family.

I said softly, grabbing her hand, "You can feel like that. You're right."

She turned to me. The side of her mouth dipped down. "What are you talking about?"

"Malinda, David, and Mark—they are your family. They're your *legit* family."

"Mason—"

I stopped her with a gentle grin on my face. "No matter what, yes, Logan and I are your family. We always will be... even if something happens to you and me."

Her eyes got big.

I said quickly, "Not that I want that to happen, but if anything were to happen, I'll still be your family. Logan will still be your family. You're *in* with us. No one gets in with us, and you did. But, having said that, David and Malinda are parents to you. Your real mom's a bitch. You finally got what you've always wanted—a loving mom and a loving dad. It is normal for you to want to defend that. You've reached gold, as far as I see it. Protect the gold. Shit. Hoard the fucking gold. Loving families aren't as common as some people think. And since we're sharing here, I have to admit that I'm a little jealous of your setup with David and Malinda."

"You are?" A tear slid down her cheek, but she ignored it.

I didn't think she noticed it. Her eyes went back to sparkling. A little bit of pink moved back to her cheeks, too.

"My parents love me, but they're a mess. James is off with your mom. I've not seen him in months, and Helen's gone back to traveling ninety percent of the time since Logan and I are three hours away. You got parents coming for parents' weekend, and they aren't coming with an agenda."

"Oh, Mason."

I saw the sympathy creeping in and shook my head. I didn't want to see that in her. "Don't pity me. I've got a trust fund in the millions. I'm hoping to go pro football, but if I don't, I'll still be fine. I'm best friends with my soul mate and my brother. I'm damn blessed, too. I'm just reminding you that you shouldn't feel guilty about protecting your family."

"You're my—"

She started to reach for my face, and I caught her hands, bringing them to my lap, as I laced our fingers.

"I know. We're family, but you can have two families. You can enjoy having a mother, too."

More tears slid down her face, but she only gazed at me. She was sitting sideways, and she rested her head against her seat. "It's a weird feeling."

"What is?"

"Healing."

And right there, that word from her, took my breath away. *Fuck the dorm deal.* I shoved the other concern away. I'd deal with it on my own terms.

I started the vehicle.

"Where are we going?"

"You're staying the night." I flashed her a grin.

She smiled back, and the sight of it was a gut punch. She was damn beautiful. My dick was already hard, and I couldn't think about all the positions I wanted her in, or I'd be pulling over in some other lot. Instead, as I left the lot, I glanced up where Sam's room was, and I wasn't shocked to see the roommate there.

She'd been watching us, but as I met her eyes, she shifted back and let the curtain fall.

Caught you.

CHAPTER SEVENTEEN

SAMANTHA

A cake, balloons, groceries, flowers, and an inflatable chair greeted Summer and me on Friday morning. They were piled in front of our door when Summer got up to leave for the restroom.

"Uh…" She stepped back and cleared her throat. "Sam?"

I had no words. "Um…"

"Oh." A bright laugh came from the hallway. The inflatable chair was picked up and lifted before Malinda's flushed face was seen. "Happy parents' weekend, Samantha!" She shoved the chair behind her and waded through everything else.

Her arm was thrown up, and I had a second's notice before she crossed the room's threshold, grabbing me in the tightest bear hug I'd experienced in a long time.

She rocked me back and forth, smoothing a hand down my hair. "You look surprised. Good." She pulled back and patted me once on both shoulders with her hands. "Mission accomplished. I wanted to have you wake up with a delight. Now," she leaned forward, took a sniff, and wrinkled her nose, "I see I really did beat you to the punch. You need to brush your teeth, honey."

"Malinda," I started.

"Nope. I won't have it. Mom…" Her voice faded. "Well, maybe Mama Malinda? I don't want to push you. I'm sorry. Malinda is just fine."

She was hurt, and I was a dipshit.

"Sorry." But I couldn't bring myself to say the *mom* word.

And Mama Malinda was Logan's nickname for her. Knowing I couldn't appease her that way, I hugged her once more. This time, it was me who held her for a moment longer than necessary.

She melted and murmured under her breath, "Oh, sweetie."

The tears were there. I heard them in her choked voice, but she cleared her throat and stepped back.

Wiping at the corners of her eyes, her smile never wavered. It was from ear to ear. "Thank you for that. I do love you, my new daughter."

"Should I…" Summer was still studying the pile of gifts in the hallway. She was clutching her shower caddy in one hand, and a robe hung over her other arm.

"You must be Summer?" Malinda didn't give her any choice.

Summer looked a little alarmed, but Malinda swept her up in a hug similar to mine. She released Summer right away though and started grabbing the items one at a time.

"It's so nice to meet you. Here. Let me grab all of these and get them out of the way." She grabbed the flowers first and passed them to me as she said to Summer, "I'm Malinda, by the way. I married Samantha's father."

Summer started helping, putting her robe and caboodle down. As I put the flowers on my desk, she brought the balloons over. Malinda passed by her, starting with the bags of groceries.

Summer said, going back to help bring in the rest of the food, "I'm Summer. It's really nice to meet you."

"You can call me Mama Malinda." She paused next to me, her hand resting on my shoulder. The touch was gentle. "That's what Logan calls me, and it's stuck. I like the nickname. I even got Mason to call me that one time."

"You did?" I asked.

She nodded to me. Her cheeks were flushed, and her eyes gleamed from excitement. "I about choked on my coffee that morning, but I think he wanted to shock me. He did that usual face when he thinks something's funny, but he doesn't want to show it." She mimicked him, standing like a statue, letting the corners of her mouth lift up and drop back down immediately. Her face was stoic before she broke out laughing. "You know how he is. He looks like a pissed off robot half the time."

Summer was bringing in the last of the groceries, and she burst out a laugh but muffled it, coughing over it. "Wha—never mind." She gestured to the hallway, reaching for her caboodle again. "I'll be back in a bit." She paused, grabbed clothes from her closet, and disappeared, shutting the door behind her.

"Is my dad coming, too?"

Malinda waved that off. "He was worried about that scene, catching any of the girls too early in the morning, if you know what I mean. My word, Sam." She blinked several times at me, pressing a hand to her chest. "Your roommate is gorgeous."

"Oh." I laughed. "She used to be a model."

"I had no idea. You talked about her, and Logan said she was gorgeous, but I didn't realize how beautiful she was. That's a relief."

I started to pick at the bags of groceries. If my nose wasn't deceiving me, I could smell some coffee somewhere. I asked, reaching for another bag that seemed heavier than the others, "Logan? Relief?"

"Well, yeah." She plopped down on my bed. "I know you've had a hard time with girls being jealous of you. I was a little worried about how your roommate would handle your looks and your closeness to Mason and Logan. Not a lot of girls could handle that, but she seems like a very self-assured girl herself. That's a relief for you."

Aha! Coffee and a coffeemaker. Mama Malinda was my new favorite person.

I pulled the maker out of the bag and got right to work getting it set up.

"Samantha?"

"Huh?" I paused and looked over at her.

She fixed me with a look.

I slowly lowered the coffee machine to the desk as I asked, "What did I miss?"

She didn't answer. She stared at me. Her brown hair was tamed under a red silk scarf. Gold thread weaved through it, somehow reflecting off her complexion. I stopped and really stared back at my new mother. Her love was right there. It was swimming on the surface with a few unshed tears in her eyes. Her lips were struggling not to smile too wide, and she pressed a hand to her cheek.

She huskily murmured, "Nothing. You've missed nothing. I'm just being an emotional mess over here."

"Huh?"

"Go ahead." She stood and waved at me. "I knew you'd find that first. I brought water for you two gals, too. You can use that to make the coffee."

It wasn't until later that I realized what happened. My new mom brought me stuff to college, and I'd dug right in, looking for the goodies, while she sat and got emotional.

I had been normal.

Right?

I asked Summer when her parents were coming, and she didn't answer right away. She'd been quiet about her family since the first weekend. Both her mother and stepmother were there, helping her move into the room, but they barely talked to each other. Her father was, too. I hadn't thought much about it. Who was I to be nosy about someone else's family? Mine was crazy enough, but now, getting no response from my roommate, I started to wonder why.

I got the answer that night.

I'd just gotten back from dinner with David, Malinda, Logan, Mason, and Nate. Nate's parents came with us. I hadn't known they were in town, but they were tight-lipped. There were a lot of looks between Mason, Logan, Nate, and his parents. Malinda and David hadn't been oblivious. They'd caught on to the undercurrents, whatever they were, but Malinda pretended they weren't there. I'd caught her studying Nate's mother a few times with a speculative look in her eyes. I couldn't be sure what she saw, but I was glad that Malinda hadn't pushed to know what was going on.

Nate's parents gave me the chills. They reminded me of Helen—wealthy, pretentious, and just plain stuck-up snobs. However, they couldn't snub their nose at Malinda. She had her own wealth, coming from her father, and she was connected. She ran in those hoity-toity circles that Mason and Logan's parents had as well before the divorce and the implosion of my family on them.

At one point, Nate's mother inquired about where Helen was, if she'd be attending parents' weekend as well.

Logan snorted in laughter. "Are you kidding me? Pretty sure the formerly absent mother has returned back to her absent status." He asked Mason, "What? She's in Paris now?"

"Venice."

Logan snorted again but in disgust. He let out a sigh. "I've lost my appetite now."

For the only time that night, Nate's mother lost her holier-than-thou air for a moment. She'd looked to be at a loss for words, but she'd folded her hands in her lap and kept her head down for twenty minutes after that.

Malinda pressed her lips together, still eyeing the other woman with hawk-like focus, but only reached for her wine. Nate's father asked David how the Fallen Crest Academy football team was going to do for the rest of the season.

Things progressed a little more smoothly after that. Nate's father and David conversed about football, asking Mason about his season so far, while Malinda informed Logan and Nate how Mark was doing at his college.

I remained quiet.

The whole dinner was unsettling. Nate's parents never said or did anything wrong to me, but they reminded me too much of Helen's disdain for me, which reminded me of Garrett and what my professor said. She knew my biological father, who I hadn't heard from since leaving Boston last Christmas.

The time with him had been...okay. I was there. He was there. We'd shared a few dinners. I'd explored the coffee shop down the same block and the bookstore it was attached to while he'd worked at his office during the day. My nights had been spent on the phone with Mason and Logan. When Garrett dropped me off at the airport, the good-byes had been respectful. That was the best word to describe them. I wasn't angry with him. I didn't feel close to him, but he wasn't really a stranger anymore.

I hadn't thought about him until that night again, so when Summer dropped her bomb, it floored me.

Really floored me.

I gaped at her, my mouth hanging open. "Wha—huh? Say that again."

"My father and stepmother have a house here, but my dad has a bunch of houses. He does business in Boston." Her head was down. Her eyes were averted.

I watched how she tucked her hands under her legs, and her shoulders slumped down.

A bad feeling, a very bad feeling, started in my stomach.

I shook my head. "What? I mean, I'm still lost."

"You talked about that professor who knew your biological father. Remember?"

"Uh, yeah." Why was she remembering? That was the real question. "What does this have to do with your dad and stepmother?"

She looked up, biting her lip. The fear that crossed her face took me back. I quieted. My mind was reeling. I knew that Mason would've figured this out in one second. He would jump five steps ahead to the real reason Summer was suddenly so nervous. I wasn't there. I was still back where she'd said her dad did business in Boston.

"Wait." I held up a hand. She'd been about to say more, but I needed to go slow. "Your dad does business in Boston?"

She nodded.

I asked the second question, "But he has a house here, too?" What did that have to do with my professor? As she started to nod again, in mid nod, I asked my third one, "Does your dad live here? Or is it like a vacation home or something?"

"He lives here. My mom does, too, but he travels to Boston for business."

Things were starting to connect, but I didn't like the feeling I was getting. This was becoming too fucked up to be a coincidence. "Your dad knows Garrett, doesn't he?"

She sucked in a breath but forced her head to slowly move up and down. The trepidation spreading over her face was a little too much for me. I had a sense I wasn't going to like what else she would say. I had a sense I was going to hate it.

She said, "My father and stepmother invited us for dinner tomorrow at their house. Your father and his wife are going to be there. They'd like for us to come."

She wasn't telling me the truth. She wasn't telling me what I really needed to hear.

I could forget about Garrett and why he hadn't said a word to me about this, forget that he knew her parents or that they'd been in the same city this whole time, forget the fact that Summer never conversed with her parents—that I knew of. There was something nagging at me. I couldn't get it out of my head.

I said, "Summer."

She froze, hearing the sudden seriousness from me. She turned her head away.

"Summer."

She didn't look at me.

"Look at me." It was an order, one that I needed her to obey. And she did. Tears along with raw agony filled her eyes.

I didn't let it faze me. I couldn't. "What else are you keeping from me?" There was a link somewhere that connected everything. It would all make sense. I just needed to find it.

Her tears fell, as if my question had given them the final push to fall free. "Come to dinner tomorrow night. You'll understand all of it then."

That was the answer I got. *Well then...*

Mason had a game the next afternoon. I told David and Malinda there that Garrett was in town as well, and I was going to have dinner with him and his wife. They were quiet. I didn't get the barrage of questions I'd assumed Malinda would have.

Instead, she murmured, "Well, that's nice of him to come."

David gazed at me. I felt the questions from him, but he didn't ask them. During halftime, I went back to the dorm to get ready. Summer wasn't in the room, but she texted with the time to be ready and when she would pick me up.

I sat on the bed and waited.

Nothing. No text message. No phone call.

After waiting another hour, I had enough. I changed back to jeans and a Cain University sweatshirt with Mason's football number on the back. I was heading through the lobby to go to the game when my phone buzzed in my hand. I was tempted to ignore it. Fuck whatever shadiness my roommate was doing. I'd get to the bottom of it, but my parents were in town. I wanted to see them, not deal with people who were lying to me—including Garrett.

He should've called. Hell, he should've called a long time ago, like after I had flown back to Fallen Crest, or after I found out he wasn't moving anymore and was going to stay in Boston. I got that golden nugget of information from Malinda who heard it via her friends at the Fallen Crest Country Club.

There'd been no word from Garrett at all, so I moved on.

David was my real dad. I didn't need Garrett. Just like Analise, he wasn't important enough to be a part of my life. The fact that both my biological parents were absent wasn't lost on me. It was funny, in a sick and sad way. The parents that mattered to me weren't blood, but they were my real family now.

A black vehicle pulled up to the dorm as I was coming out. I was passing by when the back door opened.

"Sam." Summer was there, half coming out of the door. She paused there and waved for me. "I'm sorry I'm late. My car broke down, so I had to call for a ride. My mom sent the car, and it took longer to get here because of traffic on game day."

Ah, yes, all the extra traffic because of my boyfriend's football game.

I gritted my teeth. "Fuck this, Summer. I waited. I'm over it. I'm going to spend the day with people who don't lie to me." I turned to go past the car.

"Please, Sam." The break in her voice had me pausing.

I wanted to curse again. I was turning back.

Fuck me. I was never going to learn.

But I went to the vehicle.

Summer lit up before she scooted back and made room for me. She said, as I climbed in and closed the door, "I promise that, after this dinner, I will explain everything. I mean, *everything*." She reached over, her hand squeezing on my arm as she said that last word. "I've wanted to come clean about some things for a *long* time. After this, no lies. I promise."

Considering the fact that I hadn't known there were lies, I was more than okay with that.

One dinner to hear the truth. That was easy. I could do that.

CHAPTER EIGHTEEN

We were driven through the city and turned into a gated driveway before coming to a stop. Summer was nervous. That was obvious from how she was fidgeting with her hands, how she only glanced at me before skirting away again, and the number of times she readjusted her clothing. Her shirt was pulled up, then pulled down, and then flattened over her stomach. She'd repeated that process over and over and kept scratching her forehead.

I kept my mouth shut. I knew the answers were coming—or they'd better be.

Her house was huge, but I wasn't surprised. Summer came from wealth. I hadn't known it for sure, but I figured it out by the time we got there. It wasn't any bigger than Mason and Logan's house when I'd moved in with Analise. That place was a mausoleum, and so was this.

Summer led the way, casting me another look, before swallowing, rolling her shoulders back, and heading inside.

Marble tile, a statue of a nude woman on a horse, and the color of gold greeted us. The gold was everywhere. There were small gold flecks on the walls, but they sparkled and matched the gold that had been woven into the marble tile. The horse's halter had gold in it, and so did the woman's hair. There were hints of gold glitter on her body as well.

I felt like rubbing my eyes raw and dousing them with salt water. Too much gold, just too much.

"I know." Summer moved around me to close the door. She glanced around the foyer and winced. "It's a bit…much."

"You live here?"

"Hell, no." Her eyes got big. "I live in the dorm."

"But before that?"

She stared at me, confused. Understanding dawned. "Oh, no. I lived with my mother. My dad recently had this built. The stepmonster has a complex, obviously." She pointed at a flourish on the horse's halter. "See? There's even a goldfish in the middle of that swirl thing."

I didn't want to look. "Can we not? I…I'm not trying to sound like a bitch, but if this is all to impress me with your family's 401(k), it's not working."

"What?" She blinked a few times. "Oh, no. I mean, sorry. Yeah. Let's go in."

It was a grand hallway. I was led past portraits of people and could recognize Summer in a few of them. Another couple—I guessed the father and stepmother—were in others. There was a family portrait with a boy, but I couldn't get closer to study who he was. Summer hadn't mentioned a brother. I took a step toward it. There was something about him…about how he was looking back at me…

Summer bumped into me. She said under her breath, "I'm so sorry, Sam."

"What?"

I was about to ask more when I heard my name coming from farther down the hall, and I tensed. I had known, but it'd been so long since I last saw him.

Garrett was striding toward me. Instead of the business suit that I'd gotten used to him wearing in Boston, he was wearing a polo shirt and striped shorts. This was why I wasn't impressed by Summer's family. My biological dad fit right in with them. He was dressed down, but his clothes still screamed money.

My mouth pressed into a flat line.

He was getting closer, wearing a friendly smile, and he paused right at my side. He skimmed me over, but his smile didn't fade. He turned to Summer. "Thanks for getting my girl."

His arm was going to curve around my back.

I sidestepped him and shot him a glare. I wasn't his girl. I was barely a blood relation.

Garrett's smile dimmed. He said, "Samantha, I—"

"Can we talk in private?" I cut him off. To Summer, I asked, "Is there a place?"

Her eyes were like saucers again. "Yes, yes." She scooted around and pointed to a side hallway. "Follow this all the way down to the last door. It's my own study room. You can use that."

I started off. I wanted to get this done and over with. I was going to call a cab and try to figure out where to tell the driver to pick me up.

Garrett said from behind me, "We'll, uh...thank you, Summer. I'll show her to the backyard when we're done."

"Okay, Mr. Brickshire."

I paused. My back was turned. I was still livid, but she'd sounded so small there.

Garrett added to the betrayal when he said, "You're the best goddaughter I could have. Thank you again for looking out for her."

I'd been stuck by a hot poker. The end was dipped in fire, and it burned inside of me. I was robbed of breath. I could only stand there, my arms firmly crossed over my chest, and try to suck in air.

She was his goddaughter.

My roommate, who I had come to trust, knew my biological father more in the daughter sense than I did.

I was almost paralyzed.

That lasted two seconds.

A blast of fury flared up, shoving the betrayal from my body, and I was full-on raging by the time I heard Garrett coming behind me.

He thought he could come into my life and then disappear? Never. He thought he could do it again? Hell no. This was the third time.

He was done. *We* were done.

He paused beside me. I felt his uncertainty now. No doubt, he was seeing my rage. I wanted him to see it.

"Can we talk?" he asked again, his tone more wary.

Yes. My insides rejoiced. That small triumph was a lot, but the fury was still boiling in me. I clipped out, "Go ahead." I indicated the door. "Let's do this."

He opened the door but paused at my last statement.

I swept past him. I didn't pay attention to Summer's own personal study room. There was a desk and a couch. The colorful room was clean, and she had all the technical toys I assumed a rich kid would have. I turned my back to all of it and waited for Garrett to shut the door.

As soon as he did, he looked at me.

I didn't give him time to start. I started, "This is the third time."

He didn't ask what I meant. His head hung down. "She's pregnant."

My rage paused. "Who?"

"My wife." Stark eyes looked back at me. "She miscarried twice, but she's pregnant again. It's why I haven't called or e-mailed you."

"No." I started shaking my head. "No, no, no. You always do this. Always! The first time was because you didn't know about me. The second time was because you went to get your wife back. And now this—this is the *third* time, and this is the excuse?"

My chest was heaving. My eyes were wild.

I was on a roll.

I kept going, "I cannot believe you. You're having a kid. Congratu-fucking-lations! Now, you can do it right, maybe?" I started for the door but swung around again. "But here's a tip. Don't disappear. You'd be amazed at the relationship you could have if you were around to have one!"

I stormed out.

I was done, and damn it, I needed to call a cab to come get me wherever I was.

"Sam?" Summer was waiting, fiddling with her shirt. When she saw that I wasn't going to stop, she jerked forward from the wall and hurried to walk with me. "What happened? What did he say?"

"He's having a kid. They're having a kid." I kept going. Fuck him. Fuck any relationship with him. I already had a dad.

"What? That's great. Sharon's been…" She stopped, catching the warning I'd sent to her. She gulped. "Look, I don't know your relationship with him. I mean, it's weird. You never talked about him, but now seeing how mad you are, I'm sorry." She tugged me to a stop. We were alone, right in front of the door again. Her hands twisted around each other, and she tugged at her sleeves, pulling them into a tangled mess. "Garrett knows my dad. They're all friends. There's a huge group of them, and there are others, too. But…" She glanced down to the floor before looking back up to me.

A decision was made. I saw it. She came to some conclusion.

Her chin lifted higher. "Screw it. I'm going to tell you everything—"

"Summer, darling?"

She swore before whipping around. Her whole body tensed. "Molly. Hello." Her tone was guarded. Her chin went from determined to bracing.

A woman in a yellow dress was coming toward us, holding two flute glasses and wearing a large white hat. The hat was a third of the woman's weight. It could've toppled her over, but she kept coming with a graceful smile on her face. When she stopped in front of us, wide, blue eyes ignored Summer and were transfixed on me. She was a stunning woman, but the term *airhead* seemed appropriate to describe her.

She wouldn't hold a candle to Helen or Malinda or even Analise.

"You must be Samantha." She thrust both of the flute glasses to Summer, saying, "Here, dear. I brought you each a mimosa." As soon as her hands were clear, she reached for me. "I have to give you a hug. I have heard so much about you from Sharon. She's raved about how beautiful you are, and she wasn't exaggerating. You, my dear," she held me in front of her, enraptured, "are just stunning. Absolutely stunning. Summer mentioned you were pretty, but she didn't do you justice. You look so much like Garrett. I'm in shock."

That snapped me out of it. My eyes went flat. "I'm nothing like him." I rolled my arms, loosening her hold on me, and I stepped back. "Not to be rude."

She didn't look offended. Her smile only increased. "Yes. You have the same fighting spirit as him, too. I can see it in you. You're so much stronger than Summer here. Summer, dear, you should be taking lessons from your roommate. I can't help but be charmed by you, Samantha. I'm so glad that Summer finally invited you to our family dinner."

Finally? I threw Summer a look. *Finally?*

She wasn't looking. Her eyes were fixed on something in the distance. Her throat trembled. I got the impression she was fighting back tears. A wave of remorse rolled through me—no, forget that. She lied to me.

She was Garrett's goddaughter.

That was enough to bring back the anger. Once it clicked back into place, I felt safe again, and I said, "Well…" I searched for words. There were none. I wanted to get out of there. "I'm leaving. What's your address?"

"Why?"

"I'm going to call a cab."

"What?" She asked Summer, "Did you do something to upset her?"

Summer sucked in a breath and let it out, her cheeks flaming red, "You, woman, are a piece of work. You know why I haven't been able to tell her the truth. You guys even approved, telling him it would all be worth it." She pointed at me. "It's not worth it. She's upset! And Garrett's here. I heard her yelling. He hadn't even told her about her little sister until today. She has every right to be angry."

Sister…

I have a sister coming?

Summer and Molly were snapping at each other, but their voices went away to the distance for me. I couldn't believe it. *A sister.* He said a baby, but I hadn't really thought about it. Another excuse. That was all I'd heard. Another excuse for his absence, but now…it was seeping in.

The corner of my lip twitched. I was going to be a big sister. *A real sibling, with my same blood,* I closed my eyes, *not one from Analise.*

Garrett was whatever he was. Distracted, forgetful, neglectful—I didn't know. But he wasn't Analise. That child wouldn't have what I had—my mother.

Good for her. Relief poured through me at the thought of what my sister would be saved from.

My little sister got a shot at a good family with two parents. A lump formed in my throat, and I swallowed it, shoving it down. Garrett would be a good dad. My jaw firmed. I was going to make sure he would be.

"Samantha?"

It was him, and I pulled myself out of my reverie.

He stood to the side, frowning fiercely at me. "I'm sorry that I haven't called. I really am."

Molly sighed, grabbing ahold of Summer's arm.

He continued, "I didn't grow up in a family where phone calls were a common occurrence. It's not an excuse. It's just…I don't think about calling because I'm an idiotic father, and I have no idea what I'm doing. It's not worth much, but I wanted you to know that I didn't *not* call on purpose. Well, I did, but it wasn't to hurt you or keep you out of the loop. We didn't know at first. Sharon didn't want to say anything. Miscarriages run in her family. She said she'd probably lose the baby, so I didn't want to get anyone's hopes up. Then, she did."

He blinked rapidly. Some moisture built up in the corner of his eye.

He ignored it. "It hit us harder than we'd thought. It hit me harder than I'd thought, but we kept trying, and it happened almost immediately. The second one…we thought we were good to go. I called David, but you were on a run. He told me you were getting ready to go to Cain University. It was a month before or maybe more than a month. He told me when you were moving there and everything. I was going to surprise you and help you move in, but I wanted to wait again. I wanted to be sure to have good news for you, but we lost the second one." His voice grew hoarse.

His emotion was thick. I felt my own rising up, blocking my vocal cords.

"I didn't show up. I meant to. David thought I would be there, but I wasn't, and I'm sorry for that. I was mourning, and that's no excuse. I've been messing up nonstop since I found out about you, but with this one…"

His head hung down. The charismatic and charming Garrett that I'd witnessed at times morphed into an unsure little boy. He was vulnerable, and he'd meant every word he said.

I held my breath. I hoped he'd meant every word. It meant he was flawed, not intentionally a fuck-up.

I shook my head. *What was I doing? But a sister…I was going to be a big sister.*

He started to speak, but I cut in, "You can't *not* call anymore."

He looked back up. A shine of tears was on his eyelids, ready to spill. He cleared his throat. "What?"

"You have to call. Once a week."

He wiped at the corner of his eye. "I know. I got an earful from Sharon when she found out I hadn't been calling you. She'd thought I had. Her mama bear stuff has been coming out with you, too."

I cursed in my head. I knew, after hearing that, that I would be getting another mother in my life. A wary chuckle left me. I didn't know how I was going to handle any of this, but a sister…I never thought about it.

I asked, "Is she here?"

"Sharon?"

I nodded.

"No." He gestured to Molly and Summer, both dabbing at the corners of their eyes. "She said I needed to make things right by myself. She'd sweep in and smother you with kisses. She's been waiting for a long time, but now, with the baby, there's no holding her back anymore. She was going to find you whether or not I made things right today with you."

Mama Malinda would approve.

A small grin was on my face. I didn't try to hold it back. "I'm still so pissed at you, but…" I pressed my lips together. "A little sister?"

"Yeah." A proud expression crossed his features. "I got lucky. Two daughters now."

"Do you have a name picked out?"

"Ah!" Molly stuck her fingers in her ears and turned away. "I don't want to hear. Sharon didn't want anyone to know."

Summer groaned. "Oh my god. I'm sorry. Here, we'll go in the back." She searched my face, taking hold of her stepmother's elbow. "This was part of the reason I didn't say anything. We all knew he wanted to tell you himself. I am sorry for deceiving you."

I waited until they were out of earshot before murmuring, "You're really close to Summer's family?"

"What?" Garrett was grinning from ear to ear. "Oh, yeah, I am. She really hasn't said a word?"

I shook my head. "Not a word."

"Wow. She said she'd keep quiet, but I didn't think she really would. She's a good goddaughter. She's excited about little Seb."

"Seb?"

A car door sounded behind me. I heard it in the back of my mind, but I wasn't paying attention. "You're naming her Seb?"

Garrett laughed. "No, no. Sabrina, but her nickname will be Seb. Sharon's already calling her that. We're not quite out of the first trimester, but I knew I needed to let you know what was going on. I mean, we're hoping you'll be her godmother."

More emotion. More tears.

My heart was melting.

I coughed, trying to clear some of the pressure weighing on my chest. "Of course."

The door opened behind me.

I was going to be a godmother. *My word.* I knew my smile was spread from cheek to cheek. I couldn't wait to tell Mason and Logan.

A male voice sounded behind me.

"Uncle Garrett, I forgot you were coming today."

Wait...

A sickening feeling took root.

Garrett laughed and reached around me to shake a hand. "I wouldn't have missed it for the world. It's your birthday. Plus," he clasped me to him, bringing me around to face who

I already knew it was, "I can finally introduce you to my daughter. Samantha."

I wanted to vomit.

Garrett introduced, "This is my godson, Sebastian."

Looking down at me, his eyes laughing at me, was Park Sebastian. One corner of his mouth lifted into a cocky smirk and he drawled, "Happy birthday to me."

CHAPTER NINETEEN

I punched Sebastian.

My hand was in a fist, and I was swinging before I realized what I was doing. When I did, I swung harder. I glared at him, silently daring him to do something about it.

Sebastian kept staring right back at me.

I'd made contact with his cheek, and a red spot was already forming, but he hadn't done anything. He hadn't flinched. He hadn't hissed. He hadn't stepped back. He took the hit and never broken eye contact with me.

Well, if he was going for scary...I thought about doing it again.

He must've sensed my intent. He warned, "Don't you dare."

I huffed out, "Really?" And I swung again. I didn't care about the girls-can't-hit-guys-because-they-can't-fight-back rule. That was bullshit.

Park Sebastian deserved all the punches he got.

"Samantha!"

I stopped, my arm in mid swing, and let it fall back to my side. I'd forgotten Garrett was there.

He looked shocked. His eyes were arched high, and his head was craned backward. "What are you doing? You can't hit people."

Sebastian snorted.

I rounded on him. "You use cars, dude. They use fists. One grossly outweighs the other. You can defend yourself against a hand. You can't against an oncoming car."

"Wait—" Garrett's head was swiveling between us. Back and forth. Back and forth.

"Really? What about a house being burned down? What did I do that was worse than that?" Sebastian shoved his face forward, right into mine. He stopped with barely an inch separating us. "He took my house away. My house. That was everything to me."

"You tried to take his future away."

"No." He laughed, and it sent a chill through me. "His future isn't his career. Oh, no. Someone else is his future, and you're damn right. I—" He stopped. His eyes went wide, and a look of panic flared there before he jerked backward. He raked a hand over his head. "Shit. I…" He shook his head. "I didn't mean that, Samantha. I didn't. I'm sorry."

Someone else. I didn't need two guesses to know that I'd been right this whole time. He wanted to hurt Mason via me. I was that 'someone else.' I held my hands up and started around him. "I've heard enough. All you did was confirm my suspicion."

Garrett asked, "What just happened?"

I shoved out the door, the second one for the day, and stalked down the driveway. Whatever. I'd get to the street, walk to an intersection, and phone a cab from there.

I was around the first bend when Summer started shouting behind me, "Sam! Sam!"

I clipped my head from side to side. I wasn't having it.

Her feet pounded on the pavement, running behind me.

My teeth ground against each other as she came to my side. I could *feel* her caution, and I snapped, "Don't! You lied to me." *Screw it. If we're going to do this, it might as well be when I am heated.*

She stopped, her face pale. One of her hands lifted, as if to ward me off, but she let it fall slowly back down. "I did."

"He's your brother. Your fucking brother."

She winced. "Okay. One, he's not my *fucking* brother. He's my brother. That word makes it sound gross and twisted. He's my brother. That's it."

"You have different last names."

"I took our mom's maiden name, and he kept our dad's last name. If you haven't figured it out, I'm not close to my dad or his family. I can't stand Molly, and most days, I can't stand Parker either."

"Parker?" I snorted in disgust. "Is that like a reverse nickname you have for him? Instead of shortening the name, you add to it?" My top lip curled up. "How unfucking cute."

She reared back and cursed. "I knew you'd be mad, but you're not holding any punches."

"I don't have to!" That was enough. My hands formed fists, and I kept them tight against my sides. They dug into me the more I talked. "You lied to me. Did you know who I was the whole time?"

She didn't respond, not at first. Then, a quiet, "Yes," came from her.

My hands flew up. I knew it. "What was the plan? Were you supposed to spy on me? My god." A new and so horrifying thought came to me. "Were we even supposed to be roommates? Did Sebastian do something to switch our roommates? I got my dorm assignment late." My gut clenched. I felt like I'd been kicked in the stomach. "Was that because of your brother?"

Again, there was no answer.

The guilt was there. I knew enough.

I shook my head. "I can't believe you. I can't believe any of it."

"Yes. Okay?" A new frenzied plea was in her voice as she surged toward me. "He didn't inform me about the feud. I had to see it for myself, that first day of classes. When I saw how you guys reacted to him, I knew something was up. I already really liked you, so I didn't say anything. I didn't want to lose a potentially great roommate.

"When I cornered him at the house the next week, he told me everything. It was why he hadn't shown up on moving day. He was supposed to help me move in. He explained everything, talked about how Mason burned down his fraternity house, and how he started a fight and beat up a bunch of his brothers.

"I don't know what my brother's done, but I'm guessing he's done something. He claims that he hasn't, but I'm not an idiot. I love my brother, but I'm not blind to the things he's capable of. I know he can be ruthless, and I begged him to leave it all alone. He said he would, and then Logan crashed his party and started a massive brawl."

"Logan did?" A harsh laugh ripped from me. "Really? Sebastian went to the trouble of making us roommates, of planting a spy in my own *room*? You think your brother was going to drop everything, but it's Logan's fault. It's because Logan crashed a party and started a fight. That's why your brother won't drop this whole thing?"

My hands were up. My eyes were bulging out. My face felt

hot, so it must've been red all over. I wanted to grab ahold of my hair and try to pull it out.

Instead, I yelled, "Are you an idiot?"

She jumped back, startled. Her eyebrows bunched together.

"All of this started because Mason wouldn't be some stupid trophy for your brother to use. Sebastian couldn't control him. That was it. Because of that, he tried to run Mason down with a truck."

Summer's mouth fell open. A dumbstruck expression had her pinching her lips together. "No." She started to shake her head. "No, he wouldn't. That doesn't seem like—"

"You're clueless."

Her eyes jumped to mine. A cloud of disbelief was there, and I saw another *no* forming on her mouth.

"Yes." I clipped my head up and down. "Not *no*. Yes. Your brother tried to get Mason and hit Marissa instead, his stalker. Sebastian paid her off, and she transferred colleges. He and his friends jumped Mason last year too." An easy wave rolled over me. "Did you…" I was scared to ask. The thought sickened me. "Did he ask you to spy on me?"

"Uh-huh. But no, I wouldn't do that."

My eyes narrowed. She'd answered that too quickly.

"What did he ask?"

"No, Sam. I told you. I wouldn't do that to you."

"But he did ask?"

"Sam…" Her voice broke.

I had her, and she looked away. Her jaw was starting to tremble.

I grew quiet. "What did he ask, Summer? I have to know."

"He asked about your family—your mom and dad. He

wanted to know about your stepbrother. That was it." Her eyes swept down and to the side. The corner of her mouth twitched.

There was more. "Summer?"

"He came over one night."

He'd been in the room. I was trying to tell myself that was logical. She was his sister, but my entire body clenched. An ice storm blasted in my veins. He'd been near my desk, my bed, my clothes. I'd leave my purse in the room sometimes.

Beads of cold sweat formed on my forehead, but I had to ask, "Was he alone in the room?"

"No." She shook her head, but her gaze was still turned downward. "I might've gone to the restroom."

"Summer!"

"He wouldn't do anything," she argued.

I shot back, "He already has."

She flinched, letting out a deep groan. "I'm so sorry, Samantha. I really am. I didn't want to tell you because I knew you'd freak, and I liked you. I didn't want you to move out, not until you got to know me."

"It's too late." The fight started to lesson. I had to move out. An ironic laugh bubbled up my throat. "It's funny. The very guy who I need to be kept safe from is the only other guy besides Mason who has a key to our place." I fixed her with a look. "Sebastian *does* have a key, doesn't he?"

She didn't respond but nodded, jerking her head up and down. "I'm so sor—"

I waved her off. "I got it. You said it, but the damage is done. I don't trust you. First, Garrett, and now, your brother. How am I supposed to live with you after this?"

"I—" She tipped her head back, and a muffled scream came

out. Her hands grabbed the sides of her head, and her fingers sank in, taking hold of her hair.

"My god, I want to murder my brother. He put me in this spot. He changed my roommate assignment, but I like you. I'd met the other girl, and I would've hated her. I thought he was helping me, and I was grateful to him. He manipulated me. I'm going to rip his balls off." Another guttural scream burst out, and she followed it with a litany of swear words that Logan would've written down. "Trust me, Sam. I get it. I do, and I'm raking my mind, trying to think of ways to make it up to you. I can't think of one thing—"

"Tell me his secrets."

"What?" She eyed me, one corner of her mouth sinking down.

"Tell me his secrets. Tell me everything."

"But isn't that the same thing? Instead of getting information through me about you, I'm passing information about him to you?"

My eyes closed until they were slits. "You said you wanted to make it up to me. Tell me everything about him, all the gory details."

She remained quiet but didn't look away and didn't walk away. Then, her head slowly lowered back down.

I had her.

Sebastian wanted to use me to his advantage. Maybe I could use his sister to my advantage instead.

I never told Mason and Logan about Summer.

I should have, but my friendship with her would've been done immediately. They would've labeled her a traitor, and would never trust her again. She'd lied to me, but she hadn't betrayed me, at least I hoped she hadn't. So a part of me didn't want to move out, not yet anyway. The other part of me was trying to be Mason-like, all cold and ruthless. I wasn't on his mastermind level, but I felt I wasn't hurting too much.

Summer wasn't sure what would be helpful, so the next couple of weeks were filled with random information. If she thought of something, she would tell me. If I thought of something, I would ask. She'd answer everything with no hesitation, and she never broke eye contact.

"What are you going to do when Mason and Logan find out about me?" she asked me one night.

"Tell them the truth, the whole truth, and nothing but the truth." It would be game over. I was in a stall-and-evade battlefront right now. I asked her, "What did you tell Sebastian?"

Her jaw hardened. "Nothing. He doesn't deserve to know a damn thing."

That sounded good to me, and there'd been no sightings or even a phone call from him since I left their parents' house, but I knew my luck would run out at some point.

When I got home from my class one day, that day came.

I opened the door, and there he was. Park Sebastian was standing inside our dorm room, looking at something on my desk. His hand reached out, and he turned a piece of paper over.

"Get out." The door was about to slam shut behind me. I stuck a foot out, stopping it, and folded my arms over my chest. "Now."

A slow grin was his response. "Long time no see, Samantha."

"Step away from the desk."

He laughed but did as I'd asked. I pulled a shoe out to keep the door propped open, and I went to see whatever he'd been spying on. It was a note Summer left.

Sam,

Went to eat with my mom. Be back tonight.

Summer

P.S. I called campus security. They're going to change the locks.

I looked up at Sebastian, whose smile turned smug.

I read the rest of the note.

My brother won't have a key anymore.

XOXO

"Give me the key." I held my hand out.

Crumpling the note up, I tossed it in the garbage as Sebastian made a show of leaning forward and inspecting my hand.

Another irritating chuckle came from him. "My sister forgot that I have the same connections she does. She should remember to use a different key guy the next time she wants to pull a fast one on me."

"You shouldn't have a key anyway. I could report you."

He studied me, pursing his lips together, and shook his head. "No, I don't think you will. Kinda like I don't think you want anyone to know I'm in here."

As he said that, he kicked the shoe out from the door. It went into the hallway, and the door shut. He turned around now, blocking the door, and I was a captive in my own room.

My nostrils flared. "Get. Out."

"No."

I grabbed my phone and unlocked the screen. "I'm not bullshitting. Leave, or I'll call 911."

"Mason will find out."

My shoulder lifted. "Game's over. Get ready for a new kind of fight."

Suddenly, whatever teasing attitude he'd had was dropped. A dangerous glint showed in his eyes, and the air in the room seemed to drop five degrees. I felt a chill graze over my skin.

"I'm not the bad guy here."

"Yet, you're in my dorm room, blocking my door, telling me you're not the bad guy?" My chin lifted. "Like I already said, get out." I waved the phone at him. The threat was still there.

"Fine, I'll go, but just remember that your boyfriend was the one who burned my house down. He got away with that."

"Really?" I rolled my eyes. "Do we have to list off who's worse than the other one? Oh, and by the way, it was so nice of you not to tell your sister everything you had done. You tried to control Mason first. You started all of this."

He grew quiet. "You might think you have my sister on your side, but you're forgetting another thing."

"Oh, yeah? What's that?"

"She's family." He opened the door, his gaze trailed over my shoulder. "You'd be surprised by what you do for family."

He left.

I had a sick feeling as I glanced behind me. Right there, in the smack center of my desk, was a picture of Mason, Logan, and me. The picture was taken at David and Malinda's wedding. All three of us had our arms around the others with wide smiles facing the camera. It'd been on my shelf among the rest of my photographs.

Sebastian put it there on purpose. A shiver wound down my spine.

CHAPTER TWENTY

Pins and needles.

That was the feeling over the next few weeks.

Everyone was waiting for the big explosion because it was coming. Everyone could feel it. I was waiting. Mason and Logan must've been waiting. Sebastian and Summer, too. And even Heather. When we went back to Fallen Crest for Thanksgiving, she'd asked if anything had happened yet. Nothing. It was the calm before the storm.

When we went back to school for the last month before the long holiday break, it was more of the same.

Waiting.

Tension.

There were whispers of a threat. People heard that Logan set fire to a car. He and Mason weren't saying anything, so I assumed that was a rumor. The next gossip claimed that Nate tried to get Sebastian expelled from school, but again, Mason and Logan didn't say a word to me.

What did I do?

What I was doing right now. Studying and wanting to rip my hair out because there was no way I could memorize every famous psychologist, all of their theories, laws, and principles, and every tiny function of the brain.

The door to our study room in the library was kicked open.

Logan had a pizza in one hand, his bag thrown over his shoulder, and a grocery bag filled with energy drinks in his other hand. He proclaimed, "I'm here, bitches. Let's get the studying going."

Before anyone could say a word, he dropped everything on the table and pumped his arms forward and back, like he was a machine gun. And for the grand finale, he swung his leg over an empty chair, slid down into it, and his arms crossed so that his elbow landed on the table at the same time as when his palm propped up his head. He batted his eyelids at Summer. "What's happening, hot stuff?"

She dropped her pen into her book. "Did you just quote *Sixteen Candles* to me?"

His eyelids fluttered, and two dimples showed in his cheeks. "Does it make you horny?"

"No." She scowled.

He didn't care. His cocky grin went up a notch. "My name could be Long Duck Dick for you. Does that make you horny?"

"You're messing with me on purpose. Stop it." She poked at the pizza box. "We can't have food in the library."

"Yeah, we can and I haven't even started. Do you like cupcakes? Because I do, and ass-skirts. Just putting that out there." She sent him a warning look and Logan dropped the flirting, his grin deepening. He leaned back, hooking his fingers behind his head. "How do you think I brought it in here? Walked right past the librarians."

"You can't have food like this. Sandwiches, salads, bags of chips—we can have those. But a large pizza? You're going to get us kicked out, and I don't know about the rest," she cast Mason and me a look, her eyebrows locking together, "but I can't study at my dorm. Kitty and Nina have a rotating schedule of their meltdowns. If Kitty's not crying about how she's going to fail poli-sci, she's comforting Nina with her full-blown dry-heaving panic attacks. Like I said, I can't study there."

Logan frowned. "I was joking before, but seriously, you need to get laid. You're wound too tight to get any real studying done." He wasn't looking at her as he said that. He reached forward and flipped the pizza box open.

I didn't move. I waited, watching my roommate. Beside me, Mason was doing the same. Her scowl morphed into blind panic as Logan talked, and it changed to speculation.

She was going to do it.

I saw the wheels spinning, and as Logan took a slice of pizza and started eating it, she studied him. Her eyes slid over him, taking in his hair and how he got a crew cut, going down his throat as he was swallowing the pizza, moving to his hands and how he folded the pizza in half. He took one, large bite, devouring half the slice right there. Her eyes lingered on his shoulders, which were accentuated by the shirt he was wearing. His shoulders were broad, and the shirt showcased how his bicep muscles were cut and sculpted, rippling as he leaned forward for another bite of pizza.

She shoved back her chair, throwing me a pleading look. "Don't think less of me."

Logan looked up. "Huh?"

Summer grabbed his hand and yanked him behind her. "We need to find a closet."

His eyebrows shot up in the air, but he flashed us a grin and waved the pizza at us while Summer led him around a bookshelf. Right as they did, he stuffed the rest of the pizza down and hurried, catching up with Summer, his hands on her hips.

Mason grunted as he got up and shut the door again. "We got thirty minutes."

I laughed, focusing on my laptop again. "I say twenty." A large envelope was tossed on the desk, and I grew distracted. "What is that?" It was wrinkled from wear and tear. One corner of the envelope was ripped open, and the edge of a photograph peeked out. My mouth dried up, and my tongue felt like a lump of coal.

This was not good.

Mason leaned back. I felt his gaze on me, but I was too scared to look. I had a suspicion of what might be in those pictures.

Swallowing over a lump, I asked, "What are those?"

He shoved them closer to me. "Why don't you take a look?"

My gaze lifted to his. *Bull's-eye.*

Contained anger stared back at me. He was heated, really heated.

I licked my lips. "Mason—"

He interrupted, "I hired someone for you."

"What?"

"The day after you moved in, I called a company that my dad uses. I wanted someone guarding you because I was worried about you. Sebastian can hurt me in a lot of ways, but you and Logan are where I'm most vulnerable."

"Did you..."

"Yes," he answered the rest of my unspoken question. "I hired a security guy for Logan, too, but he doesn't know it."

A headache was pressing behind my forehead. "That means that you..." *Summer. Her parents' house. Garrett even.* I hadn't said a word about any of it. I didn't know how to explain that I'd seen Sebastian or how I knew about my little sister or Sebastian.

Mason knew who Summer was.

He was staring back at me, pinning me down.

A memory came back.

"My dad has a weakness for weak women."

Again, there was no judgment. It was a fact, and he said it as such. The truth of it held more power because of the lack of emotion with him.

My throat went dry. "You called my mother weak."

"Isn't she?"

His gaze was searing into mine.

My chest tightened. My throat clamped up. "I, uh—"

He snorted in disgust. "You think so, too, but you can't say the words, not to me. That's all right. I understand. She's your blood."

He looked away, and again, my whole body almost fell from the chair. It was as if he had pinned me in place, but now I was free from the hold.

My hands curled in on themselves, and I couldn't stop my fingers from trembling. I tucked them between my legs and took a breath. I needed to gain control of myself again.

In that moment, I realized that he always had that effect on me. The ice façade I reined over myself would be plucked away whenever his attention was on me. He'd reach over and take it away, like I was a baby with candy.

"Does my mom know you don't like her?" It was a weird question, but I wanted to know how he thought. I wanted to understand him.

He grinned at me. The power of that look with his piercing eyes, perfect teeth, and square jaw had me pinned against my chair again. I couldn't breathe for a moment.

Mason could always see inside of me. Of course, he had known. Of course, he'd had a plan.

I closed my eyes. "What do you know?"

"I didn't hire someone to spy on you. It was for security measures, but he came to me before break and gave me those."

He opened the envelope and began lying out the photographs. It was what I'd thought. The first one was Summer and I going into her father's house. The next was of Sebastian arriving. I was leaving the house in the third. My face was pale. Tears were streaming down my cheeks. I touched them now. I hadn't realized I was crying. Summer ran after me. The two of us were talking in the next few.

We walked back to the house where Garrett and Sebastian were waiting for us. Both of them were sitting down, their elbows resting on their knees. They'd stood as we approached. All four of us stood in a group, but that'd been when I was saying good-bye. I had Garrett drive me back to the dorm, and even after I'd decided to use Summer to get close to her brother, I had my phone out. I was about to call Mason and Logan to help me move out of the room. I sat in Garrett's car for thirty minutes, trying to decide.

I said to Mason, "He went to school with Summer's parents. There's a professor here they know, too."

"The one who asked to see you after class?"

I nodded. It stung to tell him everything I kept secret, but it was freeing. The more I told him, the faster it came out. I was rushing at the end, barely able to get a breath. I felt bad. I didn't know what else to do. I wanted to protect him—at any cost. Summer could be trusted. Summer loathed her brother.

"There's more."

Mason was unreadable, which was never good. But he was waiting.

"Sharon's pregnant."

"Garrett's wife?"

I nodded. "I'm going to be a big sister, Mason." I grabbed his hand. "I'm going to have a little sister."

He was quiet. No congratulations came. No, *I'm happy for you*, or, *That'll be great*. He was just silent, watching me. My eyes fell back to the envelope, and one more picture was in there.

I kept one item to myself.

He took it out and laid it before me. I sucked in my breath. My chest was tight. It wanted to implode in me, but there it was—the one picture I knew Mason would be livid about. It'd been taken through my window from outside. Sebastian was inside my room, standing next to my desk, and I was coming into the room. The door looked closed behind me, even though it hadn't been. I put a shoe there, but the picture hadn't caught that.

I couldn't talk.

My throat was burning.

"Did he touch you?"

My head whipped up. I was horrified. "No!" *Did he think that?* "No. God, no, Mason. He was there, but I think he wanted to intimidate me. That was it. All he said was that he wasn't the bad guy." I told him the rest, "Summer tried to get the locks changed that day. He had a key. When she came back that night, I told her about it, and she looked like she wanted to cry. I think him showing up was more about scaring her than me. He said to tell her that she should've used someone new, that she wasn't the only one with connections at the school. I assumed the whole thing was about changing the locks."

"She went against him?"

"Yeah." I frowned.

He was still so cold. There was no heat in his tone. He didn't touch me, to reassure or comfort me. He was like a stranger.

An ice-cold shiver wound down my spine.

This was the dangerous and calculating Mason everyone was scared to go against. I was with him in the room. For once, I wasn't protected by him. I knew Mason loved me. I knew he wouldn't do anything to harm me, but I felt what others felt. It was within his ability to destroy them.

My pulse was pounding. I could barely hear over it. And Mason was still withdrawn from me, lost in his thoughts now.

I murmured, "You protect me." My voice was a hoarse whisper. "I wanted to protect you back."

He shoved back his chair.

He was leaving. I already felt the sting of his absence.

"Mason, please."

He stuffed his textbook, his notebook, his pen into his bag. His laptop was last, and he paused, holding it, as we heard laughter coming from the bookshelves. Logan and Summer were coming back. The door was made of glass, so I turned, keeping my head hidden so that they couldn't see signs of my distress.

Mason was still guarded. "I don't want a word of this to Logan."

I nodded, but I didn't respond. It hurt too much to even attempt to talk.

"If you think you can trust her, you're wrong." Mason finished putting his laptop into his bag.

He was acting calm, which made the pain press even harder down on me. Sliding his bag onto his back, he went to the door, but he held it, so Logan and Summer couldn't get in at first. I couldn't look, but I knew he looked back at me.

"I know—fuck it. I need time." His voice was clearer.

"Dude." Logan knocked on the glass. "She won't let me go for another round, so can you let us in? I'm finals-stressed, too."

Mason didn't let them in. He said to me, "She's his family. Don't assume that wasn't a big act for you, showing that she was going against him."

I frowned. "But—"

And it didn't matter.

Mason opened the door, an easy grin on his face, as he waved Logan and Summer back in.

Logan clapped him on the shoulder. "Record time, big brother."

"I wouldn't brag about that."

He shrugged, dropping back into his seat. "She said to stuff it in and pump until she came. I meant, a record time for *her*." Logan didn't down his cocky smirk. "I do believe I made the Kade name proud tonight."

Summer groaned, coming in and sitting beside Logan. "Don't tell me you measure your manliness by your lengths."

"Uh," Logan held a finger in the air, "again, I wasn't lying when I said my name was Long Duck Dick, but we don't. We measure our manliness in how satisfied our women are."

"Shut up." Summer moaned again, shaking her head. She grabbed her book and got busy highlighting it.

She was not looking at the rest of us, so Logan turned to Mason, and his grin slipped a bit. He looked to me, and his grin vanished completely. He lingered on Summer's bent head.

Nothing was said, but Logan knew.

We weren't that great of actors.

Mason met my gaze. He was still holding everything back, but I caught a glimpse of his rage. I saw anguish, too. I hurt him, and that had a lump forming in my throat again.

I never wanted to hurt him. I only wanted to protect him.

He left, and Logan looked back to me. He was going to demand to know what just happened, but I had no clue what I was going to say to him.

I was suddenly so very tired.

Logan waited until we got back to the dorm. Summer stayed behind, claiming she needed to study more, and she might've, but I caught the uneasy look she cast in Logan's direction. I had a hunch she wanted to avoid that whole situation. When we went inside the lounge, I thought he'd start in or go home. He walked with me upstairs.

Ruby's door was open. She saw us, and immediately shoved it closed.

It swung open a second later, and Blaze popped his head out. His eyes lit up when he saw Logan. "My man!" Wearing only gym shorts, he came out with his fist up and ready to be pounded. "How's it going?"

The two bumped fists. Logan threw me a look. He was annoyed, but he replied with an easygoing grin, "Hey, man. It's good. How are you?"

Blaze patted him on the shoulder. "Are we partying anytime soon?" He stepped close and lowered his voice. "There's a rumor that Sebastian's having a big end-of-finals blowout. The location's secret, but I think we can find out where. You up for it?"

"Are you kidding me?" The fake easygoing facade was dropped. Logan stared at him, long and hard.

Blaze's smile slipped, and he stepped back. "What are you talking about?"

"You're going to seek out a party and do what?"

Blaze glanced to me. He was asking me if Logan was playing with him. He wasn't. I leveled him with a dark look, too. I didn't know what was going on, why Logan was acting like this, but I had my own problems. Mason had been cold to me. Mason was never cold to me. I had to make that right.

Blaze was laughing again, a forced note in there. "Nah, man. I mean, like last time."

"Last time wasn't planned. Sebastian's crew wasn't prepared for us."

"Yeah...I mean..." Blaze's eyes darted around. He lifted a hand to scratch his chin. "We could do it again. More guys, too."

Logan bit out a laugh. "Really? You think it's just like that? A bigger crew. You crash his party, and what? You'll walk out like a man? Because you started another fight?"

Whoa. What?

Ruby came to stand at her door. I heard more doors opening. Kitty and Nina poked their heads out, too.

Blaze took another step backward. His hand fell from his chin to his shoulder. His arm looked like he was shielding his bare chest. "That's what you did. Why not?" He lifted a shoulder. "It could happen. What's wrong with that?"

Logan's eyes flashed in anger.

I remembered the bruises on Logan's face at the home game. Sebastian's face had bruises, too.

"Because there's been no blowback."

"Yeah?" Blaze reared his head back. He was clueless. "So? That's good, right?"

"There's always blowback." Logan's jaw firmed. "Haven't you ever been in a fight before? You wait for the blowback. You don't search it out. Whatever he's got going, he'll be ready for another fight. Trust me on this."

"The location is top secret. He's not going to expect anything." He jerked his head in my direction. "Sam can get the location."

I sucked in a breath. *Oh, shit.*

Logan paused, stiffening, and turned to me. He was suddenly thoughtful now. I knew he was remembering whatever spat I'd had with Mason. He asked in a too quiet voice, "And how would Sam get the location so easily?"

"Because of her roommate. She's Sebastian's sister."

Ruby gasped behind him.

Blaze quieted. The sides of his mouth sank down. He looked from her horrified face to my very still one and to Logan's darkening expression. One last step backward, Blaze muttered under his breath, "Oops." He disappeared inside Ruby's room.

She snapped at Kitty and Nina, "Get back to studying!"

Both of them hurried inside, slamming their door behind them.

More doors closed softly, and at the end, it was Logan and me.

He ground out, his eyes flashing in anger, "Mason knows?"

It was Confession Time 2.0. I jerked my head up and down. "Yeah."

"That's what your tiff was about?"

"Somewhat."

He didn't reply to that but asked, "How long?"

"Mason told me he knew before the break."

"That was two weeks ago."

I swallowed over a knot. "I know."

"How long have you known?"

"Longer than that."

"How long, Sam?" he clipped out. A vein in his neck twitched.

"A few weeks." It'd been three before that—one week where I was scared shitless, wondering what the hell I was doing; a second week where I was racked with guilt and shame because I was lying to my family, and they were the only ones I shouldn't have been lying to; and the third week where I felt like everyone was going to find out. I wouldn't have been able to make it all worth it. Everything would've been for nothing, which was happening right now.

"A few weeks?" he parroted.

I cringed, hearing the same emotion that Mason had masked in the library.

I'd hurt both of them now.

My door opened. I saw it. I didn't believe it, and it didn't register at first.

Wait, my roommate is still in the library.

There was only one other person...

I burst into action. *Screw this.*

Logan was going to see him. There was no way I could've gotten him to leave the hallway, and there was no reason to lie anymore.

I shoved past Logan, going for my room. I was almost there when Sebastian's head cleared the doorway. I cried out, "You were in there again?"

"Again?" I heard from behind me.

Sebastian saw me. His eyes trailed past me and rounded.

That was all I saw before Logan was around me. He grabbed Sebastian's shirt, hauled him into the hallway, and slammed him against the wall. "Again? You were in Sam's room before?"

Time slowed. I ground to a halt, and I saw it happening, but I couldn't stop it. I couldn't do anything. Someone started screaming, and I might as well have heard a bomb going off.

All the undercurrents of violence, the tension, and everything that had been building over the last month were coming to a head. And it was going to happen in my dorm hallway.

Logan's face was scrunched up. I glimpsed his eyes. He wasn't holding back. No matter what Sebastian said, it wouldn't change a thing. Logan was going to hurt him, one way or another.

But nothing else was spoken anyway.

As soon as Sebastian's head hit the wall, Logan's fist was coming up to punch him.

Sebastian saw it. He wore the same look as Logan. Snarling, his nostrils flaring, he brought up an arm to block Logan. He hit Logan with the other hand in a crosscut. Logan's head snapped back. I was grabbed and jerked out of the way.

Whoever was screaming kept screaming.

I rolled my arm up and around, breaking the hold on me.

The screaming stopped.

I rushed forward. I stopped thinking. Logan couldn't get hurt, but he must've sensed my intention.

He yelled, not looking away from Sebastian, "Get her away from him! *Now!*" He dodged Sebastian's hit and landed an uppercut to Sebastian's rib cage.

The fight was on after that.

I tried getting free and running in, but I couldn't. Whoever was holding me had a cement-like grasp on me.

Sebastian threw Logan off, going with him against a wall and raining punches to his side and stomach. Logan doubled over, his arms up to block the hits. Sebastian switched, bringing his elbow down on Logan's head, but Logan feinted, caught Sebastian's elbow, and slammed him into the other wall. He was on the offense this time. Sebastian went on the defense until they switched again.

It was deathly quiet in the hallway. No one was saying anything. No one was doing anything. Sebastian and Logan kept exchanging punches until we heard a stampede of feet coming up the stairs. We felt them at first, and the crowd looked back.

It was a bunch of Sebastian's friends. They were coming to help him.

The hold on me disappeared, and Blaze stepped out in front of the guys. His hands were up. "Hey. Whoa, whoa. That's no longer a fair fight."

The friends didn't care. The guy leading their charge took one look at Blaze. An ugly grin appeared, and he knocked Blaze out. He didn't break his stride. Then they were all on Logan.

"No!" I took off and screamed over my shoulder, "Call the police, Ruby!"

She was glued back against the hallway, her phone clutched in her hands. The blood drained from her face long ago.

I screamed one last time, watching with a sickening feeling, as I saw Logan get picked up and slammed back down on the floor. They started to kick him.

"*Ruby!*"

Kitty grabbed the phone from Ruby's hands and punched in the numbers. She yelled at the guys, "I'm calling the cops, you assholes!" She twisted around. "Nina, tape those fuckers."

Help was coming. I tried telling myself that, but they kept kicking Logan. It wouldn't come fast enough.

I was going in. I had to try.

"Sam! No!"

I didn't know who yelled at me, but I looked around for a weapon. There was nothing—until I saw the fire extinguisher. It was big. It'd have to do.

Nina was ahead of me.

She was coming out of her room with her phone in hand, pointed right at the group, and a bat in her other hand. I took the bat and shattered the glass. Nina took the bat again while I pulled the extinguisher out.

"Here." Kitty gave Ruby's phone to Nina. "Talk to them." She took the bat from Nina and shared a look with me.

It was the two of us.

I nodded, gripping the extinguisher with a firm hold. She nodded and started forward with me.

I pulled the pin, aimed the extinguisher, and squeezed the trigger, sweeping from side to side. It hit the guys, and they fell back, slightly stunned. It didn't faze the others, and Kitty ran in. She lifted the bat, already swinging. One guy bent down to hit Logan's head. Kitty swung the bat, getting the guy clear under his chin. He snapped back, and she hit two of his friends. She kept going.

I kept squeezing the trigger, using the extinguisher on them. When I was out, I took the handle and began swinging like Kitty.

The guys could've taken the weapons from us. It would've been so easy, but they seemed dazed by the sudden turn of events. We waded in. I got close enough to Logan, and I swung one last time. I clipped Sebastian on the forehead, but he grabbed the extinguisher. I let him have it, even shoving it at him. He was pushed off-balance. As he was knocked backward,

I grabbed Logan around the arm and dragged him into my room.

"Kitty!" I yelled.

Her back was to me. She jumped there to protect us, and she was swinging the bat again. She couldn't hear me. I tugged her backward.

I yelled at Nina, "Get in your room, so they can't take the phone."

After that, I slammed my door shut, locked it, and sank down with my back against it. My pulse was racing. My arms and legs started trembling, but I had to keep it together.

Logan still needed me.

"Kitty," I croaked.

She was standing above me, her chest heaving. She was holding on to that bat like they were going to shove their way inside. "What?"

"I need you to call someone for me."

She looked down at me. I couldn't even hold on to my knees. Even my teeth were rattling against each other.

"Okay." She patted me on the head. "I'll call your boyfriend for you."

I looked up, my jaw trembling. "Thank you."

CHAPTER TWENTY-ONE
MASON

Logan got his ass kicked by Sebastian and four of his friends. They'd beaten my best friend. I gazed at Sam over Logan's hospital bed and knew she was next. They might not physically beat her, but they were going to beat her down somehow. She was right in the aim of fire. If she didn't see that, she was an idiot.

No matter who got hurt, I was Sebastian's main target. I'd been sitting back this whole time. I had been waiting. Sam was going to be his weapon against me. I knew it. I was just waiting for the warm-up before he struck.

That time was now.

Logan was kept for observation overnight and released.

That was the beginning of his troubles. The school board asked the police department to step back. It was between college students and occurred on campus. They wanted to deal with it internally. Because Cain University was powerful and a Division One school, the department stepped back, which everyone was happy about—except for Logan and everyone on his side.

The board found Logan guilty of the altercation between students. He'd swung first. He got the blame, and the meeting today was to officially determine if he'd get expelled from school or just suspended. And because it stemmed from my own run-ins with Sebastian, I was called to testify. I knew what I was walking into. They were going to ask me questions about Logan's past—if he was violent, if he started physical altercations. What else had he done? Had he been arrested? How many times was he arrested?

Logan could get expelled for the mere fact that he'd swung first, but the real agenda was to discredit him so that he looked like the *only* guilty perpetrator. They didn't want to suspend Sebastian.

"Is your dad coming today?"

I looked up from fixing my tie. Sam was on the edge of our bed, watching me in the mirror.

Since Logan's attack, she'd been different. The fight left her. Her cheeks were gaunt. She seemed more fragile. I knew she hadn't been eating, and her runs had been back up to two hours, sometimes more. I'd started driving around, looking for her, and so many times, I'd find her limping back. She always climbed into the vehicle, and I would bring her home. I'd tended to her while Malinda came and tended to Logan until our mother got in from Italy. That'd been two days ago. Malinda hadn't wanted to leave, but we'd return to Fallen Crest within a few days anyway.

Finals were done.

Football was done. We hadn't gotten to the championship game, even though Drew won The Heisman.

The only thing I had to deal with was this meeting…and Park Sebastian.

"Mason," Sam said again, tucking her hands under her legs.

She'd been doing that a lot lately, always hiding her hands.

My mouth twisted, and a jolt of anger started in me. She was still rattled from the fight. She would shake at night, tossing and turning. Some nights, she'd wake up, screaming. I hadn't been there, and I'd have to live with that for the rest of my life.

She leaned forward, still searching my face in the mirror.

I cleared my throat, finishing the tie, before I turned around. "I hope so. I think so. Helen said she got ahold of him."

She relaxed visibly, her shoulders softening. "Oh, good."

Sam and I hadn't resolved what happened in the library when I found out she knew Summer was Sebastian's sister. I didn't care who Summer was, but I cared if she hurt Sam or not. I also cared that Sam hadn't told me, but even that…I understood that, too. She and my brother both protected me this year. It was still their mission. Sam and I needed to smooth things over, but I didn't think either of us had the energy to approach that conversation yet.

I sighed and reached out for her hand. "Come on. Let's go deal with these board dickheads."

Sam's cheeks grew pink, and she linked her fingers through mine, squeezing my hand. She walked beside me out the door and remained by my side the entire drive to campus and into the building.

When we got inside, everyone was ready. My dad wasn't there, but he was coming. I hoped. There weren't a lot of times when I needed him, but I did for these moments. My jaw hardened, thinking about needing my father. I hated it, but I couldn't do anything about it.

"Mr. Kade." A woman in a business skirt opened the boardroom doors.

I recognized her from the last time I'd been called in there. That meeting was eerily similar. It was after Sebastian and his buddies jumped me, but instead of questioning if only one of us should be expelled, they decided to suspend both of us.

Some anger grew in me, but I nodded, my entire body tense.

Sam squeezed my hand once more, and I skimmed a soft kiss to her forehead, hugging her to my side. As we stood there, the lady went back inside. Right before the door closed behind her, I got a glimpse of Sebastian. He was sitting at the same table as before, wearing a business suit, with two others beside him. He'd brought a lawyer.

I growled, "This isn't supposed to be a trial."

"Mason?"

Sam hadn't seen him, and I didn't want her to.

My hand found her hip, and I gently moved her back. "I'll be back. Love you."

"Love you, too."

I heard a small wonder in her voice as she said those two words, but I couldn't do anything about it. I turned abruptly and went inside. She sensed my anger, and I knew she wanted to help, but she couldn't.

This was my mess to clean up. The first step to do that was going into the boardroom and sitting at the table.

"Thank you for coming in, Mason."

There were six board members. All of them sat across from me with their stern asshole faces. It'd been the same after my fight with Sebastian and his buddies. I hadn't struck first with my altercation. Logan had. That was a big difference in their eyes, but they were stuck-up pricks. They weren't taking the common factor into account—the dick sitting at the table on my right, Park Sebastian. His crew, his fault.

"Mason," the spokeswoman prompted me again.

I scowled. "Am I going to be able to have my say in here?"

Surprise flitted across her face. Her lips mashed together. Her eyes blinked a few times, and her head moved back an inch. She cleared her throat. "Why wouldn't you?"

"Because you've deemed my brother guilty already."

"Well." She looked up and down her table.

The other members all gave varying motions of support. One nodded. Another moved his head down. A third gave her a slight grin. The fourth lifted his finger in the air.

She was reassured and said further, "Guilt goes to the first aggressor. In your situation, it was Mr. Sebastian and his friends. In your brother's case, it was your brother. He struck first. We have witness testimonies and a video clip that speaks to that."

I snorted, cursing. "The video clip didn't show my brother hitting Sebastian first. The clip showed him on the ground while Sebastian and four of his friends ganged up on him. The rest of the clip is where my girlfriend and her friend waded in to save him. And why did you bring up the video clip? You threw it out, said it wasn't helpful."

"Mason," she spoke in that pretentious and condescending manner that my mom used.

I was gritting my teeth. I interrupted her, "Stop, lady."

The other members sat upright.

One pointed at me, leaning forward from his seat. "You'll show respect, son."

"I'm not your son," I whipped back to him. "Can we just drop the fucking act here? You want to expel my brother, but you don't want to piss off Sebastian by suspending him. Sorry. Anytime there's one against five, the one guy isn't kicked out."

"There wouldn't have been an altercation if your brother hadn't started it."

"Bullshit." I jerked a finger in Sebastian's direction. "There was an altercation last year with me. Same guy. Same scenario. I took on six of his friends."

"Yes, and you were both suspended for that."

"Both of us, even though they hit me first."

"Mason," the spokeswoman started to say again.

I shook my head. "No. No. I'm not your friend. I'm not your son. You don't know me. The only things you care about is my record on the football field and if I go pro next year or not. That's the only reason you brought me in here. Own up to that. You don't want to piss me off either."

They were quiet. I was right, and the slight guilt on their faces told me that.

"Who do you think I am? You think you can pull me in here, and what? Brainwash me to sell out my brother? Manipulate me? Is that what this is about?"

"Mr. Kade," the guy on the end spoke up. He sat forward, placing his folded hands on the table. His striped business suit looked like it was bursting at the seams. He was the type who was pissed that this meeting was cutting into his time with his mistress before going to see his second mistress while his wife got drunk and ordered a new mare for their neglected teenage daughter.

I said before he could continue, "You all are forgetting some things. I don't push my weight around like Sebastian does, but that doesn't mean I don't live in your world. None of you scare me. I grew up throwing water balloons filled with piss on people like you while you attended my father's sleazy parties. You're that type of people. The money in here can't push me around because—sorry, Sebastian, but I'm pretty sure your father's not in my dad's league—if that's what this is about, be prepared for me to push back."

"Mr. Kade—"

"Mason." A new voice filled the room.

My football coach came in. He stopped inside the door and stared at me, his chest heaving up and down. He jerked out the chair beside me and sat down. His breathing was ragged. "I've never heard you speak like that."

"This is what you're playing?" I ignored him, addressing the board. "The football card? You think my coach is going to make me heel?"

"Mason!"

I started to shove back my chair. This was enough. They were putting me in a corner, and I wouldn't go there. I wouldn't make it okay for them to expel my brother while Sebastian got away, scot-free.

The second woman snapped her fingers at me and pointed to the chair. "Stay there."

She was different. The others looked like they thought they were important. They kept glancing at Sebastian and whoever's support he had. The looks were nervous and cautious but not this woman. She was leaning back in her chair the whole time, only giving support to her fellow board members

She was calm. Her voice was soft as she spoke now, "I'm going to do something that will shock the pants off you."

I doubted that.

She laughed, waving her finger at me. "You've got some spunk, Mr. Kade. I can see how you look at us, and I'll tell you something." She leaned forward over the table. Her pearl necklace fell, grazing across the top of the table. "You're completely right."

"Miriam," the other spokeswoman gasped. "What are you doing?"

Miriam ignored her and ignored the mutterings from the other men on the board. She waved at them, looking at me. "I do think it's horrid how they've ignored Mr. Sebastian's history, and it's not just with your family. Mr. Sebastian is a regular visitor to these meetings. Everyone up here knows that he's the problem, even though I highly doubt that you and your brother are saints. A certain house that burned down where no one could prove that it was by your hands is one example that comes to mind, but yes, in the grand scheme of things, the problem is Mr. Sebastian. However, the other problem for us is his father. Do you know what happens every time Mr. Sebastian comes in here?" She rubbed her finger against her thumb, grinning at me. "Money, Mason. His daddy comes in and writes a big-ass check for the school."

"Miriam!"

"Shut it, Aggie. This kid is a straight shooter, so I'm telling him the facts, not like anyone else in here will argue this anyway." She shot all of them a warning look before addressing me again, "You know what else his daddy does? He drops a lot of names, reminding us how connected he is, and this board does the same thing every time. We let him push us around—just like we're going to let him do again. One, it's good for the school, and that's always our main priority, but the other reason is because his father will continue to support this school even after his son has graduated. Because we have endured so much shit for this kid, Mr. Sebastian will come back and support the college financially long into his life. The cycle will continue. His kids will be pricks, too, just like him, but he'll come in and write a big check. That kid will be given a pass, over and over again. It's the way of life for some of us here."

She tapped her finger on the table and held it there. Her eyes looked right at me. They were alert, intelligent, and focused. One of her eyebrows lifted. "What are you going to do, Mr. Kade? You're a hell of a football player, but that's all you're giving us. With all those politics and all that money, why would we choose you over Mr. Sebastian here? Give it to me straight, just like I did with you." She leaned back and folded her arms over her chest. "Give me a good argument, so we can suspend your brother instead of expelling him."

My eyebrows bunched forward. They already deemed him guilty. This meeting was about getting Sebastian suspended. Now, she was saying Logan could be saved?

I was taken aback, and so were the others, as their heads snapped to attention, craning to look at Miriam. She wasn't looking at them, only at me.

She held out her hand to me before folding it back under her arm. "Let's hear it, Mr. Kade. The floor is yours."

"Mason."

Another new voice spoke up, coming into the room. This time, I closed my eyes. My shoulders sagged in relief.

He came up, his hand a comforting weight on my back, as he patted me there before clearing his throat. "May I sit beside my son, please?"

"Oh." My coach stood abruptly and moved down a seat. "We've never met before. I'm Mason's coach."

"James Kade."

They shook hands.

My father turned to the board. "I'd like the boys to both be excused." He spoke right to the Miriam lady, "I believe I have what you're asking for."

Her lips pursed together before lifting into a knowing grin. She waved a finger at the other board members. "I say that's fine with all of us here. Mason, Park, you both can go to the waiting lounge."

Sebastian pushed up to his feet but didn't move from the table. "What is going on here?"

"Nothing for you to worry about." She gestured to the door. "When your father comes with his checkbook, you'll let him know that he can contact my office directly. You can leave. Now." She pinned me down with her gaze. "It was a pleasure, Mr. Kade. I am not bullshitting you when I say that I hope you'll continue to have a promising future at Cain University and, hopefully, after you go on to your future pursuits. You're a straight shooter, and we need more of them around here. You could be a real asset for the university."

I nodded and started for the door.

"Mason," my dad caught my arm, "don't leave. I'd like to talk to you after this."

"You're going to make them keep Logan, right?"

"Of course." He nodded. "That's one thing I've always done well over the years. Sam looks ready to cry out there. She needs you."

That was an understatement. I wanted to hug my dad, an emotion I hadn't felt for a long time, but I went to the lounge.

Sebastian went ahead of me, so Sam and Nate were on their feet, waiting for me. She was fidgeting with her hands, watching Sebastian with a nervous look through the corner of her eye, before she saw me. Her whole body seemed to pause. Nate, too. They were both waiting to hear the decision.

I said, breaking out into a grin, "My dad will take care of it. Logan will probably just be suspended."

"But..." Nate turned sharply to Sebastian, who stepped to his group in the far corner.

A bunch of his douchebag pals were there along with their girlfriends. I scanned the room, but there was no sight of his sister.

I said, "No. He's still here."

"But..." Nate sputtered some more, his face flushing red. His hands formed into fists before he roughly rubbed at his temples. "This is bullshit, Mason." He raised his voice, pointing at Sebastian. "This is bullshit, Sebastian."

His friends rallied around him.

One retorted, "Shove it, Monson. Our deal with you was between you and the house. You brought them in, not us."

Nate's arm went back down. "What are you talking about?"

"You left us."

Another guy said, "You turned your back on us. The shit could've been handled in-house, but you didn't give us a chance to fix the problem. Park gave you an ultimatum, and you left, like a bitch."

"He was speaking for the house."

"No," a new guy, who was taller and bigger, spoke up.

He had a girl pressed against his side. Her arm was hanging off his arm folded over his chest.

"Park doesn't speak for everyone in the house. He's got a crew, yes, but not all of us would've followed him. You didn't give us a chance to even decide that though. You ran to him." He jerked his chin in my direction.

Nate's eyebrows were permanently locked together. He was staring at the last speaker, almost fixated on him, before he asked, much quieter, "Are you for real? You would've backed me up on that issue?"

The big guy scoffed, jerking a shoulder up and down. "You'll never know now. You're out, Monson. We're here to show support to the brother who didn't hightail it out of the house."

Nate glanced at me before his eyes slid down to the ground. His head hung there. He was going over everything they'd just said.

Sam pressed against my side, watching the exchange. I felt her trembling, and I swept a hand out to catch her on her hip. I anchored her to me. As soon as I did, her body calmed. She grew firm, as if taking my strength into her.

I met the bigger guy's gaze and asked, "What's your house policy on girls?"

"What are you talking about?" But the bigger guy glanced at Sam. He knew.

Sebastian looked back at his fraternity brother. He moved forward a step, getting between the two of us. "Stop meddling in our business, Kade."

"None of us would be here if you hadn't tried to meddle in mine."

"Nate was our brother—"

I shot him down, "I'm not talking about Nate."

"What are you talking about?" The big guy moved forward, brushing off the girl.

Sebastian shot him a nervous look.

The big guy didn't care. He said to me, "What do you mean?"

"His politics." I nodded in Sebastian's direction. "He wanted to use my name and connections. He never said anything outright, but it was there. I know when a piece of shit is trying to manipulate me into being one of his patsies. That's what I'm talking about."

A lot could be argued there. I was bringing up undercurrent dynamics, and most could pretend to be ignorant of them.

This guy didn't. He nodded slowly, casting a side look at Sebastian. "That's not what he said to us."

"I'm the president, Clint."

"No." The big guy shook his head, turning to squarely face him. His arms folded over his massive chest again. "You were the president, but the house is gone."

Sebastian sputtered, "Come on. We're not really gone. All the old positions hold—"

"No." His head moved forward. He was almost in Sebastian's face. "They don't. The old positions were disbanded when that house burned down, and we were given the ultimatum to remain as students and not as brothers or remain brothers but not students. You could've gone to another chapter. You didn't. You chose to stay, but the old way burned down when the house did."

"Clint—" Sebastian looked at the rest of their guys.

A few guys shuffled, showing their support for Sebastian. A lot of them didn't. They didn't move an inch. Their faces were impassive.

"Look, this is business we can deal with outside of here." Clint skimmed over Sam, Nate, and me. "Especially now that new information has come forward."

"Clint—" Sebastian started again, a more authoritative bark to his voice.

But the doors opened. My father, my coach, and Sebastian's representative walked out. The board members were with them. They all paused in the waiting room to shake hands. My dad shook each member's hand. All of them were grinning, even Sebastian's representative.

Miriam was the first to leave, passing by me. She slowed and remarked, "I meant what I said in there. I do think you have a promising future, and your father just made it even more promising. Come and see me at my office sometime. I'd like to speak with you."

Sebastian's representative went to him. Their heads bent together before Sebastian reared back, shot me a hostile look, and stormed out. The rest of his friends, Clint included, followed behind at a more sedate pace. Everyone trickled out until it was Nate, Sam, my father, my coach, and me.

My father shook hands with my coach at the door.

My coach said to me, "Keep up with your off-season training, Mason. I'll be seeing you."

When he left, I asked my dad, "Logan's okay?"

James let out a deep breath. "Yeah. He's resting at the house?"

I nodded.

"I'd like to go see him, but yes, you're both fine."

"How much did you pay?"

James cringed. "A lot. Let's just leave it there." He clasped me on the arm and squeezed. "It's good to see you, but I haven't missed these meetings. You boys used to be hard on the bank account, and you still are." He became somber. "I have a feeling things aren't going to be just fine."

He turned to Sam. "Can I talk to you in private for a quick second?"

She straightened, and her mouth opened slightly. "Sure. Uh, yeah."

Nate and I followed them outside. James and Sam migrated toward his vehicle. Nate and I went to mine, but we didn't get inside. We stayed there, leaning against it, as we watched James and Sam talking.

Nate mused, "So…it's our move next?"

My eyes narrowed. I was studying Sam as she continued talking to my dad.

I murmured, "Yeah, it's our move."

Finally.

CHAPTER TWENTY-TWO

SAMANTHA

Here we were.

Mason, Logan, Nate, and I were all in the living room, each in a different corner, as we looked at each other. There was a moment of silence. It was a few hours after the board meeting.

Logan hadn't been ecstatic about Sebastian's lack of punishment, but he couldn't argue with only getting a suspension. James hadn't stayed long. He'd come in, spent an hour talking with Mason and Logan, and taken off again. He mentioned he was going to Fallen Crest and seeing David, but I hadn't asked. The less I knew about Analise, the better.

"Do I need to have a drink for this talk?" Logan broke the silence. He didn't wait. He snapped his fingers at Nate. "My gaysome twosome, get me a beer." He chucked a pillow at him.

Nate chucked it back. "You can walk. Get it yourself."

Logan extended his middle finger.

Nate laughed and then the moment was done. They both quieted and turned to Mason and me. It was time. A shift happened in the air. It went from lighthearted and joking to a grave seriousness.

The butterflies started in my stomach. They weren't the nervous kind. They were the kind where I wanted to puke and run for the next four days straight. The showdown with Sebastian wasn't going to be pretty. I flattened my hand against my stomach, trying to calm those butterflies. I couldn't lose anyone. That was all I was worried about.

"Okay." Mason sat forward.

Everyone tuned into him.

He swept his gaze over the group, lingering on me for a moment. A dark emotion passed in his depths, but I couldn't name it. My mouth became dry.

"We have to move against Sebastian." Mason seemed unwilling to say more. He looked at Nate, Logan, and me again before he stood up.

I asked, "Where are you going?"

Mason stopped in the hallway to his room. He said to me, "I'm getting everything I have on Sebastian. It's time to share it with you guys."

"You have stuff on him?" Heat flared from Logan.

But Mason didn't respond. He returned a moment later with a box in his hand. Putting it down on the coffee table, he stood back and said, "I didn't just hire security for Sam. I hired a private investigator to look into Sebastian. He's connected, and I wanted to know how connected."

Nate pulled some photos from the box, musing, "You mean, to whom he's connected, right?"

"Holy shit," Logan muttered under his breath. He pulled out a pile of papers. His forehead wrinkled. The sides of his mouth turned down. "There are some big names here, big brother. Who did you hire for this job?"

Mason sat down again. "The same guy Dad uses."

"Right on." Logan bobbed his head. "Are you the future Mrs. James Kade? Does Analise have her throne threatened by his own son?" Logan winked at me. "Not to be a dick, but Mama Psychopath scares the shit out of me. I don't think I'd be up for another round against her. I think we were safe to escape with our clothes on our backs from the first round against her."

I reached inside the box when I saw a picture of Garrett. He was with my professor, the same one who said she already knew him. That wasn't the surprising part of it. What caught my eye was the other person in the photo.

I showed it to Mason. "This was taken when they were in college?"

Mason was waiting for me. He nodded, his voice quiet, as he said, "Yes."

I pointed at the other female. "Is that who I think it is?"

"She went to college with Garrett."

"That wasn't an answer." I didn't need him to tell me though. I knew who it was.

Logan asked, "Who is it?"

"My mother."

"Oh."

Another hush of silence fell over the room.

Logan said quietly, "Are you sure?"

Nate darted him a look. "Dude."

I shook my head. "It's okay." And it was.

I already knew that Analise and Garrett went to college together. It wasn't just the three of them in the photograph. She was the one I'd singled out, but as I looked over it, I picked out Sharon, Garrett's now wife, Sebastian's father, and others. They were posing for a group photograph somewhere. It was sunny. Most of them wore sunglasses. They were all dressed for warm weather in tank tops, T-shirts, shorts, and loose skirts for the girls.

I couldn't stop looking at my mother.

Her black hair was pulled up into a braid. She was smiling, but unlike the others, there were no sunglasses to block her eyes. She was looking sideways, up at Garrett, with her hand resting over her stomach. He was standing next to her but not looking at her. His shoulder was forward, so his back was turned slightly toward her, and he had his arm around Sharon's shoulders. His head was angled down, like he'd just shared a secret with her.

Analise wasn't showing, but a sixth sense told me that she was pregnant.

That was me.

I glanced to Mason.

He'd been watching me the whole time, and he nodded. "The PI thought so, too. The timing's right."

I was speechless.

"What?" Nate asked us.

Logan skirted between the two of us. "What's going on?"

I handed him the picture. "I think my mom was pregnant there."

He looked at it and hooted in laughter. "Your mom was sneaky. Holy shitola. And he's still with the other chick. That's his wife now, right?"

I nodded as he passed it to Nate.

"Oh, man." Nate shook his head. "Wow. That's…" He said to me, "Sorry, Sam. That's gotta be weird to see."

It was. A lump was clogging my throat, but I shrugged. "I'm fine."

I wasn't.

I knew it. I heard about it, but the proof was right there. Garrett was still with Sharon. He cheated on her, like how she'd cheated on him later. And Analise...it was just further proof about what type of person she was.

I'd come from two cheaters. I was a product of them.

I felt like I'd been gut-punched, and I couldn't breathe for a moment.

"Sam," Mason softly said my name.

He was going to reassure me, but I didn't want that right now. I knew what Analise was capable of. Tears stung my eyelids, wanting to be shed, but I refused to let them free. I refused to cry over her. This wasn't just about what she did, but what she'd continued to do, what she had done to me all my life.

Lie. Cheat. Hurt. Destroy.

That was my legacy. That was where I'd come from.

"Sam, stop." Mason came over. His hands slid under me.

He was going to pick me up, but I pushed him.

"Stop." I scrambled to my feet and scooted away. My arms crossed over my chest. I couldn't stop looking at that photograph.

"Sam. Come on."

Logan and Nate grew quiet. Nate was still holding the photograph, but Logan grabbed it from him and ripped it in two.

He stood, showing me both pieces. "See? Whatever's in your head, shove it out, Sam. This piece of shit isn't you." He gripped the photo above Analise's head and ripped it again. She was torn in half. "I was joking before. I'll take your mom on any day of the week. I know Mason's ahead of me, and Nate's with us, too. Stop thinking." He showed me the ripped pieces again. "This isn't you."

I looked at Mason. I didn't know what I needed, but he'd have it. He always did, and he came to me now. He pulled me into his arms and sat down on the chair behind him.

I was cradled on his lap as he spoke, "I have to tell you guys what my PI uncovered, and some of it has to do with that photograph."

"The one I shredded just now?"

"Yeah."

"Oh." Logan looked at it again. "Oops."

Nate pulled out some negatives from the box. "We're good. If we need it, I bet we can get it again."

Logan's head lifted. His shoulders bounced up. "Never mind me as I go to burn this piece of shit, and yes, I mean literally. Analise is a piece of shit."

"Logan," Mason called after him.

He was heading to the kitchen but backtracked. "Yeah?"

"Stay here for a bit. You all need to hear this just so you know what we're going up against."

Logan's eyebrows locked forward together. "That doesn't sound good."

Nate grunted.

Mason added, "Because it's not. Park Sebastian is connected in ways that we can't fathom, but we have a card on our side." He grew quiet.

I was perched on his lap, listening, when Logan and Nate both looked at me. Their gazes stopped and settled on me. I felt Mason's attention before I realized he was staring right at me, too. Those butterflies picked up once more, and I swallowed that lump.

I said, "Okay. What do I do?"

And an hour later, the plan was hatched, but things needed to be smoothed over between Mason and me. By an unspoken agreement, we both got up and headed for his room.

Mason closed the door behind us, and I went straight for the bed. Sinking down on his bed, I picked at my shirt while he stood away from me, studying me.

He asked softly, "Are you sure you want to do this?"

That wasn't the question. I had to. I was their only in.

I sighed and looked up at him. "Ask me what you really want to know."

There was an elephant in the room with us, and both of us hadn't talked about it over the last week. Logan's ass-kicking put everything on halt, but here it was. Here we were. It had to be talked about before we could take Park Sebastian down.

Mason let out a soft sigh, sitting on the bed beside me. It sunk under from his weight. I waited, expecting his hand to cover my knee, but it didn't. He sat next to me. His side touched me, but he didn't reach over. In some ways, that felt like a rejection. I yearned for it. I could relax into it, feeling the weight of his hand and arm over me in bed. He shielded me just by touching me. Without it now, I felt cold.

A shiver racked through me. Goose bumps appeared on my skin, but it wasn't from the weather.

"Sam," he started, leaning forward. His elbows rested on his knees, and his head bent over them. He clasped his hands together, forming one big fist, and he reached up, his forehead touching them for a split moment. "Fuck." He expelled a deep breath. "Why did you lie to me?"

There it was—my deceit.

I shot back, "Why did you lie to me?"

"What?" He shifted, looking at me.

I raised my chin. "You heard me. You lied, too."

"I lied for your protection."

"Bullshit."

"What?"

I felt bad about it—at first. Then, I started thinking, and the anger I shoved down was coming up. Mason was addressing it, which meant all those emotions could finally be dealt with.

I said, "You lied to me, too. You hired security."

"Sam—"

I ignored that. "You hired a private investigator."

"I did that for—"

It didn't matter. I clipped my head from side to side. "No way, buddy."

His lip twitched up. "Buddy?"

"I was protecting you, just like you were protecting me. And I know you. You always think you have to protect Logan and me. Well, back up because, this time, it was us taking care of you. You can't do anything. Your football career is like you're a politician. One wrong move, and you're done. That means, it was up to us, and you have no room to judge Logan or me about how we've been trying to take care of you." I stopped for a breath before I kept going, "It's because we love yo—"

Mason slammed his mouth to mine.

That shut me up.

The hunger took over. I was lifting my arms around his neck as he was pulling me onto his lap. My legs opened, straddling him, and Mason swept a hand under my shirt. His touch was addictive. My mouth opened, answering his back. He was demanding. His tongue went in, but mine was there. I was battling him. I wanted as much of him as he wanted of me. Desire and lust took over, shutting my mind down.

All the arguments.

All the heated accusations.

I could protect him like he'd protected me.

All those statements melted away.

It was him and me. We were together on the same page again.

Mason rolled me over and laid me down. His lips were still on mine as he held himself above me. His weight wasn't on me and I grabbed for him. I wanted it there. That was home to me, but he shook his head. I felt him lifting his head and caught the back of his head. My fingers twisted into his hair. I held him there. I still wanted him. I wasn't done.

Mason pulled up, lifting me with him. I was moved to a sitting position, my hand still in his hair.

He gazed at me, smiling, raking his eyes all over me. "Sam."

"Enough talking." I tried to pull him back down. "I want you."

"I know." His hand grazed down my arm and took my hand in his. He pulled my other one from his hair, and he held on to it, entwining our fingers. "But you're right. I wanted to tell you that."

"What?" The addiction to having him inside of me was overwhelming, but I shoved it back, slightly. Some logic filtered in. I gaped at him. "You're saying that I was right."

"You were right."

He waited for my reaction.

"Well, it's about time." My hand reached for him again.

He laughed, pinning my hand down. "I'm trying to tell you that you were right. I was wrong. I shouldn't have kept the security guy or the PI from you guys."

"Why did you?"

Mason grew quiet, thoughtful. He pulled his hand back and moved so that he was sitting next to me instead of holding himself above me. Wrapping an arm around me, he pulled me up so that I was straddling him again. I reached above him, grabbing on to the headboard. Mason held my gaze. His hands grabbed my arms, but he only held on to them. He didn't move them back. He didn't take over our position. I was dominating him, and in a small way, a thrill wound through me.

"Mason?"

He lifted a shoulder. "I didn't know what I would find. I don't have a good reason for keeping you or Logan in the dark. I mean, all of this happened because of me. I wanted both of you to enjoy your first semester at college as normal students—or as normal as you could. All of this was because of me. I went against Sebastian last year, not you guys. I just pulled you into it with me."

"But, Mason," I murmured, my insides rolling over into mush. "We're with you. When something happens to one of us, it happens to all of us."

"I know." He frowned. Regret flared over his face. "I-it was another battle because of me, you know? Yes, you had to deal with some shit because of your mom, but that stopped when you moved out. You were done and away from her. It all kicked up again because of me. She was trying to break us up, and you went to battle for me. The shit happened with Kate. That gutted me, what they did to you. That was all because of me. And again, with Broudou. Do you know how it killed me that he wanted to hurt you because of the mere fact that you were my girlfriend? None of that would've happened if you hadn't been with me.

"I just…I wanted you to be normal for a little bit. I always get in some war. I always will. I know that, because it's me. People try to dominate me, and you know me, that shit won't fly. I don't know what the future will bring, but I know there will be more battles, more fights, more of you getting hurt." His hand brushed the side of my face.

I closed my eyes, moving into his touch.

He slid his hands over my cheek and cupped the side of my face. His thumb brushed back and forth over my skin. He said, "I'm too selfish to let you go, but I'm selfless enough that I will always protect you." He leaned forward, pressing a kiss to my lips. He breathed there, saying, "Because that's my job. I will love you. I will take care of you. I will worry about you, and I will do everything in my being to make sure you are okay."

"Mason," I started.

He tugged my lips down, back to his. "I know that we're going into this together. I know we're equal, but let me protect you. That's what I'm supposed to do."

My fingers slid into his hair, cupping both sides of his face, and I leaned back. "You and me."

He nodded, his eyes lit up with love. "You and me."

"We protect each other."

He nodded again. "We do."

"And you're not mad at me because I didn't tell you about Summer right away?"

"No." His eyes closed for a moment. His forehead rested against mine. "I did the same to you. I lied to you, too."

"Okay." I nodded to myself. "As long as I know you're aware that you fucked up."

The corner of his mouth curved up. "I fucked up?"

I gave another nod with a stern look on my face. "You did. You completely fucked up."

"Oh, yeah?" The other side of his mouth lifted into a playful grin. He started to lean toward me.

I leaned back until my head rested against his knees. I was flushed, growing warm, as a tingle of excitement started.

Mason laughed and opened his legs from beneath me so I was on the bed. He shifted so he was above me. His hand brushed over my forehead, tucking my hair back. He grinned at me, and his eyes held mine. And he was doing what he always did.

He was looking into me.

He was reading my insides.

He murmured, "I fucked up, huh?"

"Completely." I closed my eyes.

His lips touched over mine again, a soft caress.

"Totally," I added.

"I won't do it again."

"You'd better not."

He pressed harder. His kiss grew more commanding.

I took hold of his face. He started to pull away, another teasing comment on his lips, but I stopped him. I tugged him to me, and I took over the kiss.

Enough talk.

It was time to show him how much I loved him, and so I did.

CHAPTER TWENTY-THREE

The mission was to get invited to Park Sebastian's party.

I'd accepted the mission, and when I returned to my dorm room the next morning, I had no idea how to do the impossible. I walked in, saw the bare desk, the empty closet, the empty dresser drawers, the one box on the floor, and the bag on the stripped bed. Summer sat beside it. She pushed it aside and folded her hands in her lap. She looked down at her lap for a split second before lifting her gaze again, biting down on her lip and tucking a strand of hair behind her ear.

"Summer? What's going on?"

"This was all a lie." Her voice was trembling, and she wouldn't look at me. She kept her head down. "But I can't participate in this anymore."

"What do you mean? You already came clean." My insides were twisting. I felt like I was approaching a wounded animal, and I proceeded inside with caution, closing the door with a soft click. "I know you're Sebastian's sister."

"No, Sam." She wiped a hand over her cheek. Wetness glistened from the top of her palm as it went back to her lap. "All of it was a lie. I wasn't even going to come to college. I came because Park convinced me. He made you, Mason, and Logan sound like a scene from *The Exorcist*."

"You weren't going to come to college…at all?"

"No. The modeling thing was true. My contract ended with an agency, and I was going to sign a new one, but he got in my head. He said I was perfect, that I would be ingratiated with you immediately." Her shoulders dropped another inch, closing together. Her size seemed to shrink from a six-foot-one model to a tiny little girl. Her hair fell over her shoulder, and she grabbed a chunk of it, wrapping it into her sleeve, as she began picking at the end of her shirt. "He picked me because of Heather."

"What?" I was so far behind. "Heather?"

"I'm just like her. That's why he picked me. Said my personality was like your best friend. There was no way you couldn't *not* trust me. He said you'd trust me without realizing it even. I'm so sorry, Sam. I really am." She waited a second. Her shoulders lifted as she took in some air. She started again, "He wanted me to come clean because he wanted me to further gain your trust. It was all a part of some mind game he's playing with you guys."

"Okay." I frowned. A headache was forming behind my temples. "How was that supposed to gain my trust?"

"He said that it was going to come out anyway. He wanted me to tell you before it did, and he said that we could spin it. The whole changing-the-key thing—that was part of the charade. He was supposed to show up. I was supposed to get mad at him. Someone would use me against him, but he didn't think it'd be you. He thought Mason would try to get information from me. Not you. None of his plans have gone the way he said they would." Her chest heaved up and held. She fisted her hands in her shirt. Her shoulders dropped, and a sob wrenched out.

My chair was a few feet from me, and I slowly edged closer before sitting. I never turned away from her. It wasn't that I thought Summer would move against me. I didn't want to spook her. She'd run away, and I wanted more answers. She was right. The charade was done.

"Summer." I held on to the back of my chair. My nails dug into it. "Tell me what was the truth."

"What I've already said. I do like you." She looked up now. Her tears left trails through her makeup, running down her face. Her mascara was in clumps under her eyelids. "And I do like football. I always have, but all my weirdness around Mason wasn't because of his stats. It was because of my brother. He made Mason out to be a villain. Park said he hated Mason because Mason wanted to destroy everything for him. Sebastian even said that Mason would try to hit on me. Park wanted me to sleep with Mason."

My eyes got big with that one, but I held back. I couldn't scare her away.

"But Mason didn't. It's so obvious how much he loves you and Logan." She sighed. "Park said that Logan would hit on me, too, and he did, but it wasn't like how Park said it would be. Logan...there's more to him. He's not the asshole my brother portrayed him to be." A defiant glint showed across her features. "And I don't regret sleeping with him. My brother isn't entitled to know everything. It's none of his business."

She was going to spill more about Logan. I needed to know more about Sebastian, how it pertained to me.

I urged gently, "Summer, what else was a lie?"

Her head went back down. More sniffles wheezed from her, mixed with tears. "I don't know why I'm a mess. I mean, it's you. You're not even mad. I'd be livid, knowing my roommate was lying to me. I love you. You have no idea. I can't be your friend, but I want to be. My brother said it's him or you, but fuck him." That defiant look was back.

"I'm leaving, Sam." She gestured to the box and bag and around the room. A sad and bitter laugh left her. "Not that you couldn't see that yourself, but I'm leaving school permanently. My mom is going back to New York. I'm going with her. I'm going to go back into modeling." She paused, glancing up at me from underneath her eyelids. "If you ever come out there, please call me. I'd love to see you again. Or you could stay with us. My mom's not like my dad. She's not involved with that college group they have. She doesn't believe in using their connections. She said it's all one big scandal that's waiting to be taken down anyway."

My mind was buzzing. I needed to get an invite to Sebastian's party, and Summer was the only avenue for that to happen. But she was leaving…

My shoulders slumped down.

"I'm supposed to invite you to his party tomorrow."

My head popped up. "What?"

"I know. I know." She waved at me, wiping at her nose. "It's completely stupid, but Park said to make it happen. He doesn't know I'm leaving. I should be in New York by the time he finds out, and it'll be too late. He doesn't dare take our mom on. He has our dad wrapped around his finger, and Molly, too, but not our mom. My mom loves Park, but she thinks he's a manipulative weasel, which he is." She groaned. "There it is. That's the last of my confessions. I'm sorry, Sam, but I told Park everything you told me. He already knew about Garrett because we know him, obviously, but Park knows everything else. He knows about your other dad, David, and also Malinda.

He knows about Mark. He knows Analise is in a psych place, but to be fair, he knew about your mom before I told him. I have no clue how. Wait." Her lips puckered up, and her forehead bunched together. "Your mom went to college with all of them, didn't she?"

"All of whom?"

"My dad, my mom, your parents, Professor Baun." She waved her hand in the air. "There's more, but you know about all of that, right?"

I cocked my head to the side. My fingers were digging into the chair now. I didn't dare show her my card. I wanted her to spill everything, so I murmured, "Oh, yeah."

"That's the other reason for me, you know. You're in The Network by default, like me. Your mom, too, but all her stuff is known I guess. There's not much they can blackmail her with." A dry chuckle slid from her lips. "Oh. Hold on." Digging in her bag, she pulled out a flash drive and handed it to me. "That's for you."

"What is it?"

Her eyes fell on it, now in my hands, and she was quiet for a moment. She shrugged. "It's whatever you want it to be."

That sounded ominous. "Summer?"

Her jaw was firm, and she wiped the last of the tears from her face. "After what they did to Logan, I can't be a part of this anymore. I've done nothing in my life for them to blackmail me with, so I'm walking away now." She indicated the flash drive. "That's for you to do with as you please. If you can decrypt it, it's yours."

Oh, holy shit.

I didn't dare breathe.

She'd realize she was making a mistake. That was her family in the end.

As if hearing my thoughts, Summer shook her head. "I don't know what's on it, but it's important. I took it out of Park's safety deposit box. I know he's my brother, but I can't support him anymore. He's going down a dangerous path. Whether he wants to look at it this way or not, this is my way of trying to save him. He deserves whatever happens to him." Her chin started to tremble again. "It might even save him from something worse."

"Summer?"

She stood, still not looking at me. Gathering her bag and box, she held them. She didn't leave. She didn't do anything. She waited by the bed for a moment before she dumped them. "Oh, to hell with it."

Her arms wrapped around me in the next second. I was pulled in for a tight hug.

She buried her head into my neck, saying, "I am so sorry for everything my brother has already done and anything he does."

I was so shocked at the turn of events. My arm was crushed against my chest. My fingers hadn't closed around the flash drive yet. I was still holding it in the palm of my hand.

She hugged me again before she moved back. Her hand closed my fingers over the flash drive. "Use this. Whatever is on it, use it. I hope it helps you."

She went back to her bag and box. She was leaving.

I almost shouted, "Wait!"

She stopped at the door, turning back.

I said, "Where's his party tomorrow?"

Her eyebrows bunched together. She started shaking her head. "No, no, no. Don't go there, Sam."

I shoved the flash drive in my pocket and rolled back my shoulders. "Tell me where it is. I'll go without you."

"No, Sam. I can't. Park...he's...he has something planned for you tomorrow. Don't go." Her eyes were pleading. "I mean it. Don't go, Sam. Please."

"I'm not going in blind. I know he has something planned. My eyes have been wide open this whole time."

"They weren't. Not with me."

"Not at first, no, but once you told me, they were. You might think you've spied on me, but you haven't really. Sebastian could've found out any of that information himself."

"No, Sam. I told him things that I know you wouldn't have wanted me to." She clasped the box to her chest, holding tightly. "I have to go. I'm sorry, Sam. I really am. Don't go to that party tomorrow."

"Summer?"

She left. The door slammed shut behind her. I went after her, but the phone started to ring behind me. We both used our cell phones, but the dorm installed a landline. I never used it and was going to ignore it this time, too, but a thought occurred, and I held back.

Picking up the receiver, I asked, "Hello?"

"Is my sister there?"

It was Sebastian.

I gritted my teeth but replied in a cheerful voice, "Nope, but she just talked me into going to a party you're throwing tomorrow?"

"Oh, good. That's what I was calling about. Now," his voice dipped down, "Samantha, I know that there's been some bad blood between us, but I want to make things right. You're friends with my sister. Your father is close to my family, and we've all been supporting your mother."

The last statement churned my blood. I gripped the phone tighter. "What do you mean?"

"Just that this silly battle I have with Mason and Logan doesn't need to extend to you and me. I mean, we're practically family anyway." He laughed into the phone.

The smugness had me seeing red.

"It must have been difficult to go through everything you have. You don't just have Mason and Logan to lean on, you know. There's a whole network of people you can lean on. We'll support you through anything. That sounds good, doesn't it?"

It sounded condescending. I went with it. "Oh, yeah." My sarcasm was kept in check. Sugary sweetness here. "I'll take any support I can get."

"See? I know my sister was hesitant to bring you in, but I think it's time you found out about everyone else. I wasn't lying when I said there's a whole network of people you can call family. In fact, you're more connected than Mason and Logan are. I think you have a really great future ahead of you."

"Oh," *fucker*, "yeah, that sounds wonderful." My knuckles were white. I had to keep from breaking the phone. "Hey, can you let me know where the party is? Your sister seemed distracted when I asked for the directions, and I just wanted to double check with you."

"Sure. Are you ready?"

After jotting it down, I signed off with a cheerful, *Fuck you*, in my head.

I dialed Mason immediately after.

As soon as he answered, I said, "We have a problem."

CHAPTER TWENTY-FOUR

MASON

Sam said Garrett and his wife were staying with the Sebastians. I figured I needed somewhere more private than my house to have this meeting so I booked a suite at a hotel. This was all Sam's idea. Once we hatched the plan with Nate and Logan, we were good to go until she woke up in the middle of the night.

"What's wrong?" I sat up next to her, rubbing her back under her shirt.

Tears ran down her cheeks and she raised her knees up, hugging them to her. She rested her cheek against her knee and looked at me. There was such sadness in her gaze, and it tugged at me, sinking deep in my chest. Wiping some of the wetness from her face, I asked again, "What's wrong? Tell me."

"Garrett."

I frowned. Her dad? My hand paused on her back. "What about him?"

"He's a part of all of this." She sniffled, but she didn't pull away from her knee. She just kept looking up at me. She wasn't seeing me. She was seeing him. My jaw clenched, realizing that. The sadness was for him.

I asked, "What do you want to do?"

She hesitated and her teeth sank down on her bottom lip.

My hand rested against her cheek, and I said softly, "No more lies. No more trying to protect each other. What do you want to do? We'll do it together. What are you thinking?"

Her head lifted, and a surge of strength flared over her features. Her chin lifted. Her eyes took on a fierce determination, and her entire body grew stronger. She said, "We take the flash drive to him. We make him do the dirty work for us."

It was a gamble.

"Are you sure?" I asked.

She nodded. Her eyes were lidded with fear, but she murmured, "We have to try. He is my father, after all."

Garrett was connected to whatever was on Summer's flash drive. We still didn't unencrypt it, but he was involved. He could warn them against us, before we even made our move, but this was Sam's call. She wanted to go to her biological father first. And he was here.

The hotel door buzzed.

Sam was sitting in the corner of the room, wringing her hands together, and chewing the inside of her cheek for the last hour. She sucked in her breath and her eyes whipped to mine. I nodded, standing from my seat, and I crossed the room to open the door.

Garrett was on the other side. No welcoming smile came. No question lurking in his depths. He skimmed over my face and then looked inside for his daughter. Once he saw her, he looked back to me. He was waiting for me to invite him in. I nodded, stepping back, and he came inside. Shutting the door behind him, as he stopped behind a couch, I passed him to stand beside Samantha. We were on one side of the room. He was on the other, his hands fell to rest onto the couch. He let out one short breath before clearing his throat. "I take it this isn't a social call?"

Sam stood next to me, her hand slipping into mine. She wanted me to be the spokesman, but I knew some of the talking had to come from her. In a way, Sam was exposing herself completely here. Garrett came into her life twice, and left twice. This was his last and final chance. If he rejected her again, that was it. She hadn't shared that sentiment with me, but she'd been quiet the entire morning. She barely said a word. I knew Sam. I knew what this was going to do to her and if he chose wrong, I'd make him pay.

He looked from me to Sam, lingering on her. "Sam?"

She held my hand in a death grip, but her voice was sturdy. "Give him the flash drive."

"What?" Confusion crossed over Garrett's face.

But she was talking to me. I tossed it on the coffee table between us.

He didn't grab it. He just looked at it. "What is that?"

I waited. When Sam didn't say anything more, I moved forward. It was my turn. She would jump in when she was ready. "It's information on whatever you're involved in with the Sebastians."

"What?"

I waited with my eyes narrowed. He wasn't showing much. Sam inherited some of her emotionless expressions from him, I saw that now, but he was rocked. My gut was telling me that, even though I couldn't tell from observing him. I felt it, though. My gut was never wrong.

"You heard me." I added, "It's encrypted, whatever it is, but it came to us straight from Park Sebastian's safety deposit box."

"You're lying." His nostrils flared, just an inch.

I tried to tell if he was pissed or scared. I didn't know this dad of Sam's, so I couldn't get a good read on him. Again, I had to rely on my gut. I didn't think he was pissed. I hoped not, for Sam's sake. "You can take it with you. It's a copy. We have more, but we were given that by someone close to Sebastian."

Garrett still didn't move to pick it up. He switched so he was watching me instead. I felt his gaze probing me. He was trying to figure out if I was bluffing or not. I wasn't. I let him see that. There was no hesitation. I wasn't hoping he'd buy a lie. I wasn't doing anything. The only thing I was nervous about was what he did when he left this room, but as to what was on the flash drive—even though I didn't know what it was, I knew it was important.

Another beat passed as Garrett was studying me, then his scrutiny dropped. His shoulders slumped down and he raised a hand to wipe at his face. He let out a deep pocket of oxygen. "If that's what I think it is, you both could be in a lot of trouble."

"That's why we called you." Sam's hand loosened. It fell from mine and she moved ahead of me, one step. "We're going to release that, but whatever it is; you're on there. Aren't you?"

His gaze switched to his daughter's. He didn't reply. Another moment passed before he nodded, slowly. It was like he was surrendering to us with that motion. "It's the blackmail list, if it is what I think it is."

"Blackmail?"

"For The Network."

"The fuck?" Sam's eyebrows lifted high.

I hid a grin, feeling she channeled Logan with that question.

"The Network. That's the name. It's not original, but that's the point. If you're in it, you're in it. If you want out—" He nodded at the flash drive. "—they use whatever's on there against you." He was dead serious. He asked us, "Do you have any idea how bad this is for you two? Whoever gave that to you was handling dynamite. Who was it?"

"No way." Sam shook her head. "You're not getting that from us."

"Samantha." A warning growl came from her father.

I moved forward, urging Sam back a step. She was going to take this down a different path. Her 'fuck you' attitude about Garrett was close to the surface. She was going to make it about that, but he was right. Whatever The Network was, they were dangerous. We needed to keep it about that, not making it personal between father and daughter.

I gestured to the flash drive. "Will you help us?"

A second growl emanated from him. It was cut short, but he wasn't happy. "You guys are nuts. You can't take The Network on—"

"It's because of Park Sebastian." I stopped him. My own anger was starting to simmer under the surface. "We didn't come to you to get lectures. You're not the adult to treat us like we're children in over our heads. We didn't want anything to do with this. Our fight isn't The Network. It's Park Sebastian."

"What are you talking about?"

"Sebastian wanted something from me last year. He never outright said what it was, but I knew he wanted to manipulate me and use me. I've been around enough people trying to use me to know what it feels like. I might not have reacted the right way, but I wanted nothing to do with him. That pissed him off."

Garrett grunted, shoving his hands into his jeans' pockets. "I'm not surprised. I love my godson, but he does have an ego on him."

He loved him? That hit a nerve. I shared a look with Sam. She told me Garrett was like family to them, but he loved his godson? That shut it down. I shook my head and moved back. "Never mind. This isn't going to work."

"What?" His hands came out of his pockets. He gripped the couch in front of him. "What are you talking about? What just happened?"

I said to Sam, "He's too close to them."

She darted forward, grabbing the flash drive before Garrett could, but her biological father never tried. His jaw was set forward, and he wore a deep frown. He asked, "What did you just decide about me?"

"Nothing." Sam answered for me. Her hand closed over the flash drive, and she backed up to stand next to me. Her shoulder hit my chest. Her hand lifted, and I took the flash drive from her. "It's nothing…Dad."

His eyes sharpened on her. To my knowledge, it was the first time she called him that. She was manipulating him. He was the enemy, and he knew we had something on his side, on The Network.

"Whatever you guys are going to do, fill me in on it. You're my daughter, Sam. Please let me in. Please." He was pleading.

She bit down on her lip. If she could have stepped backward, she would've. She was plastered against me, leaning her whole body on me so I was supporting her as she was staring at her father. I felt the struggle inside of her. She told me about her little sister. Sam was going to love that little girl. She already did, but our next move could sever that tie between her and her sister. Garrett was on the flash drive. He was going to be hurt by it, and now he knew that we would be behind it. He knew Sam was behind it. It would be up to him, with what he decided to do afterward.

He could take her sister away from her.

I asked, "You want to be in Samantha's life?"

"You know I do."

"Then prove it." Sam stepped forward, straightening from me. "This information is going to come out. When it does, have our backs."

"You guys have no idea what you're about to do, do you?"

"No." I clipped my head to the side. "We're not little kids. We're not teenagers. Fuck. We're not even regular college students. Fighting. Battling. Waging wars—this is what we do. The Network, or whatever the hell you guys call your group of people, it doesn't matter how connected you are, it's always the same thing. Someone comes at us, we go back at them. As for how we do it, a little faith here. It'll come out, but you're the only one who will know it came from us." I waited a second, then added, "I guess Sam will have her answer with how you handle that information."

He didn't say a word.

His head lowered a little bit. He stared at Samantha for another full minute before he finally just turned and left. I waited for a breakdown or an explosion, but nothing came. It was going to hurt her. There was no way around that. Whatever Garrett did afterward, if he exposed us or if he kept quiet, I still knew that his reaction in the hotel room struck Sam deep.

"You okay?" I asked her later in bed.

She nodded. "Same shit, different day."

Brushing back her hair, I tucked it behind her ear and my hand lingered, cupping the side of her face. "I'm sorry about Garrett."

"Don't be." She took my hand in hers and then lifted both of them to my face. She cupped the side of my face instead and smiled at me. There were shadows in her eyes, but there was love. So goddamn much love. She added, simply, "I don't need him. I have David back in my life. I have Malinda. I even have a brother in Mark, but more importantly, I have you and Logan. I have you." She pressed our hands more firmly against my face. "I need you. That's all I need."

A tear welled up on the inside of her eyelid. It stayed there. She didn't shed it, and her eyes gleamed bright, promising to me. "You are all I need."

I lifted up with my other hand and touched the side of her eyelid. The tear slipped, falling onto my hand. "You'll know your sister. We won't let him keep her away."

"I know."

That was it. That was all she said. We were one unit again.

SAMANTHA

The party wasn't what I expected. I'd assumed to see boozing, beer pong, chugging contests, and half-naked chicks running around the lawn. When I pulled past the opened gate at the end of the driveway, I felt like I was driving into the Fallen Crest Country Club.

Maseratis, Corvettes, Ferraris, BMWs, Rolls-Royces—those were among the cars in the parking lot. As an attendant waved me to the house, I saw there was valet parking.

Well, shit.

Park Sebastian really did own his own country club.

"Ma'am." The attendant held his hand out, looking younger than me.

I sighed and handed over the keys. My little Corolla had been with me since the beginning. I patted the front as I rounded the car and said, "Be nice to her. She's revved up for the evening. She might be a little tense."

He frowned, pausing, and then he rounded the opened door right before he got behind the wheel. I felt his eyes on me. I ignored them and headed inside, but I stopped as soon as I passed the threshold. A large chandelier hung from the ceiling.

A waiter greeted me right away. He offered a tray of champagne. I was tempted to take the whole thing.

Shaking my head, I murmured, "No, thank you."

He didn't seem to care, extending it to a group of people before me. They, however, didn't hesitate. The tray was empty within seconds, and the waiter tucked the tray under his arm, bending his head down. He slipped away. Another waiter appeared, as if magically summoned. He held a tray of champagne as well, but a second waiter was beside him. That one was filled with chocolate-covered strawberries along with some other crepe-looking desserts. It was all very fancy.

I skimmed an eye over the group still in front of me. They hadn't moved forward, so neither had I. The entire foyer was packed with people, and all of them were dressed to go along with the fancy theme.

Some women wore dresses. One was a sequin dress even. The men were dressed for a casual business dinner, with a few wearing dinner jackets. The whole country club vibe was resounding loud and clear to me.

I was in jeans and a white shirt. I looked down at my V-neck. It was nicer than I normally wore—thanks to Malinda, who updated my wardrobe—but it was plain, compared to the dresses the others were wearing. Not to mention, I was the youngest in the foyer. Everywhere I looked, they were middle-aged and older. No, wait. I saw a couple of others who looked like they were my age, but they were standing next to the older people. They looked like parents or even grandparents.

What the fuck?

What kind of party is this?

"Samantha." Sebastian waved from a side room. He grinned at me above all the heads and shouldered his way to me. "I'm so glad you came."

I was in a twilight zone. That was the only explanation. He helped beat Logan down. Mason told him to fuck off in the board meeting. We were chums now?

My jaw wanted to fall to the floor, but I just nodded, flashing him a grin. "Uh-huh. Yeah. How are you?"

"I'm better. I'm better."

He reached for my hand, but I stepped back, knocking into people behind me. A woman sucked in her breath, indignant, and a few others protested. I ignored them all, only staring at Sebastian, who stilled when he saw my reaction. I swallowed. I couldn't look away.

How would he react?

He didn't. His mouth froze but twitched into another grin. He cleared his throat, gesturing where he came from. "I'd like to show you around, if that's okay with you?"

It wasn't. I went anyway.

Sebastian didn't touch me, only kept looking back to make sure I was following. He led the way through a living room and then a second living room. A dining room. A second dining room. We were in a third sitting area, but it was smaller than the other two. This place was ridiculous.

Finally, he stopped and looked back. His smile seemed more genuine, growing, as he gestured to another room. "In here."

I craned my neck, trying to see beyond him. I only saw people. Everywhere.

I shrugged and shoved past some ladies wearing too much makeup. They were weighed down by their jewelry and clutching drinks that—I caught a whiff—weren't champagne. Sebastian was standing next to an older guy. Two other men were there, but they left as I approached.

Sebastian was almost beaming. "Samantha, I wanted you to meet my grandfather."

My hand had been reaching for him but stopped. *Grandfather?* "Uh..." This was a party for The Network. Dread was starting to line my veins, plunging through my body. My father would be here. Garrett was here...and he knew. He could stop this whole thing even before it came out.

I cleared my throat. "Is my—is Garrett here?"

"I don't believe he is. Park?"

"No," Sebastian said. "He called from the house. Sharon wasn't feeling well. They were going to head back to Boston, I believe."

"Ah. Well, there you have it, but no worries." The older man raised a weathered hand. "Your father isn't here, but your grandfather is, and you can call me Gerald."

My eyes shot to Sebastian's grandfather. "What?"

"Garrett's father," Sebastian explained, frowning slightly. "Isn't that why you came today?"

I couldn't look away from his grandfather. I had my own

grandfather. Somewhere, that would make sense but not with my life.

"Sam?"

The corners of Gerald's eyes turned down, and his head cocked to the side. He murmured, "You didn't know about your grandfather?"

I found myself shaking my head.

Gerald glanced at Sebastian. "You were supposed to tell her." His tone was disapproving.

Sebastian flushed, tugging at the collar of his shirt. He sent me a furtive look under his eyelids before lifting his shoulders high. "I thought Garrett had. He said he was going to see his daughter last night. Plus, I told you there were other issues going on."

"You're talking about James Kade's boys?" his grandfather barked back. If he'd been patient, it was all used up. Sharp impatience flared up in his face, and he was almost glaring at his grandson. "I told you to deal with all that nonsense long ago. I want James Kade in. Are you telling me that you haven't dealt with that?"

"Well..." Sebastian sent me another quick look. "I...no, I haven't. James Kade's sons hate me. I thought you knew that. They wouldn't want to come in anyway—because of me."

"James Kade was approved to come in long ago."

"Grandpa," Sebastian started.

"No, I don't want to hear it. I'll be talking to your father, but you are not above the board's decisions."

"I'm your grandson. They hate me, literally hate me. Mason's the one who burned my house down last year."

"Good."

I stumbled back a step.

The force of that word spoke volumes. Gerald Sebastian commanded authority, and judging from this sharp exchange, he wasn't used to not having someone do as he told.

Gerald stabbed his finger in the air, snapping at Sebastian. "That means he has initiative, and he's someone we want in the organization. You were given an order. You have failed with that order."

His voice kept rising in anger, but no one came to see what the problem was. Conversations quieted. People were looking over, now watching, but no one seemed surprised.

"She's here." Sebastian flung his arm out toward me. "I brought Ben's granddaughter into the fold."

"Bullshit," Gerald grunted. "You've been using your sister this entire time. Don't try to pull one over on me."

"But—"

"Your job was to bring Mason Kade in. Through him, we were going to bring James Kade into the fold."

Sebastian looked away, but he folded his hands together in front of him. He slightly turned away as one foot shifted backward. "Grandpa," he said again, his lips pressed tightly together, "I think it's a mistake. James Kade doesn't need to be brought in. He's attached to Analise Strattan, and everyone knows her background. She can't be given the support The Network would be handing to her. She's been watched. We're all aware of how she's acted throughout her life."

"Don't you dare try to tell me what to decide. You're in the wrong, Park. The decision was made long ago. Ben wasn't aware of Analise's deception when she and Garrett were in college. All these years, he's been cheated from knowing his granddaughter. I won't stand for it any longer. Now," Gerald gestured to me with the same stabbing motion, "take her to the meeting room and fill her in on everything. I want the Kade boys here within the hour, too." He turned to me, gentling his tone a little bit. "When this boy is done, you come and find me. I'll personally introduce you to your grandfather."

I didn't know what to say, so I nodded, feeling dazed.

"Good." He clapped Sebastian on the shoulder. "Go on. Fill her in, and drop whatever silly issues are going on between you and her boyfriend." He moved his head up and down in a slow and exaggerated motion. "You know what to do."

Sebastian's shoulders dropped an inch, and he nodded back, his head hanging down. "Yes, sir." Everything about him was submissive.

I was holding my breath. The exchange I'd just witnessed was overloading my senses.

Sebastian's gaze found mine when his grandfather left the room. He nodded behind me. "It's down that hallway."

"Sebastian, what's going on?"

"I'll explain everything." He moved around a couple. "Just follow me."

We went through the kitchen and out to another hallway that led to an adjoined building.

As we moved past a pair of French doors that opened outside, I asked, "I need to know where we're going. Enough of this crap. Start filling me in on something, or I'm not going anywhere with you."

He stopped right before a closed door and looked back at me. I remained by the French doors. When he didn't say a word, I folded my arms. I meant business.

A short chuckle left him, and he jerked a thumb over his shoulder to the room. "We're here."

"Oh." I unfolded my arms. My mind was scrambling. "I have to pee. Is there a bathroom close by?"

His head tilted to the side. He studied me and then sighed as he gestured to a door on his right. "You can use this one, but come here first."

"Why?" My feet didn't move.

"Because what I have to tell is top secret." As he said that, he opened a cupboard on his left that was directly across the small hallway from the bathroom. As he opened it, he told me, "There's a rule of no cell phones. You have to lock yours in here before hearing everything."

Holy shitola, as Logan would say. I was about to be inducted into a secret cult.

Edging closer, there were a bunch of small drawers in the cupboard. Each of them had a key code in front of them.

Sebastian said, "Pick a drawer. Put your phone in there, and code in whatever you want. Same thing as a safe in a hotel. Only you have the code to get your phone, but that's the rule." He opened the door for the main room and stepped inside. "Take a piss, put your phone away, and come in."

"Where are you going to be?"

A dry laugh came from him. "Making myself a strong drink. I need it after getting my asshole chewed off by my grandfather."

I waited until he went in and closed the door. Then, I went and made sure the French doors were unlocked. They were, but to make sure nothing went wrong, I went into the bathroom. I hadn't come to this party alone. Mason and Nate were waiting for me. Not far away, they pulled off the road.

I texted Mason now. Not only was it safe for him to come

to the party, he was also invited. I said enough in the text to let him know that Sebastian's grandfather was pro-Mason.

He texted back,

> I'm pro-grandpa, I guess.

I thumbed back,

> Ha-ha. French doors are left open. Go all the way to a second building. It's all connected. In the room at the end of the hallway.

And with that last text, I had a dilemma. Actually put my cell phone away or not? If I didn't, Sebastian could use it as an example to pat me down, making sure the phone was away. I didn't want to deal with that, so I opened the door. Sebastian looked up from behind a bar. I waved my phone in the air and made a show of putting it into one of the drawers. Cupping my hand over my other hand, I put in a code and stepped back.

My phone was now locked away. It was just Sebastian and me—until Mason would join us. I didn't know how long that would be, but okay, here I went.

Sebastian was watching me as I stepped inside. He slid a drink across the counter to me. "I'm surprised you actually put the phone away. After Logan and the board meeting, I would've assumed you wouldn't trust me at all."

Yes, a sane person would have that reaction.

I let out a shaky breath, rubbing the palms of my hands down my legs. "Yeah, well, as you apparently know, a little craziness runs in my blood."

"Yeah, about that." He stopped, waved me in, and said, "Shut the door, please."

I did, a full knot forming in my gut. "I'm in. Now, start talking."

He opened his mouth, started to lift his drink, and then paused. "No." He put it back down. "You start talking."

"Excuse me?"

His eyes narrowed, and his nose crinkled up. His eyebrows furrowed together. "Why are you here? My friends and I beat the living shit out of Logan, someone who you call family and claim to love. What's the plan? I'm protected here. There's no way Mason can come in and punch me." His lip curled up in contempt. "I doubt he'll set fire to *this* house."

Ah, fuck. We were doing truth talk, huh? Okay.

I nodded to myself, stepping forward. "Fine, yes, your sister told me that she was supposed to invite me to this party, but she wasn't going to. She was honest about that—right before she left." I pretended to check my invisible watch, tapping my wrist instead. "And right about now, she should already be in New York."

He straightened from the bar. His face instantly dropped to an impassive mask. "Bullshit."

"I see the word is a family favorite."

"My sister wouldn't go to New York."

"She did, and she went with your mother."

A savage curse slipped from him.

"And I can see that she told the truth about that. Your mother's not a big fan of yours?"

"She's inconsequential." Anger was glaring back at me. His eyes were almost sparkling from the emotion. "What did you say to my sister? She never would've left otherwise."

"Nope." I clipped my head from side to side. "Not going there. You can't put that blame on me. I liked your sister, even after she'd told me she was your sister. She went on her own free will. Apparently, when she saw what you did to Logan, that was the last straw for her. You know, because she actually liked us and liked Logan, too."

His head lowered. He kept his eyes pinned on me. "I don't believe you."

"I don't need you to. It's the truth. She's gone, Sebastian."

"Then, why are you here?"

I countered with, "Why did you invite me? I didn't see any of your fraternity buds out there."

He smirked. "Because this has nothing to do with the fraternity. I used my fraternity to go against you guys. This party?" He indicated the door behind me. "All of that is completely separate from the fraternity—or the lack of a fraternity, thanks to your boyfriend. As for why you were invited?" He grunted, lifting a careless shoulder. "You heard my grandfather. I was given orders to invite you. Though I'm shocked as hell you came. I hoped you wouldn't, and all my problems would have been solved." He relaxed back against the bar and picked up his drink.

The small satisfaction that I had been feeling went away. "You mean, you didn't think I would come?"

"I mean," he gave me a chilling smile, "I was banking on the fact that you wouldn't, but here you are. And whatever you have planned, it won't work. What am I going to do with you now?"

It clicked with me. Whatever his grandfather wanted, Sebastian had his own agenda.

I said, "You're not going to do what Gerald wanted, are you?"

He shook his head, finishing his drink. "Nope. How did you say that? 'Not going there. You can't put that blame on me.'" He laughed shortly to himself. "Yes, my grandfather will be upset, but there isn't a thing they can do about it. For one, they never reach out to do their own bidding. It's the grandchildren who reach out. The elders, and even my father—those guys all think it's beneath them. You see, it's during college. That's when the bonding happens. That's when people are supposed to become friends, do stupid shit together, and all for the main purpose of fucking up. You," he fixed me with another glare, "are supposed to be brought into the fold, and we are supposed to become the best of buds. Well, Summer was supposed to be the best of buds with you."

"What are you talking about? I thought you were the one who got Summer to befriend me?"

"I was, and here's where everything goes sideways. Summer doesn't even fully know what's going on. She knows a little bit. She knows that your father is close to our family. She knows about your grandfather, but she doesn't know everything. She was supposed to be initiated with you. And everything was supposed to be all happy, happy, joy, joy for the next four years until both of you learned the real truth." He gestured around the room. "Look at this place. Look at the walls."

Mason showed the photographs of Sebastian talking with his dad, his grandfather, and other men outside of a large house. "The private investigator found this."

Logan shot forward from the couch, grabbing the photograph. "What the fuck? Is that a basketball player?"

"Dude." Nate leaned over to see.

Logan shouldered him back. "Space. I've got broken bones here." Nate scowled at him.

Logan rolled his eyes and handed the photo over. "It pains me to know that one of my basketball faves is a slimeball like Park Sebastian. Seriously," he patted where his heart was, "it hurts me right here. He took away my healthy bones. He took away my, probably, deluded thought that I could take five fraternity assholes at once and walk away still swinging. And," he shot a finger in the air, "if my ego hasn't been wounded enough, I'm in pain from knowing that I will not be able to go to that house to see all those celebrities. Can you imagine? I could get everything autographed, sell it online, and use that money to buy a shit machine. I'm talking a literal shit machine— where it goes and then flings that shit at the target. That'd be my revenge against Sebastian. Mount that crap on his front lawn and put, like, circling tigers around it, so no one could remove it. Best plan ever." He pretended his hands exploded like a bomb and fell back slowly against the couch cushion.

"Really?" Mason lifted an eyebrow. "That's your plan for revenge?"

Logan didn't care. He folded his arms over his chest, winced, and then let them drop back to his sides. "Whatever. I should trademark my ideas. I bet someone will do it. Hashtag revenge shit machine. That video would go viral."

"Oh my god." I groaned from next to Mason. "Can we please get back to all these people Sebastian is connected to? Because that's really concerning."

Sebastian wanted me to look at the walls, so I did. The entire room was set up in a circular layout. The room was square, but the couches were positioned to form a circle, and the walls were covered in portraits. I hadn't considered them when I first came in. All eyes and focus had been on Sebastian, but now that he'd pointed them out, I started putting names to faces.

A senator.

A celebrity—no, a couple of celebrities.

Wrong again.

I recognized more and more of them. Actors. Producers. Singers.

My gaze fell on one in the back corner. My father. Garrett was smiling at the painter. My gaze slid over to the painting beside him. Sharon. And on the other side of her was my mother. This was how they knew Analise.

I murmured, "You said it all starts in college."

"It does. You're starting to figure it out, huh?"

"What happens in college?"

Sebastian chuckled. The sound sent chills down my back.

He said, "You do anything and everything. You screw each other. You don't screw each other. You get drunk. You don't get drunk. It's a normal college experience, but that's where you make the mistakes. And you're supposed to make those mistakes with, who else? Your best friends. I mean, say, for example, if someone raped a girl, who else is going to have your back to cover it up?" He pointed at a portrait of a young man and then to another one of a well-known actor. "Your best friend gives you the alibi. There's no way you could've raped that girl because your buddy is vouching that you were at his house. If you want to cheat on a test," he crossed the room to a portrait of a singer and pointed to another portrait of a senator, "your best gal pal, who's the teacher's assistant, will either get the test for you or cover your back. If a professor gets suspicious, the teacher's assistant will let you know to do a few wrong answers on purpose. And so on and so on. That's what this all is. Connections."

He swept his arm around the room. The walls were covered in the paintings. There was no empty space.

"No, we're not some cult group or anything. It's not blood in and blood out. It's just...blackmail and IOUs. That's what it is, and my family holds all the keys. My great-great-great grandfather started everything, so that's how I'm in the unique position of knowing what the hell is going to happen after each class graduates."

"So..." I frowned. "My mother..."

"No, no." Sebastian shook his head. "Your mother is the *mistake*. She was considered to be inducted. She was initiated, so she knew of the connections. That's what you're told in the beginning. You and Summer would've gotten the same speech. We're all here for each other. Everyone will support you. If you need money, we'll give it to you. If you need a house, here's a mansion. If you need a mistress, we'll get you two who will do anything you want. The speech is custom-made. You and Summer are both girls, so you probably would've been promised success in whatever career you chose. If you wanted to be famous, they would've made you both famous. If you wanted a business, they would've had one ready and waiting for you once you graduated. Hell, if you wanted a husband, they would've introduced you to other members of The Network. And all of it would've been sold with the statement that we're all family. We all love each other. We all take care of each other—along with our mistakes, too. We take care of those, so don't hesitate to reach out if something happens. No matter how horrible the crime is, they'll take care of it."

As he kept talking, Sebastian was going from one painting to the next. A full glow radiated from him, while he was laughing. The effect had my insides turning into ice. I backed all the way to the door and reached behind me for the door handle. If I had to, I'd make a run for it. The nightmare he was promising wasn't going to be given to me. But what else did he have in store then? I knew, without a doubt, that it would be much worse.

He kept on, "Families who started in are automatically chosen to be inducted, but we can choose others, too. My grandfather chose your grandfather to be inducted, so that meant that Garrett was inducted as well. He was an automatic, but your mother wasn't. Garrett chose to induct her, and my guess is that was when they were screwing."

"And Sharon? Her portrait is up there."

"She was inducted later because Garrett broke it off with Analise. He went back to Sharon and eventually married her. After that year, a rule was made. No girlfriends. Only wives."

"But you said my mother was the mistake somehow?"

"Yeah. She was initiated, but she skipped town. She never graduated. When you showed up two years ago, they all realized why. She was pregnant, and Garrett had already gone back to Sharon. Who the hell knows why your mother didn't come clean? She knew she'd be taken care of, but she was a mess. They let her go. She's up on the wall, but she hasn't gotten any of the benefits. Then again," his head moved forward, "she's never shown up to claim any of the benefits either. If she did…I cringe at just wondering what the board would do to her. She's considered a disgrace. All of these people help build The Network. They've all toed the line and used their power to help the others."

"Where's the other foot? When does that drop?"

He laughed again, pointing at me in the air. "It drops when, and if, you deem that you don't need The Network. If you refuse to do something, you find out really quick that, fine, if you choose to go alone, whatever mistakes you've committed from college and onward are yours, too. Information gets released. Testimonies are taken back. You're hung out to dry, and all because you might not have wanted to help a brother get his sister to be roommates with a certain Samantha Strattan at Cain University."

He was staring at me hard now.

"That's how you did that." And that was the blackmail material Garrett said we must've had. That was what was on the flash drive. My fingers wrapped around the handle. I was ready to go at any second.

"What's the plan? You're going to upload all these photographs and e-mail them to the cops or something?"

Nate asked the question, but I was thinking it, too.

Logan added, "Not to be a dick, but if we did that, we would be dicks. We can't narc on these assholes."

Mason countered with, "Even if those assholes are going to hurt us someday?"

Nate nodded. "Mason's right. We're going to go against someone in this organization at some point in our lives. We should let 'em get away with this?"

"Get away with what?" Logan argued. "We don't know what they've done."

"Because jumping all three of us at three different times isn't enough? Or setting up his sister as a spy on Sam?" Nate gestured to me. His disgust was evident. "All of those are good enough reasons for us to go to the authorities with this."

Mason shook his head. Logan was right. They didn't narc to the authorities. It'd been their code for so long, but that didn't mean they couldn't narc at all.

"What about if we let them know?" I said.

"Let them know what?" Logan started to lean forward again, resting his elbows on his knees.

I frowned. "Are you completely forgetting the brace on your chest? Stop moving around so much."

Logan shot me a grin. "Stop looking for ways to undress me, woman. You're my brother's mate."

Mason covered my hand with his and said in a warning, "Logan."

"Okay, okay." Logan shot him a look. "We hear you loud and clear. Mason," he indicated his brother, "what's the plan?"

Mason held up the box with all the information we had with his free hand. "We're going to upload all this information and e-mail it to them."

That was the plan.

Logan snorted. "Genius." He didn't hold back his sarcasm.

Sebastian was staring at me, long and hard. He just revealed how he got Summer to be my roommate, and he echoed softly, "That's how I did that."

I took a breath. My nerves were stretched tight. I needed to stall him so Mason could upload the flash drive. It had to be from a computer as close to Sebastian as we could get. Once he was done, he'd be coming through that door. I looked at it now, wondering how long he would be.

"You can't run, Samantha."

"What?"

"You think you can run, but you can't. The door is locked until I choose to unlock it."

"You opened the door—"

But he hadn't.

I was rewinding everything in my mind. He hadn't opened the door from the inside. I opened it from the outside.

"People can come in?"

"Sure." He shrugged. "But they won't."

"Why not?" He was too casual, too confident.

Mason was coming.

"Enough with my truth. I told you all about The Network. I didn't want you to come today. I thought, after what had happened with Logan, that would've cemented it. Even if someone else reached out, you'd have nothing to do with us, but here you are. You came to the party. You came to this room. You heard about everything. Now, it's your turn." He paused and leveled me with an intense look. "Why are you here, Samantha?"

My mouth was dry, and my heart was pounding. It was my turn to spin a web so I started with my first lie. "I came in here to record a confession from you."

His eyes were still narrowed, but they relaxed slightly. "Really?"

Mason taught me well. The first step to lying was, give a lie that would be believable.

I nodded, steadily holding Sebastian's gaze.

That was the second step—I remembered what I had to do. *Don't look up, don't look down, and don't look to the side. Look them in the eye, and calmly say the words. No tone inflections. No awkward pauses. No heated motions. Talk like you're sharing your most intimate secret with someone.*

My insides were churning, but I envisioned Mason was in the room already. I felt stronger, more sure, feeling he was already here. Pretending he was behind Sebastian, I said, "I wanted to hear the words that you were the one responsible for having Nate beaten up and that you were involved when Logan and Mason were both jumped. I wanted to hear all of it."

He lifted an eyebrow, chuckling to himself. "And how were you going to make that happen? Why would I open up to you?"

I shrugged. "I was hoping to drug your drink."

"This drink?" He held up the glass in his hand.

I gritted my teeth. "I'm not saying the plan wasn't foolproof, but yes, that was the plan." I started for the bar. "But you beat me to it. You already had a drink." And speaking of, my mouth was like the Sahara. There was a water bottle in the mini refrigerator, and I grabbed it.

"Help yourself."

I ignored his sarcasm, taking a big sip. "Thanks."

"You were telling me..." he prompted. His hand moved sideways in the air. "I was going to confess everything to you?"

"You would've." He never would've. I continued to lie, "You would've admitted to the hit-and-run, too. Mason was the target, not Marissa." My stomach rolled over on itself. Sebastian bought her off, but all the pieces fit together now. An abrupt laugh ripped from me. "That wasn't the fraternity, was it?"

His smugness rose a level. He was almost grinning at me. "What do you mean?"

"Last year, Marissa never came forward against you guys. She didn't charge you. We thought it was the fraternity, but it wasn't."

I looked at the portraits. It was like they were looking down at us. They were laughing. We were center stage for them.

"It was them, wasn't this? This network. You guys got to her somehow."

"My, my." Sebastian's voice as soft. "You really are piecing things together."

"But…" I knew there was more. "What else? What else have you done?"

"You're right. Marissa was paid, and when the money wasn't enough, she was threatened. I will admit to that."

I knew there was more. I pushed. "What else?"

"You're eager to know everything, huh? Are you sure, Samantha? Are you sure you want to know all the dirty secrets? That's what they are. They're all dirty." He moved a step toward the bar, intently watching me. "Have you thought about what will happen to you afterward? Because you know too much now?"

There it was. My eyes held his. I couldn't look away. I couldn't shrink against the bar like I wanted to, so I just held on to it. This ride was going to get a little bumpy.

"Maybe that's your other truth," I said.

"What's that?"

He was enjoying this now. I was a mouse to him. He was playing with me before eating me—or whatever he had planned. He was a sick fuck.

I said, "You know what I'm saying."

"I do." He laughed, and the sound filled the entire room. I heard an echo even. "And you're right. I do have something planned, but it's not as sophisticated as what you might think. It's almost primal." He paused, and his eyes narrowed again.

My hand clutched the water bottle, and I drank half of the water in one gulp. I didn't know if I was heated or if I was becoming sick from being in Sebastian's proximity. Either way, I licked my lips and finished the rest of the water. My head was swimming.

"Go on," I croaked. "I want to know your plan."

"That was it."

"What?"

He took another step closer and nodded at the water bottle in my hand. "Right there."

"What?" I still wasn't following. My stomach felt like it was dropping out of me. My hand pressed there. I needed to calm down. My head needed to be clear. "What are you talking about? The water...oh, shit."

The light bulb turned on as he laughed. "I thought it was ironic that you were going to drug me, considering..." Another step closer. He pointed at the bottle again. "You know.

Mason said, "We have to fight smarter." He looked at Nate and Logan. "That means, no more physical fighting, not if we can help it."

Nate nodded in agreement, rubbing his hands together.

Logan rolled his eyes. "For real? I'm not signing up to run for the senate. You can't fight, Mr. I'm Going into the National Football League, and Everyone Will Watch Me." He pointed to himself. "I can still fight. High school wasn't the best years of my life. I'm planning for college to be that time. Sorry, Mase. I love you. I'm with you, but if I feel a good fight coming on, I'm not holding back." He jerked his head upward, his chin nodding to Mason. "And don't even try arguing with me. You love fighting as much as I do."

Mason didn't agree, but he did say, "With this group, we fight back smart. Okay?"

I hadn't been smart. Sebastian outsmarted me.

I thought, *Fuck me.*

"I figured you wouldn't drink. You'd be coming into enemy territory, and Mason would've coached you better. That meant a clear head, but I also knew this would take a long time. There's a lot to explain, and I'm not even done. I still have more to enlighten you about. I knew you'd want some water. The only problem was that." He gestured to a cupboard behind me.

My arms were growing heavier the more he talked, but I opened it. Two cases of water sat there. I could've grabbed one of those twenty-four bottles. I'd taken the single one in the refrigerator.

Sebastian said, as his hand rested on top of the bar an inch from mine, "But I eliminated the risk and put only one in there."

"How?"

"A syringe," he said so matter-of-factly. "If you turned your bottle over, a very, very small leak would show up. It was big enough, though, for what I needed."

Everything was getting even heavier. I wanted to lie down.

"Sam?"

I wanted to shake my head. I didn't want to hear the rest. He hadn't won. He just thought he had, but he'd find that out in the morning. I started to look around. I needed a chair. I would tell him where his plan wouldn't work out when I woke up.

I needed to rest.

"You're not going to fall asleep."

That was not what my eyelids were saying. I grinned, laughing at my stupid joke. My eyeballs, my legs, everything in me wanted to check out and go away.

"You're going to stay awake."

Pfft.

He was an idiot. I took a step around the bar. That couch was my goal, but my body went the other direction. Sebastian grabbed me.

I didn't want him to touch me. I tried to swing my hand at him. Nothing. I slapped my other arm. I started to shake my head, but the room turned to the left. It wasn't upside down. It was just sitting at a side angle.

He helped me to the couch. His touch was soothing. He cradled the back of my head, and I was placed on a pillow.

"There you go. See? That's not too bad."

Asshole.

I wanted to growl at him.

I couldn't do a thing, except hear him and stare at him.

My body was almost paralyzed. He could do as he pleased. This…this was what he thought of when I came to the party.

He'd drugged me, and he was going to rape me.

"Ah, yes." His head floated right above mine. He was staring down into my eyes, waiting. "I see it now. You know what I'm going to do, don't you?" His hand ran down my forehead and traced the side of my jaw, tucking a strand of hair behind my ear. It was almost loving. "My grandfather and The Network want Mason and his father in with them, but that can't happen. Mason pissed me off, so no, he won't be brought in. I'm going to do everything in my power to stop that from happening. I thought the little battle would be over in a few months. I underestimated you guys. All of you. Mason. Logan. You. Even Nate. All four of you were together in this against me. I don't know how to fight like that. It's me, but I realized I could use the fraternity against you. When Nate left the house, it didn't take me much to stir up resentment. The hit-and-run was my idea, and of course, Mason was the target. He already knew that, and he knew why. I wanted to hurt him, but I wanted him to live with it. I thought football was his obsession. I was wrong." He sighed to himself. His hand fell to my arm. He began rubbing it in circles, caressing me.

A tear welled up in my eye. I couldn't do a thing. I wanted to run. That was all I wanted.

Sebastian continued, "I realized it was you. I needed to find a way to destroy you. Summer was supposed to help me, but everything she told me about you, none of it seemed to matter. I already knew about Analise. Your other father and stepmother—they weren't weak. Your only weakness is yourself. Once I knew what I had to do, I guess you brought it about. When you came here, that was the perfect time to do this."

He looked down, skimming up and down my body. "You really are beautiful, Sam. All that running has kept you toned. I can see why Garrett fell for your mother. With your eyes and how your face is framed, you're both stunning to look at. There's a light inside of you."

He sat up and leaned over me, so his head was directly above mine. His eyes went dead. "And I will enjoy taking that light away from you because that's how I'm going to destroy Mason. I don't need a camera. I don't need to record anything for blackmail. Just me, violating you over and over tonight. That will do enough damage. You'll never get over it. You'll never be whole again because that's what rape does to a person."

Mason…

He wouldn't be here in time. This was going to happen now. He'd be too late.

Sebastian laughed to himself. "At least, that's what the psychologists all say. Now, let's get to it."

I started to go somewhere else.

He was taking his clothes off, so I closed my eyes. It would be Sebastian's body, but it would be Mason in my mind. Sebastian would be raping me while Mason would be holding me.

It'd be Mason.
Where was Mason?

CHAPTER TWENTY-FIVE

MASON

Upload the information. Click Send to everyone in The Network—or those we knew.

That was the plan and I got inside, uploaded everything to the closest computer I could find to Sebastian's location, but once I heard Sam's voice coming from the vent, the plans changed. I heard what Sebastian was going to do to her.

That wasn't going to happen.

Opening the door, I stood there for a minute. He didn't hear me come in and he was bending over her now, stroking her face like she was his damn child. It was tender and loving.

It made me sick.

"I told myself I was going to be smarter," I murmured. My hands were flexing into fists, then relaxing, and flexing back again.

His head jerked up. His eyes went wide. Blood drained from his face, and he stumbled away from the couch, moving back a few feet. "Mason."

I stepped inside. His gaze went to the door, and my head tilted to the side. Fear and panic were there.

Good. I wanted him to be pissing himself. His pants should've been drenched already.

When he kept looking at the door, I laughed to myself. It sounded sick and twisted to my own ears, but there was rage, so much damn rage.

I mused, "The door wasn't locked from the outside, but I know Sam. She would've left if she could've, so that means the door was locked. Let me guess." I moved farther inside and shut the door behind me.

"No!" He surged forward, his hand reaching in the air, but he caught himself.

I smiled at him. No joy. No fun. The only part of this that was enjoyable was what I was going to do to him. My smile made him shrink backward.

I said, "And, yes," I tried the door, but it didn't move, "it locks from the inside." I paused a beat. "Why would a door lock from the inside? What kinds of things might happen inside a room where the door has to be locked that way? Where the occupants couldn't leave?"

My foot moved forward. My eyes were trained on him, and I kept my hands at my sides—for now. "Why do I get the feeling that other nightmares have happened in this room? Maybe this is the house I should've burned down?" I lifted an eyebrow at him.

He didn't react. The fear was gone, instead replaced with resignation.

"What's wrong, Sebastian? You've had a lot to say every time I've seen you. Why are you quiet now?"

"This is my grandfather's home." His tone was almost timid.

"Yeah?" I held up my hands. "So what?" My jaw clenched. "What does that mean? Tell me. Why should I be scared that this is your grandfather's house?"

The fear came back. It flashed across his face. His mouth fell open, and his shoulders hunched down.

A brave front appeared. His shoulders lifted back up. His mouth closed again, and his eyes narrowed. "Do you know who you're messing with? Do you really have any idea who I am, what I can do to you?"

"Why haven't you?" I shot back.

I moved forward, stopping by Sam's head, where she seemed to be sleeping on the couch. She looked peaceful, but her fingers were tucked into her palms. Even in her sleep, they were curled inward. I knew that if I unraveled them, blood would come from the palm of her hands. Her nails were digging into them. I skimmed over her, making sure the rest of her looked fine, and it did.

I saw a little droplet of blood. It pooled on the underside of her palm.

He made her bleed. He would've done worse. I'd been keeping the rage contained, but a little bit slipped out there.

"She's unharmed." His voice shook, and he coughed, clearing his throat. He tried to sound strong as he added, "As you can see, I was checking on her."

"Really?"

"She had too much to drink. That's all."

"You're lying out of your fucking teeth." My eyes narrowed. "I heard everything, Sebastian."

He slammed into the wall behind him, upending one of the paintings. It fell onto his shoulders, rolled to the side, and crashed onto the floor. Sebastian's gaze was glued to mine. He never reacted. I didn't think he realized what he had just done.

"You're weak, Sebastian," I murmured lightly, casually glancing around the room.

He was scared, and he was backed into a corner. A wounded animal that couldn't break free always lashed out. He was going to try. It was inevitable, and I knew it was coming sooner than later, but I was ready. Hell, I was going to use it to my advantage.

"You weren't weak while hiding behind your fraternity buds. You aren't weak when you're trying to hide behind your connections."

"Screw you."

I paused. There it was. Some heat came back into him. He wasn't such a wounded animal. There was some fight still left in him. That was good. I had more time.

"Screw me?" A soft laugh slipped out. "That's what you were going to do to Sam."

He seemed to shrink again.

"Weren't you?"

"I wasn't going to hurt her."

Ah.

A baseball bat was mounted on a wall, underneath a professional ball player's painting. It was signed, too.

I crossed the room for it and said, "Stop lying, Sebastian. There's no reason for it anymore. I know everything."

His eyes darted to where I was going. "What are you doing?"

I lifted the glass box that the bat was in and grinned at him. "No worries. I won't throw the box at you."

His eyes fell to the bat, and he scooted over until he was in the farthest corner of the room. Samantha was between us, and he looked at her. I pulled off the back of the glass box and grabbed the bat.

Pulling it out, I pointed it at him. "You'll stay back from her."

I didn't want to scare him too much. If I did, all this would be over. He'd lunge for her, and I wouldn't hear what I wanted to hear.

"I can't let you hurt her. This is between you and me." I kept my tone calm, casual even, and it worked.

He held my gaze, weighing my words.

His shoulders relaxed. The fear was leaving him.

Enough was enough. "Like I said before, I was trying to be smarter this year. No burning houses. No cars put on fire. No brawls. Nothing like that." I tapped the side of my head. "Act smarter. Think smarter. *Be* smarter. Those were the basic rules I tried following when I came back."

My gaze fell back to Samantha. She seemed more vulnerable than ever, lying there, where he could've done anything he pleased.

If I hadn't been here...

I couldn't finish that thought. I'd murder him here and now. I drew in a breath, trying to keep the rage at bay. *This asshole...*

I shook my head. "Logan and Sam have been trying to protect me this whole time. They knew all eyes were on me. They did anything they could, but this wasn't their battle."

It was mine.

I locked eyes with him again. "You went after me, not them. They were collateral damages."

"They were weapons against you."

Finally. That was the truth, but I needed more from him. I wanted to hear as much as I could before I hurt him.

I nodded. "You hurt them to hurt me."

He said further, a soft sigh leaving him, "I was supposed to recruit you. That's the kicker. I never wanted to use you for your power. We wanted to *give* you that power."

He was in control now. That was fine. I could get more out of him like this.

More. I still needed to hear more.

I shook my head. "You're wrong. I'll be fine, no matter what I do. I'm a fighter. I don't and didn't need anything from you. It was the other way around. Isn't that what you guys really do? You find people like me, Logan, Sam, and you latch on to them before they realize the game? You *take* from them. You don't give them anything."

"You're wrong."

"I'm not. Even you know I speak the truth. It's why you don't want us in. Right? You don't want us to have the benefits your network could provide us?"

Sebastian shook his head, looking down for a minute. His hands were folded together, and he stood like that before lifting his head again. "It wouldn't have worked with you guys. You, Logan, even Sam. The three of you were wanted, but the program would've had to work where you trusted us. We needed to obtain dirt on you in order to hold that against you, to use you later in life. But it never would've worked because the three of you never would've let any of us in. The three of you don't trust anyone."

He was right.

"Trusting means being used." I skimmed him up and down. I'd heard enough. I needed to take that control from him.

His head lifted up and down in a smooth nod, and he ground out, "I tried telling my grandfather that, but he wouldn't listen to me. He kept insisting, even today, that I was supposed to bring you in. This has gone too far for that. I told Samantha everything, but I already knew that I was going to ruin her, so she wouldn't have ground to stand on against me. I didn't think you'd have the balls to come here with her."

His eyelids twitched, and his gaze fell to the ground behind me. "I've underestimated all of you this entire time." His eyes went to the bat in my hand. "You should know that it was me the whole time. The Network had nothing to do with the hit-and-run and when me and the fraternity went after you, Nate, and Logan. That was me. I used the fraternity against you guys, and I did it because…" He faltered now, lifting his head.

He was calming again.

No.

I chided softly, "Because I turned you down. Because I wanted nothing to do with you." I moved closer and hardened my voice. "Because I decided that you were *beneath* me."

"I hated you. Who are you to go against me? Who is Nate to think he's better than me? Who were you to think you could take one of my fraternity brothers away from me? You're nothing! You're no one," he ground out, spitting at the floor. "You are beneath me, Mason Kade." Disdain sparked in his eyes. His mouth tightened, stretching at the ends, and his eyes narrowed to slits.

"No one turns you down, right?"

Because he was the best. Everyone else was less than him.

"Exactly." He flared up. The coward was gone. The wounded animal side of him left. This was the real Sebastian. "Who are you? Who are any of you?"

He came toward me.

I'd fanned the flames, and he took the bait.

I murmured, "Your grandfather chose us over you."

"He did." He became like a statue. His shoulders grew rigid. His hands slowly curved inward, forming fists.

"Even your own sister chose us."

His nostrils flared, but he didn't reply. I was getting to him.

I added, "She slept with Logan—" I had more to add, but his head whipped up.

There it was. The anger was taking over him. I moved closer. Samantha was still between us, but I was in control.

"She told Samantha that she didn't regret it."

He sucked in his breath.

I advanced. "She was stressed about finals, and he offered to have sex with her as a joke. Screwing her was a joke to him."

He was breathing hard now. He couldn't look away from me. The anger was almost to a rage now.

I added more, "They went to a janitor's closet, and they were back within an hour."

"You're lying."

"No." I shook my head.

He could read the truth from me.

"I'm not. She'd do him again, too. She invited us to call her up whenever we're in New York. She wants to remain friends with Sam."

"Shut up, Kade."

His breathing was ragged now. His hands were pressing into his sides, and his head was bent down. He was trying to keep calm, but he was unraveling.

My hands gripped the bat. It was almost time. One swing— that was all I was going to do.

Act smart. Think smart. Be smart. All that was down the drain.

He was going to shatter Samantha. No one would walk away from that.

"What's the worst insult to you, Sebastian?"

He stopped breathing, but he was still listening. His vein was throbbing in his neck, and his feet moved, so he had a wider stance.

I waited, ready. "The fact that I won or the fact that you underestimated us? Or is it that, even after today, we'll still be welcomed into your family, and you can't do a thing about it?"

That was enough.

Sebastian lunged for me, but I was ready. This was what I wanted, and I ducked, ready to hit him when the door burst open.

"Stop!"

Garrett raced into the room. His hand was stretched out, but he stuck his leg out behind him to catch the door. His eyes were wide and alarmed, a look of panic in them. His mouth was open, and he was panting. He said a second time, "Stop."

I didn't.

I reached up and grabbed Sebastian's arm, then flung him into the wall.

"Mason," Garrett yelled. "Stop."

"No." I reared back to swing at him.

Garrett was there. He was on me the next instant, wrapping his arms around mine, and he pulled me back before I could hit Sebastian. The bat fell from my fingers. I bent over and threw Samantha's father off me. He bounced against the wall but was on his feet the next instant. He shot a hand out to me again. "No, Mason, I mean—I need him conscious."

Both Sebastian and I threw him a look. "What?" we both asked together.

Garrett turned on him and moved so he was standing next to me. He straightened to his fullest height, and he narrowed his eyes before he cut to where Sam was on the couch. "I know

Mason wouldn't do that. Sam wouldn't do it to herself. That leaves one person."

"You're my godfather," Sebastian started.

"And you did that to my daughter!" He thrust a finger in Samantha's direction with each word he yelled. "You, Park. You did that to her. She's my daughter."

"He was going to rape her." My patience was wearing thin. Sam's dad had three seconds to say what he needed. If it wasn't enough, I was knocking Sebastian unconscious. I didn't give a shit about his plans. "Why do you want him awake?"

"I wasn't going to—"

"Shut up!" Garrett lurched forward.

For a second, I thought he was going to hit him for me. I didn't know if I wanted that, but I waited. Sebastian and Garrett both seemed surprised by the movement. He caught himself, reining backward and let out a disgusted sound. It was a groan, but a growl at the same time. "I swear, Park," his chest heaved up and down for control, "you will be quiet, or I will let Mason do whatever he wants to you."

He moved forward and poked him in the chest as he said the last three words. The second poke was harder than the first, and with the last one, his finger never lifted from Sebastian. It stayed there, drilling into him.

Finally, after another ten seconds of staring into Sebastian's eyes, Garrett stepped backward. He said to me, his head lowering, "I wasn't aware you were going to make your move today. I sent Sharon back home where she was safe. I was coming back to tell you guys I would help you, but Logan told me at the house where you really were. I almost got into two accidents speeding here."

I snorted. "I'm sorry. Were we supposed to run it by you first?" My sarcasm was thick.

"No. I'm just saying that I would've been here. She…" He snuck a look at his daughter. His jaw clenched, and he looked away immediately. "She wouldn't have been hurt. I wouldn't have even let either of you in."

Another snort from me. "I'm sure you wouldn't have."

He glanced up, holding my gaze. "I mean it, Mason. I would've done the dirty work for you."

That surprised me, and I held my next retort. Instead, I replied, "He's like family to you."

"He's not." His head lifted again, and he was almost glaring at Sebastian, who seemed to wither in place, his shoulders scrunching together. Garrett clipped out, "Samantha was an innocent, as were you. I don't know what he's done to you, but I talked to Gerald. His grandfather told me something about a house being burned down?"

"He used his fraternity brothers to jump me, my best friend, and my brother. All of us at separate times. They tried to hit me with a car last year, too."

"I see." Garrett's eyes narrowed to slits. He stepped toward Sebastian, asking, "Is that true?"

A guttural, "Yes," came from deep in his throat. "Yes."

"All of that on top of what you were going to do to my daughter?"

Sebastian was staring at him, then he tried again, "Uncle Garr—"

"I'm not," he snapped at Sebastian. "I'm not your uncle anymore. I'm not your godfather anymore. I'm nothing to you. Like you'll be nothing."

"Garrett?"

He ignored Sebastian's one-word question and turned to me. "Take Samantha. Take her home. I'll deal with Park."

"What will happen to him?"

"He'll be cast out. All the blackmail material The Network has on him will be used against him and," he cast a scathing look at him, "I believe there's enough to strip him helpless. He'll have no power. The Network will turn on him. Rape of another member is never allowed."

"She's not a memb—"

"It doesn't matter!" Garrett roared back at him. "She's my daughter, and you were going to hurt her."

I heard enough. Picking up the bat again, I knew what I was going to do, no matter what Sam's dad was saying. It wasn't allowed because she was going to be a member? That was it? Because she was Garrett's daughter? What if she weren't? What if she was someone else's daughter, not someone from The Network? I'd been repressing my fury, but it was done. I didn't care what happened after this. Whatever Garrett was going to do, it wasn't enough.

I turned and swung, clocking Sebastian clean in the face. He dropped like a bag of weights, and I kicked at him, double-checking. He was unconscious.

"Mason?"

The bat fell to the floor again. I knelt down and rummaged through his clothing. Feeling his phone inside of his pockets, I took it and stepped back. I pointed at the door, which Garrett left propped open. "Take him. Get him out of here before I do something permanent to him."

He glanced at the phone. "What are you going to do?"

"If you want Samantha to be in your life, you will protect her after this."

"You're not going to tell me?"

I didn't have to. He'd know in a second, and after that, Sam would know, too, if he was going to actually step up as a dad or hang her out to dry. Either way, it was going to end after this. I gestured to the door again. "Take him."

I waited thirty seconds until he was gone before I did what I needed to do. Once it was done, I picked Sam up in my arms and left. Nate was in the car, waiting for us, and when I got inside, I never let her go. I held her as I told Nate, "Go to the hospital."

He took off, but looked in the rearview mirror. "Is she going to be okay?"

I nodded. "Yeah. We all will be."

Then he asked, "Did you do it?"

I nodded again, resting my head against the seat's headrest. Yeah. I used the passcode Summer told us her brother used for his phone. Once in there, I clicked on the e-mail I sent from the computer upstairs to Sebastian's phone. Then I sent it to his entire list of contacts titled The Network.

Everyone within The Network would see the blackmail material the organization had on them, and on everyone else. What they did with that, was up to them. When they would look into it, there would be no evidence linking me to the e-mail. Everything was connected to Sebastian. He would say it was us; I knew that much, but now everything was in Garrett's hands.

He would lie for us. He would protect Sam.

Finally.

CHAPTER TWENTY-SIX
SAMANTHA

I was dreaming about flowers, weddings, and candles. Mason got up from the bed, and the mattress dipped from the movement. That woke me up as he padded barefoot to my bathroom. He didn't turn the light on. The sun filled the room enough, and I waited one moment, guessing that it was eight thirty-two in the morning before I opened one eye, seeing that I was right from the clock on my nightstand.

The smell of pancakes and coffee told me the time more than how bright it was in my room. Malinda would've gotten up around seven. By this time, it would be the second pot of coffee, and I sat up, waiting for it.

"Mama Malinda, you're looking fresh this morning." Logan's voice could be heard all the way down to my room in the basement. A faint grin came over my face, and I snuggled back down underneath the sheets.

Home. That was where we were.

I woke up in the hospital where they got the drugs out of my system. I told them I'd been at a party, and it must've been slipped into my drink. After a few hours under intense scrutiny, they released me to go home with Mason. It helped when Garrett came later to check on me, stating that he was my father. He brought my phone too. When Mason was finally allowed to take me home, Garrett followed behind to the house. There, with Nate and Logan, we all sat around the table, and he told us Sebastian's fate.

"I didn't even tell them about Sam." His gaze lingered on me before casing a sharp look to Mason beside me. "You already leaked the e-mail."

Mason smiled at him. "What e-mail?"

Logan sucked in his breath as a wide smile started to grow. "Oh, damn."

"It's like that, huh?" Garrett's eyebrow lifted up.

Logan coughed into his hand, "Burn."

Mason started to speak, but Logan cut in, leaning forward and placing a hand onto the table, "We never admit. To anything." He made a show of looking Garrett up and down, and his top lip curled upward. "You know, so we can't be incriminated for things we *don't* do."

Garrett's eyes grew lidded, but he nodded. "Fine. Whatever your 'policy' is, I'm here to tell you that once the e-mail was leaked, everyone went into chaos. They blamed my godson—"

Logan opened his mouth, but Mason held up a hand, putting it in front of his brother's face. He said first, "Which they should. It came from his e-mail. Right?"

"It did, indeed." My biological father had a knowing spark in his eyes. It was like he was realizing Mason wasn't a normal college student.

I glanced down to my lap, slid my hand from underneath Mason's, and tangled my fingers together. Mason and Logan weren't normal. I wasn't either. When they burned Sebastian's frat house down, I knew things were different. Or I knew things were going to be different, and they had been. We all went our own paths during this semester. Each of us tried to protect the other, but all in our own ways. I didn't want that to be the normal routine. I enjoyed, relished even, the feel of Mason and Logan always having my back. I didn't know why, but I frowned to myself. We were individuals, but we were family. Mason and I—we were individuals, too. Yet, we were together. I knew nothing would get between us, not unless we allowed it.

This was a different feeling than before.

I had changed.

I didn't need them in a way like before. Mason and Logan were there for me. Seeing my biological father across the table, he stood for the other parents in my life. All of them abandoned me. I was left with no one. That was when Mason and Logan came in. They became my real family. I was related to Garrett and Analise by blood. David raised me, and Malinda would be there for me for the rest of my life, but Mason and Logan—they were the real deal for me.

Going into that house, stalling Sebastian so that Mason could upload the flash drive—no. Not even that. I was different. I just felt it in me. Sebastian was going to rape me, and he might've if Mason hadn't been there for me, but it wouldn't happen again. I knew I wouldn't allow that. If I were in a room with my enemy, I'd be watching everything. How he moved, what facial expressions he had, where he looked, how he said things, and yes, most definitely if one bottle of water was left in the refrigerator. I'd be aware of my surroundings. That was one lesson Sebastian taught me, but I knew there were more.

Garrett was a person. He was a fuck-up dad, but he was a person. That'd been another lesson. And the other main lesson: I was going to be okay. No matter what happened. I just escaped a near-rape, and it hadn't changed me. From all the crap I'd been dealt over the years, that was almost nothing. Still. I might start carrying a bat with me, or maybe it was time I learned more than a few moves of self-defense.

I think it was time I became a badass fighter like Mason.

Having that thought, I glanced at him from the side of my eye. All that time in the arena, learning those defensive and attack moves, I rubbed my lips together. It might take a while for me, but the whole training process would be fun. Hell, it'd be delicious, and I couldn't wait to start.

Garrett informed us that Sebastian was blamed for the e-mail leak. He denied until he was blue in the face that it was him, putting the blame on us, but my biological father vowed Mason was nowhere near the house. There was no way Sebastian could blame this on him. As for me, apparently I had been scanned when I came through the front door by some hidden machine. No flash drive was on my body, so they knew it wasn't me.

Then we heard the best part.

Sebastian raped a girl his freshmen, sophomore, and junior years of college. That wasn't the good part. It was the evidence The Network had on him. In true casting-out fashion, all that evidence was leaked to the authorities. And that meant Sebastian was going away to prison for a long time.

When he would be released, Garrett informed us that more blackmail information would be released. Sebastian did more than rape a few girls, and if he saw the outside of a prison, there was more information that would send him right back.

In short, Park Sebastian was screwed. Literally.

We never had to worry about him again, and we were home for holiday break. That meant an entire month of being here, having Mason next to me every night, and not worrying about next semester. Right now, hearing Malinda laughing above me from the kitchen as Logan's laugh followed a second later, I was happy.

I was content.

Mason asked from the bathroom doorway, his toothbrush in hand, "You okay?"

Was I? I smiled at him and didn't hold anything back. "Hell to the yes. I'm more than okay."

He lifted up an eyebrow before grinning from the corner of his mouth before he putting away his toothbrush, and coming back to the bed. "You and me, we're okay?"

We lied to each other. It was wrong. I said I wasn't going to do it. So had Mason, then we did it, but we were protecting each other. I needed to remember that, and I sat up, pulling the bed sheet against my chest as I reached to touch the side of his face.

He was mine. No one else's. We weren't perfect, but we would do whatever it took to protect the other. I didn't know another couple who could say the same thing. A surge of love filled me, and I nodded, feeling choked in the throat. "We're good. We're great."

He took my hand in his and leaned down, resting his forehead to mine. He murmured, gazing deep into my eyes the entire time, "You're strong, Samantha. You kick ass. You don't flinch when someone's coming at you, and you'll go back. You'll always go back, no matter the consequences, if it means protecting someone you love. I am lucky to have you. I am lucky that you love me."

I was feeling the tears coming. I pulled back, my smile almost taking over my entire face. Holy shit. I didn't think I could love him more than I did at that moment. "No more lies, right?"

He grinned, laughing softly. "You would've thought we had learned, right?"

"Yeah."

His forehead moved against mine, a gentle brush as he nodded, echoing my word quietly, "Yeah."

Screwed up or not, I knew we'd be fine. We always would. I was thinking about pulling him down to the bed with me when someone knocked on my door. Mark's voice sounded through it, slightly hesitant, "Uh...Sam? You have a visitor."

Mason sat back, still gripping my hand. He asked me, "He's not talking about Logan?"

That didn't sound right. Logan didn't get announced by others. Logan did the announcing. I started to climb out of bed and called out, "I'm coming. I'll be up in a bit."

Ten minutes later, still dressed in my pajamas, but refreshed for the day, I stepped into the kitchen, holding Mason's hand behind me. Malinda looked over, a worry line sticking out from across her forehead.

I frowned. She'd been laughing twenty minutes ago.

I cast Logan a look. He wasn't paying attention to us. He was standing, staring at whoever was at the front door with a scowl on his face. When he realized we were there, he said, "The code word is strangle. You say it, and I'm there for you. I'm not letting her hurt you again."

Her? Then I remembered what James said to me after Mason met with the board for Logan's punishment hearing. He drew me to his vehicle ...

I was remembering the conversation, as I was moving in slow motion.

My heart slowed.

Everything stilled.

His words came back to me as I stepped around Logan, and I saw who was waiting just inside the doorway, huddled against the wall with her arms hugging herself.

He had said, "The doctors are pleased with your mother. Her progress has been incredible over the last six months."

It was *her*.

His voice droned on, dipping down an octave, "They said she might be able to come home. I'm not sure when that would be, but I wanted to let you know. We'd be coming back, Sam. I wanted you to be the first to know."

I blocked out what he said.

That was the truth. With Sebastian and knowing we still needed to deal with him, everything James told me went in one ear and out the other. I couldn't digest it. So I hadn't.

I just couldn't deal with it, but here she was.

I took a step toward her. I felt like I was walking through invisible mud, and I said, my own voice sounding muffled and unclear to my ears, "Mom?"

Her head came up. She was huddled in the doorway. Her arms were wrapped around herself. Her hair was pulled back in a low ponytail behind her head. She looked...I couldn't process it. Natural. Her eyes lifted, clearing from whatever emotion she was feeling, and her entire face became radiant. She had no make-up on and she pulled her sweater even tighter around her frame.

"Samantha." She beamed at me. Then she said it—the words I didn't think I ever wanted to hear. "I'm home."

For more information, go to www.tijansbooks.com

Stay tuned for Fallen Crest Six (untitled), but until then, here's a sneak peek at Logan Kade.

SNEAK PEEK

(This teaser is not in Logan's point of view.)

We were only two pitchers in when the party came to an end. Jason and I had taken up position on the front lawn. We were on two lounge chairs, and he'd just come back with our third pitcher when a girl walked around from the back of the house for the cars. Before she could slip through them, a group of guys stepped out. They seemed to have materialized from the road. The girl started backing up as the guys continued moving toward her. They weren't chasing her, but they weren't holding back either.

"Oh no." Jason sat straight up. The pitcher was forgotten.

"What?"

"That's Samantha."

"Who's Samantha?"

He didn't answer. I swung my head over and saw why—he wasn't there. "Jason? Where'd you go?" It didn't matter. He really was gone, and I wasn't going to be able to find him. People were starting to come around the house.

"I'm leaving. I suggest you get out of my way."

The girl from before said that. I frowned, surprised. She wasn't scared. She was annoyed. The rest of the crowd began to form around her, and I walked over as well. If she was going

SNEAK PEEK

to be hassled, I wasn't going to stand for that. The complete pitcher I downed myself may have been assisting my bravado, but I tucked that away. I would've done this sober too, or I hoped I would've.

I stepped closer, and then recognized the girl. It'd been the same girl that had been with Logan Kade earlier. Her hands were beside her, her feet set apart. Her shoulders were back and ready while she watched the guys warily. She was getting ready to fight. I recognized the signs, and a nervous flutter started in me. She meant business, but so did the guys. I didn't know who they were. I frowned, scratching at my forehead. I didn't think they were at the party, but who knows. They could've been. Either way, this girl wasn't happy with them.

"Get Logan."

"Where's Logan?"

I heard other people saying the same thing, but I was focused on the girl. She really was stunning, even more so up-close. She raised her chin, and a warning flashed in her eyes. "Touch me. I dare you."

The three guys were unfazed. All tall, and not to be stereotypical, but they looked like preppy douchebags. If I found out later they all belonged to some Ivy League secret society club, I wouldn't have been surprised. Each of them was gorgeous with bodies built like they rowed every morning for hours. They also looked like money. It was dripping from them, from how they dressed. Their jawlines looked rigid enough to form glaciers. Their eyes were icy, too, as they stared back at the girl.

They weren't backing down.

I started to break from the crowd, to stand next to her. If they were going to screw with one girl, they were going to take on the rest of us too. Girl power and all, but before I could, the crowd broke in half. An actual opening formed, and Logan Kade strode forward.

My foot jerked back in its spot. I was still holding judgement, but it looked like I didn't need to link elbows with this girl and form a wall.

As Kade stopped beside the girl, the three guys turned their attention to him. They didn't move or say anything, but the air shifted. It went from dark and ominous to dangerous. I felt a battle brewing. My gut was telling me that these guys didn't want to mess with Kade. I remembered Jason's words from the backyard. Kade started fights, and he finished fights. At that moment, I hoped that was the case.

"Kade." One of them finally spoke, grating out his name. His nostrils flared.

Kade's eyes narrowed. He glanced at the girl, and then settled back on the spokesman. "What are you doing here?"

"It's a party. We were invited."

"And that's why you're facing off against Sam?" Logan moved forward a step.

"We weren't facing off against her."

The girl snorted, folding her arms over her chest. "Yeah, right. That's why you wouldn't let me go past to the car, because you weren't 'facing off' against me. You could've walked around me, dickhead."

A little laugh slipped from me. I might like this girl.

Kade threw me a sideways look.

I clamped a hand over my mouth. Not my fight. Not my place to interrupt. When his eyes lingered on me, I started to wave a hand for him to go back to his confrontation, but he turned back before I could. I felt more laughter bubbling

SNEAK PEEK

up, so I slipped backward into the crowd, then turned away. I was being inappropriate, but then again, I was drunk. Jason said to get drunk like we were back in high school. I wasn't so appropriate back then, either.

Mission. Accomplished.

Douchebag One said something back to Kade, but I couldn't hear it. The crowd was starting to get louder. Kade replied, but again, couldn't make it out.

"Come on. Who invited them?"

"Who are these guys?"

"Park's lackeys, and they aren't invited."

More and more people were talking. They were annoyed. An excited buzz was filling the atmosphere. People wanted a fight. They wanted to see some action. The three douchebags threw looks at the crowd. Two stepped back. They were becoming more wary, but the third snapped his attention back to Kade. His top lip curled up in derision, and his mouth moved, saying something I couldn't make out.

Oh boy. I swallowed.

Whatever he said, they were fighting words. I recognized the look in his eyes. His anger wasn't fading. It was increasing—then it didn't matter.

As soon as I recognized it, Kade's fist flew up, punching the guy right in the face. Douchebag One's head flung backward, and he stumbled a few steps before recovering. His two friends shared a look, both unsure what to do, but Douchebag One made the decision for them. He wiped the back of his hand over his mouth, locked eyes on Kade, and charged.

The fight was on.

"No, no, no." Jason shoved his way through the crowd. He yelled over them, "Cops were called. Everyone scatter—"

Before he finished talking, the sounds of sirens were heard. They were faint, but he was right. They were coming.

Douchebag One reared back. He was going to hit Kade.

"Stop!" I yelled out.

Kade heard me, his head whipping to mine. I pointed behind him and he ducked, turning at the same time. Douchebag One's arm went over his head. Kade caught it, twisted around, and rammed his elbow into the guy's gut. He hit him with an uppercut and then bent over and tossed him over his back. The other two douchebags ran and pulled their friend to his feet. They took off with the scattering crowd.

I paused, frowning. We weren't in high school. I didn't think we really needed to worry about getting in trouble with the law, but Jason grabbed my hand. He yanked me after him, saying, "Come on. There's illegal shit here. We don't want to get caught. Trust me."

"Well," I wrinkled up my nose but went with him. "Forget that."

Kade looked back at me. His eyebrows furrowed together, but Jason and I zipped past him.

"Logan," the girl called out from farther down the road.

She was waving from an Escalade. Jason veered toward them. I wasn't sure what he was doing, but he soared right past the vehicle. I glanced back and watched as Kade sprinted for the vehicle. He leapt, took hold of the top of the Escalade, and somehow threw himself into the opened seat. The girl was clambering to the backseat.

Kade reached out and pounded on the top of the vehicle, barking out one command. "Let's go."

The driver took off and they were past us in two seconds.

Claire pulled up next to us, coming behind the Escalade.

SNEAK PEEK

Jason hurried into the passenger seat, and I threw myself into the backseat. She gunned the engine, and we were pulling onto another street as the cop cars turned to where the party was.

"That was close."

I wasn't sure who said it, but it didn't matter. We were all thinking it. Then I grinned. I'd had fun. That was all I cared about, but I kept my opinion to myself. Something told me my friends wouldn't have understood.

(Coming winter 2015)

CPSIA information can be obtained
at www.ICGtesting.com
Printed in the USA
LVHW030733170320
650283LV00013B/199